TONOPAH

ALSO BY CHRISTOPHER A. LANE

Eden's Gate
Appearance of Evil

An amazing discovery in a forbidden Nevada
military zone erupts into a deadly quest for truth.

Christopher A. Lane
Best-selling author of *Appearance of Evil* and *Eden's Gate*

ZondervanPublishingHouse
Grand Rapids, Michigan

A Division of HarperCollinsPublishers

Tonopah

Copyright © 1999 by Christopher Lane

Requests for information should be addressed to:

ZondervanPublishingHouse
Grand Rapids, Michigan 49530

Library of Congress Cataloging-in-Publication Data

Lane, Christopher A.
    Tonopah / Christopher A. Lane.
      p. cm.
    ISBN: 0-310-21568-4
    1. Title.
PS3562.A4842T66 1999
813' .54—dc 21   98-49556
                                                                  CIP

Interior design by Sherri Hoffman

Printed in the United States of America

---

99 00 01 02 03 04 05 /❖ DC/ 10 9 8 7 6 5 4 3 2 1

To my little T. rexes, Micah and Christopher
And to their new baby sister, Shoshanna

PRELUDE

THE PREDAWN DESERT WAS A SEA OF DARKNESS, ALIVE WITH UNSEEN predators hunting unseen prey: hawks swooping down upon unsuspecting mice; bats chasing insects through the warm air; hungry owls scanning the rocky ground with keen eyes; humans obsessively stalking the technological future.

The trailers seemed out of place in the wild, unbridled environment. Huddled together on the plateau, their windows gave off a dim, yellow glow. Inside each of the short, squatty units, men were bent over monitors and electronic instruments, busying themselves with their work. Their senses dulled by concentration, they failed to notice as a pack of coyotes lifted their heads to the quarter moon.

Just 3.2 miles northeast of their position, a steel tower rose up from the flat, barren terrain. Perched atop the simple, three-hundred-foot structure was a canister the size of a fifty-five-gallon oil drum. Within, a banshee waited to be loosed.

The mesa itself was quiet, save a hot summer wind that gusted and moaned through the scrub cedar, causing the rabbitbrush to sway and dance. It was a serene, even peaceful night until the countdown reached zero.

On cue, electrical current raced from the control point to the tower, setting off a series of explosive detonations. The hollow, pewter sphere at the core of the device imploded, shrinking to two-thirds of its original size. Solid gave way to liquid, liquid to gas.

The product was twofold: heat and radiation. Even before the flash, the storm of energy reached a hellish 389,000 degrees, 200 billion curies and 6,500 trillion neutrons spewing into the air, blanketing the desert with invisible death.

For a picosecond the tower was bathed in an eerie, violet fluorescence—a phenomena referred to as the Teller Light. This brief sheen told those observing the shot that gamma rays and neutrons were ricocheting through molecules of air, moving the reaction in the intended direction: toward supercritical status.

The purple radiance flickered, flared, and in the next instant was replaced by a burst of stark, blinding light—an artificial sun so bright that it was visible for 240,000 miles. Beneath it, the sand dissolved, melting into smooth glass. A ball of fire rushed forth, consuming the tower like a vengeful demon.

Milliseconds after the detonation, the glaring isothermic flash was masked by an expanding band of superheated, opaque air. As the mushroom cloud seethed into the sky at two hundred miles per hour, a pressure wave leapt forth, pushing one ton of force per square inch toward the horizon in every direction. The shock front was actually visible, concentric rings moving out from the hypocenter, driving dust and debris across the landscape. Hills shook. Mountains trembled. Rivers fled.

Less than ten minutes later, a dark, unsettling calm had returned to the land. The white flames had retreated, quickly burning themselves out, the shock waves slowly subsiding. The desert was silent once again, except for the wind. Lifting its voice intermittently, it kicked up dirt and tickled the sagebrush, ushering the cloud to an altitude of nearly thirty thousand feet before carrying the five-mile-long stream of radiant particles eastward, toward a sleeping town.

One

"THIS WAS A JUNGLE?"

The question hung in the air as the four occupants of the Land Rover surveyed the land spread out before them: flat, sandy earth; a scattering of dwarf trees; low, barren hills; uneven patches of scraggly gray brush. The highway formed a long black ribbon that disappeared into a cloudless horizon, dividing the bleak, rugged terrain into two neat halves.

"More of a rain forest, Gill," Melissa replied, eyeing the speedometer. They were cruising at a smooth seventy-four miles per hour north on U.S. 95. There probably wasn't a patrolman within fifty miles, but she eased up on the gas anyway.

"A rain forest, huh?" Gill wondered. He poured another handful of Corn Nuts into his mouth. "I know about the inland sea," he mumbled, chewing. "It shifted back and forth through this area sixty-five to eighty million years ago. Was the jungle before or after the sea?"

"Maybe instead of," Melissa asserted, watching as the speedometer arrow nudged its way under seventy.

"It's in chapter fourteen," Beth chirped. She was riding shotgun, grinning smugly as she downed Lay's potato chips.

"You did read your assignment, didn't you?" Sydney asked in a singsong voice. She was sitting in the back seat, next to Gill, drinking a diet pop.

Beth offered chips over the seat. Sydney shook her head and declared, "I'm on a diet." Tipping the scale at nearly two hundred pounds, she habitually made a point of letting everyone know that she was in the process of shedding the extra weight.

"Yes, I read it," Gill said tentatively. "It's just . . . I don't remember anything about a jungle."

"A rain forest," Beth corrected proudly. "With a pink sky."

"A what?"

"A pink sky," Sydney said matter-of-factly, as if every schoolchild possessed this knowledge. "The sky wasn't blue like it is now. It was pink. All the time."

"Pink?"

"You didn't read the material, did you, Gill?" Melissa asked, already knowing the answer.

"No, Ms. Lewis."

Gill peered out the window at an outcropping of scrub cedars, a twisted expression on his face. Beth and Sydney rolled their eyes at him. Melissa had no doubt that they had both completed the reading in advance of the field trip—as requested.

"Gill, I assigned it well before the break," Melissa chided. "And I specifically stipulated that anyone interested in going on this excursion familiarize themselves with the 'early earth' concept and the theory of 'catastrophism.'"

"Yes, ma'am, I know," he groaned. "But Ms. Lewis, you wouldn't believe how busy I've been." He paused and sighed dramatically, as if he were suddenly exhausted. "I've had tons of homework for my other classes. Two research papers, an English exam, a math quiz . . . I had football tryouts. My part-time job. There was after-school band practice two afternoons. I had to—"

"You had to make out with Diana Perkins at Skate City on Saturday night," Beth announced with a straight face. Sydney burst out laughing.

Gill glared at them, his cheeks flushing bright pink.

"Sounds like you're a busy guy, Gill," Melissa observed, suppressing a chuckle of her own. "But since you'll be tested on the material when we go back on track next week, I advise you to make time for it."

"Yes, Ms. Lewis," Gill replied glumly. He sighed again, then asked, "So why was the sky pink?"

"I brought my text, Ms. Lewis," Beth told her helpfully, ever the teacher's pet. She dug it out of her backpack. "The intro to chapter fourteen is very descriptive. Want me to read it to him?"

Gill groaned softly at this. "Please . . ."

"You don't have to—" Melissa started to object. But Beth was already clearing her throat. She repositioned herself in the seat, her back unnaturally straight, as if she were preparing to deliver an important address.

"'The sky is pink, a glowing iridescent dome stretched over a mass of heavy, moist air,'" she read with a sense of melodrama. "'A mist drifts playfully across the valley, reaching its wispy limbs down ravines and arroyos, leaving in its wake a sea of waxy green leaves. The ground is dense with foliage, a tangle of thick ferns, draping vines, flowering branches, their stalks straining toward the sun.

"'In the distance, the gentle slopes of a low mountain fall away to a pristine lake, its miniature waves sparkling like liquid jewels in the afternoon light. At the water's edge, a gangly giant with pillar-like legs cranes its long neck to reach the fruit of a towering date palm. One hundred and thirty feet long, its one-hundred-ton frame causes the earth to shake with each step. The rest of the Seismosaurus herd grazes lazily in a sprawling meadow.'"

"Can I read?" Sydney interrupted.

Beth frowned, but handed the book over the seat, pointing to the place where she had left off.

"'The hot, smothering air is alive with the calls of a thousand species of birds: caws, whistles, musical trills,'" Sydney read. "'Abruptly, their songs fade, then die away as an ominous silence sweeps across the valley. Branches rustle as countless birds take flight, squawking a shrill warning to the animals below.

"'An adolescent Velociraptor springs from its hiding place, darting gracefully toward a nearby field like a gazelle evading a lion. A horrible roar arises. To the left, trees part like stalks of grass and a forty-ton Tyrannosaurus rex stomps and snorts into view. Tail parallel to the ground, it takes up chase, narrowing the distance with long, confident strides. Lunging forward, it snaps its powerful jaws, clamping seven-inch, serrated teeth around its victim. The Tyrannosaurus shakes its head violently before dropping its prey and going about the messy task of ingesting it.'"

Beth retrieved the book and cleared her voice again. Flipping stray hair back from her face, she lifted her chin to recite the lesson.

Melissa checked her rearview mirror to see how Gill was reacting to all of this. He was looking out the window, disinterested. He'd obviously had enough of Smartie I and Smartie II, and their thinly veiled efforts to impress the teacher.

"'In the foreground, another creature studies the scene with rapt interest,'" Beth read with a pretense of suspense. "'It stands perfectly still, watching, listening, sniffing the air. When at last it chooses to move forward, it does so carefully, on only two legs.

"'In its hand it holds a long shaft of wood to which a sharp stone point has been fastened with a thin gut string. As it creeps forward, its eyes shift from side to side, searching. Its mate and offspring waiting back at the village are hungry. Tired of berries and nuts, they long for meat.

"'There is a sound off to the right. The man freezes, straining his ears: birds! He circles slowly to ensure that he is downwind for the attack and two quiet minutes later spots the nest. Raising his spear, he pauses to finger the fetish slung around his neck, whispering a brief prayer to the god of sustenance. Before he can strike, something flashes at the edge of his vision: a tiny sun streaking across the pink sky.'"

Sydney reached a chubby hand toward the book, but Beth pulled it away, just out of reach.

"'Suddenly the ground begins to move,'" Beth continued, "'waves of solid earth rising, falling, rippling across the forest. On the horizon a mountain erupts in flames, spewing black plumes high into the air.

"'Looking up, the man realizes that the sky is aglow with lights: stars falling from the heavens. As they strike the ground, the flaming missiles explode, igniting brush fires that envelope the valley in flames.

"'Overcome with panic, the man tries to run, but each step sends him staggering into trees, stumbling down ravines. Clouds of ash descend upon the forest, filtering through branches, turning the sky a dull gray. Light fades, ushering in a premature dusk.'"

"My turn!" Sydney whined.

Beth handed the book over the seat again.

"'When the tremors subside momentarily,'" Sydney read, "'the man jumps to his feet and fights his way through the jungle, lost, desperate for a landmark. He hears a noise like that of a rushing river and seconds later is met by a hellish wind. Surging to speeds well in excess of gale force, it growls and moans like a raging ghoul.

"'Night overtakes afternoon. Though the sun is still high in the sky, total darkness now prevails. The man rubs his stinging eyes, cursing the ashes, praying for deliverance. The gods are angry. Will any creature survive?

"'He reaches the meadow, recognizing this only because he feels the tall grass swirling around his knees. Something brushes his arm— something rough and cold: a reptile. Another invisible beast pushes past, its breathing labored. Hideous growls mix with the shouts of the wind.

"'The man does not see what happens next. As he takes his last futile steps, tripping his way across the black, featureless meadow, a wall arises to the west, a towering new horizon that rushes toward him like an ocean swell. Stone, soil, and volcanic fire meet together, only to be thrust heavenward, energized by a colossal subterranean disturbance. The result is an earthen tidal wave.

"'The man runs, screaming, somehow certain that he is about to die. In his very footsteps, creation is stampeding—great thunder lizards, oversized mammals, gigantic birds, innumerable rare species fleeing for their lives, yet destined for a sudden extinction.

"'The wall of molten rock crests, then crashes down, burying the valley in the blink of an eye, covering the forest, drowning its inhabitants under—'"

Beth snatched the book back, a wicked grin pasted on her face.

"'Under layers and layers of heavy geological strata. With the fresh crustal plate still rippling and virgin mountains and valleys issuing clouds of steam, droplets of moisture begin to fall. The sprinkles give way to rain, rain to sheets of hail. High-atmosphere winds direct the torrential downpour, giving birth to waterspouts. A hurricane spins and whirls into being, its crest twenty miles above the earth's surface. Its winds rage in excess of five hundred miles per hour.

"'The oceans rise. The dry land disappears. The Flood has begun and with it judgment—swift and severe.'"

Beth snapped the text shut and gleamed at her mentor.

Melissa ignored this, pretending to concentrate on the road.

"That was fascinating," Gill muttered sarcastically. "So why was the sky pink?"

"It was pink because—" Beth started to answer in a voice that conveyed superiority.

"Anybody see a mile marker?" Melissa interrupted. Slowing the Rover to fifty, then forty, she began hunting for the unmarked dirt road that would lead them to the site.

"The one we just passed was number 149," Sydney submitted.

"Then the cutoff we're looking for should be . . ." Her voice trailed off as she studied the road. A quarter mile later she slammed on the brakes and the vehicle went into a skid, fishtailing to a stop crossways in the road. Thankfully there were no cars in the vicinity—the straight, flat highway was clear from horizon to horizon.

"There. I think that's it," Melissa announced. The four-wheel drive was pointed east, at a single-lane dirt road that ran away through gray-green rabbitbrush, toward the Cactus Mountains. It rolled and twisted before disappearing behind a series of sharp earthen mounds.

"Nice turn," Gill noted, admiring the black skid marks behind them.

"Thanks," Melissa said, shifting as they left the highway. "Now, back to your question. Why was the sky pink? Because of the canopy. Do you know what the canopy was?"

Gill shook his head. "No."

Two

$\int$TAGE THREE ALERT!"

Vaughn looked up from his newspaper and glared at the intercom speaker, waiting for confirmation.

"Stage three alert!" the deep voice repeated. "This is not a drill. Contact in the zone. Officers to the control room!" The red light above the door to the lounge blinked and an annoying siren erupted.

Vaughn's assistant, Phil Parish, cursed at the announcement. "Never fails."

"Come on," Vaughn grumbled. Setting aside the paper, he took up his Styrofoam cup and started down the hall. Parish followed.

Vaughn was in his mid-thirties, trim, with closely cropped brown hair. He had been told by more than one woman that he was handsome. But, as Parish liked to say, even a stiff was attractive to a certain segment of the female population—if it was wearing a military uniform. Parish was short and wiry, a scrappy African American with round, wire-frame spectacles that he thought made him look scholarly, but which more often than not brought to mind comparisons with film director Spike Lee.

"Probably just coyotes again," Parish complained, tossing his cup into a trash container.

"Probably," Vaughn agreed, sipping lukewarm coffee.

They continued down the sterile hallway at a leisurely pace. Despite the siren, the red strobes, and the animated loudspeaker announcement, a stage three contact was nothing to get excited about. Especially nowadays. "Threes"—an uncommon occurrence just months earlier—happened routinely now, sometimes a half-dozen times a day, thanks to the new, hopelessly flawed security system.

Stage one alerts were called when an NTS—Nevada Test Site— secure area had been physically breached. Stage two alerts meant that an uninvited guest was approaching a secure area. Stage threes meant simply that someone—or something—was moving around in what was informally designated as "the zone"—the wide, restricted perimeter surrounding vital NTS locations. Ninety-nine percent of the "threes" turned out to be nonhuman: a stray herd of antelope, a large jackrabbit, a coyote scavenging for his next meal, or some other harmless, four-legged intruder. The new sensors were extremely touchy, and on occasion even the wind set them off. The few viable contacts were usually either tourists stopping for an off-road picnic on their way to Vegas, truck nuts innocently four-wheeling through the hills, or rock hunters looking for valuable gems.

Miles from civilization, hours from water, food, or gas, the barren, godforsaken region was seldom visited, much less threatened by humans.

"I thought you told Jimmy to reconfigure the sensors," Parish said as they neared the control room.

"I did," Vaughn answered. He shrugged, then pressed his thumb against the pad next to the door. "Captain Steven R. Vaughn," he told the device. "08871." A green light flickered on.

Parish pressed his thumb down on the pad. "Santa Claus—five goose eggs."

The device buzzed at him, the light blinking red. "Access denied," a computerized voice announced.

"Phil!" Vaughn urged.

"Lieutenant Phillip T. Parish," he tried again in a bored monotone. "08862."

Satisfied that the two officers were who they claimed to be and were therefore worthy to enter the control room, the computerized security system beeped at them. The bolting mechanism slid back and the thick steel door swung open with a swoosh.

"Whattya got, Jimmy?" Vaughn asked, stepping into the darkness. The room was small and cramped, illuminated only by the glow of the sensing and monitoring equipment.

"A three in the zone," a deep voice replied sleepily.

"Aroo!" Parish called, mimicking a coyote. He slid into his chair and began scanning his screens for activity. "How many howlers this time, Jimmy?"

"Just one," the voice answered.

Vaughn took the chair next to Parish and eyed his screens. "Yucca's all quiet."

"So's Central," Parish reported.

"Where's the—" Vaughn started to ask.

"Quad 217," the low voice told them.

Parish reached up, followed the grid numbers with his finger, then tapped a tiny red dot. "Thar she blows."

Vaughn leaned in to inspect it. "Mineral, vegetable, or animal?"

"None of the above, sir," the voice answered. "This one looks legit." A chair squeaked in the shadows and an enormous figure lumbered slowly across the room. Sergeant James Albert Donohue, the resident computer tech, constituted nearly three hundred pounds of enlisted man. Nicknamed "The Truck" by his comrades back at Nellis, he had once formed most of the front line for the Brigham Young University football team. A knee injury early in his junior year had ended dreams of a pro career—as well as an athletic scholarship. In the absence of tuition money, the freckled, strawberry blond hulk had joined the marines, enrolling in a software design training program. Still a maniac in the weight room despite the bad knee, his shoulders were nearly twice as wide as Parish's, his towering frame a full head taller than Vaughn's.

"It's hot, sir," he explained, leaning over Vaughn's chair. "And it's moving."

Parish smiled at this. "All right!"

Vaughn stared at the dot. It disappeared for a moment, then reappeared a fraction of an inch higher on the grid map. "Another glitch? Maybe a wildlife reading?"

"I don't think so, sir," Jimmy said, squinting at the screen. He reached a beefy arm past Vaughn and fiddled with the resolution. "I reconfigured the whole system last night, specifically to circumvent that problem. Even installed a new utility to screen out incidentals. The lasers might still pick up four-leggers, but the smart sensors are supposed to download so the program can analyze the contact against the data bank library."

"Meaning?"

"It should be able to differentiate between, say . . . a bunny rabbit and a Russian tank."

"Let's hope so." Vaughn watched the blip.

"Why Washington can't cough up the bucks to patrol this place properly, I will never understand," Parish lamented.

"Credit the end of the Cold War," Jimmy observed.

"Yeah," Parish sighed. "We're lucky we have a roof over our heads after all the budget cuts. If they really want to keep people out, they need to build a ten-foot chain-link topped with rolls of barbed wire. And then electrify it."

"Yeah, right," Vaughn scoffed. "Then we wouldn't have to bother with this invisible fence system. We could just drive around in trucks and load the remains of trespassers into body bags."

"I'm serious. Fence off the entire site. Then post some billboard-sized signs. How's the public supposed to know it's off limits if nobody tells them?"

Vaughn shrugged at this, watching the blip.

"Then we put up closed-circuit cameras—so we can see who or what's in the zone."

"Nah," Jimmy said with a shake of his head. "Heat sensors. They can be programmed to preset body and vehicle limits. The computer would kick out a warning whenever a contact so much as looked into the zone, and it would classify it for us. Sort of like the sonar computers on subs. Then we could verify the target with, say, spy sats. You know, a grid of synchronous space eyes. We could position and coordinate the sats on-line, in real time, from right here in the bunker."

"The Pentagon would never go for it," Parish lamented. "Way too pricey."

"It's not the State Department that's the problem," Jimmy said. "It's the Department of Energy. They're the cheapos who want this place guarded but won't appropriate the funds to do it right. This system we're running is . . ." His voice trailed off and he punctuated the thought with a curse.

Vaughn wasn't listening anymore. He was studying the red dot, a frown pasted across his face.

"Better question is why D.C. wants to eyeball the zone in the first place," Parish continued griping. "It's just an ugly strip of empty desert."

"An ugly strip of empty desert that happens to surround two nuclear testing facilities and Dreamland," Jimmy noted.

"But you can't even see those sites, much less any of the Air Force's new toys, from the zone," Parish argued.

"True," Jimmy nodded. "Quad 217 is light years away from anything classified."

"Course, if the Russkies dropped a battalion or so of troops into the zone, we'd be ready," Parish said, patting his sidearm. "The three of us could hold off Yeltsin and Company with our six-shooters until the cavalry arrived."

He and Jimmy shared a laugh over this.

"Want me to call it in, sir?" Jimmy asked, one of his treelike limbs reaching for the phone.

Vaughn considered this. "One blip . . . You're positive it's viable, Jimmy?"

The Truck's muscular shoulders rose to his thick neck. "Not positive. But . . ."

"No way it could be a plane or a convoy, right?"

"No," Jimmy chuckled, his waist jiggling. "With this particular configuration, we can't pick up aircraft anymore. Nellis has to. As far as a convoy . . . Anything over a couple or three jeep-sized trucks and the system would go ballistic. It would sound like the start of World War III around here."

Vaughn took a gulp of coffee, thinking.

"Sir? Do I call it in or not?" Jimmy wanted to know. His long, thick fingers were poised over the telephone buttons.

"If we alert Nellis, and they send out the elite fighters to do a fly-over, and it turns out to be a four-legger again," Parish offered, making a face, "General Henderson will have all our butts in a sling."

"That's what I'm worried about," Vaughn sighed.

"I'm telling you it's hot," Jimmy argued. "That's no coyote."

"Maybe not." Vaughn crumpled his cup and shot it into the darkness, in the general direction of the waste can. "But let's do a visual anyway. We'll swing over for a look-see, confirm the contact, then call it in."

"Whatever you say, sir." Jimmy shrugged, replaced the phone, and moved back to his station.

"Come on, Phil," Vaughn said, rising.

"Yes, sir," Parish said, springing out of his chair. "Personally, I don't care if it does turn out to be a howler. Any excuse to get out of this dungeon."

"Jimmy, mind the store."

"Yes, sir, Captain, sir."

Five minutes later the outer door of the underground control bunker groaned upward and a Hummer rolled out. The square, boxy vehicle accelerated to forty miles per hour, kicking up a rooster tail of dust that hid the tall, flexible rear antenna.

Strapped into the passenger's seat, Vaughn twisted the controls of the onboard computer. The tiny screen blinked, then glowed a bright green, displaying the same grid they had studied in the control room, with the same red blip. He thumbed his headset. "Homebase, this is Recon One. Jimmy, you with us?"

The frequency came alive with static. "Roger," Jimmy's low voice replied. "This is Homebase. I read you four by four."

"Ten-four. Recon One is linked and running," Vaughn said. He looked over at Parish. "All right, Phil, this is our position." He tapped the screen. "And this mesa is where we need to be to intersect the contact and do a visual—assuming the contact continues on the same general course." Another tap. He read the coordinates to Parish. "Get us there, LT."

"Yes, sir," Parish replied with a brisk salute. He shifted gears and stomped down on the pedal. The Hummer leapt over a small rise, all four wheels leaving the ground.

"In one piece!" Vaughn added, bracing himself for impact.

THREE

W HEN GOD CREATED THE EARTH, HE PLACED A THICK LAYER OF WATER in the atmosphere," Melissa explained.

They were headed down the dirt road, doing a bumpy thirty-five, a yellow-brown cloud rising inside the cab.

"The Bible says that?" Gill wondered, rubbing his eyes against the dust.

"'And God said, Let there be a firmament in the midst of the waters,'" Beth quoted pompously. "'And let it divide the waters from the waters. And God made the firmament, and divided the waters which were under the firmament from the waters which were above the firmament: and it was so.'"

"Well, that explains everything," Gill muttered with a scowl.

"Actually," Melissa said, "those verses from Genesis do give us insight into the original state of the earth. The 'firmament' mentioned there is thought by many creationists to refer to an atmospheric layer that suspended an envelope of moisture around the earth."

"In the textbook it says it was like a ball of water," Sydney said.

"Right," Melissa nodded. Gearing down, she twisted the steering wheel to avoid a boulder. "And if that were the case, this 'canopy' of water would produce many interesting characteristics."

"Like a greenhouse effect," Beth announced proudly.

"Long-wave radiation would be scattered by the canopy," Sydney chimed in. "Therefore light would reach all latitudes with equal intensity."

"And radiated heat from the earth's surface would be trapped by the canopy," Beth explained, "creating a global, subtropical climate."

"Are we almost there?" Gill groaned.

"See that low mesa?" Melissa said, pointing through the windshield. "The site we're looking for is just beyond it."

The road had degenerated into nothing more than a glorified trail: two overgrown wheel tracks running away through pale, loosely packed soil. They rode in silence for the next few minutes, bouncing through ruts, all four tires spinning, shooting pebbles high into the air.

"So why was the sky pink?" Gill finally repeated.

"The canopy was made up of a pressurized layer of water," Melissa explained. "Under pressure, the hydrogen in the water took on metallic characteristics. In fact, the Hebrew word used in Genesis to describe the firmament is *raqiya*, which literally means to 'pound together into metal sheets.'"

Gill sniffed, clearly unimpressed.

"The canopy reflected light," Melissa tried again. "Kind of like a sunset. As the light from the sun passed through, it took on a pink hue."

To this, Gill nodded, still nonplused.

"The whole concept of a canopied earth is fascinating," Melissa continued. She paused to shift again, this time navigating the Land Rover across a shallow, dry riverbed. "With an envelope of water in place, the earth would be shielded from short-wave radiation—the harmful kind that causes degenerative genetic changes to the chromosomes of cells."

"That means no sunburns, right?" Gill asked without enthusiasm.

"Well, for a start. But the aging process would also be decelerated. And that, in turn, would enable creatures to live longer and grow larger."

"Which is what we find in the fossil record," Beth interjected.

"Reptiles, mammals, fish, birds—everything was big back then," Sydney agreed.

Gill was looking out the window, ignoring them. "I'm hot."

Melissa laughed at this and reached to crank up the air conditioner. "You think you're hot now, just wait." It was only 9:30 and the temperature was already approaching ninety. If the meteorologist on KJZZ was right, the temperature would climb to a stifling one hundred and twelve back in town. Out here on the high desert, two thousand feet above Vegas's altitude, it was expected to break one hundred before the day was over. A typical late June heat wave. That was why they were all wearing shorts, tank tops, and hats. And that was why Melissa had packed several bottles of number thirty sunscreen and a twenty-gallon barrel of water.

"So this place was a jungle, the sky was pink, " Gill reviewed skeptically. "And this canopy thing—it just disappeared?"

"During the Flood of Noah," Melissa added.

"What about the meteor that hit Mexico?" Gill asked. "Carl Sagan said that's what did the dinosaurs in."

"He may be right." She nodded, bracing as they encountered another set of deep ruts. "The two events aren't mutually exclusive. The theory you're talking about says that a meteor—a piece of space rock some five to eight miles wide—collided with the earth and set in motion a global cataclysm. In your text—if you'd take the time to read it—you'll find a complimentary theory that sets this meteor strike at the time of the Flood."

"But it rained during the Flood," Gill objected. "The Bible doesn't say anything about meteors."

"Not specifically. But the way it describes the Flood implies a global cataclysm," Melissa explained. "It says that the windows of heaven were opened. 'Fire and brimstone'—meteoric iron, cosmic hydrocarbon gases, flaming tar, and bitumen—came showering down. It also states that the fountains of the deep broke up. This suggests volcanic eruptions. And it rained for the first time. In other words, the canopy collapsed. Thousands of feet of ice and snow were deposited on the magnetic poles. Tidal waves deposited layers and layers of horizontal strata across the surface of the earth. The crust rose and sank, giving birth to new mountain ranges.

"The destruction was sudden, burying millions of animals and plants instantaneously."

Gill considered this. "But if that's the case . . . If all that happened during the Flood of Noah . . . Wouldn't that mean that dinosaurs and man . . . wouldn't that mean that they . . ."

"Coexisted?" Melissa asked, her eyes on the narrow, bending road. "That's what the scenario in the text was getting at. Men may well have walked the earth at the same time as the thunder lizards."

"Boy, the evolutionists would have a field day with that one," Gill said with a smirk. "I'm no expert—"

"No kidding," Sydney threw in.

Gill shot her a dirty look before continuing. "I'm no expert, but if that were true, if dinosaurs and men were around at the same time, wouldn't we find fossils to prove it? Scientists have found plenty of dinosaur bones. And they've found lots of skeletons of ancient man. But they're always on different levels."

"Stragma levels," Beth reported with a cock of her head.

"Strata. That's strata levels, Miss Brainy," Gill corrected. "Anyway, I've never heard of a T. rex found with the predigested remains of a caveman in his belly."

"Neither have I," Melissa conceded. "But there have been sites where dinosaur footprints and human footprints cross paths on the same strata level."

"Really?" the three students asked in unison.

"Sure. It's not that uncommon. There was a neat find in Texas a few years back: two tracks on top of each other—one Homo sapiens, the other an Allosaurus. Makes you wonder, huh?"

The Land Rover skirted the edge of the mesa, struggling northeast.

"Not only that, but the strata system—the geological column used for dating—is suspect. If there was a global cataclysm, thousands of feet of strata could have been laid down at one time—in a matter of hours rather than millions of years. Instead of being separated by vast spans of time, mammoths, Stegosauruses, and men could have been contemporaries."

"I don't know, Ms. Lewis," Gill said. "That's pretty far-fetched. Besides, that's not what any of the leading paleontologists say. None of them believe men and dinosaurs lived together. Dinosaurs are from the Mesozoic period. Men didn't come along for another sixty million years. You could learn that much from *Jurassic Park.*"

"Like *Jurassic Park* was a documentary," Beth scoffed.

"Hey, it was based on research by John Horner," Gill argued. "He's one of the guys who popularized the 'dinosaurs are more like birds than reptiles' theory."

"So you do read," Melissa teased.

"I've been interested in dinosaurs since I was a kid, Ms. Lewis," Gill answered. "I've read all of Horner's stuff. His and Bob Bakker's. And Nigel Kendrick's. Those are the three big names in paleontology right now."

"You're right," Melissa admitted, silently hoping the conversation would turn to something else—anything else. She tried to ignore the name, to pretend that hearing it didn't inflict pain. But the mere mention of Nigel Kendrick was enough to unleash a whirlwind of conflicting emotions.

In the next instant, her students, the Land Rover, the desert, everything disappeared and she was suddenly back at the University of Colorado—an aspiring doctoral student intent upon earning her advanced degree in paleontology. She was young again, fascinated with prehistoric life, zealous for the field, wanting nothing more than to spend her life on her knees in the dirt, searching for clues to the past. She remembered the unbound elation of serendipitous discovery, the thrill of holding a fossil that had once been part of a living, breathing creature, of examining a bone shard that had been embedded in the earth for untold millennia. She remembered wrestling with the evolutionary perspective pushed upon her by her profs, ultimately discarding it in favor of a view that complemented her faith: creationism. More than any of that, however, she remembered him.

A friend had introduced them at a luncheon/lecture. It was surprising that they hadn't met before—they were both on the same academic track, both two years out from their Ph.D.s. That first encounter was memorable in itself: the way he had looked at her, the way he had made her feel—alive, electric, on fire. She had never given much credence to the idea of love at first sight—until that moment. In the days that followed they had quickly moved from being acquaintances to being close friends, to being . . . more than that. A rich sense of compatibility grew and blossomed, infatuation evolving into a deeper, lasting bond. The intoxication of their romance carried them along, rushing them toward a lifelong commitment.

Six months after entrancing each other, Nigel had proposed. And for a week, she had walked around in a dream, a ring on her finger, her head in the clouds.

Why had she changed her mind? Why had she changed her heart? The answer seemed silly, even foolish in retrospect. He had been the love of her life, the only man she had ever cared for—*could* ever care for?—with that intensity of desire. And yet she had jilted him, handing back his ring, telling him that she couldn't marry him. Why? Because of a single Bible passage? Had she really turned her back on the relationship, hurting him, injuring herself, simply because two thousand years earlier a church leader had written a letter urging believers not to be "yoked together" with unbelievers? No. It was more than that. Paul's words to the Corinthians had provided the foundation for the decision, but it all came down to a difference in lifestyle—a difference in identity. Nigel was a dyed-in-the-wool atheist, certain that God did not exist. He was proud of this belief, unwilling to change, unwilling to entertain her faith, even if it meant losing her. He had made his choice: humanistic science. She had made hers: God.

Abandoning her doctoral work, Melissa had left both the university and Nigel, turning her attention to education. It was a sacrifice in more ways than one. Not only did it mean giving up a life partner, it meant giving up the serious study of paleontology. She had laid down her dream, never to pick it up again. In turn, she had taken up the teacher's mantle, accepting a position at a private Christian high school in Las Vegas.

The disappointment and sorrow of the abrupt transition were still with her, tender wounds that refused to heal, despite the passage of six long, difficult years.

"Kendrick found the twelfth rex," Gill was saying.

I know, Melissa thought, but didn't say. *I was with him.*

"The what?" Beth asked.

"There have only been twelve T. rexes discovered. Dr. Kendrick found the last one. I think he was still a student when it happened. Anyway, now he's a professor. At . . . the University of Colorado, I think. You went there, didn't you, Ms. Lewis?"

The Land Rover was jumping up and down on its shocks, protesting the state of the road. Melissa acted as though she hadn't heard the question.

"You went to CU, didn't you?"

"Yeah," she sighed, fighting to control the vehicle. The steering wheel was spinning back and forth on its own, reacting to the rock trail. "Go Buffs."

"Dr. Kendrick teaches there, right?"

"Uh-huh."

"Did you take any classes from him?"

"No. He wasn't an instructor when I was there."

"So you never met him?"

Melissa sighed at this and was trying to come up with a suitable answer—something truthful yet vague—when she saw the site up ahead. "There it is," she announced, glad for the diversion. "That's our site."

The four of them looked ahead at a shallow indentation in the earth. "Doesn't look like much," Gill said.

"It isn't," Melissa responded. "Just a hole in the ground. About twenty years back a geologist found a bone fragment out here. He showed it to somebody in the science department at UNLV. Somehow, it wound up at the University of Montana and the paleos there had it analyzed. Apparently they decided that it might have come from a sea-dweller. But it was really too small to tell. Anyway, a team came out here and excavated to try and find more bone."

"Did they?" Gill asked.

"Nope. It was dry. That's why we get to come out and poke around. The pros aren't interested in the site."

"What if we find something?" Beth asked. "Do we have to tell the pros and let them dig it up?"

"Basically. It's always prudent to let a trained paleontologist extract a fossil. Unless it's a trilobite or a loose piece of shell or something. If you happen upon a bone, you stop and call in the specialists. They're trained to document finds, preserve them, and remove them without destroying anything. Besides, a great deal can be learned from the position of a fossil in the strata. If you jerk it out, you can lose important information."

Melissa pulled to the far side of the hole and put the Land Rover in first gear, switching off the ignition. After engaging the emergency brake, she popped open the door and started to get out.

"Oh," she said, leaning back into her seat, "before we get started, let's pray."

Gill frowned at this, but the two girls joined hands and bowed their heads obediently. Melissa took Gill's hand and directed him with her eyes to take Beth's. Gill begrudgingly complied.

"Father," Melissa began, "you are the Creator of all things. We are in awe of you. And in awe of your creation. That's why we're here today. To honor you and to explore what you have made. Please give us wisdom and insight as we undertake this expedition. Guide us and help us to learn more about you and this world of yours."

"And help us dig up an Apatosaurus or something," Gill threw in.

The two girls grimaced piously at Gill. But Melissa laughed. "I'll second that, Father. We wouldn't mind stumbling across a dinosaur skeleton or two. In Jesus' name."

The foursome closed the prayer with a unified chant: "Amen."

FOUR

"THAT'S OUR MESA." VAUGHN AIMED AN INDEX FINGER AT THE GRID ON the miniature computer, then up at the ridge.

They were rumbling down a narrow arroyo, using the craggy walls for cover as the Hummer neared the intersect coordinates. The contact had stopped, the blip blinking strong and steady on the northwestern edge of Quadrant 217 for the past twenty minutes. Now it was simply a matter of making a stealthy approach.

"Take us two-thirds of the way up the backside of the mesa. We'll recon on foot from there."

Parish nodded, twisting the wheel. Instead of easing out of the arroyo, he gunned the engine and assaulted the wall head on. The Hummer tilted, compliantly scrambling up the steep bank. There was almost no object it could not crawl up and over.

Vaughn shook his head, smirking. "You think this thing's a dune buggy, don't you?"

"Isn't it?"

Once out of the ravine, Parish used the same strategy on the mesa itself, barreling straight up the side. Five minutes later, with the vehicle resting at an awkward forty-degree angle, he switched off the engine and began collecting his gear.

"Recon one, in position to intersect," Vaughn told the radio. "Now leaving the vehicle."

"Roger that," Jimmy replied through the static.

Parish slipped on his pack and smiled at Vaughn. "Ready to rock and roll," he reported.

"Glad you get such a kick out of this," Vaughn told him as he donned his own pack and they started up the hill. "Until Jimmy gets the system squared away, we'll probably be doing plenty of field maneuvers—if we want to keep General H. off our backs."

"Fine with me," Parish said, clearly relishing the experience. He had picked up the pace and started to jog.

"Slow and easy," Vaughn cautioned as they neared the crest of the mesa. The top was flat but surprisingly narrow, a thin plateau that fell away sharply to the north. "We don't know what we're chasing."

"I'm betting it's a detachment of Iraqis—a crack force of Hussein's best paratroopers," Parish joked, unsnapping his holster. "Either that or Ninja assassins from Tibet. Maybe even Mutant Turtles."

"Weapons locked," Vaughn told him. He waited while the lieutenant cursed softly, then resnapped the leather flap. "We're not cleared to go in hot."

"Yeah, yeah. No unauthorized force. Don't fire unless fired upon," Parish groaned. "What I would have given to see some action in the Gulf War. Even Bosnia."

"Action is highly overrated," Vaughn assured him. "And very dangerous."

"We could use a little danger. At least danger is exciting. I've been suffering from adrenaline deprivation ever since officer training."

"Uh-huh," Vaughn grunted. His unit had been among those deployed on the ground in the Gulf and had seen plenty of "action." For some, that had translated into a trip stateside in a body bag. Despite his love for the marines, Vaughn found the business of war to be highly distasteful. Exciting, it was not.

"Over here," he said, pointing to an observation point that promised a clear view of the valley below. They moved toward it slowly, bent at the waist, heads hunkered into their shoulders. When they stopped, Parish snaked into a cluster of tumbleweeds, flattening himself against the sand. Vaughn performed an identical maneuver next to him. Each dug a pair of binoculars out of their equipment pack.

"Dirt, dirt, and more dirt," Parish reported, scanning the area. "Told you it was coyotes."

"Those coyotes are riding in style these days," Vaughn said. "Check your eleven o'clock, LT."

"What? Eleven o'clock . . ." He moved the binoculars to the left, then back and forth. "We got mountains a few hundred clicks north. Piece of the highway off to the west."

"Closer to home. If they were rattlesnakes I'd be reading the first-aid manual, figuring out how to save your life."

Parish panned the area again, then looked directly down the ridge. "Yikes."

"Yikes is right. Lucky that isn't a truckload of Charlie commandos."

They studied the scene for a moment.

"I make two females—about fifteen or sixteen years old," Parish finally offered. "One male, same age. One female around . . . thirty? And she's not bad looking. For a white woman," Parish joked.

Vaughn ignored the lame stab at racist humor, repeating the information into the radio. He added, "Vehicle is an old Land Rover—white, Nevada license: Echo, Bravo, Zulu, 6–6–3."

"Roger, copy that," Jimmy's voice responded.

"Should we roust them, Steve?" Parish asked. "They look pretty dangerous."

"You'd love that, wouldn't you?"

Parish's eyes lit up and he nodded enthusiastically.

"Homebase, this is Recon One. We call no-threat. Repeat: no-threat."

"Roger that. Homebase copies a no-threat."

"No threat?" Parish gasped, binoculars fixed on the contact. "But Steve, those are obviously Russian spooks disguised as harmless Americans. Probably preparing to launch a counterintelligence strike against the NTS. National security is in the balance, I'm sure of it."

"Mmm-hmm."

"Okay, how about Mom and the kids out for a picnic?" Parish suggested.

Vaughn frowned at this. "No. The woman's too young to be the mother of teenagers. Besides, the kids are too close in age. And they've got shovels. My guess is it's a rock-hunting club."

Parish shrugged his agreement.

Vaughn thumbed the radio button again. "Homebase, this is Recon One. Classify the no-threat as rock hounds."

"Rock hounds. Roger."

"Homebase, inform Nellis, contact verified. Recon One, returning to base."

"Roger that."

"See ya in seventy-five, Jimmy."

"Take your time, sirs. I want to catch a nap. Homebase out."

Vaughn and Parish watched as the woman told the kids something, gestured to their surroundings, then to the ground, and began hacking away with a shovel. They were too far away to hear the impact, but they could see the handle bend with each stroke. The blade didn't seem to be doing much damage to the sun-hardened soil.

"Looks like loads of fun," Parish frowned. "Digging a hole in the middle of the desert during a summer heat wave."

"Come on," Vaughn said, repacking his binoculars. "Let's go—"

"Recon One, this is Homebase, over," the radio interrupted.

"What is it, Homebase?" Vaughn asked.

"Contact has been reported as no-threat, sir." There was a burst of static, then, "Nellis wants you to sit on it."

"Huh?" Parish grunted.

"Say again, Homebase?" Vaughn asked, his brow wrinkled.

"Nellis wants you to sit on it."

"Sit on it?" Vaughn repeated in a whisper. He hit the radio switch and asked, "You're kidding. Did you tell them it was just some kids and a lady in an old Rover?"

"Rock hounds. Yes, sir. They said sit on it. And they want video."

"Whose orders?"

"Direct from General Henderson," Jimmy explained.

"Payback," Parish grumbled, frowning.

"What?"

"I'll bet money it's payback for the wild-goose chase we sent his fly-boys on yesterday—running down those antelope."

"I wouldn't doubt it."

The frown on Parish's face quickly disappeared. "Course, if he wants to leave us out here—on the open range—instead of sending us back to the bunker to stare at those blasted monitors, who are we to argue?"

"In case you hadn't noticed, Phil, it's hotter than blazes out here. We'll bake our brains."

Vaughn took another look at the contact: a woman and three teenagers . . . One small step above four-leggers in terms of threat level. Sure, they were in the zone, and there was a chance they might stray closer to a restricted area. But that could be monitored and reacted to from the bunker—where the temperature was nearly thirty-five degrees cooler than it was out here. Parish was right. This was clearly Henderson's revenge.

"Homebase. Recon One. Will continue surveillance until further notice," he glumly told the radio.

"Roger."

Vaughn squinted up at the sun, then glanced at his watch. It was only 11:00 and already the heat was suffocating. "I know Henderson is peeved, but this is cruel and unusual punishment."

"We've got desert supplies in the Hummer," Parish reported, digging a miniature camcorder out of his pack. "Let's set up a bivouac. At least that'll give us a little relief."

"Yeah." Vaughn called Henderson a derogatory name under his breath.

"What's the big deal, Steve? We hang out for a while, maybe even get our uniforms dirty—for once. My guess is, Henderson will make us sweat for a bit, then call us in. He's a bear. But he's not a monster. Either that or the rock hunters down there will pack up and leave. Another hour or so, and it'll really start to get hot."

"And what if we wind up spending the entire day out here?"

"Then we work on our tans." He laughed at this as he adjusted the camera. "Course, I've got a head start on you there, Steve."

Vaughn shook his head. "Work on our tans," he muttered.

"You're a Vegas boy."

"So?"

"So you should be used to this weather."

"Used to it, sure. Do I like it? Huh-uh."

Parish punched a button and the camera emitted a beep. "I'll bet it never bothered you as a kid," he said, eye to the viewfinder. "You probably ran around barefoot all summer, playing baseball when it was hot enough to fry eggs on the sidewalk."

"My sister and I used to spend our summers holed up in the house—next to the air conditioning vent—watching TV."

"It hardly ever got this hot back in Minnesota. If it made it to eighty-five, we called the day a scorcher. But in the winter . . ." He cursed for emphasis. "Talk about cold. Maybe that's why I like Nevada so much. I'm still thawing out."

"Tell you what, Phil," Vaughn said, scooting backwards through the dirt. "You can thaw out by taking the first watch."

"Fine." He was busy playing with the zoom rocker.

Vaughn rose carefully and started back down the side of the mesa, his shirt already dark with sweat. "Call if you need me. I'll relieve you at twelve hundred hours. If you haven't already melted into a puddle by then."

FIVE

"MAYBE THERE JUST AREN'T ANY FOSSILS OUT HERE, MS. LEWIS," BETH pouted, scowling at the dirt.

"Oh, they're here," she replied, prodding the earth with a trowel. "We just have to find them. And you've got to get down here to do that."

Melissa was on her hands and knees in the depression that had once been a dig site, the sun stinging the back of her neck despite a fresh layer of sunscreen. Gill was by her side, squatting, raking through the soil with a short garden hoe, sifting the loose sand with his hand. The two girls were standing, taking turns complaining about the heat, the lack of modern conveniences, the dust—just about everything. After more than two hours in the field, they had yet to so much as bend over to inspect a rock. Beth claimed this was because they didn't want to get dirty. Melissa had decided it was because they were lazy. Any hopes she'd had that the girls might be budding paleontologists had long since evaporated.

"How much longer until lunch?" Sydney asked.

Melissa ignored this, concentrating on her work. She didn't expect to find anything on this outing. It was more of a learning opportunity than anything else, a chance for the kids to get out and experience paleontology firsthand. For most people, *Jurassic Park* was as close as they ever got to a real dig. Their knowledge of dinosaurs was fueled by movies, cartoons, even Barney, the simple-minded purple cheerleader. Few people cared enough or were curious enough to delve into paleontology. Despite the outward appeal of tracking "terrible lizards," the life of a paleontologist was dull. For the most part, they spent their professional lives looking for but not finding secrets hidden beneath the surface of the earth. When they were lucky enough to stumble onto a significant discovery, months, sometimes years were invested in raising capital for the venture, organizing the dig, setting up a base camp, extracting the fossil, studying it, and transporting it to a museum. It was a tedious line of work with few rewards and almost no financial compensation. There were never more than fifty to a hundred grant-funded dinosaur hunters roaming the globe. The work was too time consuming and unprofitable to draw any but the most ardent, determined scientists.

It was already clear that Beth and Sydney would probably never enter the ranks of serious-minded fossil hunters. They obviously harbored no great love for the field. Gill, on the other hand, had all the marks of a hungry paleo. He was bright, intuitive, and could be very tenacious—when something captured his interest. He would, of course, most likely outgrow his interest in dinosaurs—most people did. But there was always a chance ...

Wouldn't that be something? Melissa thought. Gill represented precisely what was missing from the field of paleontology: God-fearing, Christ-centered young minds.

"It's almost noon," Beth said. "Can't we stop for lunch?"

Stop whining! Melissa wanted to say, but didn't. Instead, she chipped away with her trowel.

"It's not almost noon," Gill told them. "It's ..." He checked his watch. "11:27."

"But we're hungry," Sydney chimed.

"And bored," Beth added. "There just aren't any fossils around here."

"Go right over there," Gill told them, pointing at a craggy outcropping thirty yards away. "Pick up ten of those rocks—any ten—and look at them. I'll bet there's a fossil in one of them."

"I don't bet," Beth proclaimed with disdain. "It's sinful."

"Just go look at the rocks," Gill groaned.

Beth sniffed at him, then motioned for Sydney to follow her over to the rocks. They leaned over gingerly and began picking through the selection.

"You lose. There's not—" Beth started to say.

"Look!" Sydney shouted. "Look! A shell thing." She displayed her discovery as if it were a precious jewel.

"Wow!" Beth exclaimed. She outlined it with her finger, then returned to the rocks, checking each one over before discarding it. A minute later, she had her own fossil. "I got one!"

"It's not a shell," Sydney announced.

Beth trotted to the hole and presented it to Melissa. "What is it?" Gill looked up, a half-grin on his face. "Leaf. Nice one, too."

Beth and Sydney beamed at their treasures for a moment. Then Beth asked, "Can we have lunch now?"

"GENERAL HENDERSON, LINE ONE," THE SPEAKER PAGED.

Gerald Henderson was standing in the control tower at Nellis Air Force Base, watching as the air wing performed an alert-one drill. Six stories below him, pilots were sprinting across the tarmac like startled quail, helmets and flight bags in hand, hurrying to their aircraft. Outside the closest row of hangars, crews of mechanics inspected the support planes, pumping fuel, adjusting bay doors, adding ordinance.

"General Henderson, line one," the voice on the speaker repeated.

"General . . ." Colonel Johnson prompted.

Henderson silenced him with a finger. The general glanced at his stopwatch, then back down at the field. Two jets were already moving, heat waves issuing from their tails as they rolled toward the takeoff area. The ten remaining fighter jockeys were in the process of pulling their canopies shut and calling their birds to life.

The inside of the tower was quiet. A dozen uniformed controllers gazed down at circular radar screens, speaking softly into headsets as they organized the launch.

"General Henderson, line one."

Henderson ignored the page, his attention focused on the first pair of F-15 Eagles as they taxied to the end of the runway and paused, waiting for a green light from the tower. Moments later they jerked forward, propelled by the thrust from their powerful Pratt & Whitney turbofans. They accelerated to one hundred and fifty knots before lifting their tire-clad feet from the ground. Thirty seconds after taking flight, the pilots punched their afterburners, sending the jets into parallel, forty-two-degree climbs. The resulting roar rattled the windows, sending ripples through Henderson's coffee.

He clicked his stopwatch. Not bad. When the other jets had followed suit and the entire wing was airborne, he clicked the button again and inspected the face, noting the elapsed time from the scramble siren to ABA—"all birds aloft." Pretty good. The team could use a little work though. Tomorrow he would oversee a drill at Indian Springs. Monday he would goose the boys over at Dreamland and see what state of readiness they were maintaining. Then on Wednesday, he would start over and drill Nellis again.

"General Henderson, line one."

He put the watch back into his pocket and took a long draw of muddy liquid before picking up the phone.

"Henderson here."

"Gerald, this is Robert DiCaprio."

The general stood up straighter, an instinctive reaction to authority. "Yes, sir."

"Drop the 'sir,' Gerald," DiCaprio said.

"All right . . ." He paused, uncertain whether to call the secretary of energy Robert, or Rob, or Bob—none of these seemed appropriate. "Good to hear from you . . . Mr. DiCaprio. How does your wife like Washington?"

"Loretta? Oh, she absolutely loves it: the parties, the schmoozing, hobnobbing with the beautiful people—she's so glad to be away from Vegas she can hardly stand it."

Henderson laughed politely. DiCaprio was extremely well connected. At the age of forty-seven, he appeared to have a long and illustrious political career ahead of him. Aside from being the son of Guido DiCaprio, an influential union leader back East, and the nephew of Anthony DiCaprio, a hotel/casino magnate in Vegas, he also held a doctorate from MIT in nuclear engineering and had evidenced a keen affinity for administration. After just fourteen years with the DOE—much of that as chairman of the operations at the NTS—he had climbed into the secretary's office. Rumor had it that he and the president were already "tight" and that DiCaprio was being groomed for a second-term cabinet position.

"What can I do for you, sir?" Henderson asked, slipping back into the role of subordinate.

"Gerald, I've got your report sitting here on my desk."

Henderson tried to think. *Report? What report?*

"Somebody snooping around in Quadrant 217?"

"Oh, that. Right. We have a surveillance team in position," he assured DiCaprio. He couldn't help but wonder why in the world the man cared. Better yet, how on earth did he know? As a matter of procedure, Henderson had reported the contact to his superiors and notified the folks over at the DOE. Also as a matter of procedure—and a gratifying means of sticking it to the marines in the control bunker—he had stationed a watch. Henderson glanced at his watch and tried to calculate how much time had passed since the contact was first called in. It couldn't have been more than a couple of hours. Yet somehow the report had moved, like lightning, up the chain of command—all the way to the desk of the chief of the department of energy.

"Good. Well, I'm sure it's nothing to worry about. Especially if your people are on top of it, Gerald. But I need a favor."

"What's that, sir?"

"I'd like you to handle this one personally."

"But, Mr. DiCaprio, this is a stage three contact, out in the—"

"No questions, all right, Gerald? Just do this, as a personal favor to me."

Henderson hesitated, mostly out of curiosity. It was a strange request. Why put a brigadier general in charge of running down a three in the zone? "Yes, sir," he finally replied. "Listen, if you'd like us to bring the contact in for questioning or—"

"No, no. Just keep me posted. Keep an eye on the situation and let me know when the zone is clear. And I'd like a full report tonight."

"Certainly, sir," Henderson answered, knowing that "I'd like" was DiCaprio's way of saying "Do it."

"Good. Well, then . . . I'll be waiting to hear from you."

Henderson replaced the phone, blinked at it, then swore softly.

"What is it, sir?" Johnson wondered. Henderson was not given to profanity. A fourth-generation Mormon, the big man often raised his voice and could be counted on to blow his stack in a fit of anger at least once a day—he had a short fuse and it didn't take much to light it—but he very seldom cursed.

"D.C." he mumbled in response. "The Sec. DOE is worried about a rock-hunting club doodling around in the zone."

"That was DiCaprio?" Johnson asked with wide eyes. It was his turn to swear. "Just what we need."

"Precisely," Henderson grunted, obviously displeased. "Something's up, Bill. D.C. doesn't give a hoot about the zone. Shoot, they hardly even care about the secure sites nowadays. They wouldn't blink an eye if a foreign army planted themselves smack dab in the middle of Frenchman's Flat."

"Does sound a little odd," Johnson agreed. "Remember when that nut from Reno managed to sneak into Dreamland a few years back?"

"Remember? I was the assistant base commander. That turkey nearly cost me my job."

"And Washington barely even noticed."

"But let a lady and a few kids stray into 217, and all hell breaks loose. What's up, Bill?"

The colonel shrugged, his expression sour.

Henderson shook his head at the call, dismissing DiCaprio with a sigh. "Bureaucrats. Now that he's on the rise on Capital Hill—one of the anointed few—there's no telling what's motivating him."

"How about greed, power, control, ambition," Johnson tried, smirking. "Those political types are all obsessed with something. Maybe DiCaprio's just practicing up for the White House."

Henderson grimaced. "Old Bob was a hands-on guy while he was overseeing the site—a real pain in the backside. I thought we'd seen the last of him. But something tells me he'll be giving us grief long distance from here on out." The general took a deep breath, then barked, "Get me Major Wallace."

Johnson reached for the nearest phone and began dialing.

Henderson's gaze was fixed on the horizon where a dozen specks had just materialized: the elite fighters returning. They magically grew to the size of gnats, then became tiny airplanes as they rocketed toward the base at Mach Two. "Inbounds."

"General," the nearest air controller said, "wing leader requests a flyby."

Henderson shrugged. The drill had been a success. "Why not. Let the hot dogs have a little fun."

The controller nodded and relayed the information, then shouted, "Flyby!" Everyone in the room instinctively placed their hands over their ears. Seconds later three perfect formations of F−15s and F−16s screamed by, their jet engines shaking the very foundations of the building.

When the thunder had subsided, Johnson handed Henderson the receiver.

"Major, this is General Henderson. Drop whatever you're doing and get me all the intel you can find regarding Quad 217."

The general paused, listening to the major's question.

"Beats me. But the brass in D.C. are buzzing. We had a contact in 217 this morning and somebody somewhere hit the panic button. I want to know why. Leave the files on my desk. I'll read them when I get back," he said before hanging up.

"Back, sir?" Johnson asked. "From where?"

Henderson sighed. "We're gonna hop up to the bunker."

"We?" The blood drained from Johnson's face. "I'm going?"

"Yep. Do you good, Bill. You need to get over that air-sickness problem. Set it up."

"Yes, sir," Johnson groaned. He picked the phone back up and began making the necessary arrangements.

Henderson smiled as the fighters circled back and prepared to land: losing altitude, reducing airspeed, floating earthward like majestic birds of prey, wheels unfolding beneath them. As a decorated pilot, he loved watching them perform. It was the next best thing to being in the cockpit himself, throttle in hand.

"Send a few of those birds out over the zone," he told the controller. "Tell them to buzz 217—low and fast. And have them get movies of the contact."

"Yes, sir."

Henderson picked up another line and grunted, "Tonopah Control." He frowned at the idea of going all the way up there. What a waste of time. But at least it gave him an excuse to take his own bird up.

On the heels of that pleasant thought, another struck him. This one brought a smile of contentment to his rugged face. Obeying DiCaprio's directive to keep a close eye on the contact meant that the bunker rats would be spending more time in the sun than Henderson had originally planned. Captain Vaughn and Lieutenant Parish would be posted out in the scorching heat until the contact called it a day and decided to make its way back to safer ground. And on top of that, when the rats finally made it back to the bunker, they would be welcomed home by one of their least favorite people: the commanding officer of Nellis Air Force Base.

Henderson almost felt sorry for them. Almost.

ſix

ſTABS OF PAIN PULSATED DOWN THE RIGHT SIDE OF HIS LOWER abdomen, fanning out in a network of thin, fiery fingers. He clenched his jaw, pushing a fist against the offending region. His ulcer was acting up—again. It didn't seem to take much to set it off lately: an impending deadline, a rough budget meeting, any manner of crisis—which the DOE seemed to face on a daily basis. Even a spicy Mexican meal could give him cause to reach for the antacid.

Rising from his desk, DiCaprio ordered the breach in his intestinal wall to stop bothering him, then leaned against the floor-to-ceiling window as his belly burned with renewed vigor.

Outside, the buildings bordering the Mall appeared pale and faint in the hot, humid afternoon haze. The sidewalks were thick with people: tourists braving the weather to visit the Smithsonian, crazed locals walking and jogging themselves toward heatstrokes. Suits—politicians, lawyers, and others representing the federal government—hurried from one air-conditioned building to the next, never pausing to acknowledge, much less appreciate, the looming presence of the Monument, which rose like an ivory tower against the smoggy sky, a white exclamation point at the end of the long, grassy park strip.

The scene always reminded DiCaprio of an ant farm: tiny insects busying themselves with frantic, seemingly mindless actions. They appeared to be going in circles, accomplishing nothing of importance.

He fished a bottle of sodium bicarbonate out of his desk, unscrewed the top, and took a long swig, knowing full well that it would have little if any effect. This flare-up wasn't the result of poor nutritional habits or run-of-the-mill stress.

Suddenly, he craved a drink. *What a time to be on the wagon*, he thought, watching the ants do their dance of insignificance nine floors below. *A martini would come in handy right about now.*

He looked over at the phone, expecting it to ring. Waiting for it to ring. Certain that it would ring. Dread—that was the emotion that had caused his ulcer to kick him in the stomach.

Slipping into the chair behind his desk, he leaned back and closed his eyes, intending to review the situation and find a solution. There had to be one. His experience as a manager told him that there was. And as one of the best trouble-shooters in the Capital, he would find it. Wouldn't he?

"If *I* know . . . *they* know," he thought aloud. He had no idea how they did it, what system of inside sources they tapped, but somehow they always managed to stay abreast of events. They were often better informed than he was. In the case of Quad 217, DiCaprio had a red flag in the DOE computer, calling any and all contacts—no matter how incidental—to his immediate attention. Minutes after a contact was reported, he was electronically alerted. But, mysteriously, so were they. And it would do him no good to pretend to be unaware of the situation; they would react poorly, he was certain of that.

"If I can't keep this quiet and/or feign ignorance, then I . . ." He stared at the ceiling, as if it held the answer. "I instill confidence that I'm on top of it, that everything is under control." As he said the word "control," his voice wavered. He swore at this. They would see right through him. Even he wasn't convinced that it was under control.

"Worst case scenario," he told the ceiling tiles, "they get tough, put on the pressure, threaten to drag a few skeletons out of the closet. I balk, cower, kiss up, promise to take care of it."

He slammed his fist on the desk. They had him. And they always would. No matter how high he managed to climb—the cabinet, the senate, the White House—they would always own him.

DiCaprio aimed a series of expletives at them, took a deep breath, then continued his problem-solving session. "Best case scenario: Those really are rock hunters and they'll go away without doing any damage—except to my ulcer.

"Why did they have to pick Quad 217?" he asked the empty room.

He was in the process of reaching for the phone, intent upon having his secretary run out and grab him some Zantac from the drugstore—and maybe a fifth of vodka?—when the thing buzzed at him.

He flinched, then glared at the device. After two deep breaths, he punched the button.

"What is it, Patty?"

"Call for you, sir."

"Who is it?"

"They wouldn't give their name. I told them you wouldn't take a call unless—"

"Put it through," he said, propping his elbows on the desk.

"Robert?"

"Speaking."

"What's this I hear about a problem?"

DiCaprio swallowed hard. Despite his education, rank, and ascending career, these people still intimidated him.

"Four people entered our quad at approximately 1200 hours Eastern time today," he reported.

"Our quad?" the voice on the other end of the line questioned.

He ignored this. "Nellis makes them out to be rock hunters. Just a club out looking for rare stones. Nothing to worry about."

The caller snorted at this. "Nothing for *you* to worry about, maybe. Rock hunters dig, don't they?"

"Well, sure, but what are the odds—"

"I don't play the odds, Robert. What if one of the rock hounds happens to dig up something they shouldn't? What then?"

"That won't happen. And if and when it did, I would—"

"I think this is a matter for our people to take care of," the voice announced. "We've had more experience with this sort of thing than the DOE has."

DiCaprio was buoyed by a sudden surge of courage. "The DOE takes care of its own," he argued. "The zone is my territory. Let me handle it."

There was a pause, then, "Have it your way. But if things go awry and you don't handle it, Robert, I'm pulling rank."

"But you can't—"

"I can do whatever I want to," the caller reminded him. "Now fix it. Do what needs to be done. Got that?"

The phone went dead, and as DiCaprio replaced the receiver he was struck by a wave of paranoia. What if the line were bugged? What if the FBI was listening in? What if his political dreams were being compromised—by a foursome of rock hounds? It sounded ludicrous. But stranger things had happened.

Seven

I'M GETTING TIRED," SYDNEY GROANED. "AND HOT." SHE SIPPED WATER from a paper cup, her chubby face flushed.

"Me too," Beth agreed.

"What was that, girls?" Melissa asked the question from the far side of the dig site. She was hunched over in the dirt, trowel in hand, sifting the earth—the same basic position she had assumed for the past four hours. Her neck and the back of her legs were sunburned, despite several applications of sunscreen, and the hair beneath her hat was matted with sweat. Her knees ached and her skin was covered by a fine layer of dust. It felt good to be back in the field again.

"Nothing, Ms. Lewis," Beth said. She and Sydney finished their water, put the cups back in the Land Rover, and returned to Melissa's side.

"Got anything yet?" Sydney asked in a bored monotone.

"No." Melissa shook her head, smiling up at them. "Except maybe heatstroke."

The thermometer in the car registered one hundred and thirty-two degrees in the sun—meaning the air temp was somewhere in the neighborhood of one hundred and two—and a scorching wind had begun to blow, whipping sand into their faces with every blast.

"We need a bulldozer," Beth remarked, covering her eyes as another gust of sand peppered them.

"Or one of those computer mapper things," Sydney said. "Like on *Jurassic Park.*"

"You mean a thumper?" Melissa asked. She paused to adjust the vibrant purple bandanna tied around her neck, pulling it up over her mouth to keep the dirt out of her teeth.

"A bumper?" Sydney asked.

"No, a *thum*-per," Melissa said, overenunciating the word through the bandanna. "That's what that thing was. It shot a vibration into the ground and then mapped the return. Great device. Only thing is, they're pricey. The University of Colorado has one. But it's a little beyond the salary of a high-school teacher. So we have to look for dinosaurs the old-fashioned way: on all fours. The closer you get to the ground, the better your chance of finding something.

"As for a bulldozer . . ." Her words trailed off as she waited for the wind to die down. "As for a bulldozer, that would be too intrusive. We don't want to displace that much soil. It might harm any fossils that are hiding down there. And it would most certainly knock them out of position. It's important to study their orientation in the strata and in relation to other fossils. We can learn a lot just by the layout of a skeleton: how it died, how it moved . . . So the idea is to probe carefully, remove layers of soil—one at a time—then slowly unearth whatever fossils might be hiding down there."

She took a deep breath, siphoning air through the fabric barrier, then groaned as she tried to rise. "My back is killing me."

"Why would anyone want to do this? For a living, I mean?" Beth asked.

Melissa shrugged, stretching. "Different strokes for different folks, I guess. I happen to enjoy being out here. I think I could probably live in the field and dig every day."

"But you just said that your back was killing you," Sydney argued.

"Backaches, kneeaches, headaches, stinging eyes, sunburn—it's all part of the fun."

"Yeah, right, fun," Beth scoffed. "I already miss air conditioning. And we've only been out here half a day."

Melissa smiled at them. "It's like fishing. It's no fun getting up early, digging worms, baiting hooks, then sitting there shivering in the dark, swatting mosquitoes at five in the morning . . . unless you get a bite. Once you catch something, it takes on a whole new meaning.

"Paleontology is the same way. Coming out here to the middle of nowhere to kick rocks and shovel sand when the mercury is up in the hundreds isn't exactly my idea of heaven. But back in college, I was lucky enough to be on a few digs where finds were made." She paused, shaking her head. "It's . . . It's hard to describe how it feels . . . to stare down into a grid and see the skull of a prehistoric sloth or the limbs of

an Apatosaurus . . . To find the tooth shard of a Tyrannosaurus, and watch
as a team resurrects the rest of him . . . It's . . . exhilarating. An incredible high. And it's humbling. You realize just how long this world has
been around, and how short your own life really is—how big God is,
how complex his universe is . . . how little and seemingly insignificant
you are. What the Bible says is true, you know: we're all just vapors—
here today, gone tomorrow."

The girls looked back at her quizzically. She could see that they didn't
have a clue what she was talking about. But then, they were teenagers.
How many teens really had a sense of the timeline of history, a sense of
their own mortality? Most kids naturally assumed the world was custom
built for them and that they would never grow old, much less die.

"Where's Gill?"

The girls turned toward the Land Rover, then shrugged, like synchronous mimes.

Melissa scanned the area: mesa directly west; low mounds covered
with rabbitbrush to the north; mountains on the horizon to the east;
flat, windswept earth to the south. Not a tree in sight. No Gill either.

"Stay here," she told them, handing Beth the trowel.

"Can we sit in the Jeep?" Sydney wanted to know.

"Sure," Melissa answered. "But it's a lot hotter in there than it is out
here. And it's not a Jeep. It's a Land Rover."

She set out toward the edge of the mesa, following the dirt track
until she could see behind it, across the valley to the highway. Without
binoculars, it was difficult to make out any distinctions in the terrain.
The light brown dirt, rocks, and clumps of tall grass all blended together.
She stood for a moment and watched for movement. Nothing.

As she headed back to the dig site, she realized that she was growing irritated. As if the girls' constant complaining weren't bad enough,
now Gill had wandered off. Where had he gone? Better yet, why? She
had specifically instructed them to stay close to the hole.

Passing the site again, she walked north, crossing a wide, steep-sided
ditch before ascending the first mound. From the top she would be able
to view the entire area. With each step the annoyance grew, now tinged
with anxiety. What if something had happened to Gill? There were
plenty of rattlesnakes around. And scorpions. And coyotes. If he had
decided to go exploring, he was . . . well, stupid. In this heat, in this
desert, he wouldn't last long.

But Gill wasn't a stupid kid. He was intelligent, a good student when he wanted to be. Surely he wouldn't . . .

She reached the top of the mound and stopped to catch her breath, suddenly exhausted, ready to give in to the girls, pack up and call it a day. Turning slowing, she surveyed the mesa, the site, the plains. She was about to continue on to the next mound when she saw it: a red object in a ravine directly below her. The ditch was obviously the work of an extinct river, a deep cut in the crust of the earth that ran in a ragged line from the mesa toward the mountains. It was just the sort of trough that you didn't want to be in during a rainstorm for fear of a flash flood. Melissa had actually traversed a branch of it in order to climb the mound. Gill was standing in the main channel, his red tank top illuminated by the harsh sun, a mere hundred yards from the site.

"Gill!"

It took her voice a few seconds to reach him. When it did, he turned around. Placing his hand to his brow, he searched for the source of the summons.

"Gill! Up here!" She waved at him.

He waved back. "Ms. Lewis! I think I . . ." The rest of his words were stolen away by the wind.

"What?"

"I found something!"

"What is it?"

"Looks like . . ." Another gust cut his sentence short.

"What? I couldn't hear you. It looks like what?"

He cupped his hand to his ear, then lifted his hands, palms to the sky, clearly unable to discern her question.

"I said . . . What is it?"

Gill shook his head and waved for her to join him.

Melissa began her descent, resisting the urge to head for the Rover. Gill's position was out of her way. And he had probably found a snake hole or something equally innocuous. She checked her watch: 2:27. The desert would heat up another few degrees over the next hour. She was dripping with sweat, tired—it was a good time to flange things up and start the three-hour drive back to Vegas.

The bottom of the ravine, she soon learned, was like a beach: deep, fine sand that made walking a chore. Whirlwinds were lifting the sand into the air with such vigor that for a few moments, she lost sight of Gill and the mesa and the sky. When the gusts subsided—albeit temporarily—and she had rubbed the grit from her eyes, she reoriented herself and hurried over to him.

"What's up?" she asked.

His back was to her, his face toward the cliffside.

"Look at this, Ms. Lewis!" He stepped away from the ravine wall and Melissa saw the focus of his attention: a sharp, vertical rift. It appeared to be the result of a recent mudslide. The slide had exposed a thin chasm that displayed a neat stack of strata layers.

"Wow. Quite a geological column," she said with a pretense of interest. "Listen, don't wander off like that. Are you about ready to go? The girls are fried and . . ." Her voice trailed off as her eyes followed Gill's pointer finger.

"Could that be a bone?" he asked, tapping a lump in the strata.

Melissa leaned forward to inspect it. The gray-yellow bump looked a little like bone—either that or a dirt clod.

"Mmm. I'm not sure, Gill."

"What about this?" He pointed out another bump. "And this . . . And this . . . And this . . ."

Melissa took a step back. The gash in the ravine was covered with small, rounded protrusions. There were hundreds . . . thousands . . .

"Those have to be rocks," she said, staring.

"There's something else in there," Gill told her, gesturing into the rift. "Turn sideways and squeeze in."

She responded to this with an expression that said: *You must be joking.*

"Seriously, Ms. Lewis. You can't see it if you don't."

Melissa sighed, then began pushing into the rugged break in the wall. The rift was deeper than it looked. Almost like a narrow cave. It continued back, getting smaller and wetter, until it disappeared in darkness. Just the sort of setting snakes and bats liked to call home, she thought. "What am I looking for?"

"See where there's a hole down at the bottom, towards the back?"

"Yeah. Rattler City, by the looks of it."

"Well, back about . . . three feet. There's a clump of dark soil. Looks like hardened mud. And there's something sticking out of it."

Melissa located the mud. There was a short, rounded stick in the middle of it. A tree branch? A funny-shaped stone? Or a . . . No. Couldn't be.

"I couldn't quite reach it," Gill told her. "Maybe with one of the shovels we could get it out."

She extricated herself from the crevasse and brushed the dirt from her shorts. "You'll have to run back and get one. I only have one trip to the Rover left in me."

"Okay. Hang on." Gill sprinted off.

While he was gone, Melissa used a pocket knife to work one of the knobby protrusions loose. It couldn't be a bone, she told herself as she chipped at the surrounding earth. There were too many of them. They had to be small, rounded stones. But as she slowly exposed more and more of the knob, she realized that the object was longer than she expected. It extended back into the wall of the ravine and resisted her efforts to dislodge it. Two minutes later, with a full six inches exposed, she changed her mind about the object's identity. It was definitely bone. The question was, what kind?

Gill returned bearing a shovel and a trowel. "How do we do this?"

Melissa shrugged. "Knock away a few of these rocks, push back in there, and snag the thing with a shovel handle."

Gill made a face. "Snag it? I don't remember Horner or Kendrick using that term."

"This crevasse is too skinny to perform a by-the-book extraction," Melissa explained. "We don't have the equipment or the time to do anything elaborate. Let's just see if we can get a shovel on it."

"You're the boss, Ms. Lewis."

Gill banged at a few of the more obvious rock obstacles, then stepped into the gap, grunting as he forced his way inside.

"Watch out for snakes," Melissa cautioned. "Can you get to it?"

"Almost." He grunted again and tried to squeeze further in. "I can almost . . . Oh, great!"

"What?"

"I dropped the shovel. And I can't reach it." He withdrew himself from the rift, one side of his face caked with dirt.

"Let me try," Melissa told him. "I'm smaller." She sucked in her breath and slid in. "What are Beth and Sydney doing?" she asked, panting as she struggled forward.

"Sitting in the Jeep."

"It's not a Jeep. It's a—"

"I know, Ms. Lewis. I was just kidding. Do you see the shovel?"

"Oh, I see it all right. How did you manage to get it way back there?"

"Talent, I guess."

"Hand me the trowel." She reached a hand backwards, blindly.

Gill placed the instrument in her hand, like a nurse assisting a surgeon.

Melissa flailed the trowel at the shovel head. There was a clank as metal met metal. Another clank. Another. Then: "Got it."

"The bone or the shovel?"

"The shovel. Here." The trowel came Gill's direction again. "Now . . ." Melissa positioned the shovel carefully. "I can touch it, but I'm not sure how to extract it. I need a grabber."

"A grabber? Is that another technical term, Ms. Lewis?"

"Yeah. I need a grabber to snag the thing."

"Well, I don't have one of those."

"Maybe I can . . ." She tapped the object, tugging it gently in her direction with the shovel. "If the mud was softer . . ." More tapping, more tugging, a lot of body English. Finally the object began to move. "Hey! Here we go. Just a little more . . . A little more . . . I can almost . . . Got it! Here." She sent the shovel out, handle-end first.

Emerging from the crevasse, she presented the bone to Gill. It was thick, about a foot and a half long, rounded on one end, sharp and ragged on the other.

"Wow! What is it?"

"Good question." She leaned against the wall of the ravine, studying the find. "Bone. Not human."

Gill beamed, his eyes wide. "Do you think it's a T. rex?"

Melissa frowned at this. "Doubtful. Of course, it's been so long since I was around a dig site that I couldn't tell you for sure. I probably wouldn't recognize a T. if it jumped up and bit me. But . . . well, it's unlikely."

* "Why?"

"You're a self-proclaimed student of Horner. You tell me."

Gill looked at the bone, then shrugged. "Wrong size?"

"Forget about the bone. Tell me why it would be a surprise to find a skeleton of a dinosaur—much less a Tyrannosaurus—out here, in the Tonopah desert."

He considered this for a moment, his face contorted by thought. "Because . . . they lived mostly up in Montana and Wyoming?"

"And Colorado, the Dakotas, Nebraska, Alberta . . . ," Melissa added. "This area was covered by the inland sea."

"I thought you didn't go along with evolutionary theory."

"I don't. In my opinion, the 'sea' they talk about may well have been the result of the Flood—a temporary rise in the water level that covered all dry land, mixing up terrestrial and sea creatures and depositing them in various strata. But . . . Well, for now the fossil record lends support to the 'transitional sea' theory."

"Either way, no Ts have been found this far west, have they?" Gill asked, his shoulders sagging.

Melissa shook her head. "But then again, maybe this will be the first," she said, trying to cheer him up.

Gill glared at the bone. "Probably just a sheep or an old milk cow that got caught in a flash flood." He started to discard it.

"Hang on. It's fossilized bone," Melissa consoled. "I'm rusty, but even I can tell that much. Which means it couldn't have come from a contemporary carcass." She shrugged at it. "Just because nobody's ever found any of the bigger lizards down here doesn't mean they weren't here, at one time or another."

"Yeah," Gill muttered, obviously disappointed.

"The prudent thing to do is to take it back home with us," she told him. "I can check its size and shape against some of my old college texts. Who knows? It might turn out to be important."

Gill frowned at this, unconvinced.

"We'll photograph the site where you found it, and you can write up a fossil report. It'll be good practice. How's that sound?"

"Okay."

"I don't suppose you'd like to run back to the Rover and grab the camera?"

Gill nodded. She handed him the shovel and he jogged up the ravine.

Melissa examined the bone again and found herself hoping it had once belonged to a dinosaur, if only for Gill's sake. Though unlikely—there were so many other prehistoric land and sea creatures to consider—it wasn't out of the question. Say a Brachiosaur had collapsed on the shore of the inland sea. After the scavengers had finished with it, bits and pieces of the skeleton were carried west. Or maybe they had

settled in the Utah mud and were later swept to Nevada by a ri
There was really no way of telling at this point.

She set it carefully on the ground, squeezed back into the rift, and
procured two small, neighboring stones that appeared to be resting in
the same strata level—in the off chance that the find was significant and
they wanted to perform a radiometric dating test. Then she went back
to work on the bone protruding from the ravine wall. This bone, she
thought, wiggling it free, was . . . what? Part of the same creature? But
what were all of the other knobs? If each bump represented a bone . . .

She turned the extracted bone over in her hands. It was much
smaller than Gill's. But it was intact: both ends rounded, fossilized to
stone. This one could have passed for human. Hmm . . .

Three minutes later Gill reappeared, out of breath, bearing Melissa's
old Olympus.

"Thanks." She took it, checked the film and flicked on the light
meter. Pushing her way into the crevasse, she set the f-stop to 1.8, the
shutter speed to thirty, and steadied herself to snap pictures in the semi-
darkness. Satisfied that she had captured the scene, she stepped back out,
adjusted the settings, and clicked off another six frames of the knobs
covering the wall along the opening to the rift.

Handing Gill the large bone she took a step backwards and said:
"Smile."

"Huh?"

"We have to have a shot of the amateur paleo who found it. If it
turns out to be something big, you'll be famous," she joked.

Gill nodded, giving her his most charming grin.

She snapped off a shot. When she tried another, the shutter button
refused to depress, signaling the end of the roll. "One will have to do. I
have another roll, but it's in the Rover." After replacing the lens cap, she
slung the camera over her shoulder. "Ready to call it a day?"

"Yeah," Gill replied. He was cradling the find as if it were a new-
born babe—precious and fragile.

As they started up the ravine, back toward the site, he said, "I know
it's crazy, but wouldn't that be wild if this was a T. rex, Ms. Lewis?"

"It certainly would."

"Imagine us finding number thirteen . . ."

"Imagine."

EIGHT

VAUGHN WAS HIKING BACK UP THE MESA, MENTALLY PREPARING TO TAKE his second watch on what Parish was calling "Hell's Tower," when he heard it: a chorus of throaty baritones echoing up from the south. In the time it took him to turn his head, the four camouflage-painted F–15s were upon him, streaking north/northeast just a few hundred feet above the desert floor. As they passed directly overhead, their rumbling engines caused Vaughn's entire body to resonate. The fighters performed a hard right turn, the diamond formation moving in complete unity, before disappearing over the Cactus Mountains.

The sky was quiet and empty again, a dome of perfect blue lorded over by a blazing yellow orb, when Vaughn finally topped the mesa.

"Catch that flyover?" Parish asked from his seat in the brush. He was hiding beneath a green and brown desert hat with a wide brim, eyes closed against the glaring sun.

"Hard to miss," Vaughn grumbled.

"Henderson's way of rubbing it in."

"And you said he wasn't a monster," Vaughn scoffed, tugging at his shirt. It was hanging on him with twice its usual weight, heavy with perspiration. He took a long, refreshing drink from his water bottle before offering it to Parish.

He accepted. Removing his hat, he poured several ounces into his hair. It dripped down his face, into his lap.

"Thawed yet, Minnesota boy?" Vaughn teased with a smug grin.

"Oh, I'm thawed, all right. I've had about all the fun I can stand for one day."

"What're the rock hounds up to?" he asked, digging out his binoculars.

"The two girls are in the Rover," Parish reported with a sigh. "Don't ask me why. It has to be a sauna in there. Anyway, the guy and the lady are down in that riverbed." He pointed at a dry ravine.

Vaughn followed Parish's index finger with his eyes, then lifted his binoculars. "I don't see 'em."

"Big gash in the ground—'bout two clicks from the Rover."

"I see the riverbed. I just don't see anybody in it."

"They're up against the near wall. The kid wandered down there first. Then the lady went looking for him. She walked over here." He pointed left. "Then went up that hill. When she finally spotted him, she went down and looked at whatever it was he was doing. The kid came back to the Rover for a shovel, then again for a camera."

"Did you get it on video?"

"Oh, yeah. Exciting stuff." He paused, shaking his head. "Classic military operation, Steve. Probably laying land mines. My guess is these are Chinese communists preparing for a full-scale invasion." Grumbling something under his breath, he opened his own water bottle and took a drink. After pouring water over his head again, he cursed the heat for the tenth time that day.

Vaughn was watching the riverbed. In a minute he said, "Here they come."

Parish picked up the video camera and hurriedly adjusted the focus.

Two figures climbed out of the riverbed. The woman was carrying the camera and the shovel. The teen was holding something in his arms.

"What's the kid got?" Vaughn wondered.

"A rock?" Parish suggested, squinting into the viewfinder. "You said it was a rock club."

The figures reached the Land Rover and loaded the item into the back.

"Bone," Vaughn announced. "That was a bone. A big one. They're fossil hunters."

"Fossil hunters?" Parish said, making it sound like a swear word.

The woman and the boy climbed into the four-wheeler and moments later it lurched in a half-circle, turning back toward the highway. Picking up speed, it rolled west.

"Scratch one contact," Vaughn said, watching the vehicle disappear down the dirt road.

"Hallelujah!" Parish exaggerated with a wide smile that made him look like a faithful Southern churchgoer. Then his expression shifted, turning serious. "And once again, the United States Marines have successfully defended America's freedom from the likes of the ever-dangerous ... fossil hunters," he deadpanned. "Can we go home now, sir?"

Vaughn thumbed his radio transmitter. "Homebase, this is Recon One. Contact is bugging out. Repeat, contact is bugging out—leaving the zone. The fossil hunters are headed back to the highway."

"Roger that, Recon."

"Homebase, call Nellis and get us permission to come home. ASAP. We're dying out here."

After a brief pause Jimmy replied, "Recon One, this is Homebase. Permission has been granted. Come on in."

Vaughn shot Parish a look of relief.

"Tonight. Ice cold brewskies. McCormick's," he announced, stowing the camera. "I'm buying."

"After a nice cold shower," Vaughn stipulated.

"Recon One . . . Uh . . . There's something else," Jimmy added. Even through the static they recognized the ominous tone to his voice.

"What's that, Homebase?" Vaughn asked, not sure he wanted to hear the answer.

"We're about to have company."

"Company?"

"General Henderson is inbound—as we speak."

Parish let loose with a curse.

"Henderson?" The smile on Vaughn's face disappeared as his jaw dropped. "He's coming to the bunker?"

"Yes, sir."

"Why?"

"Something about a debriefing."

"Debriefing?"

"He didn't explain, sir. Just said he was paying us a visit."

Vaughn muttered his own expletive. "Roger," he groaned. "ETA to bunker . . . seventy-five minutes. Recon One out."

"Homebase, out," Jimmy chimed.

"We're dead," Parish said, gathering his gear. "Henderson will clean and fry us, Steve."

"For what? What did we do?"

Parish shrugged at him.

"A debriefing?" Vaughn wondered. "What's that supposed to mean?"

"Beats me," Parish said. He took the lead as they started down the mesa, toward the Hummer. "But in an hour and a quarter, we'll find out."

Nine

"HOW MUCH LONGER?"

"When are we gonna be home?"

Both questions were phrased in the form of a whine, each girl applying an artificially high, especially irritating lilt to her voice. They had asked the same things, in the same annoying way, for the past ninety minutes. And unfortunately, Vegas was still over an hour away.

So this is what it's like to have kids, Melissa thought as she watched the heat waves rising from the highway. Beth and Sydney were fourteen years old. That put them at the outer edge of poor car travel. Just imagine if they were younger! Think about driving several hours in a small, enclosed space with a couple of, say . . . six-year-olds. Though she was not Catholic, Melissa decided that car travel with small children must be something akin to purgatory: an expiation of sins by suffering. How did parents endure it?

Parenthood . . . It was something she couldn't relate to, and most likely never would. She had resigned herself to the depressing fact she would probably never bear children. Not at this rate. Not in the absence of anything even resembling a serious relationship with a man. There was always hope, of course. But unless things changed radically . . .

She and Nigel had discussed children at length and with great energy. Nigel wanted a family, at least three children. Melissa had been excited by this prospect, but wondered if they could keep up with their careers and raise three children too. She was also concerned about finances. Could they support that many kids? She had voted for a more manageable two. In the end, he had agreed, and they had even outlined a budget and college savings plan.

It seemed funny in retrospect. They had been able to agree in the often touchy areas of family planning and finances, but not on the seemingly simple issue of religious belief. But as Jesus had once said, he came not to bring peace, but a sword: his identity becoming a violent source of division. It had certainly divided her from Nigel.

Since she doubted that she would ever marry and have children, the occupants of the Land Rover and the other members of her classes—her students—were her offspring. Robbed of the chance to spawn a lineage of blood and smother her own flesh-and-blood with motherly love, she was determined to hand down a legacy of knowledge and faith to a budding, fresh-faced generation.

"I'm hot," Beth complained.

"Me too," Sydney agreed.

Melissa eyed the temperature gauge. Despite the heat, the engine was running cool, the needle frozen just below the midway mark—right where it should be. As she reached to crank up the air conditioner, she gave herself a mental pat on the back for filling the radiator with new coolant. A thin, cool breeze fought against the warmth in the cab.

"How much longer?" Beth repeated.

"We're sixty-seven miles from home," Gill reported.

"How do you know?"

"See that?" He pointed down the road at an approaching guard house. When it had whizzed past, he said, "Mercury. The gate to the Test Site. It's sixty-seven miles from the city limits."

"How do you know?" Sydney asked, frowning. "I didn't see a sign."

"My dad used to work there," Gill said. "Before they shut it down."

"If it's shut down, why do they need a gate?" Beth wondered.

Gill shook his head at them. "How can you live in Las Vegas and not know what goes on at the Test Site?"

"My father works for DigiCom," Beth responded proudly. "He makes $200,000 a year."

"As if we cared," Gill muttered.

"I thought they just cut back at the Test Site," Melissa said. "It's not totally shut down, is it?"

"Well, not quite," Gill conceded. "I guess they're still doing something. But after the budget reductions and the atomic testing treaties, the Department of Energy laid off something like three-quarters of the employees. My dad was one of the last to get the ax. They kept telling him his position wouldn't be affected."

"What did he do out there?"

"He's a nuclear engineer. He was working on classified projects."

"What's he doing now?"

"Working for a chemical company. It's an administrative job. The pay's crummy, though. He tried to get reassigned someplace else in the DOE. But they didn't have anything. So my mom went back to work as an accountant. That helps pay the bills. But—I don't know. We may be moving if he can get a better job somewhere else."

Melissa tried to think of something to say, something comforting, but couldn't. The silence stretched. Beth and Sydney, obviously sobered by this revelation, wisely decided not to joke or tease Gill about his father's work situation. Finally, Melissa said, "Let's pray about it. You want to, Gill?"

Gill nodded. "Okay."

They spent the next ten miles asking God to intervene in the situation. Melissa led, the girls followed with short, well-meaning prayers, and Gill concluded with a blunt petition for help.

"Thanks," he said when they had finished.

They topped a low rise and watched as the barren, scorched earth stretched toward the horizon. A mile ahead, a nonexistent lake beckoned them forward.

"Why didn't the dinosaurs make the cut?" Gill suddenly asked.

Three heads swung toward him, each bearing a puzzled look.

"The Flood. Ms. Lewis, you said they were destroyed all at once in the Flood."

Melissa nodded, not sure what Gill was getting at. "Yeah."

"Why? How come alligators and camels and zebras survived, but dinosaurs didn't?"

"Because they were too big to fit into the Ark," Sydney submitted, apparently serious.

Gill laughed at this. "Oh, so it was a space problem. There just wasn't room for them on the boat. They didn't book their seats far enough in advance, so God let them drown."

"That's not what I meant." Sydney glared.

"Maybe they showed up late and it was first come, first serve—you know, festival seating. Or they just forgot their boarding passes and Noah left without them."

"Shut up!"

"Gill has a point," Melissa admitted. "God could have saved all of the dinosaurs if he had wanted to. It was certainly within his power to do so."

"Right." Gill nodded. "So why didn't he?"

The question was answered only by the hum of the straining air conditioner and the singing of the tires as the Rover raced down the highway.

After a minute had passed, Melissa said, "Answer that one, Gill, and you can write a book. A best-seller."

"Nobody knows?"

"There are some theories. But nothing concrete."

"What sort of theories, Ms. Lewis?"

"Well . . . Before you can get into the theories themselves, you have to remember the early earth scenario. You've got the canopy—resulting in increased life spans, increased sizes—supporting dinosaurs and similarly large creatures and plant life. We'll also assume, for the sake of discussion, that dinosaurs and men coexisted. Now, we have to take into account the Fall."

"The Fall? What do Adam and Eve have to do with dinosaurs?"

Melissa stared at the road as she gathered her thoughts. "If we go back to the Creation account in Genesis," she began, "we find that on the fifth day God made birds and sea creatures. On the sixth day, he made land creatures. Let's say that dinosaurs and sea-dwelling reptiles were included in that. After God finished creating on day six, the Bible says that he 'saw that it was good.' In other words, he was pleased with his work."

"Sure, but—" Gill interrupted.

Melissa waved him off. "Hang on. Now, God's next creative act was man. God made man in his own image—endowing him with abilities and attributes that mirrored his own."

"Right, Ms. Lewis, but—" Gill tried again.

She silenced him with her hand. "Here's where the theories come in. One line of thought says that Adam and Eve—before the Fall— were super-extraordinary creatures. Not just because they were human. They were also supremely intelligent, perceptive, highly advanced beings that put today's finest scientific minds to shame."

Melissa paused as Gill digested this. Beth and Sydney were listening with blank stares.

"Contrary to popular, secular thought," Melissa continued, "the first man and woman were not monkeylike cave dwellers or grunting Neanderthals. They were wise beyond imagination, knowledgeable beyond belief, gifted in understanding the secrets of the universe. Drawing on the full capacity of their complex brains, they were undoubtedly the most brilliant, insightful human beings ever to walk the earth: Godlike in the true sense of the term. Until the Fall.

"Free will was perhaps their most astonishing trait. God created Adam and Eve with an ability to choose the depth and quality of their relationship with him. Unfortunately, they chose poorly."

"But, Ms. Lewis, being ejected from the Garden of Eden for eating an apple has no bearing on the fact that T. rexes are extinct."

"It probably wasn't an apple," Melissa corrected playfully. "And actually, the Fall may have had quite a bit to do with the extinction of the dinosaurs."

Gill was leaning into the front seat, waiting for an explanation.

"Instead of our evolving from the primordial ooze," Melissa continued, "moving from a one-celled blob, to a fish, to a land dweller, to a mammal, to man over the course of millions of years, several theorists believe that the Bible supports an entirely opposite movement: a de-evolution from near perfection to a state of chaos. We see this in the universe itself—the principle of entropy: everything moving from available energy to a state of disorganization."

"I don't get it."

"Instead of getting smarter and smarter, becoming more civilized and advanced, mankind is moving backwards, degenerating. Consider some of the marvels of the ancient world: the Great Pyramids, the Hanging Gardens of Babylon, Easter Island . . . We can't even figure out how to build these using modern technology. So it's been suggested that aliens from other planets or galaxies may have helped construct them. But if the theory of de-evolution is true, if ancient man was incredibly advanced rather than primitive . . ."

"That's interesting," Gill admitted. "But is any of that actually in the Bible?"

"Adam named all the animals," Melissa asserted. "So he was apparently quite knowledgeable in the area of veterinary biology. He and Eve also took care of the Garden of Eden—they must have had a pretty good grasp of animal husbandry and botany. Their son, Cain, built an entire city: Enoch. A little later a guy named Jubal invented musical instruments. Another guy by the name of Tubal-Cain invented all manner of bronze and iron tools."

"But they were bronze and iron," Gill pointed out. "Not steel or aluminum."

"Sure. But these folks were starting from scratch. We're talking about a metallurgist ushering in the metal age a few short generations after the creation of the world."

Gill shrugged his approval of this. "Okay. So where do the dinosaurs come in?"

Good question, Melissa thought. She took a deep breath. "The motivation for their destruction could have come from a number of areas. This is where the theories get iffy. Mostly because they consist of speculation—taking what we find in the Bible and extrapolating."

"Extrapolating?" Beth asked with a twisted face.

"Making assumptions. Remember, the Bible isn't exhaustive. It is Truth—true knowledge. And it is totally reliable. But it doesn't tell us everything—only the things we need to know in order to be reconciled with God. The Bible is God's Word to fallen man. Its purpose is redemptive, not scientific. It's not an encyclopedia. More of a love letter, really: a heartfelt message from the Creator to his prized creation. So when we hypothesize about things that it doesn't fully explain, we're on thin ice."

"Back to the theories," Gill prodded.

"Right. Well, there's one called the Gap Theory. It says that there is a huge gap of time—eons—between the creation of the world in Genesis 1:1 and the 'formless and void' state described in verse two. The idea is that something catastrophic happened in this period—such as Lucifer's fall from heaven—thereby causing the destruction of the original earth. Perhaps the dinosaurs were the result of Satan tampering with God's original creation."

"Do you believe that?"

"No. I don't buy any of it—the gap or the idea that dinosaurs were something outside of God's preordained plan. Another theory says that demons gave rise to dinosaurs by cohabiting with women and/or reptiles."

"Yuck!" Beth flinched.

"That's gross," Sydney added with a twisted face.

"Yeah, it is. I'm not too hot on that theory either. Though the Bible does say that such cohabitation did occur and that one of the products was a race of giants referred to as the Nephilim.

"What you have to realize is that the Fall affected more than just Adam and Eve. It perverted the entire creation. I believe that, before the Fall, the universe was *not* running down. Death did not exist—not for mankind, not for animals, not for stars and planets. There were probably not any carnivores. No predators. Everything coexisted in a peaceful state. By rebelling against God, Adam and Eve managed to throw the whole thing out of kilter, sending the universe into a downward spiral toward destruction."

"I thought you just said that you didn't think dinosaurs were outside of God's plan," Gill prodded.

"I did."

"You make it sound like the Fall was unexpected, that it messed up his plans."

"In a way it did. But it wasn't a surprise. He was ready for it."

"How do you mean?"

"First of all, God gave man freedom of choice. A free will. I'm sure he realized the inherent danger in that. Instead of fashioning a robot that would comply to his every whim, God had created an independent soul capable of disobedience and rebellion.

"Second, the Bible says that Jesus is the Lamb of God—chosen before the creation of the world, slain from the foundation of the world. God obviously knew what would happen when he gave mankind free will and had already taken steps to undo the damage. When Adam and Eve broke relationship with him, he immediately set about mending the relationship through Jesus."

Gill nodded. "I believe that too, Ms. Lewis. But the dinosaurs—they still aren't in the picture."

"Sure they are. The Fall twisted all of creation: tame creatures became wild; safe, kind beasts became predators; plant eaters began to seek meat. Death entered the system and mankind had to struggle to survive. That was all part of the curse. We're still seeing the results of that today, entire species becoming extinct as the ecosystem sputters and stumbles along, out of control."

"So you're saying that the dinosaurs disappeared as a result of Adam's sin?" Gill wondered.

"Basically. Maybe they had reached a place of de-evolution that was detrimental to man," Melissa suggested. "I don't know. But the Bible says that by Noah's day, man had grown so very wicked that God was sorry he had made him. The earth was corrupt and full of violence. That included the animal kingdom. God decided to wipe the slate clean and start over. This purging action was aimed at men, animals, reptiles, birds . . . the entire creation apparently. And we know from the fossil record that many species didn't survive the Flood."

Gill was obviously unsatisfied with this. "They didn't make the cut," he muttered.

"I don't pretend to have all the answers, Gill. Nobody does. But the bottom line is that God created it all—including the dinosaurs—for one purpose: to give him glory. Why he chose to allow or even orchestrate their eradication, who can say? He's God. He has his own reasons."

She let this statement hang, wishing she could offer something more specific. Then she added, "The Bible does describe some creatures that sound an awful lot like dinosaurs, though."

"It does?" Gill asked skeptically, raising one eyebrow.

"In Job it talks about a plant eater and a carnivore."

"Right," Gill sighed, rolling his eyes.

"You don't believe me? Look it up."

Beth pulled a Bible from her backpack. "What chapter, Ms. Lewis?"

"Oh . . . I don't know. Try the end of the book. Around forty or forty-one, I think."

Beth paged quickly to the section with skilled hands and began scanning the pages. "How about a 'behemoth'?"

"That's the place. Read it."

"'Look at the behemoth,'" she read. "'which I made along with you and which feeds on grass like an ox. What strength he has in his loins, what power in the muscles of his belly! His tail sways like a cedar; the sinews of his thighs are close-knit. His bones are tubes of bronze, his limbs like rods of iron.'"

"That's talking about a hippo," Gill argued.

"Maybe," Melissa consented. "Maybe not. Skip down the page, Beth."

Beth did. "What about a 'leviathan'?"

"I heard about that." Gill nodded. "Somebody said it was an alligator."

"Doesn't sound like an alligator to me," Beth said, scanning. "'His snorting throws out flashes of light; his eyes are like the rays of dawn. Firebrands stream from his mouth. . . . Strength resides in his neck; dismay before him.'"

"A fire-breathing dragon?" Gill snorted.

"Listen to this," Beth said. "It sounds like one of your dinosaurs, Gill. 'When he rises up, the mighty are terrified; they retreat before his thrashing ..."" She skipped down the page."'He makes the depths churn like a boiling caldron ... Behind him he leaves a glistening wake ..."'

"Not a dinosaur," Gill said, still unconvinced. "Even if it isn't an alligator, it would be a sea dweller. If it got into the water and swam around, it wasn't a dinosaur."

"'Nothing on earth is his equal,'" Beth finished, "'a creature without fear ...'"

"Well ..." Gill conceded reluctantly. "It does make you think."

"Might make a good topic for a paper," Melissa offered. "'Dinosaurs and the Bible.'"

Ten

I DON'T SEE IT," VAUGHN OBSERVED, SQUINTING THROUGH THE BLOWING dust towards Frenchman's Flat.

They had just crested the last in a series of steep hills and were making a bounding descent toward the chalky, cracked surface of the dry lake. As the Hummer jolted along, never flinching at the grade or the rugged terrain, the unmarked location of their underground bunker slowly came into view.

"Maybe he didn't come after all," Parish submitted hopefully, gripping the wheel with both hands. "Maybe he changed his mind."

Vaughn wanted that to be true. Seconds later, he saw it: a Harrier III double-seat fighter, wings and fuselage gleaming in the afternoon sun.

Parish aimed a curse at the craft, then tried meagerly, "Somebody else's jump jet?"

There was no mistaking the general's favorite mode of transportation. Though Harriers were relatively common in the navy and marines, Henderson's was one of only three in the entire Air Force—and the other two were experimental prototypes at Dreamland. And if the size, shape, and configuration of the craft weren't enough to announce the general's arrival, the clean, polished exterior was. Despite the wind and dust, the helicopterlike attack jet was always as spotless as its owner's boots. Word had it that Henderson employed an entire crew to keep the plane in a constant state of readiness, servicing and washing it every time he ping-ponged between Nellis and Indian Springs.

"Think he brought Johnson with him?" Parish wondered, steering the Hummer around a ditch.

"Let's hope so. The colonel seems to have a calming effect on him."

Five minutes later they were inside the bunker, toting gear from the garage area down the long, bleak corridor toward the locker room. After stowing their packs and equipment, they warily approached the lounge. It was empty.

"Must be in the control room," Parish said, frowning.

"Must be."

They made the last leg of the trip in silence, like two men forced to walk to their own execution.

"Captain Steven R. Vaughn." He pressed his thumb against the scanner until the green light blinked on.

"Lieutenant Phillip T. Parish," his partner said glumly, still playing the role of a condemned prisoner. He slapped the scanner and waited.

The light blinked green, the readout declared "access approved," and the door slid back.

The room was dark and cool. Vaughn squinted, peering into the shadows for signs of life. Nothing, just the eerie glow of the monitors. But someone was there. He could feel them watching.

"Captain."

He recognized the voice. So did Parish, who cursed softly under his breath.

"General Henderson," Vaughn replied, offering a salute to the invisible guest. His eyes finally began to adjust and he saw two figures standing in the center of the room, arms folded across their chests. "Colonel." Another salute.

Parish followed suit, his hand moving sharply out from his brow.

"Gentlemen, please have a seat," the general said. He retreated to one of the four desk chairs and sank into it. The cushion and back piece squeaked in protest as he adjusted himself. He was a large man, husky once—back in his younger days—but now merely portly.

Vaughn and Parish found their usual seats and wheeled them over to Henderson. Johnson looked for a place to sit and, not finding one, leaned against the wall.

"Sir," Jimmy grunted, bolting up to offer the colonel his chair.

Johnson shook his head. His face was a pale, sickly green in the glare of the monitors. "I'll stand," he grunted.

Vaughn shot Parish a look of veiled panic. Johnson was the ever-congenial nice guy who always told bad jokes and was seldom without a smile—if he was in a bad mood, there was no hope. Henderson would eat them alive.

"How was your day in the zone?" the general asked through an evil grin.

"Hot . . . sir," Vaughn replied.

"I'll just bet it was." He laughed heartily, then the grin disappeared, replaced by a daunting glare. "I should kick your butts all the way to Reno for the bogus crap you've been reporting for the last couple of weeks."

Vaughn and Parish braced themselves for a verbal lashing.

"But I'm not going to. I know it's the equipment." His voice sank to a whisper. "Congress. They expect us to run a top-notch testing grounds but won't give us the money for decent sensors. The dimwits . . .

"Anyway, that's not why we're here. It's about today's contact," he explained. "I understand it was viable." He bent forward and began inspecting the concrete floor.

"Yes, sir," Parish replied, nodding a little too enthusiastically.

"A stage three, sir," Vaughn added. "In the zone. We tracked it. Nothing to worry about."

"Yeah, well, let's go over it anyway, shall we?"

Vaughn shrugged his approval. Whatever.

"What time did you first detect the contact?" Johnson asked. With the characteristic joviality absent from his voice, he suddenly sounded like a trained interrogator.

Vaughn began recounting the events as they had transpired, pausing to listen to Henderson's questions and Johnson's humorless requests for specific information. Parish and Jimmy spoke only when called upon.

After nearly an hour had passed, the story of the contact having been told three or four times in mind-numbing detail, Henderson issued a summons for coffee.

Jimmy beat Parish to the punch, smiling as he exited the room. The back of his shirt was dark with perspiration. Vaughn watched him escape, wondering when and if "The Truck" would return. Just how long could refreshment preparation be drawn out? Pretty long, knowing Jimmy.

The general was hunched over, still examining the floor. Behind him Johnson looked almost ill, as if lunch had disagreed with him.

"If you don't mind my asking, sir," Vaughn finally said, "since when does a three require a debrief—by senior commanders?"

"Since we said it does," Johnson retorted grumpily.

Must have had a short night, Vaughn decided. Maybe his wife was leaving him or something.

"It was a routine contact," Parish assured them. His statement was met by two cold stares.

"Where's the tape?" the general asked.

Vaughn fished a tiny videotape cartridge out of his pocket and handed it over. Henderson took it and relayed it to Johnson, who fed it into a nearby player. The four men watched as color bars filled the screen, flickered, then disappeared, replaced by a square of dark brown.

"What's that?" Henderson wanted to know.

"Uh . . ." Parish leaned toward the screen, wondering himself. "Oh," he said as the shot slowly zoomed out. "My boot."

Two boots and a pair of fatigue-clad legs came into view. The camera jiggled violently and the picture dissolved in static before a new scene appeared. This time it was steady, almost like a still photo: desert, hills, tiny specks in the distance. The focus adjusted radically, then the frame zoomed in. The specks became a vehicle and a group of people.

"There they are," Parish narrated. "Our four fossil hunters and their Rover."

The general was unimpressed. "Fast forward, Bill."

Johnson toggled the "ff" button and the home movies jumped into high gear, the people doing a jig around the Land Rover. Every few seconds, the picture bounced awkwardly. The subjects dug, rested, ate lunch, dug some more. Finally two of them got into the truck, the other pair wandering off. There were more jolts; a single ant climbed one of the hills, hiked into a ravine. Finally, a pair of specks clambered out, returning to the Rover.

"Let it play," the general barked.

Johnson backed away from the equipment and the picture jerked into what looked like slow motion.

"What's that kid carrying?" Henderson wondered aloud.

"We assume it's a fossil sir," Vaughn offered. "Maybe a dinosaur bone."

"Run it back."

Johnson did and they watched the figures approach again, bone in hand.

"Stop it there."

The colonel complied, transforming the people into statues.

"Print that. We'll take it back to the lab and have the boys enhance it."

Johnson grunted, fumbling to find the appropriate buttons. The video printer whirred to life and seconds later a thick photo curled into the tray. Johnson handed it to the general.

"Fossil, huh?"

"We think so, sir," Vaughn stipulated.

"Even with enhancement, I don't think we'll have much," Henderson said, his lips pursed.

What's going on? Vaughn wanted to ask. Parish looked puzzled too.

"What about the flyby, sir?" Johnson said.

"What about it?"

"The 15s took high-res."

Henderson smiled for the first time. "That's right. Let's get back and go over that. Maybe they picked up something."

The phone buzzed just as the general was rising from his seat. Parish answered it.

"Sir," he said, extending the phone. "Nellis. For you."

Henderson took it and barked, "What is it?"

He paused, listening. Vaughn thought he detected a brief flash of surprise in the general's eyes.

"Patch him through." Another pause. "Mr. Secretary."

Vaughn glanced at Parish and mouthed: Mr. Secretary? They both looked up at Johnson. The colonel's face was blank.

"Yes, sir," the general continued. "My aide and I debriefed the men personally."

Aide? Vaughn wondered how a bird colonel liked being called an aide.

"Yes, sir. Yes, we've got video. Uh-huh. If you'd like to, certainly. We can feed it into the computer and modem it out to you. Yes, sir. No, just some fossil hunters—as we originally thought. No. No, they dug around a little, found what appeared to be a bone, and—How big? Oh, I'd say . . . I don't know . . . two feet long. Oh, about . . . three or four inches thick. No, sir. No, sir. We couldn't tell from the video if there were other bones. No, sir, we did not detain them. But—But you asked us not to. Yes, sir . . ."

Vaughn listened with a sense of growing curiosity. He had never seen—nor imagined—the hard-nosed, controlling General Henderson behave with such obsequious deference. Though Vaughn had no idea who was on the other end of the line, it was clear that whomever it was had pull—someone with major clout. He was still trying to decide what sort of "secretary" it might be—defense? state?—when the conversation ended.

The general slammed the phone down and seemed ready to swear. Instead, he emitted something of a roar. No one dared speak. Even Johnson looked fearful.

After several minutes of silence had passed, Jimmy came whooshing through the door with a tray of coffee. "Oops," he said as he surveyed the faces. "Bad timing?"

The general ignored this and stepped over to take a mug. "Listen, gentlemen," he said in a tone that bordered on civility, "I don't know what's going on. But Washington is concerned about this contact." He paused. "No. Let me rephrase that. I've had no military response whatsoever. The Pentagon is quiet. But the DOE . . ." He took a deep breath. "The secretary is about to wet his pants over this thing."

"Over a three—in the zone?" Parish wondered aloud. "Why?"

"That's the question of the hour, Lieutenant. Pompous, airheaded bureaucrat," he muttered angrily. "Inform Nellis that we're headed back," he told Johnson. Then he turned to Parish and Vaughn. "At any rate, we need to stay on top of it until he cools off, got that?"

They nodded.

"I think it will blow over in a day or so. But who knows? So don't go anywhere. If you're scheduled for extended leave, consider it canceled—for the time being. And when you're off duty, stay close to home."

"Yes, sir," they answered in unison.

"You too, Sergeant."

Jimmy nodded emphatically. "Yes, sir, General, sir."

Henderson aimed a thumb at the door. "Ready, Bill?"

The colonel swallowed hard, took a deep breath. The blood drained from his face. After another gulp, he managed, "Yes, sir."

The general patted him on the back. "Chin up, Bill. Air sickness is nothing to be ashamed of. You can chew on some saltines when we get back to the base," he consoled as they marched out of the control room.

When they were gone, Parish wondered, "What was that all about?"

"Are we in trouble or not?" Jimmy wanted to know. His eyes were wide, white cue balls with tiny black pupils.

"Don't look at me," Vaughn said, sinking into his chair. "I have no idea what's going on."

"A three?" Parish wondered aloud, his brow furrowed. "The bozos in D.C. are hot and bothered by a three?"

"Not just any bozos,"Vaughn said. "The chief bozo. So it's no fluke. It's got something to do with the NTS."

"Maybe they've got something hot going on up north," Jimmy suggested. "Maybe they're running tests in violation of international treaties again. And Secretary DiCaprio is jittery about getting caught."

"Nah," Parish said, shaking his head. "They do that sort of thing all the time—developing new weapons, setting off secret bombs . . . Why do you think they need us? No. It's not just the usual security paranoia. Something's up. Something . . . odd."

"I'll second that," Vaughn half-chuckled. "General Dragon didn't breathe fire on us. He was actually halfway friendly. And the head man in the Department of Energy is worried about a group of dinosaur hunters. It's odd all right. Downright strange."

Eleven

IT HAS BEEN OPERATING OVER BUDGET FOR DECADES. WASTING UNTOLD billions, even trillions of taxpayer dollars. Adding to the national debt. Conducting environmentally hazardous research that we are now spending billions to clean up: Hanford, Rocky Flats, Three Mile Island—fiascos! Misguided blunders motivated by Cold War paranoia! The nuclear bomb has been perfected. We are now quite capable of destroying the planet many times over. Atomic energy has yet to make sense—even on paper. And we are ruining large regions of our nation by turning them into radioactive dumping grounds.

"Therefore, it is my contention that we shut down the Department of Energy—lock, stock, and barrel. Today! Close the shutters, lock the doors. Stop pouring money into a black hole. The DOE has become an unnecessary burden, a monstrous bureaucracy without a purpose or a goal. I submit to you: it's time to kill the beast—before it kills us!"

A half-dozen listeners applauded politely as Herman Jefferies, the longtime congressional representative from Utah, gathered his notes and stepped away from the podium. They seemed relieved that he had finally finished his droning monologue. The rest of the chamber took little notice of his departure. They were engaged in hushed conversations about everything from impending bills to the NBA playoffs. Aides were scurrying back and forth, shuttling paperwork. Committee members sat in clusters sharing laughs. Though it had the appearance of an ill-behaved elementary school classroom, the current session of Congress was in full swing, attending to the business of the land.

DiCaprio watched Jefferies plod up the aisle, toward the exit. The man was rotund, in his late sixties, with a sagging face and a bald head that gleamed in the television lights. He looked like a congressman, like the sort of person cable viewers expected to find blathering dull, life-less rhetoric when they flipped past C-SPAN.

Jefferies had been calling for the death of the Department of Energy for years. As a resident of Utah, he had long decried the atmospheric and underground testing conducted at the Nevada Test Site, blaming nuclear fallout for nearly every malady his constituents suffered: from cancers and thyroid problems to birth defects and mental retardation.

The flack over DOE projects, misappropriations, and its huge operating budget had begun in earnest four years earlier, just before DiCaprio took the helm. Consequently, his first actions as secretary were directed toward saving the Department. He had instituted a progressive schedule for severe downsizing, cutting a full third of the personnel in a six-month period. Another quarter of the work force was given the ax the following year. This pattern continued until DiCaprio was convinced that he had honed the DOE into a lean, mean, efficient machine. And yet the critics still weren't satisfied.

Jefferies's voice was growing louder, and to DiCaprio's dismay, other members of Congress, as well as the Administration, were rallying to the cause, seemingly anxious for the opportunity to participate in the demise of the DOE.

Another representative, a woman of about forty whom DiCaprio didn't recognize, stepped to the podium and took up where Jefferies had left off—arguing that the Department of Energy was nothing short of the anti-Christ.

He watched her face grow red as she shouted into the microphone. Surveying the room, he realized that despite her emotion and volume, no one was paying attention. They were all impatiently waiting their turn, champing at the bit for a chance to do what every good politician did best: take the floor and assume the center stage spotlight.

Taking a sip from his water glass, DiCaprio checked his beeper. Nothing. They hadn't called . . . yet. But it was only a matter of time.

As the woman launched into a vigorous recitation of the DOE's numerous sins, her voice echoing from wall to ceiling to floor, he closed his eyes and mentally prepared himself for the call. They would want an update on the situation. What would he tell them?

First and foremost, that everything that could be done was being done. He would remind them that the area was under careful surveillance by a capable team of marines as well as the vast resources of Nellis Air Force Base. Motion sensors guarded the quadrant. The contact had proven to be a no-threat: fossil hunters out looking for lost dinosaurs. Totally innocuous. Nothing to worry about.

Second, he would go over the response. The contact had been closely monitored: videotaped and photographed with powerful, high-resolution cameras. These materials were being scrutinized now, analyzed with computer-assisted image enhancement equipment.

Third, he was on top of this thing. It was contained. A non-event that did not warrant their concern.

It sounded good. Still, he was somehow certain that it wouldn't be enough. Not for them. No matter how many state-of-the-art toys were employed, no matter how he scrambled to react to the breach and rule out the slightest possibility of a "problem," they wouldn't be satisfied. They had a way of pushing caution to its limits, of being careful to a fault. Everything they did was calculated to the last minuscule detail. These folks didn't believe in variables, chances, or loose ends—not even in untacked threads. Their operations were always squeaky clean.

The woman at the podium finished a statement with an angry flourish, then shifted her stance. Paging through her notes, she seemed to be building up steam for her next attack. The pause was filled with the noise of lighthearted conversation. The group closest to DiCaprio was arguing about whether or not the Lakers would sweep the Sonics if both reached the finals.

The key, he thought for the tenth time that morning, was to remain calm. Keep a lid on things, and they would resolve themselves. Or so he hoped. He was in charge. He was in control. Despite their leverage, he was the one calling the shots. Now, if he could just convince them of that.

The woman at the podium had begun shouting accusations, likening the DOE to a disease-ridden albatross, when his beeper sounded. The soft tone told him that he was being paged. Silencing the device with a thumb, he glanced down at the digital readout and sighed as he read the number. The time had come.

He rose, calmly buttoned his suit coat, and walked out of the hall. The congresswoman's diatribe faded, then disappeared as the door swung shut behind him.

Outside the building he trotted down the stone steps to his waiting limo. The chauffeur, surprised by his charge's unannounced appearance, stumbled out of the driver's side and hurried around to open the door. Once safely inside, DiCaprio lifted the phone to return the call.

Then he saw the liquor rack: an array of tiny bottles bearing dark, cool liquids, each waiting to be sampled. He should have had the rack removed, he realized too late. Dry for nearly four months, he suddenly felt a desperate, suffocating thirst. He replaced the phone.

Three minutes later, a vodka martini coursing through his veins and another spirited concoction poised in his hand, he dialed the number.

A male voice answered on the third ring. "Yeah."

"This is Robert DiCaprio."

"Just a moment, sir."

The alcohol was doing its trick, settling his nerves with the gentleness of a masseuse, taking the edge off. He took another sip.

"Robert?"

"Yes."

"What's the story?"

"No story," he began confidently, buoyed by the vodka. "The contact was a false alarm. They came, they dug around, they left. Crisis averted."

"Except that they took some sort of bone with them. Isn't that right?"

DiCaprio spilled his drink. "How did you know . . . ?"

"We're not stupid, Robert. If you know something, be assured that we do too. Now about the bone . . ."

"It was a dinosaur bone," he assured.

"And you've verified that, have you?"

"Well . . . it wasn't verified, per se. But—"

"In other words you don't know for sure."

"The team on site said—"

"You don't know for sure. Isn't that right?"

His answer came in the form of a sigh.

"I have to tell you, we're rather disappointed, Robert. You assured us that the area would be safe from prying eyes. 'Deserted.' I think that's how you originally described 217. But suddenly there are people digging around out there—and finding things."

"It was probably just a fossil," he tried.

"Maybe. Maybe not. Either way, it's time to let us handle it, Robert."

DiCaprio started to object, but there was really no point. Instead, he said, "Be discreet. Please. Please, be discreet."

The caller laughed at this. "Aren't we always? Here's what's going to happen."

DiCaprio listened, wishing he was in a position to argue, wishing he didn't have to kowtow to these people, wishing he were free. But he wasn't. They held the title deed to his life. They had made him and they could break him if they so desired. It was a distressing, powerless feeling, as if he were a puppet destined to mirror every move of his master's hand—a master he despised. And the situation seemed all the more unbearable when viewed through a fresh, depressing, alcohol-induced haze.

$($LUB BLUE WAS NOT A FIVE-STAR, AAA-APPROVED ESTABLISHMENT. Located just outside the Las Vegas city limits, miles from the infamous Strip and its collection of monstrous luxury hotels and casinos, the club was a strip joint and brothel that catered to men who worked hard and played harder. The patrons were attracted to clubs like this one because it afforded them the opportunity to sip booze, watch women disrobe, and engage in various sexual activities with the attending "hostesses"— all in a decidedly legal environment, thanks to Nevada's lenient prostitution laws.

From the outside, Club Blue was a long, cobalt-painted structure bordered by an asphalt parking area. A glowing neon sign told highway travelers that the club was open for business twenty-four hours a day. The glass front door was covered with dark blue blackout paper to discourage unpaying voyeurs. Large gold letters warned: GENTLEMEN ONLY.

The inside was dark, no matter the hour, thanks to a marked absence of windows and lights. The music was loud to the point of being obnoxious, encouraging customers to hurry into a drunken stupor that dulled their hearing. Unless the place was deserted, there was usually at least one woman dancing on the small stage, often a showgirl wannabe waiting for her "big break" to come along.

Tito and Vince were seated at their usual table next to the stage, doing damage to their third round of Long Island iced tea and Diet Coke—respectively—when the bartender waved them over.

"Phone," Tito observed. He was six foot, two inches of solid muscle with wide shoulders, biceps that strained his white, short-sleeved dress shirt, and the thin waist of a bodybuilder. A tight black ponytail trailed halfway down his back.

"Huh?" Vince was gawking at the strippers.

"The phone," Tito tried again. "It's probably a job."

"You take it," Vince mumbled. His jaw was slack, his eyes glassy.

Tito shook his head and started for the bar, wondering about his partner's addiction to sex. It wasn't that Tito didn't like women. He was considered something of a ladies' man, but preferred picking up suitable companions with his charm and good looks rather than paying for them. Vince, on the other hand . . . Okay, so the guy was dog ugly: nearly bald, a slight paunch around his waist, acne scars and assorted pocks on his face. Still, he had a way about him, a steady charismatic confidence that drew people. He didn't need to resort to prostitutes.

Hanging out at Club Blue was Vince's idea, of course. He got his kicks here and it gave them a place to lay low when they weren't out on assignment. They had the money to do better, to frequent one of the more exclusive "gentlemen's clubs," the kind that allowed only high rollers through the door and employed only the finest entertainers. But this place was relatively clean and out of the way—a fitting place to set up shop.

"Did they say who it was, Joe?" Tito asked the bartender.

Joe shook his head. "Just asked to speak to you or Vince. Like always."

Tito shrugged and took the phone. "Yeah?"

"To whom am I speaking?"

"Tito Vispeti. Who's this?"

"Sonny. Got something for you."

"I'm listening."

"Need you to shadow someone."

"Shadow?"

"Did I stutter?"

"No, but—"

"Then shut up and listen. High-school teacher. Name's Melissa Lewis." He offered physical description. "Stake out her place. Follow her if she leaves home." He read the address, a vehicle make, and a license plate number. "You writing this down?"

"Whattya think, I'm stupid or something?" Tito scoffed, gesturing to Joe for a pen. When Joe produced one, Tito scribbled the street and the number on a napkin. "Stake out. Got it."

"And you're supposed to lift something."

"What kind of something?"

"Bones."

"Huh?" He turned and looked back at Vince. The lout was still entranced by the peroxide bombshell.

"I don't know the whole story, just that this Lewis has a bone—or maybe several bones—and our people want them back."

"Bones?" Tito repeated with disdain. "Stake out this woman's place and watch for bones?"

"Right."

"Surveillance and retrieval aren't exactly our specialties, Sonny."

Sonny cursed at him. "Tell me something I don't know. Can you handle it or not?"

"I guess. What do we do if we see the bones?"

"Grab 'em."

"That's it? We don't do this Lewis lady?"

"Huh-uh."

"What do the bones look like?"

Sonny cursed at this. "What do you think they look like, smart guy?" More profanity. "Call back when you've got 'em."

The line went dead. Tito hung up the phone and returned to the table. "Vince?"

"What is it?" he asked without looking away from the blond.

"We got a job."

Vince ignored this.

"Vince! We've got work to do."

His partner frowned at him. "Can't it wait?"

Tito shook his head. "Come on." He took Vince by the arm and dragged him toward the exit.

"Talk about bad timing," Vince grumbled. When they reached the parking lot and were climbing into Tito's Corvette, he asked, "So what is it? Please tell me we get to shoot somebody." He removed an automatic from the holster under his jacket and checked the clip.

"Nope."

Vince cursed at this, snapping the pistol shut. "Then what is it?"

"Bones," Tito replied. "We're going after some bones."

TWELVE

IT WAS STRAIGHT UP SIX O'CLOCK WHEN THE LAND ROVER ROLLED BY a sign on the outskirts of town: *Welcome to Las Vegas.* Beth and Sydney were still asleep. They had nodded off somewhere around the cutoff to Charleston Peak and had dozed contentedly ever since. Gill was awake, but not very talkative. He seemed bummed that his "find" was most likely not a Tyrannosaurus.

As she slowed for traffic and admired the distant skyline of the city modulating in the heat waves, Melissa considered taking the kids out for dinner. Deep-dish pizza and a couple of pitchers of ice-cold pop would be a pleasant ending to a pleasant day. There were only two problems with that idea. First, their parents were expecting them back between six and six-thirty and would be waiting at the school. Second, she wanted desperately to go home and relax, to take a long, cool shower, put on some music, do a little reading . . .

Visions of kicking back in the solitude of her apartment won out over those of gorging on pizza in a noisy restaurant and she took a right off the highway, directing the Rover toward World Harvest Christian School. A bank sign proclaimed the temperature to be a comfortable one hundred and nine.

When they reached the school twenty minutes later, it was deserted except for two cars: a Ford Taurus and a Subaru station wagon.

"Here we are," Melissa announced, pulling into a space between the other vehicles. "Beth . . . Sydney . . ."

Beth raised her head and blinked out the window.

"We're home."

"Oh," she muttered groggily, elbowing Sydney.

"Ow!"

"Wake up. We're back."

They climbed out and mumbled, "Thanks, Ms. Lewis," before staggering to the Taurus. Beth's father waved at Melissa as he backed away.

"Yeah, thanks," Gill said. "You won't forget about those bones, will you, Ms. Lewis?"

"I'll look them up tonight," she assured him, immediately regretting the promise. She was in no mood to page through paleontology texts.

"Great. And I'll be sure and read those chapters."

"You'd better," she warned sternly. "Have a good weekend, Gill. See you Tuesday."

"Tuesday?"

"Monday's an in-service," she reminded him. "The new quarter starts Tuesday."

"Oh, yeah." A huge smile spread across his face. "Okay. See you Tuesday!"

Melissa watched him get into the station wagon. Gill was a nice kid. Bright and inquisitive. Sure, he had a tendency to procrastinate—especially when the subject didn't fully capture his interest. But then, didn't everyone?

She waved good-bye to Gill and his mother, then followed them out of the lot. As she drove the three miles to her apartment, Melissa made a mental note to get the car washed. The trip had left it filthy, caked with an extra layer of dirt inside and out. It was nearly twenty years old, the odometer boasting just over 180,000 miles, the body bearing a variety of dents and scrapes. But she wouldn't have traded it for anything. It was like a part of her family, a familiar friend that treated her well, communicating her style and avocational interests, as well as serving as a storehouse for memories—some of them painful ones.

She had purchased the used Rover while attending CU, precisely for the purpose of tooling around in the back country in search of extinct lizards. She and Nigel had bumped, bounced, and four-wheeled their way through most of western Colorado in it.

Slipping into an on-street parking slot, Melissa recognized the direction her thoughts were taking and ordered herself to avoid the subject of Nigel Kendrick. She knew from experience that it would only lead to regret and heartsickness.

After switching off the ignition, she scanned the interior of the car with a sigh. Snack wrappers, cups, and pop cans were scattered on the seats and floorboards. Clods of dirt and a collection of pebbles dotted the mats. The mess would have to wait. She didn't have the energy to clean it up now. Pulling one strap of her backpack over her shoulder, she slammed the door behind her and set out across the lawn toward her unit.

It was a newer, well-kept complex, complete with a pool and a tennis court which she seldom found the time to use. Today the pool was crowded. As she snaked past it, through the collage of pink, red, and brown sun worshipers, dodging children and Frisbees, she decided that if she could possibly muster the strength, she would don a suit and come back out for a dip.

Sweat was trickling down her brow, dripping from the tip of her nose by the time she reached her apartment. After fighting with the dead bolt, she swung the door open and stepped inside, ready to retreat into the artificially refrigerated shade. Unfortunately, what met her was a wave of warm, stale air. Her first action was to check the thermostat.

"Liar," she told it, frowning.

The arrow was pointing at sixty-eight, but it had to be at least eighty-five in there. Which meant the air conditioner was still acting up. Setting her pack on the bar stool, she fumbled through a kitchen drawer, searching for the number of the management company. It was only after she had found it and was in the process of dialing that she remembered what time it was. The office closed at five and nothing short of a five-alarm emergency would generate a return call.

"This is Melissa Lewis in 7A," she told the answering machine. "My air conditioner is haywire again. I would appreciate it if you'd send someone over to fix it—this weekend if at all possible. Thanks," she said, hanging up. It was clear from the tone of her voice that the sentiment was insincere—she was not thankful.

After opening every window that would open, she sank into the cushions of the couch and closed her eyes. As she did, two opposing certainties struck her. One, she was starving. Two, she was too tired to get up and fix anything.

That's it."

Vince examined the apartments suspiciously, squinting at the name—"Birchwood Estates"—then at the napkin in his lap.

"Yeah. I guess it is," he finally agreed.

"And that's our vehicle," Tito added, pointing a finger down the block, toward a dirt-stained Land Rover.

Vince held the napkin up and compared the number on it with the plate. "Sure is. Let's do it." He popped open the passenger side door.

"Slow down," Tito cautioned, grabbing him by the arm.

Vince jerked away, insulted. After smoothing his sleeve he gave Tito an intimidating glare. "What have I told you about touching me?"

This drew a chuckle. "Close the door, tough guy."

Vince shot him another scowl, then begrudgingly complied. Thankfully. Despite his small stature, Vince was a demon when it came to hand-to-hand combat. A former Green Beret, he had served with a special forces unit in Viet Nam, winning a medal of honor and the nickname "The Butcher" in the process. He was deadly with bare hands, a knife, or a gun. Tito, on the other hand, had prepared for his current line of employment by studying martial arts, pushing weights, and working as a bouncer at a Vegas dance club. He possessed a black belt in two disciplines—kung fu and tae kwon do—and wasn't a bad marksman. Still, he was unsure who would prevail in a fight between him and his partner. And he wasn't terribly interested in finding out.

"So what are we waiting for?" Vince asked, clearly irritated.

Tito rolled his eyes. "Try witnesses for one." He gestured toward a couple sitting out on their tiny patio, then to the courtyard full of swimmers and sunbathers.

Vince shrugged. "I'll just slip over to the car, look in, open the door, grab the—"

"First of all, the bones probably aren't in the car," Tito told him. "Second, she may have a car alarm."

It was Vince's turn to laugh. "On that thing?"

"You never know. Third, if it's locked, we'll have to use the picker."

"No problem." He reached behind the seat and pulled out the instrument in question. "I'm ready."

"We should probably wait until after dark," Tito thought aloud, taking another look at the pool area. He studied the man and woman in the lawn chairs again. The former was asleep, the latter hypnotized by a thick novel. "And I should do it. I'm better with a picker."

"Says who?"

"Says me."

"Whatever. Just do it," Vince groaned. He handed him the lock-picking device. "Be quick. I'll watch your back."

Tito sighed at this, shrugged, and hopped out of the Vette, lock picker in hand. Vince slid out the passenger side and stood leaning against the car, eyes shifting from the apartments to the street.

Tito examined the sidewalk for pedestrians, then made his approach. When he reached the Land Rover he did another head check. A pickup swung around the corner and slowed to parallel park a block away. Tito waited. When the occupants of the pickup were safely inside a nearby townhouse, he turned and went to work. A cursory glance inside the car told him that it had no alarm, so he quickly attached the picker to the driver's door lock and sucked the entire mechanism off with one fluid motion.

MELISSA HAD RALLIED HER STRENGTH AND WAS IN THE PROCESS OF throwing together an oversized tossed salad when she remembered: the bones! She had forgotten them in the back of the Rover. Leaving her knife and the crooked carrot she was peeling, she wiped her hands on a dishtowel and padded out the front door, shoeless.

The sun had disappeared below the horizon, but the air remained dry and suffocatingly hot. The crowd around the pool had grown.

WHEN VINCE SAW HER APPROACHING HE CLEARED HIS THROAT LOUDLY, without hesitation. The woman fit the description of their subject: five foot six inches, auburn hair. Even if it wasn't Melissa Lewis, she presented a threat in that she was walking directly toward Tito, who was now rifling the Land Rover.

He coughed again and Tito looked back at him. Vince made a fist and pulled an outstretched thumb toward the Vette: get out!

Tito glanced toward the woman, nodded, and quietly closed the driver's door. It clanked softly, unable to latch without the benefit of its locking mechanism.

HI."

"Hello." Melissa nodded and smiled back politely as she passed the man on the sidewalk. He was big, muscular. Good looking. Greek, or Italian maybe. A real macho kind of guy. Her head instinctively swung around to take a second look. When she did, and found him doing the same to her, she jerked her head back around, blood rushing to her cheeks.

Embarrassed, she hurriedly opened the tailgate of the Rover, scooped up the towel-wrapped bundle, and retraced her footsteps back to her apartment. As she was about to go inside, she stole a glance at the street and saw a cherry red Corvette rumble away from the curb. The tinted windows made it impossible to determine whether or not "the hunk" was inside.

NICE," VINCE PRONOUNCED. HE PUNCTUATED THIS ASSESSMENT WITH A long wolf whistle. "And she sure was checking you out."

"Bad timing though," Tito said, making the block. He pulled the Vette into a spot just around the corner from the Birchwood Estates. "Another minute and I would have been finished. Bet the bones were in that towel she took out of the back."

"Maybe," Vince muttered. He was busy playing with the 35mm SLR Tito had procured on his little expedition. "At least she didn't notice the door. Or the missing camera. We would have been in sad shape."

"Suppose there's anything worthwhile in there?" Tito asked, aiming a thumb toward the camera.

Vince shrugged. "Let's find out." He rewound the film and pulled the crank. The back of the camera popped open and a roll of 100 ASA Super G Fuji fell into his hand. "Know of any one-hour developing places around here?"

"Sure. There's a Wal-Mart about a mile that way," he offered, pointing east. "But we need to keep an eye on Lewis. If those were the bones—"

"Heads or tails?"

"Huh?"

Vince fished a quarter out of his pocket and flipped it. "Call it. Loser takes the film in. Winner gets to stake out Lewis. Who knows? Maybe we'll get lucky. Maybe she'll slip into a bikini and go for a swim."

"Heads," Tito grunted.

Vince pulled his hand away from his arm, revealing a silver eagle. "Sorry, chump." He handed Tito the film, then pulled another camera out from behind the seat, this one equipped with a thick black barrel. Pointing toward a shaded bus-stop bench he said, "Meet you over there," and got out of the car. "And don't worry." Vince displayed an evil grin and patted the telephoto lens. "If she goes to the pool, I'll get some close-ups."

As he stomped on the pedal and the Vette obediently squealed its way up the block, Tito couldn't help wondering if his partner, Vince "The Butcher" Scapelli, was a certifiable sex fiend.

Thirteen

When she finished preparing her salad, Melissa made a horrifying discovery—no dressing! After scouring the refrigerator and the pantry, she added the missing item to the shopping list tacked to the corkboard beneath the phone, then examined her creation. It was a work of art: a bed of iceberg lettuce and fresh spinach leaves decorated with slices of ripe tomato, carrots, mushrooms, and red bell pepper, and topped with strips of leftover chicken breast. But without dressing, or even the ingredients to mix up a homemade oil and vinegar concoction . . .

Determined to enjoy her creation—and similarly determined not to make a run to the store—she set about whipping together a thin paste of spicy mustard and honey. It tasted fine in the bowl, so she spooned it over the salad. After pouring herself a tall glass of raspberry iced tea, she flipped on KJZZ, the local jazz station, and took a seat on the couch, next to the window. There wasn't much of a breeze, but any movement was better than none.

The "find" from their expedition was sitting on the coffee table in front of her, still wrapped in the old towel. She stared at it as she ate, thinking that she was too tired to examine the bones tonight, much less try to match them with diagrams from a text. Closing her eyes, she chewed to the soft strains of David Sanborn's lusty saxophone.

By the time she had consumed her dinner, Melissa realized that part of her problem had been hunger. She already felt better, as if a second wind had quietly stolen up on her. No, she wasn't anxious to jump head-first into an anatomy manual. But it would be kind of fun to study the bones for a little while. Kind of.

Two minutes later, she had loaded her empty plate and fork into the dishwasher, scooped out a bowl full of Chunky Monkey, and returned to the living room. It was growing dark outside, but the apartment was still sweltering. She could hear the pool patrons laughing and splashing, and considered joining them for a swim. Maybe later.

Sinking to the floor, she took a huge bite of ice cream, set the bowl aside, and began to unwrap the bones. They rolled out onto the coffee table like driftwood, two brittle, mocha-brown branches. The larger of the two was maybe a foot and a half long, about three or four inches in diameter. Except for its surface texture, it looked like the trunk of a small tree. The other bone was tiny in comparison, just ten or twelve inches long and only a half inch or so in diameter—a tubular ruler.

Between bites, Melissa picked up the big specimen. It was remarkably light for its size. Two-thirds of the bone was stained with mud. The remainder was creamier, obviously weathered. She assumed this was because the bone had been protruding from the cliffside and this portion had been exposed to the elements: wind, rain, sun, and other forms of erosion. It had probably been exposed fairly recently via a cave-in or geological shift. Otherwise it would have been "exploded"—turned to dust—by the intense heat and dry climate.

Melissa tried to recall the type of rock the bone had been extracted from. Much of the cliff had been yellow—probably sandstone left by the extinct river. But back in that vertical crevasse it had been grayish, more like mudstone or siltstone, the kind of rock created by a flood plain. The pictures might help clear that up. Pictures? The camera!

She glanced about the room, wondering what she had done with it. After checking her backpack, she concluded that it was still in the Rover. No reason to get it now, she decided. Why not leave it and take the film in tomorrow morning?

Sandstone . . . Mudstone . . . Siltstone . . . Whichever, it was just the sort of sedimentary rock formation that fossils liked to hide out in. It struck her that she hadn't even considered that while at the site. Was she that out of practice?

Gobbling another spoon of ice cream, she used a pencil to pry off the mud caked on the end of the bone. It was hard and dry and came off in dime-sized flakes. She stopped and draped an old newspaper over the table before continuing. On her knees now, she was flaking mud off with the pencil when her hand slipped. The lead and two additional inches of the pencil disappeared into the bone. As it did, the last of the mud fell off in one big chunk.

Hollow! The bone was hollow. She leaned over the table, her face nearly touching the bone.

"More light," she muttered. Gently laying the bone on the towel, she strained to reach the light switch on the wall. When she did, she was rewarded with tiny beams of track lighting. She groaned at this. It was great for setting a mood but not for close, detailed examination of an object. Time to move to the breakfast nook. It would be even hotter in there, but at least the light from the hanging lamp over the table was strong and bright.

She spent the next minute transporting the bones to the kitchen, the following half hour hunting down her college texts, which proved to be quite a chore as her collection of science books and dinosaurology were stashed here and there in the unmarked boxes cluttering the spare bedroom. She had purposefully neglected the material, choosing not to unpack it. Much of it reminded her of school, which, in turn, reminded her of . . . Nigel.

With a fresh glass of tea by her side, she sat at the kitchen table and began flipping through the thick hardcover selections from her library of required reading: *Vertebrate Paleontology, The Dynamics of Movement in Extinct Vertebrates, Dinosaur Systematics, An Ecological Summary of Paleobotany*—the titles read like foreign languages. The terms inside were unfamiliar, the descriptions confusing. Melissa was amazed at how much she had forgotten in the last half decade.

She was paging along absentmindedly in *Basic Anatomy of Late Cretaceous Carnivores,* a book written by a former professor, when a diagram caught her attention. It was an artist's rendering of a bone that looked quite similar in shape to the one sitting in front of her on the table. The sketch was labeled: Humerus. An arm bone. But from what sort of beast?

As she read the accompanying paragraph, beads of perspiration trickled down the back of her neck. The room suddenly seemed unbearably warm. She took a long draw of tea and reread the words:

> Illustration C depicts the humerus of a tyrannosaurid. Like
> its modern, ornithological relatives, the tyrannosaurid's bones
> were hollow, made up of many small air cavities. While bone
> structure suggests very limited range of motion in the upper
> extremities, the size of the humerus implies that tyrannosaurids

possessed impressive arm strength. By examining distinctly marked muscle insertion points, researchers have concluded that the biceps of a typical Tyrannosaurus rex measured six inches in diameter—at least three times larger than the average human biceps. The humerus in this illustration would have enabled its tyrannosaurid owner to lift approximately 400 pounds.

Melissa stared at the coffee-toned bone on the towel, determined not to rush to any erroneous conclusions. Still, it was hollow and large—far too large to belong to any modern bird. She turned to the index of the book and scanned the diagram list. When she saw "Comparison of Sizes," she flipped to the page. It displayed a chart of numbers corresponding to various genera and species, listing their overall sizes and the lengths of their major bones. She found "humerus" and moved her finger slowly across the line. The lengths were all in centimeters, but even so she could tell that they didn't fit her specimen.

Her eyes raced down the chart. 72 cm . . . 78 cm . . . 83 cm . . . Too long. Four-leggers. Allosaurus—an upright carnivore of the Late Jurassic—sported a 51 cm humerus. Closer, but no cigar.

She perused the list: Daspletosaurus, Maleevosaurus, Tarbosaurus . . . All too small. Finally, near the edge of the chart, she found what she was looking for. Humerus: 62 cm. She used the muddy pencil to jot the number on a stray envelope. Jerking open the junk drawer, she hunted through the tape, scissors, screwdrivers, hole punch, pens . . . for a ruler. There didn't seem to be one. But there was a tape measure.

According to Stanley, the bone in question was 18 5/16 inches. Or forty-six centimeters. The way it sloped and curled near the broken end, if it hadn't been sheered off, it might amount to . . . about two feet of bone. Twenty-four inches. Sixty-one centimeters.

Melissa could hardly contain her excitement. Maybe she was mistaken. It wouldn't be the first time. She was pretty hazy when it came to dinosaurs nowadays. Or maybe it was a coincidence. Just because the bone was the right size didn't mean it was the right age. Short of dating it in a lab, there was no way of telling for certain when the creature that used it had walked the earth. Still . . . Her mind kept coming back to the seemingly logical assumption that, based on the evidence at hand, the bone had been discarded by a dying carnivore of the Late Creta-

ceous period, that it had, quite possibly, once been the property of a living, breathing Tyrannosaurus rex.

Perhaps Gill had dug up a T. rex after all.

By the time Tito returned with the developed roll of film, it
was dark and the bus bench where he was supposed to meet Vince was
vacant. He was about to hop out and conduct a search for his partner
when his cellular rang.

"Yeah," he grunted into the device.

"It's Sonny. You get 'em yet?"

"The bones? No. Not yet."

"Why not?"

"Lewis came out to her car while I was in the process of detailing it."

"So what happened?"

"I nabbed her camera. The bones might have been in there too. She
took something back into her apartment."

"When was this?"

"Maybe an hour and a half ago."

"Whattya been doing since then? Picking your nose?"

Tito resisted the urge to tell Sonny what to do with that remark.
The guy was a greasy little coward. He reminded Tito of Danny
DeVito—all mouth, no brawn. It would have been a simple thing to
end his puny life with one swift, well-aimed blow. But Sonny was several rungs up the ladder. For whatever reason—a combination of stupidity and shortsightedness probably—the weasel had obtained favor
with the higher-ups. Currently head of security, word had it that he
would be one of the big boys in a few short years. That frustrated Tito
to no end.

"I got the film developed from Lewis's camera," he answered
through clinched teeth.

"And?"

"Hang on a sec," Tito told him. He toggled the power button and
waited as the window slid down. Leaning his head out of the car, he
squinted up the street. Someone was perched on a fire hydrant a block
away, holding something. He eased the car into gear and rolled forward.

He cursed when he realized that it was Vince and that he was peeping into someone's window with the telephoto lens.

"Get in the car!" Tito barked.

Vince clicked off a series of photos before hopping down and taking his place in the passenger seat of the Vette. "How'd the pics turn out?" He had already picked the packet up and was leafing through them.

"No pornography," Tito joked, "if that's what you mean." Suddenly he remembered the phone. "Sonny! Sorry about that. I just hooked up with Vince. He was staking out Lewis's apartment."

"About the pictures . . ." Sonny repeated. He sounded irritated.

"Yeah. They're mostly of teenagers."

"She's a teacher," Sonny informed him. "World Harvest Christian School."

"Oh, yeah. Anyway, there's one of a kid holding a big bone."

Vince held that picture up and nodded thoughtfully.

"I guess that's what we're after."

"A kid?" Sonny swore, then paused to think this over. "They didn't mention a kid. Fax me the picture. I'll makes some calls. We'll decide what to do about him later. Right now, concentrate on Lewis. Confiscate any and all bones she has in her possession."

"Confiscate. I like that. So are we to go for a break-in?"

"You've got the green light."

"Can we do Lewis?"

"No. At least, not yet. Get that photo to me, then find those bones."

"Got it."

Tito replaced the phone and looked over at Vince, who was studying one of the photos with rapt interest.

"What is it? Another shot of the bones?"

"A shot of *her* bones," he replied with a leer. He offered Tito a glossy picture of Lewis and a group of teenagers at a pool party. The "teacher" was wearing a bathing suit with a red and orange flower print that accentuated her trim, toned figure.

"Wow." Tito couldn't help agreeing that Melissa Lewis was indeed a beautiful woman.

Fourteen

"NINE OFF THE END, INTO THE SIDE POCKET."

The crowd grew quiet, watching as Parish bent over the table, stretching to reach a cue ball stranded behind two solids. With one end of his stick high in the air, the other cradled between the fingers of his right hand, he carefully pivoted on tiptoes until he was satisfied with the shot.

Whack!

The striped ball ricocheted off a solid, careened against the end bank, and hurtled into the side pocket—as promised.

The onlookers showed their appreciation with a cheer. The opponent, an air force major, wasn't as pleased. He glared at Parish, muttering something under his breath.

"Double or nothing?" Parish asked him.

"Huh?"

"I make the eight—you owe me two hundred dollars. I miss—we're even."

The major weighed this as the crowd shouted various opinions. The majority seemed to think it was a sucker bet, that the marine would have no problem finishing the major off, no matter where the eight ball might happen to be.

"Tell you what," Parish added, smiling glibly. "I'll put the eight ball in the right corner." He pointed with his stick. "Your six will go there." The stick touched the right side pocket. "And your four will go here, here, and here, then in the left corner—nothing but net."

"Double or nothing?"

Parish nodded.

The major pulled a wad of bills from his wallet and set them on the edge of the table. "You're on."

This pleased the crowd—a mix of uniformed men and women—most of whom raised their drinks to evidence their approval of the bet.

Parish examined his cue to verify that it was sure, then began chalking up. Vaughn and Jimmy sat on stools across the room, watching the show.

"Quite a performer," Jimmy noted. "He always like this?"

"Always," Vaughn assured him. "If it isn't pool, it's darts, or hoops, or something. The guy has a serious competitive streak. And he gets a kick out of gambling on himself."

"He's one heck of a pool player," Jimmy admitted.

"Yeah. The scary thing is, he's good at just about anything he puts his mind to."

After several minutes of stalling—dabbing chalk on the end of the cue, cracking his knuckles, sipping his drink, eyeing the lay of the table—Parish finally approached the ball. The twenty or so people in the peanut gallery seemed to approach with him, all leaning into the action.

Parish frowned at the table and said, "Too easy. Maybe I should make it more of a challenge." He closed his eyes and put the cue behind his back, joking.

The crowd chuckled at this—Phillip Parish the jester, in his environment.

Businesslike again, he hunched over the table, pushing the cue back and forth through the fingers of his set hand as he concentrated. Suddenly he stood up, propped the stick against the table, and removed his glasses. "Spots," he announced, cleaning them on his shirt.

Another approving laugh. Parish was on a roll. They were eating out of his hand.

Stick in position, he gently fondled it, lining up the glossy white cue ball. Without any further antics, he pulled back one last time, then pushed the cue forward with confident force.

Crack! Crack-crack!

Balls collided. The impact of Parish's shot sent them rolling in every direction. It looked like chaos. But it wasn't. The cue ball attacked the eight, setting off a chain reaction. An instant later, the eight thudded into the right corner pocket, the six plopped into the right side. The four banked, then did a long, slow roll toward the left corner. It seemed to run out of gas, ultimately balancing on the edge of the pocket—before clunking in.

Suddenly Parish was king of the mountain, the recipient of boisterous praise, free drinks, hardy pats on the back, even a few seductive smiles from eyelash-batting ladies. The major slunk away, leaving his cash for the winner.

When his court began to break up, Parish returned to his seat at the bar. He was sweaty, out of breath, happy. He waved the bills at his buddies.

"See, Jimmy. ROTC pays."

Jimmy shook his head at this. It was his first time out with "the officers." Probably not his last, though, now that they had learned of his plans to test for non-com.

"Yeah," Vaughn added. "We can't teach you much about military leadership. But Mr. Shark here can show you how to hustle pool."

"I wasn't hustling," Parish objected. "That was pure talent. No con involved."

"Right," Vaughn muttered. "I think the major you took to the cleaners might offer a different opinion. Especially since you let him wipe you out the first two games."

"It takes me a while to warm up," Parish argued with a shrug.

"Another round," Jimmy told the bartender magnanimously. He pulled out a ten and scooted it across the bar.

Vaughn shook his head. "Thanks, Jimmy. Not for me. Two's plenty."

"We're off tomorrow," Parish reminded him, gulping down the last of his beer. "If you're worried about driving, we can call a cab if we get blasted. Right, Jimmy?"

Jimmy's head nodded, a smiling boulder rolling back and forth on enormous shoulders. He'd already had four beers.

"It's not that," Vaughn explained. "I'm just a little paranoid tonight."

"Henderson?" Parish asked.

"Yeah. His little visit was . . . strange."

"Weird," Jimmy agreed.

"I wouldn't be surprised if we got called in for more questions. And if that happens, I'd just as soon not be nursing a killer hangover."

"Good point," Jimmy grunted.

The bartender showed up with three fresh drafts.

"What I don't get," Parish said, lifting his new, frothy mug, "is: Why 217? We've had contacts all over the zone. They never got that sort of response. What's special about 217?"

The three of them had discussed Henderson's visit, the debriefing, and the contact that had prompted it all at length in the bunker, and it had been the favorite topic of conversation on the commute back to Nellis. Yet, thanks to the beer, they were ready to hash it out again. Alcohol had a way of making even the most basic insights seem revelatory.

"I still say it's a weapons thing," Jimmy offered. He paused to guzzle most of his fifth glass, then looked at them through glassy eyes. "Some special-ops business."

Vaughn frowned at this. "I don't know. Why would they be running ops out in the zone? If they're testing a new weapon—nuclear or otherwise—why not do it deep inside the Site—at Frenchman's or Yucca? That's only logical."

"Who says the DOE's logical?" Parish chuckled. He emitted a long, deep belch, then finished his beer.

"That's the key," Jimmy said. His voice dropped to a whisper. "They're not logical. And they're always up to something. Usually something dangerous."

Vaughn glanced at Parish as if to say, He must be drunk.

"I'm serious. You've heard the stories. How they put army pukes in trenches just a mile or so from the bomb tower, set off the nukes, then marched those guys right to ground zero—just to see what would happen."

"That was forty years ago, Jimmy," Vaughn argued. "They didn't understand the power or the effects of nuclear fission. Radiation was a new thing." He glared at his new beer. The glass was sweating, the foam still resting on top of the deep amber liquid. Against his better judgment, he picked it up and took a sip. "They were experimenting."

"Sure. Try telling that to my friends and neighbors back in Utah— the people who died from the fallout clouds."

"Jimmy . . ." Vaughn tried.

"I saw it with my own eyes. People with open sores. Babies born deformed. And cancer—almost everyone in my family ended up with some type of cancer. My grandmother died of breast cancer, my dad died of lung cancer, my sister died of bone cancer, my best friend died of thyroid cancer . . . I'm telling you, growing up in St. George was like growing up in Hiroshima."

Vaughn took another sip of beer, unable to think of a response. Jimmy had mentioned his family before, but only in passing. From the sounds of it, he had experienced a tragic childhood, one plagued by disease and death. As for who was responsible for it all—the government, the DOE, genetics, sheer coincidence—there was no point in arguing. Not with a three-hundred-pound ox who'd had a couple too many.

"You guys don't believe me," Jimmy pressed.

"Yeah, we do," Parish assured him. "We've heard the horror stories. It was terrible, what happened during the above-ground days."

"It didn't end with the banning of atmospheric testing," Jimmy pushed. "Just because they detonated those monsters underground doesn't mean we didn't get sprayed. The things vented all the time. And the radioactive clouds always came our direction.

"I remember one winter when it snowed fallout. The radio warned everybody to stay indoors until it melted. When it did, it took the paint off all the houses and cars." He paused for emphasis, his face animated. "Imagine walking in the dust of that stuff, breathing it in every day, drinking it in the water . . . I'm lucky to be alive."

"Hear, hear!" Parish chimed, lifting his cup.

Jimmy ignored this. "The government knew about the effects. They knew how hazardous that stuff was. But they didn't care. They just kept at it: blasting those bombs whenever the wind was right. In other words, when it was blowing towards Utah."

Vaughn waited, hoping the Truck would simmer down. He sipped his beer, then asked, "Why did you agree to work at the Site?"

"Couple of reasons. First, I didn't ask for it. I was assigned, just like you guys. My LT said that if I took it, I'd stand a better chance of making non-com someday. Second, I thought the testing was over. I thought all those treaties with Russia ended the nuclear era at the Site. I thought it was just a military zone that needed security like any other base."

"But you don't think that anymore?" Vaughn asked.

Jimmy frowned and shook his head. "Base security is one thing. But motion sensors, flybys, surveillance teams, video cameras, gates, ID checks, generals zipping around in jump jets . . . Something's going on in there. Something bad. If it wasn't, we'd be out of a job."

"I'll agree that the security is rather severe," Vaughn said, "but like we were saying, they don't use satellites or heat sensors. There are no electric fences. If top secret—meaning treaty violating—nuclear research was still being conducted, everything would be beefed up. I think we're just there to keep civilians out, to keep people away from old radioactive sites."

"Maybe," Jimmy conceded. "But that brings us back to the original question. Why do they care so much about 217? What's out there?"

Vaughn lifted his hands in a gesture of surrender. "You got me."

"They were awfully concerned that those fossil hunters were digging around," Parish noted. "Maybe something's buried out there."

"Like what?" Vaughn said.

"Like something radioactive. Barrels of nuke sludge."

"Or worse," Jimmy submitted.

"Worse?" Parish made a face. "I can't think of anything worse than stumbling onto a radioactive dump. Except maybe death."

"We need to talk to Jack," Jimmy announced.

"Who?" Vaughn asked.

Jimmy finished his beer before answering, wiping his mouth on his sleeve. "Jack Weber."

"The name sounds familiar," Parish said. "Isn't he a writer?"

"Didn't he do that controversial expose on the DOE that came out a few years back?" Vaughn asked.

Jimmy nodded. "He lives in Vegas."

"You know him?" Parish asked.

Another nod. "He's from my hometown."

"No wonder he was so peeved," Parish noted. "I didn't read his book, but apparently it painted a less than positive picture of the Test Site."

"He blasted the entire nuclear testing program," Jimmy explained. "But mostly the NTS. He's an expert on the history of the DOE and he stays up-to-date. It's his passion. The guy knows everything there is to know about the Site. If something's buried out in the zone, he'd know about it."

"Think so, huh?" Vaughn said. He had reached his limit—and then some—and was ready to call it a night.

"We can go see him," Jimmy prodded.

"Sure." Vaughn humored him, rising from his stool. "We'll do that."

"What're you guys doing tomorrow?" Jimmy asked.

Vaughn looked to Parish for help. *Not going to see some anti-government conspiracy nut,* he wanted to say, but didn't.

"B-ball," Parish answered. "We play pickup at the base on Saturday mornings. Wanna play?"

A smile consumed Jimmy's round young face. "Sure. What time?"

"Eight. At the courts by the PX."

"Great. I'll call Jack in the morning and set it up. We can drop in on him right after the game." Jimmy looked like a kid who had just been invited to a birthday party. He stood up, staggered slightly, then hiccuped.

Parish patted him on the back. "Let's call a cab."

"Great," Jimmy said, giggling. "This'll be fun."

"Fun . . ." Vaughn groaned, following them toward the phone. Getting a drunk, Herculean lineman home to bed, then getting up in the morning to visit a paranoid psycho with a thing for debunking the DOE didn't sound like his idea of fun.

FIFTEEN

MELISSA WENT THROUGH THE MOTIONS OF PREPARING FOR BED—showering, brushing her teeth, washing and applying a moisturizer to her face, donning a T-shirt—mentally coaxing herself into a state of relaxation that would make for a smooth transition to sleep. But it was no use. The heavy, nearly debilitating fatigue that had dogged her earlier in the evening was gone, replaced by a growing sense of childlike anticipation. She was wired. Between the suffocating heat and the knowledge of what she—or rather, what Gill—had found, she doubted that she would so much as doze off all night.

Throwing back the covers, she sat on the bed, already sweating again, and took up her well-worn copy of *The Business of Heaven*. Like many believers, she made a practice of spending time with God first thing in the morning. Prayer, Bible study, worship, meditation—these were staples of her daily spiritual diet. But at night, when she was in bed, she thought C. S. Lewis's devotional a fitting end to the day.

Opening the book, she found the appropriate selection and began reading. Her eyes followed the flow of words and sentences, moving line by line down the page—without the slightest comprehension of their meaning.

A T. rex! her mind shouted for the hundredth time that hour. It was remarkable! If it turned out to be true . . .

She caught herself, reoriented her attention to the top of the paragraph, and started over. Again her eyes were on automatic, reading familiar words without understanding their meaning.

If it really was a T. rex, it would be only the thirteenth T. rex ever found. Of course, the humerus might be all they ever recovered. Often in a flood plain the rest of the animal was washed away, its skeleton scattered across the terrain—a tibia here, a femur there, a vertebra over there. Still, it would prove that the grand old king of the carnivorous dinosaurs had at least visited points west of Colorado.

Evolutionists—like Nigel—would say that T. rex had followed the inland sea as it receded and eventually disappeared. That placed the species from Colorado to Alberta. Water would have prevented them from venturing west. According to the early earth/creationist scenario, however, tyrannosaurs—like most other dinosaurs—roamed a larger, more varied terrain: boundaries set not by shallow seas, but by God.

This rex—Gill's rex (if that was indeed what it was)—would stir things up. It would prove that the evolutionists were wrong—again. Perhaps this particular T. had been scavenging along a delta, or hunting river-dwelling duckbills when it was caught in a flash flood. Maybe it had even been swept away in a tidal wave of earth and mud at the Flood itself.

Any way you looked at it, this was a significant find, something that would send Nigel and his kind into a euphoric frenzy. He would manage to pull the funds together for an expedition crew and be out there, moving dirt in a matter of weeks.

If Nigel knew about it . . .

Melissa stared right through her book, imagining the look on that handsome, bearded face, the fire that would dance in his eyes when he heard the news. He was at his most charming when he was alive with the hope of fresh discovery. That was something she missed about him. One of many things she missed about him.

Shaking off the thoughts, she ordered her hyperactive mind to attend to *The Business of Heaven*. Taking a deep breath, she began the reading a third time, determined to concentrate on Lewis's message. As she digested the words, however, she found Lewis sketching a vivid picture of her ex-fiancé: the consummate rebel.

"A man who admits no guilt can accept no forgiveness . . ." That sounded chillingly familiar.

"I willingly believe," Lewis wrote, "that the damned are, in one sense, successful, rebels to the end; that the doors of Hell are locked on the inside."

Melissa could still hear Nigel arguing his position, brashly declaring his independence from anything and everything connected with the very idea of God. In effect, he was locking the door—from the inside.

"They enjoy forever," Lewis continued, "the horrible freedom they have demanded, and are therefore self-enslaved: just as the blessed, forever submitting to obedience, become through all eternity more and more free."

She swallowed hard, fighting back a wave of tears. She still loved Nigel, and the vision of him in hell—alienated from God for eternity—was almost more than she could bear. The man was resolute, adamant about having nothing to do with God—about God having nothing to do with him. He just wanted to be left alone. And alone—dreadfully, horribly alone—he would be. Forever.

Unless . . . Unless someone could get through to him. Had she ever really told him about Jesus? Not exactly. Most of their discussions had revolved around the profound differences in their perspectives. They had debated their own stances, sometimes vehemently. But they hadn't actually shared, moving past the barriers of ideology into a more intimate exchange of the issues that weighed on their hearts.

There was no hope that would ever happen. Not now.

Shutting the book, she set it on the nightstand and leaned back on her pillow.

God, Nigel needs you. He won't admit it. He may not even know it, consciously. But he needs you—desperately. You know how I feel about him. Please send someone to tell him, someone he can hear. Please prepare that rebellious heart of his to receive the Good News . . . Before it's too late.

Wiping away a tear, she closed her eyes and prayed for sleep to come.

THAT SIGN SAYS IT CLOSES AT TEN."

Tito checked his watch. It was 11:38.

"No running . . . No stereos . . . No alcoholic beverages . . . Open ten to ten . . ."

"So much for rules," Tito sighed.

They were sitting in the Vette, parked directly in front of the Birchwood Apartments. Vince was peering through a pair of binoculars, watching a dozen or so residents cavorting, dancing, drinking, and occasionally swimming in the pool area.

"Couple of babes over there," he observed.

"How can you possibly critique a woman from this distance—in the dark?"

He handed Tito the binoculars. "Night vision. Military issue."

Tito tried them out, the black night suddenly glowing green. "Whoa!"

"We used 'em in Nam. I pulled a lot of night maneuvers over there. Nearly got myself killed on a regular basis. Wouldn't be here if it wasn't for my squad. Boy, they were some of the best buddies I ever had."

"So you told me." *So you told me a thousand times*, Tito felt like saying. Not only was Vince obsessed with naked women, he was also obsessed with his "good old days" as a Green Beret.

"Those were the good old days," Vince began dreamily. "Talk about building character. That's what these kids today need—a good war to shape 'em into men. Makes for a heck of a friendship too, depending on each other to survive like that."

"Check that action out!" Tito said, hoping to derail his partner's trip down memory lane.

"Where?"

"On the right, by the chairs." He gave Vince the binoculars.

"Oh, that one. Yeah. She's a little vixen."

Relieved that his distraction had worked, Tito finished the last of his Diet Coke and fished another from the cooler.

"Get me another brew, will ya?"

He handed his partner a Coors. "Stuff'll kill ya, you know that?"

Vince scoffed at this, still ogling the bikini babe.

"You should take better care of yourself," Tito said. As a martial arts practitioner and a bodybuilder, he was careful about what he ate and drank. Unlike Vince, the human garbage can. When the guy wasn't busy desecrating his body with cheap booze, he was horsing down greasy fast food. No wonder he looked ten years older than he actually was and sported a growing beer belly. If Vince didn't take a bullet, chances were he'd die an early death from heart or liver disease.

"I'm ready to get this over with," Tito muttered, eyeing his watch again. "You suppose those folks plan on calling it a night anytime soon?"

Vince shook his head. "They look like they're just getting started. Things could get downright wild before it's over."

"Maybe we should—"

The phone interrupted him.

"Yeah?"

"We IDed the kid in the photo," Sonny's voice said. "One of Lewis's students. Apparently he was with her when she snatched the bones."

"Oh, yeah? Should we—"

"No. Lewis is still the primary target."

"You mean the bones."

"Right. As it stands, you're just after the bones."

"But that could change?"

"Anything's possible."

"What about the kid?"

"We'll have to wait and see. But if the word comes down, you guys up for it?"

"Sure."

"You don't have any qualms about doing a kid?"

"Qualms? You been taking vocabulary lessons, Sonny?"

Sonny cursed at this and told Tito what he could do with his comment. "You guys in or not?"

"We're in."

"Okay. I take it you haven't done your business yet."

"No. We got a pool party in progress. Stereo, dancing, the works."

"So? Use the noise and commotion to cover up your entrance."

"But they'll see us. We have to go right by the pool."

"They drinking?"

"Yeah."

"A lot?"

"I guess so."

"So they won't even notice. When they start to stagger, move in."

"All right," Tito sighed. "Call you when we get back to the car."

"No. I'm gonna be . . . indisposed for a while." There was a pause. "I'll call you later."

"Okay." Tito hung up the phone and stared through the window. "Sonny wants us to go ahead. Says those party animals won't be able to identify us. Not if they're drunk. Do they look drunk?"

"Yep. Another ten minutes and half of them will be on their backsides."

Tito guzzled his pop, then began rolling his shoulders and rocking his head—stretching out the kinks. "What about Lewis? You think she's asleep?"

"Maybe."

"What if she's not? Or what if she wakes up while we're inside?"

Vince shrugged. "We'll figure out something." He pulled a 9mm from its hiding place in his trousers and checked the clip.

"Hey! We're not authorized to do her," Tito cautioned.

"Yeah, I know," Vince muttered, frowning, "but a Boy Scout is always prepared, right?"

"Right," Tito sighed. He slid his own Beretta into the waistband of his gym shorts and popped open the door.

Vince stepped out of the passenger side. "If we can't hit her, what about getting her out of the apartment?"

"How?"

Sixteen

MELISSA HEARD SOMETHING. A DULL THUD. IT WAS FAR AWAY, BEYOND the realm of sleep. Her foggy, dream-shrouded mind attempted to classify it, but couldn't. Then she smelled it: smoke. And suddenly, she could feel the heat.

Opening her eyes, she gazed up at a forest of fire: angry, orange tongues licking at the walls and roof, rushing upwards, through a hole in the ceiling, into a sky of infinite darkness.

She screamed and leapt from the bed, falling to all fours. Scrambling forward through the smoke, she guarded her face with one hand and searched for the door with the other. When she found it, she pushed it open and crawled into the hallway. It too was consumed by flames, dark smoke billowing upward, a thick, gray haze floating down toward the floor. She coughed, her lungs fighting for air.

Pulling herself into the living room, she found a wide chasm where the couch and love seat had been. The walls had disappeared, cloaked in living red and black. The front door stood open on the other side of the room, across the crevasse. There was no way to reach it. She looked for a window, but couldn't find one. She started to go back, into the bedroom, but was met by a fresh, crackling blaze.

Only as she examined the hole in her floor and considered it as a means of escape did she notice him: a solitary figure at the center of what was now a deep, impassable abyss. Though his back was toward her, she could tell that it was a man. He was seated in a wooden chair, his head held high, observing the ring of fire as it squeezed in upon him. Six feet away from him was a door. Melissa could see that it was locked, the safety chain latched.

"Get out before it's too late!" she shouted.

The man heard her and casually looked in her direction. His eyes were sullen, yet defiant, his jaw clinched, lips turned down in an expression of sorrow. Melissa began to cry. It was Nigel.

She panicked, desperate to save him.

Studying the hole, she tried to judge the distance to Nigel's level. It was a good thirty feet and seemed to be growing, as if the room below her was actually sinking. Too far to jump. She frantically reached for the drapes, ripping them from their frame, then fed them into the hole like a lifeline. They failed to reach him by at least twenty feet. She was losing him.

"Get out, Nigel!" she screamed hysterically. "Open the door!"

He smiled up at her painfully, then shook his head.

The front wall of her living room suddenly collapsed and from her vantage point she could now see the outside of the door in Nigel's room. There was someone standing there, beating on it, fighting to get in. But the door wouldn't budge. It was dead bolted.

"Nigel!" the person called. "Nigel! Open the door!"

"No!" he answered, stiff-backed in his seat. "Never!"

In the next instant, the fire exploded inward, encircling Nigel like a wreath of demons. Time slowed. Melissa heard him shriek in terror. She saw the fear in his eyes and watched as his flesh was snapped at and eaten by the hungry flames. The floor collapsed, tiny splinters of wood dusting the air, and he fell: a spark disappearing into a violent sea of burning liquid.

"Nigel!" she cried.

"Nigel!" the voice outside his door echoed. Then the rescuer began to weep.

MELISSA HEARD SOMETHING. A DULL THUD. OPENING HER EYES, SHE realized that she was panting, the sheets wet against her skin. Her heart was racing, pounding out a quick cadence in her breast.

A dream, she told herself. It was just a dream. A horrible, hellish, abominable dream.

Then she heard it again. A thud. It was followed by a creak: the front door opening. She tried to breathe, but couldn't.

YOU THINK YOU COULD BE ANY LOUDER?" TITO WHISPERED, SCOWLING.
"If she can sleep through the racket from that pool party," Vince whispered back, "a little lock music won't wake her."

Lock music. Never put a Green Beret in charge of breaking and entering, Tito thought. They didn't know the meaning of the word subtle. Probably use a grenade to open a sliding glass door.

Vince moved forward slowly, shining a flashlight through the doorway. He pointed at himself, at the living room. He pointed at Tito, then at the kitchen.

Tito nodded.

LORD, PROTECT ME.

Melissa reached for the phone with a trembling hand. It slipped from its cradle, clattered against the nightstand, and then bounced to the carpet. She hurriedly retrieved it and dialed 911.

Tito waved a hand to get Vince's attention, then mouthed the words: *What was that?*

"What was what?" Vince whispered, too loud.

"That clunk," Tito whispered back, barely audibly. "It came from back there." Tito pointed down the hallway.

Vince shrugged.

Tito stepped close to his partner, then whispered, "Come on, let's get out of here. If it was nothing, we can come back in ten."

Once they were outside the door, Vince swore softly. "It's a whole lot easier when they just tell us to shoot somebody," he muttered.

THE LINE RANG TWICE BEFORE MELISSA DECIDED THAT SHE MUST HAVE been mistaken. The "intruder" was probably just a creation of her overwrought imagination: a bump in the night on the heels of a genuinely terrifying nightmare. Combine that with the raucous orgy taking place out at the pool . . .

She rose and tiptoed through the bedroom door as the line rang again. The living room was dark and empty, the front door shut. She checked it—locked, but not bolted. She had probably neglected to turn the dead bolt after coming back in from the car.

According to the clock it was approaching midnight. In the courtyard, the revelers seemed to have picked up speed, laughing too loudly, music cranked, deep bass resonating through the walls. Having fun was one thing, but . . . Someone needed to call the poli—

"911."

"Uh . . . hello," Melissa responded. With no burglar to report and the adrenaline rush from the dream and the mysterious noises subsiding, she was at a loss for words.

"What seems to be the problem?" a woman's voice prodded.

"Um . . . There are some people disturbing the peace."

The woman took her name and address, then issued a mild rebuke about using the emergency line to curtail a late-night party.

"We'll send a patrol car by," she assured Melissa before hanging up.

Returning the phone to its cradle, she sank to the edge of the bed and tried to calm her ragged nerves. The excitement she had been reeling under when she'd gone to bed had evolved into a free-floating anxiety—something along the lines of an emotional hangover.

As she sat there praying for a breeze, trying to decide whether to drag her tired body into the bathroom for another cool shower, fragmented images and disconnected feelings from the dream returned, parading through her mind like pale ghosts: fire, danger, the hole, peril, the locked door, hopelessness, Nigel—death.

It didn't take a trained psychiatrist to figure out what had generated the unholy collage. She had been thinking about Nigel, reading about hell, and imagining Nigel in hell just before she went to sleep. Voila! The makings of a real barn burner of a dream.

But what if it was more than that? What if God was actually trying to tell her something? What if he was attempting to energize her concern for Nigel, to transform a latent worry into a form of positive action? God sometimes did that with dreams.

Melissa considered this, wondering what God might have in mind, unsure of how she could play a role in communicating to Nigel—in helping to turn him away from a fiery destiny. What could she do? In the dream she had been powerless. So had the person at the door, the person trying to get in. That was clearly symbolic of Jesus, standing at the door, knocking, waiting to be invited in. Yet in this case, Jesus—if that's who it was—hadn't been satisfied with just waiting. He had been trying to break down the door. He seemed passionate, almost distraught, as if time was running out. And in the dream, it had.

Theologically speaking, wasn't Jesus able to break down any door? He certainly possessed the power to do anything he pleased. Of that Melissa was certain. But it was like C. S. Lewis had written: God had already accomplished everything that needed to be done in order for men to be saved. He had wiped out their sins at great personal cost, and given them a fresh start. That was what Calvary was all about. Men, however, had to turn and embrace that salvation. They had to admit guilt and accept forgiveness.

Despite his position and his power, Jesus could not—better yet, would not—break down a door locked from the inside. He would respect a man's choice, even if that meant a self-imposed eternity of emptiness and death.

It was a tragic reality, and Melissa wished there was some way that Nigel could be convinced to avoid that future. Unfortunately, the lines of communication were down, and the gulf between them seemingly unbridgeable. They shared nothing, no common ground—aside from a love of paleontology.

The idea struck Melissa with surprising clarity, full-blown and profound: the bones! She marveled that she had overlooked it until now. They were the bridge. They were the point of contact, a way to reestablish relationship and introduce Jesus into Nigel's life.

She examined this thought warily, held back by a web of reservations. Was she really interested in Nigel—whether he wound up in heaven or hell? Or was this some sort of selfish ploy to win back something she had lost and satisfy a hidden but ever-present longing for a companion? Was she merely afraid to be alone? And Nigel . . . He was the perfect example of a man in need of a rescuer. Was she planning on being his savior? There were women who did that, who chose rebels as partners for the sole purpose of taming them, changing them, remodeling them into the ideal man.

"Lord," Melissa sighed, "please reveal my motivations. This is a crazy idea I'm entertaining. If it's of you, show me. If it's not, tell me. Don't let me do something stupid."

In the shadow of that prayer she laid out her inner desires, examining them one by one. Yes, she loved Nigel. No, in truth, she did not expect to rebuild a romantic relationship with him. At least, not consciously. Yes, she was terribly concerned about where he would spend eternity—especially after that frighteningly realistic dream. No, in all honesty, she did not want him to do an about-face just so they would achieve a level of compatibility necessary for marriage. She simply felt compelled to speak to him, to somehow persuade him that time was running out, that Jesus was trying to break into his life. And this find—the bones—offered an opportunity to contact him on a professional level, under the guise of discussing a serious academic subject.

Picking up her Bible, she let it fall open in her lap and placed an index finger on the page at random. It was an old trick, something everyone had tried at one time or another and was in many ways utterly foolish—letting the laws of gravity and chance influence a spiritual decision. And yet, on occasion, God honored the motive behind it: the heartfelt desire to know his mind in a specific situation. He apparently was not offended by man's simplistic efforts at finding his will.

Melissa looked down at the passage, chiding herself for being so silly.

"'Go into all the world and preach the good news to all creation,'" she read from Mark. It seemed like a confirmation. Still, it could have been coincidence. She tried again, closing the book, then allowing it to open itself. This time her finger found a verse in Luke.

"'Don't be afraid; from now on you will catch men.'" Interesting . . .

On the third attempt, she landed in Second Timothy.

"'Preach the Word,'" she read. "'Be prepared in season and out of season; correct, rebuke, and encourage—with great patience . . .'"

She felt like a little girl, alive with faith, a fountain of hope bubbling up inside of her. The dream combined with the verses . . . The implication seemed unmistakable: she was supposed to tell Nigel about God. But how? Should she actually "go" as the first verse had stated? Or could she perform this task by phone?

The bones were the key, she decided. So the first step in this journey was to get them to Nigel. They would be the hook that "caught" this man and reeled him into the kingdom.

Opening the door of the nightstand cabinet, she pulled out the yellow pages and looked up Federal Express. As she called the number, she glanced at the clock: 11:53. But according to the advertisement, they picked up from their depositories twenty-four hours a day.

"Hello. I'd like to overnight a package. Could you tell me where the nearest drop-off is?"

LOOK AT THOSE TWO GO AT IT." VINCE WAS STARING INTENTLY AT A couple who had excused themselves from the pool party and were making out on the grass behind a row of bushes. "Man, talk about a lucky guy."

Tito shifted in his seat. He was growing impatient, ready to get this job over and done with. "Think we should try again?"

"Huh?"

"Lewis. Think we should try her apartment again? She must be asleep by now."

"Yeah. Guess we better." Vince took one last look at the pool area. "Hey! Oh! Oh, yeah! Look at—"

"Vince! Quick!" Tito interrupted, pointing. "Is that Lewis?"

Vince swung the night-vision binoculars. "Where?"

"On the right. Coming out of the units. By the wall."

"Yep. That's her."

"What's she got?" Tito picked up the camera and started clicking off shots. "Looks like a backpack." He watched as she reached the sidewalk, holding his breath as she approached the Land Rover—and walked on by. He cursed. "That was close."

"What?"

"I thought at first that she was getting in her car."

"So?"

"So she would have noticed that the door lock is gone, don't you think, Vince?"

"Oh, yeah."

Watching through the camera, Tito followed her progress up the street until she was out of sight. "Where in the world is she going at this hour?"

"Who knows?" Vince muttered. "Probably 7–11. Maybe she had a craving for Twinkies or something."

"Twinkies?"

"Sure. She could be pregnant."

"She's not married."

"It's happened before."

Tito swore under his breath. Reasoning with Vince was like reasoning with a plank of hardwood.

"So she's out on a Twinkie run. In the middle of the night? With her backpack?"

"Maybe it's a moonlight madness sale on all Hostess products," Vince offered, still gawking at the party around the swimming pool. "Fifty percent off on Ding-Dongs, Ho-Hos, the works. You know how women are about sales."

"Should we follow her?" Tito wondered aloud.

"Nah," Vince grunted, stowing the binoculars. He climbed out of the Vette, suddenly ready for action. "Let's do her apartment, get the bones, and blow. With a little luck, we'll be back at Club Blue in time for the 12:30 feature set. Lola's dancing it tonight." His eyebrows danced.

"Now there's a thrill," Tito deadpanned.

W<small>HAT'S GOING ON?</small>"

"What do you mean?"

DiCaprio cursed into the phone, then winced in pain. His ulcer was frantic, sending wands of pain across his abdomen. He was sitting at the desk in his study at home, the room void of light, whispering so that he wouldn't wake his wife.

"I mean," he managed between deep breaths, "what's the status of our little problem? I haven't heard squat."

"Our people are working on it."

"Working on it? In other words, it still hasn't been rectified."

"Correct. But we anticipate a resolution in the next few hours."

"What sort of resolution?"

"You don't need to know the details."

"I want to know the details," he demanded just a little too adamantly.

The voice on the other end of the line growled back, "You'll know as much as we want you to know. If we want to keep you in the dark, we'll do that." There was a pause. "May I remind you, Mr. Secretary, that you are responsible for this little fiasco."

"Now wait a minute. I didn't—"

"Oh, but you did. You made us a promise. We made you one in return. It is important at this juncture that we both keep our promises."

DiCaprio fingered his stomach. "At least tell me what's happening. Did those people in the zone find anything incriminating? Are the bones—"

"We aren't sure. Maybe. Maybe not. But we aren't taking any chances. The plan is to settle this thing quietly—if possible. The more time that passes, however, the more difficult that becomes. It may soon become necessary to take more serious measures."

"Such as?"

"You'll be informed when and if it becomes appropriate. In the meantime, rest assured that all parties involved are being closely watched. The evidence—if that's what it is—will be confiscated and destroyed. Witnesses will be dealt with on an individual basis."

DiCaprio didn't like the sound of that. Neither did his ulcer. It began radiating its disapproval.

"One thing you do need to know is that we've got a crew heading out to the Site."

"A crew? What sort of crew?"

"Heavy equipment. A convoy of road construction people. Our road construction people. They'll require clearance from you to get in the gate. Tell security to look the other way. Give the crew free run of 217 for six hours or so."

"What for? Why are they—"

"Just do it."

"Okay." DiCaprio grimaced as another wave of pain moved across his torso. "Whatever. But I can't guarantee no one will see anything."

"You don't have to. According to the weather report, the wind will be blowing like a banshee out there for the next couple of days. That'll cover our tracks and keep the peeping toms to a minimum."

DiCaprio opened a desk drawer and felt around blindly until he found a bottle of Pepto-Bismol. "Fine," he grunted, removing the cap. "Just take care of this thing. Make it go away."

"Don't worry. We will."

After hanging up the phone, he guzzled the pink liquid, then held his breath, waiting for it to coat his angry stomach. Maybe the problem would go away. Maybe they would take care of it.

Sure. And maybe his ulcer would just up and disappear of its own accord, too.

SEVENTEEN

"WHAT DO YOU MEAN THEY WEREN'T THERE?"

Tito took a deep breath and tried again. "We searched the place—thoroughly—and they just weren't there."

Sonny responded to this disclosure predictably—with a thirty-second fit of staccato profanity. When he was finished, he asked in a calm, even voice, "Where are they? She had the bones. What did she do with them?"

Tito left the questions alone, not wanting to provoke Sonny with stupid answers. He had been dreading this conversation for four hours, sitting in the car, watching the apartment, listening to Vince snore, waiting for Sonny to call.

"Give me a rundown of everything that's happened since you staked her out."

"Well, when we got here, her Rover was parked on the street. I was in the process of doing a visual when she showed up and got something out of the back of the truck—something wrapped in a towel."

"The bones," Sonny observed. "Then what?"

"I got her camera, did the film, faxed you the picture . . . Uh . . . Then she went out."

"Out? Where? What time?"

"It was around midnight. Don't know where. That's when we went in and did the place."

Sonny engaged in another swearing bout. "It didn't occur to you to follow her, that she might have the bones with her?"

"No."

Wrong answer. Sonny proceeded to tear Tito up one side and down the other, describing him and his partner with a variety of colorful terms, the least crude involving their combined intelligence and its comparison with that of a household doorknob. In Sonny's opinion, the doorknob possessed a much higher IQ.

"So the bones are gone," Sonny summed up, "and you two buffoons exposed yourselves by destroying her apartment? I suppose she called the police."

"No. She didn't," Tito argued. He'd had more than enough of Sonny's high-and-mighty attitude. "We were in and out like lightning, without so much as wrinkling the welcome mat. It was slick. Professional."

Sonny cursed at this. "I'll bet." He sighed into the phone, then swore again. "Find out where she went."

"Huh?"

"Figure out where she could have taken the bones."

"Sonny—"

"Just do it." The line went dead.

Tito glanced at Vince. He was slumped in the passenger seat, his mouth hanging open, eyes shut.

"Vince?" He nudged his partner's knee and was nearly taken out by a wild left. "Mellow! It's just me."

"What? Huh?" Vince blinked at him, then frowned. "What's the matter?"

"It's Sonny. He wants us to figure out where she went."

"Where who went?"

"Lewis."

"Oh. Good luck." He hunkered down in the seat and crossed his arms, leaning against the door.

"You watch the apartment," Tito told him.

"Uh-huh."

Tito put the picture of Lewis, the kid, and their bone in his pocket and set off down the sidewalk, retracing Lewis's steps. He paused at the corner and looked both directions. To the left were more apartments and the entrance to a subdivision. If she had taken the bones to a private residence, there was no hope of ever finding them. No matter how adamant Sonny became, conducting a search of every dwelling in the entire suburb was impossible. Not even the FBI could pull that off.

To the right, five or six blocks up the street, he could see a signal and cars racing past at high speed. Without any better ideas, he strode toward it.

Ten minutes later he was standing at a busy intersection. Despite the hour—it was only 4:25 A.M.—traffic was already building at the lights. Gas stations occupied two corners, lines of early-bird commuters waiting for a chance to use the pumps. A brightly lit restaurant held the third corner, a half-dozen cars parked next to the building. The fourth held a strip mall.

Tito eyed the restaurant, then crossed the street to peruse the shopping center. The stores were dark, the parking lot empty. He looked in on a florist, a dry cleaners, a craft store.

He was about to give up, certain that this was a colossal goose chase, when he noticed a blue neon sign hovering over the last storefront in the mall: Kinko's. From a distance, it too seemed deserted. There were no vehicles parked in front. But as he approached, he saw another electric sign promising that the copy store was open twenty-four hours a day, seven days a week. The inside of the establishment was illuminated by rows of fluorescent lights. A solitary night-shift employee scurried back and forth, dipping and ducking behind the counter, attending to the copying machines.

When Tito stepped inside, the door signaled his arrival with a bong and the counter person's head jerked up. He looked surprised, relieved that someone had chosen to enter his lonely domain.

"Can I help you?" He beamed, his eyes tired and bloodshot.

"Maybe. I'm looking for someone."

The attendant shrugged. "I'm the only one here until six."

Tito withdrew the picture and slid it across the counter. "Recognize this lady?"

He studied it, squinting. "Yeah. I think so. She came in earlier. Around . . . Oh . . . midnight or so, I'd guess." Then his eyes narrowed. "You a cop?"

"No. That's my sister," Tito lied, wondering if the clerk would buy that. He and Lewis didn't exactly bear any family resemblance. "I'm just trying to track her down."

The young man considered this. Tito could almost see the wheels turning.

"You say she came in here?"

"Yeah. Fed Exed something," he said, pointing to a Federal Express counter in the corner.

"Is the package still in there?"

"No. She made it just before the 12:30 pickup."

"Any idea what it was?"

He shook his head. "Nope. Something long. She used one of the poster tubes to mail it."

Tito walked over to the Fed Ex station and picked up a tube. "Like this one?"

The clerk shook his head again. "No. The biggest size."

"This one?" Tito lifted a tube four inches in diameter.

"Yep."

"Any idea where she sent it?" he asked, returning to the counter.

"No."

"Any way to find out?"

"Not short of opening the Fed Ex receipt box."

"You have the key?"

He shrugged sheepishly. "Sure. But we're only supposed to use it for emergencies. That's what the Fed Ex people said."

"This is sort of an emergency."

The clerk stared at him, waiting for an explanation.

"You a college student?" Tito asked, fishing his wallet out.

"Yeah."

"What's your major?"

"Pre-law."

"Great. You work here nights. Go to school days."

The clerk nodded, obviously wondering where this was headed.

"Don't get much sleep, I bet."

"Not much," he sighed. "Listen, I have work to do. If there's nothing else . . ."

"I need that Fed Ex box opened," Tito said, extending a crisp hundred dollar bill. "And I'd be willing to contribute to your college fund."

The clerk's eyes got big as he gawked at the money. "No . . . I couldn't . . . I . . . Uh . . ."

A second bill made his mouth quiver. "I could get fired."

A third caused him to cave. Snapping the money out of Tito's hand, the clerk hurried to the Fed Ex station and began hunting through the keys on his key ring. His hands were trembling, sweat already beginning to work its way down his neck.

Poor kid, Tito thought. Probably the first time he'd ever broken the law. Of course, if he was planning on being a lawyer, he'd have to get used to it.

When the clerk finally managed to open the box, he waved at the stack of receipts. "Get whatever you want," he said, his voice quivering. "Just be quick."

Tito lifted the top, most recently deposited receipt, examined it for a moment, then smiled at the kid. "One more favor."

The clerk's face dropped.

"Make me a copy. Then we can put this back where it belongs."

"Good idea." He ran to the nearest machine, placed the receipt on the glass, and hit the button. Seconds later he handed Tito a copy and stuck the original back into the box, slamming the depository shut.

"Good luck in school," Tito said, folding the receipt and slipping it into his pocket. "Study hard." As he left, the clerk disappeared into the back room.

By the time Tito got back to the Vette, the first slender fingers of dawn were reaching up along the horizon to the east. Tito climbed in and hit the speed dial button on the phone. Vince muttered something, snorted, eyes glued shut.

"The bones are on their way to Colorado," Tito announced proudly.

"Colorado?" Sonny followed this with a curse.

"The University of Colorado to be specific. The Pale . . . Paleon . . . tology Lab. Whatever that is. Lewis Fed Exed them there."

"Who was the package addressed to?" Sonny asked. "Is there a name?"

"Dr. Nigel Kendrick. Must be a prof there or something."

Sonny paused, thinking about this.

"Mailed at 12:15," Tito offered, filling the silence. "Weighed three pounds, four ounces. Cost her—"

"I could care less how much it cost!" Sonny replied. He launched into an impressive, even furious storm of profanity. When it had passed over, he sighed, "I'll have to get back to you on this. But I guarantee our people will be unhappy."

Tito swallowed hard.

"Who's that?" Vince asked. He was slumped in the passenger seat, feet extended out the window, arms crossed against his chest.

"It's Sonny. And he's hot," Tito said, covering the receiver with his hand.

"Is that right? Let me talk to him a minute." Vince grabbed the phone. "Sonny? Listen, we put our butts on the line all night, so if you've got a problem, you come on over here and I'll help exorcise it for you, buddy. I'll push your head down into your shoulders and pull it out your belly button. How's that sound? And another thing—"

Tito took the phone back. "He's hung over," he explained. "And tired."

"He's psychotic!" Sonny replied. "He shouldn't be loose on the streets."

"Don't worry about him. He's good at his job."

Sonny muttered something that Tito didn't catch.

"What about Lewis?" Tito asked.

"Stick with her. I'll talk to my boss, see what he wants to do about her, the kid, the bones, Colorado . . ." He swore at the problem. "Until you hear from me, you go wherever she goes, got that? School, church, store, ladies room, Africa—everywhere. Just don't lose her. If you do, don't bother calling in. "

"Got it." Tito replaced the phone.

"What's the story?" Vince asked sleepily.

"We screwed up, that's the story. And if we screw up again, we'll be unemployed. Or worse."

––––––––––––

MORNING ANNOUNCED ITSELF WITH A GENTLE BREEZE, A YELLOW GLOW behind faded drapes, silence. Melissa lay motionless, soaking it in, eyes closed, unwilling to break the spell that hovered over her, caressing her—mind, body, and spirit—like an angel's breath.

Her first waking thought was of Nigel. Of his need. Of God's answer to that need. Of her responsibility to deliver that answer. Without consciously seeking to, she had made a decision. She would go to see Nigel. Today.

It was crazy, sure. But God's business was often that way: odd, peculiar, risky, humbling, out of the ordinary, seemingly crazy. His ways were not the ways of man. Neither was his timing man's timing.

When she finally rolled over and squinted at the clock, Melissa was amazed to find that it was only six. No wonder it was so quiet. She should have been exhausted—especially after her middle-of-the-night trek to the Fed Ex box. And yet, for some inexplicable reason, she felt rested, refreshed . . . alive. She was brimming with expectation, anxious to see what God was up to, what he had planned for Nigel.

A short, cooling shower only added to the growing sense of contentment, and by the time she padded into the kitchen even the mundane task of preparing the coffee seemed to offer a unique satisfaction. She breathed in the aroma as the deep brown liquid trickled into the carafe. Life was good. Nearly perfect.

Standing at the cabinet, clad only in a towel, her hair still dripping wet, Melissa thumbed through the phone book. She found the number of a discount airline, dialed it, and asked for a reservation on the first plane to Denver. As luck would have it—or in her view providence—there was a seat available on the nine o'clock flight. She gave the operator her Visa number, hung up, and hurried back to the bathroom, forgetting the coffee. It was 6:22. She was supposed to check in and pick up her ticket by eight. That gave her a little over an hour and a half to dry her hair, dress, pack, and make the forty-five minute trip to McCarran International. She would be cutting it close.

Miraculously, she emerged from her apartment at exactly 7:15, bag in hand, hair styled, clothes in place. She was thinking that the day and its purpose had all of the earmarks of God's favor and blessing as she reached her Land Rover and attempted to fit the key into the driver's door. So much for the perfect morning.

Melissa stared incredulously at the neat, perfectly round void in the metal. Reality was striking back, intruding upon her slice of heaven. Stunned, she glanced at her apartment, trying to decide whether to go back and report the crime. She eyed her watch with a heavy sigh: 7:17. If she called it in, she would miss the plane. If she didn't, her car would be open game for thieves. Of course, who would want to steal an ancient Land Rover? She didn't have a sound system in it. For that matter, why had someone bothered to break into it in the first place?

She climbed in and slammed the door, wincing as it clanked loudly and swung back open with a hideous groan. Another attempt brought the same result: a metallic crunch followed by a long, wicked creak.

"I'll just have to hold it shut," she muttered to herself as she pulled the door in under her arm. Switching the ignition, she started down the street, steering and working the gear shift with her right hand, clinging awkwardly to the door with her left.

Guiding the vehicle was such a trick of coordination and concentration that she failed to notice the cherry red Corvette rolling quietly along a block and a half behind her.

EIGHTEEN

IT WAS A WAR DANCE: OVERHEATED BODIES STRAINING IN THE EARLY morning light, long, muscular limbs whipping and tangling, high-topped Nikes stutter-stepping, shoulders colliding, hips bumping and twisting, hands pushing off, a forest of arms reaching skyward. The violent asphalt ballet was accompanied by a symphony of primitive grunts, panting, curses, and urgent shouts.

The skins were ahead, one hoop away from victory. Thanks to Parish. At just five feet ten inches, he had the quickness of a small point guard, the ability to head fake one direction, then break the other, leaving his defender standing there with feet of clay. And somehow, when the game went above the rim, he followed, sprouting wings that allowed him to reel in boards on one end, skywalk slams on the other.

"Come on, big man," Parish taunted, "show me what you got." He was looking into Jimmy's eyes, smiling like a lion that had just been asked to chaperone a gazelle on a trip to the watering hole. "Come on," he urged, waving him forward. The mismatch was comical: three hundred pounds of slow-moving football lineman trying to push the ball down the court against a hundred sixty-five pounds of tawny, bespectacled energy.

Parish bobbed and weaved, teasing his prey. Behind him, in the paint beneath the chain net, four other players fought for position, bare chests and T-shirts merging into a sweaty, agitated octopus.

"Jimmy!" Vaughn called. His back was to his opponent, legs propped out at odd angles. He shook a right arm in the air. "Send it in!"

In the time it took Jimmy to consider acting on this invitation the pattern changed, bodies rearranging themselves in jerky movements. Vaughn disappeared into the organism.

The instant of indecision was all Parish needed. A hand flicked out, stealing the ball off the dribble, and before Jimmy could react the thief was gone. He shot down court, leaving the ground near the foul line and flying the rest of the way in. A reverse slam served as an exclamation point on the statement.

"Game," Parish announced smugly, pretending to yawn.

"Why didn't you send it in?" Vaughn asked, glaring at Jimmy. The gentle giant hung his head.

"Pay up, gentlemen," Parish said, hand extended.

The shirts gloomily turned to their athletic bags and began digging out their wallets. Parish beamed as he accepted a twenty from each of the three of them, then distributed the booty to his teammates.

"Nice doing business with you," he said. "Care to try again? First team to thirty?"

One of the shirts muttered something under his breath, shook his head, and started for his car.

"I'll take Jimmy," Parish tried.

The two other skins laughed and gathered their things. "See you next Saturday, Phil," one of them called.

Parish looked to Vaughn and Jimmy. "Two on one?"

The looks on their faces answered his question: pained expressions that said, "You must be kidding."

"Just trying to give you a chance to win back your losses."

"Yeah, right, Phil," Vaughn said. "Next week . . ." He paused, staring Parish down. "It's my turn to guard you. You're mine, buddy. I'll be all over you—like white on rice."

Parish laughed at this. "Let's go. Right now." He dribbled the ball from hand to hand, under his legs, behind his back. "I'm ready. Let's see what you've got."

Vaughn ignored him. "Put your shirt on." He withdrew a towel from his bag and began drying his face and neck. When he finished, he changed into a fresh T-shirt.

"Who's up for breakfast?"

"Sounds good," Parish answered.

"Great. Then you're buying, Moneybags."

Jimmy chortled at this. "In that case, I'm glad I decided to take it easy on you, Lieutenant."

"First of all, don't even try to tell me you weren't playing 110 percent, Jimmy. You were sweating a river. Face it, b-ball just isn't your game. Second, now that I've displayed my superior talents on the court—and taken your money—the least you can do is call me Phil."

The Truck shrugged at this.

"Now, about that breakfast," Parish continued, "if I'm buying—"

"Maybe we could invite Dr. Weber," Jimmy proposed.

Vaughn and Parish looked at him, puzzled. "Who?" they wondered in unison.

"Dr. Weber."

Vaughn had no idea who that was, and it was obvious from the look on his face that Parish didn't either.

"Jack Weber. Remember? The guy I told you about last night?"

Vaughn mentally evaluated the events of the past evening: bar, drinks, alcoholic stupor—a slight hangover when he got up to dress for hoops. No Dr. Weber.

"The expert on the NTS," Jimmy added, trying to jog their memories.

"Oh, yeah," Vaughn groaned. He glanced at his watch. "Actually, I've got a lot to do today, Jimmy."

"Me too," Parish said, nodding.

Jimmy frowned at them. They were avoiding his eyes, examining the fading center court line.

"I forgot to call him last night. I can call him now. We can talk over breakfast."

Great, Vaughn thought but didn't say. He rolled his eyes at Parish. Parish grimaced back.

Thirty minutes later they were seated at a window booth in Jackie's Cafe waiting for Jimmy's friend to show. Jackie's was a favorite military hangout. Located just minutes from Nellis, it offered bland meals and weak coffee at inflated prices. Even so, the fare was better than anything the base had to offer, and Vaughn and Parish patronized the place at least twice a week.

"You boys see anything you like?" The question came from a pretty brunette in her early twenties. Her name was Denise, and she made a point of flirting with the regulars. Vaughn was certain that she made more in tips than salary.

"We're still waiting on someone," Vaughn told her.

Jimmy watched in awe as she refilled their cups—a dumb animal beholding a heavenly creature.

"Who's your friend?" she asked, batting long, dark eyelashes at Jimmy. She smiled playfully, revealing two rows of perfect pearls.

Parish poked Jimmy with an elbow. Jimmy grunted, then swallowed, his face blushing. "J . . . J . . . Jimmy," he stuttered.

"Well, J . . . J . . . Jimmy," she joked, "welcome to J . . . J . . . Jackie's. Let me know if there's anything . . . anything . . . I can do to make your visit more pleasurable." She winked at him before moving down the aisle to titillate the next table.

Vaughn shook his head at her. "Denise works nights as a showgirl. Quite a performer."

"Quite a lady," Jimmy added through fat, dry lips.

Parish burst out laughing. "Quite a lady," he mimicked in a doltish tone.

"Well, she is!" Jimmy argued. His cheeks and forehead glowed a sunburned pink.

"Let's order," Vaughn suggested, eyeing the menu. No matter how much he debated, he always got the same thing: the western omelet. Morning, noon, or night, it was the only fail-safe entree. You couldn't burn or mutilate an omelet without significant effort.

"Hey," Parish said, looking toward the entrance. "That guy's waving at you, Jimmy. The guy with the box."

Jimmy was busy watching Denise make time with other military personnel.

"Jimmy!" Vaughn nearly shouted.

"Huh?" His thick head swung toward the door. "That's him. That's Jack." He stood and invited him over.

Dr. Jack Weber was a small, hairless man with a pasty complexion and narrow eyes imprisoned behind horn-rim glasses. As he approached their table, Vaughn noticed that Weber's chocolate-brown slacks failed to reach his worn black loafers, revealing two bleach-white athletic socks. The man wasn't wearing a belt and his short-sleeved, white dress shirt was stained yellow beneath the arms and around the neck. Weber's tie reminded Vaughn of the horrid shag carpeting fad of the late sixties: lime green speckled with black and yellow teardrops.

Jimmy made the introductions and Weber accepted the hands offered him in businesslike fashion, without smiling. The doctor slid the cardboard file box he was carrying under the table, took a seat, and cautiously studied the dining area.

Magically, Denise reappeared. "Another hungry man," she said, giving Weber a wiggle of her eyebrow before opening her order pad. Weber seemed oblivious to her presence. "What'll it be, boys?" she asked, pencil poised.

"Western omelet," Vaughn answered.

"Same," Parish nodded, tossing the menu toward the end of the table.

"Big guy?" Denise asked, winking at Jimmy.

"I'll have the . . ." He stopped to swallow the lump in his throat. "The hungry man special."

"How would you like those eggs?"

"Over easy."

"Toast or hash browns?"

Jimmy hesitated, unsure.

"Go with the hash browns, honey. You need the fuel to keep that big engine stoked."

He agreed with a nod, his face turning rosy red.

"And you, sir," Denise asked Weber. "What can I get you?"

"Do you have granola?"

Denise giggled at this. "No, sir. Corn flakes. Cheerios. Rice Krispies. That's about it in the cereal department. How 'bout if I get you some flapjacks?"

Weber made a face, shaking his head. "Rice Krispies. And orange juice."

Denise made a note and winked at Jimmy again before strutting toward the kitchen.

Vaughn and Parish stared at Weber expectantly. The doctor's eyes were darting about the room. He seemed worried. Nervous. Even paranoid. Jimmy's gaze was fixed on the kitchen door as he waited for "the goddess" to return and fill his morning with sultry sunshine. The silence at the table stretched.

"Well," Vaughn finally began, "tell us, Dr. Weber. Uh . . . What sort of doctor are you?"

Weber's eyes flashed. "I have a Ph.D. in psychology," he said matter-of-factly. End of discussion.

"Jimmy . . . ," Vaughn prompted, gesturing to Weber.

Jimmy gave the door a last, disappointed look, then said, "Jack, I wanted these guys to meet you."

Weber pursed his lips and nodded slowly, almost imperceptibly, as if to say: So?

"They work with me in the bunker."

Another disinterested nod.

"We had this contact in the zone yesterday," Jimmy continued.

"The zone is the area—" Parish started to explain.

"I'm well acquainted with the zone," Weber assured him.

"Anyway, it was a strange deal. Turned out to be a lady and some kids looking for fossils."

Weber waited, stone-faced.

"But the brass went ballistic. Had these guys out there doing a visual all day. And Henderson showed up at the bunker for a debrief."

"General Henderson is—" Vaughn began.

Weber waved him off. "I know the general."

"Jack here was in military intel until he retired a few years back," Jimmy explained.

"Forced retirement," Weber admitted. "It was either that or be court-martialed for copying top-secret documents and removing them from the base." He was suddenly animated. "They weren't top secret— just secure. I had a high enough security level. And I only took them home for academic purposes. It was research for my book." He gestured under the table and tapped the box with his foot.

"Is that what's in the box?" Vaughn asked, almost certain now that Weber was a true nutcase.

"Yes. I have to take it with me everywhere."

"Why's that?" Parish asked.

"Because it contains information that could embarrass the government." His voice fell to a whisper. "I've spent the past twenty-two years digging into a cover-up involving the DOE, the military, and various presidential administrations."

"Is that right?" Vaughn shot Jimmy a disapproving look. Why had he gotten them into this?

"I can't let that box out of my sight."

"How come?" Parish prodded curiously.

"Because they want it. They want to bury it. They don't want me going public with it."

"Huh," Vaughn grunted.

More silence. Jimmy was gawking at Denise again.

"Wow, look at the time." Vaughn examined his watch. "We really need to be—"

"We haven't even had our breakfast yet," Jimmy said, glaring. He turned to Weber. "So Jack, we were wondering if you had any idea what might be out there in the zone—in Quad 217 to be precise—that's so gosh-awful important. What could possibly get the higher-ups in such a swivet?"

Weber gave them a long knowing look, then bent to open his box. He pulled out a thick stack of file folders and slapped them on the table. "What's out there? You want to know what's out there?"

No, Vaughn thought, *not really. Not if it means enduring this weirdo's psychotic delusions.*

"I'll tell you what's out there," the doctor said, deadly serious. He flipped open the first folder and began paging through the material. It appeared to be a mix of poorly copied type-written pages and yellow notepaper bearing indiscernible scribbles.

When the first folder didn't have what he was after, Weber tossed it back into the box and began going through the second, then the third.

Denise arrived with their meals, setting them in the appropriate spots with her characteristic charm. She placed a miniature box of Rice Krispies in front of Weber, along with a small carton of milk, a bowl, and a tiny glass of O.J. "Anything else I can get for you boys?"

Jimmy smiled at her dopily, without responding.

"We're fine," Vaughn assured her. He and Parish dug into their omelets, both assuming that when they were finished they would be allowed to leave.

Weber was in another world, scattering pages, scanning notes with grave concentration. "Quad 217 . . . Let's see . . . Here we go. No wait . . . Yeah. Here it is. You want to know what's in Quad 217? I'll tell you what's in Quad 217."

Please do, Vaughn felt like begging. *So that we can go home.*

Nineteen

"AND THIS IS LIZZIE, MY YOUNGEST. SHE'S TWENTY-TWO. LIVES IN PALO Alto. Going to Stanford. Smart as a whip. She's dating a kid in law school, but . . . I have my doubts about those two. Don't think it will work out. Just a hunch. The boy's likable enough. Bright. Probably make her a good husband, but . . . This picture is before she cut her hair. It was a shock at first. She'd been growing it out as long as I can remember. My wife actually cried when she first saw Lizzie's new hairstyle. Now it looks like . . . like Julia Roberts in *Steel Magnolias*. You know, after she got her hair cut off. I like it. It's cute. But at first . . . I don't think I have a shot of her with short hair . . ."

Melissa nodded politely, forcing a tired smile as the man in the seat next to her dug around in his wallet. The guy gave new meaning to the word *bore*. He had begun talking to her before takeoff and never slowed down. There were a dozen photographs scattered on the tray in front of her, a loving full-color legacy of the man's five grown children and seven grandchildren. Melissa was now an authority on the entire clan— their successes, failures, degrees, vocations, hobbies . . . the smallest details of their lives.

"Oh, here's one of Joshua." He handed her a two-by-two photo of a diaper-clad toddler, a cowboy hat atop his head, a stuffed tiger in his arms.

"Cute," she said, sneaking a glance at her watch. The flight was more than half over and she had yet to do anything but smile and nod. The muscles around her lips were fatigued from grinning, her neck stiff from acknowledging and affirming her seatmate's running monologue. When a perky female flight attendant arrived to serve breakfast and Mr. Non-stop Talker had to put his memorabilia away, Melissa wanted to hug her.

"Thank you," she said, accepting a tray. Her gratitude ran deeper than just an appreciation for the greasy eggs and sausage links.

The food quieted her flying companion. The man ate hungrily, stuffing his mouth, adding extra strain to the already overburdened waistline of his bulging suit trousers.

Melissa savored the silence. Having missed her devotions that morning, she had intended to spend some quiet time on the plane. Mr. Mouth had made that impossible so far. As he wolfed down his breakfast, she tried to focus herself, listen to God, prepare for what was waiting for her in Boulder. That was the question of the hour, of course: What was waiting for her? Nigel. But what sort of Nigel? The same arrogant, opinionated man she had left six years earlier? Or had he changed? Was he more humble now? Was he—as the evangelism literature liked to put it—bowed down, searching for something to fill the God-sized void within? She hoped with all her heart that she would find the latter. And yet somehow she fully expected the former.

If Nigel had remained unchanged, she thought, picking at her food, if he was still the stubborn, unreceptive jerk he had been . . . then what? Then this was a big waste of time, money, and emotional energy.

That thought started the doubts flowing. They percolated up into her mind like bubbles, gurgling and bursting until she wondered if it was all a mistake: the dream, the inner impression that she was supposed to tell Nigel about Jesus, the midnight Fed Ex package, this trip . . . Maybe none of it was of God, all of it fabricated by her imagination. Maybe she was out of her mind—stupidly naive for even attempting such a foolish venture. As she assessed the situation from a number of angles, struggling to remain objective, one conclusion presented itself again and again: it was quite possible that her little missionary journey had been ill-conceived and was destined to fail.

Pushing the unfinished meal aside, she pulled her Bible out of an overnight bag and turned to Hebrews. No holy roulette this time. She could feel her faith eroding, her spiritual feet sinking in the wet sand of a desperate riptide. She needed solid, foundational truth and she needed it quickly, before she was carried out to sea and decided to call the whole thing off.

As was often the case, the verses of the familiar "faith chapter" jumped out at her alive and vibrant, a lifeline to a drowning soul.

Faith is the substance of things hoped for,
the evidence of things not seen.

She read the words, breathing in the meaning. She read them again and again. Then she took them apart and applied them to her circumstances. "Things hoped for." That was Nigel. His salvation. Her desire—fueled by God's prompting, she believed—to see him accept Christ, gaining heaven and eternal fellowship with God, avoiding hell's unending fury. Faith was the only substance—the only tangible sign—that Nigel would ever know Jesus. *Her* faith. "Things not seen." That must be God's work inside of Nigel, cracking away that tough, guarded exterior of intellectual snobbery, breaking through the humanistic rhetoric that imprisoned his heart, freeing him to serve the living Savior. The "evidence" of that was still invisible, residing only in Melissa's faith and God's mind. To give up would be to rob Nigel of the most precious and necessary gift in all of life.

Father, she prayed silently, *Nigel needs you. He needs the life of your Son inside of him. And if my dream was really from you, then . . . well, it would seem that he needs you now. But whether he dies and faces judgment today, or thirty years from today, the case is still the same: He will remain incomplete, a sinner headed for hell, without Jesus. So please go before me and prepare his heart to receive your Good News. Make it soft toward you. Call him home. And provide me with the words . . . with the message you want to communicate to him. Let me be the mailman—delivering your truth and love.*

"Why are you going to Denver?" The man had downed the eggs and sausage and was chasing three slippery grapefruit slices around his plate with a spoon. Apparently his appetite had been satisfied and he was ready to resume their prolonged conversation.

"I'm surprising an old friend," she answered.

"Surprise, huh? She doesn't know you're coming?"

"It's a he. And no, he doesn't know."

The man seemed amused at this. He traded the spoon for a fork, stabbed a grapefruit, and tossed it into his mouth like a shrimp. Wiping the juice from his chin he asked, "Old boyfriend?"

Melissa shrugged, then nodded. It was really none of this guy's business, but . . . "We dated in college."

"Sounds dangerous. Popping in on an old flame like that."

It is dangerous, she felt like saying. Acting on faith always was. It was risky. And you usually stood a good chance of embarrassing yourself.

"What made you decide to do it?"

Melissa considered her answer, then gestured to her Bible. The man squinted at it as if it were a new species of exotic insect.

"The man I'm going to see doesn't believe in God," she explained. "He's a paleontologist. An ardent evolutionist. I think I'm supposed to go see him, to tell him about what's in this book. To tell him about the kingdom of God . . . about Jesus."

The expression of curiosity turned to one of horror, and suddenly the man was heavily invested in spearing the last two grapefruit slices. Melissa smiled at this. It never failed. The mere mention of Jesus was enough to shut up even the most obnoxious windbag.

The man was looking out the window now, doing anything and everything to avoid eye contact. Melissa opened her Bible to the Psalms, certain that the remainder of the flight would be peaceful.

Boom-shadda-boom!"

Tito looked over the top of his *Muscle* magazine and discovered the current focus of Vince's unrestrained, overly active libido: an attractive, red-headed flight attendant approaching with a beverage cart.

Tito sighed at him and went back to his reading, thankful that he had something to distract his attention from his sexually obsessed partner. He had purchased the magazine moments before boarding. No small feat since they had nearly missed the flight. Of course not knowing they would be flying anywhere had something to do with that. Who could have guessed that Lewis was heading to Denver this morning? They had followed her to the airport, then to the gate—successfully passing through security with graphite weapons and non-reflective carbon ammo intact—then were forced to buy seats when—to their utter dismay—Lewis responded to the boarding call, produced a pass, and sauntered down the jetway with her bag.

In retrospect, the bag should have been a dead giveaway that she was going somewhere. But as Vince had reminded him several times during the past twelve hours, their expertise was not in the area of surveillance. They weren't PIs. They were expediters, specialists that were called upon when a problem needed solving—permanently. Ask them to disappear someone and they could do it quickly, quietly, without fuss or muss. They had dispatched dozens of troublemakers over the course of the past few years. Breaking into cars, searching apartments, looking for bones, following junior-high school teachers on cross-country trips—none of that was in their job description. They were terminators, not gophers.

Excuses didn't fly with Sonny, though. He expected perfection. When he found out that they had left Vegas he would have a conniption fit. He would probably—

Tito flinched as his cellular came to life, announcing an incoming call. Great. Speak of the devil.

He took a deep breath and looked to Vince for support. Vince was engrossed in his nudie rag, mouth hanging open.

"What do I tell him?" Tito asked.

"Who?"

"Sonny." He held up the phone.

"How do you know that's who it is?" He turned the page, hypnotized by the images.

"Who else would be calling us on this line?"

"Answer it. Don't worry about what to say until you know who it is—that's my motto."

Despite his study of martial arts, Tito was not a big fan of eastern religions and didn't believe in reincarnation. Still, at that moment, as he watched Vince salivate over his dirty magazine and considered his advice, Tito had to wonder if his partner had been a Neanderthal or perhaps a musk ox in a past life.

He flipped open the phone and braced himself for what he knew was coming. "Hey, Sonny."

"Tito? What's up? Where are you? Why didn't you call in?"

"Which answer do you want first?"

Sonny cursed at him. "Where are you?"

Tito swung his head from side to side then eyed the numbers above their heads. He was suddenly in the mood to be smart. After all, Sonny was several hundred miles behind him. What could the guy do besides swear up a storm?

"Approximately thirty thousand feet above . . . Utah, probably. In row . . . 33. Occupying an aisle seat. I prefer that to the window. You know, in case you have to run to the head or something."

He paused, waiting for Sonny to run out of choice expletives and steam.

"She hopped a plane to Denver," he explained. "We hopped with her, like you said to."

Sonny growled for another thirty seconds, then asked, "Is she traveling with anyone?"

"No."

"Denver . . ." he thought aloud. "Maybe she's flying to the University of Colorado."

"Maybe. But if she's going to see that Dr. Kendrick guy why did she Fed Ex the bones? Why not hand deliver them?"

Sonny didn't have an answer.

"What's with the bones anyway, Sonny? Why is everyone hot and bothered about them? What kind of bones are they?"

"That's none of your business. Concentrate on Lewis."

"But, Sonny, the least you can do is tell us—"

"Listen, this thing is complicated and it's being handled on a number of levels."

Tito tried to imagine how a couple of bones could be complicated but couldn't. "I just don't understand."

"Exactly. You're not being paid to understand."

"But if you filled us in, maybe we could do this thing right— instead of stumbling around in the dark. For instance, we'd know when things had gone too far and it was time to, say, do Lewis." When this drew no reaction from Sonny, Tito asked, "Is it time?"

"Not yet. The plan is to keep it contained: neat and tidy. If you two can come up with those bones . . . well, let's just say the rest is being taken care of."

"The rest?"

"The other loose ends." He cursed softly, contemplatively. "This whole business is getting messy. Stick to Lewis. Maybe she'll take you to the bones."

"What's the ruling on force?"

"Don't get itchy. Keep Vince on a tight leash. He's trigger happy and we don't need that. But if push comes to shove, do what you need to do."

"Okay," Tito said. "Boy, I wish we could just finish this thing— ping-ping. Put Lewis down slick and simple."

"Yeah, well . . . You may get your wish here pretty soon."

"Really?"

"Let's just say that it's been suggested that we wipe the slate clean and put this behind us. And I tend to agree. Otherwise it's just too iffy, too many leaks in the dam, if you know what I mean."

Tito did. As he hung up the phone he smiled, relieved that this strange job was finally moving back toward solid ground, to the familiar territory they had been trained to operate in. With any luck they would soon be allowed to exchange their spy hats and binoculars for hollow points and silencers.

Twenty

There were one hundred and twenty-six above-ground tests conducted at the NTS between January 27, 1951 and the signing of the Atmospheric Test Ban Treaty in 1963. What you have to realize is that each of these detonations resulted in a fallout cloud containing radiation levels comparable to, sometimes higher than, the amount released in the 1986 Chernobyl disaster."

Weber paused to breathe, then spooned in another mound of soggy Rice Krispies. The members of his captive audience had finished their breakfasts long ago and were sipping their way through their fourth, even fifth cups of coffee. Vaughn's kidneys were already screaming at him.

"These tests effectively contaminated most if not all of the continental United States," Weber explained, still chewing. He opened another folder before continuing. "Atomic tests in Nevada were responsible for poisoning milk in New England, poisoning wheat in South Dakota, poisoning the soil in Virginia . . ." He finished off his second orange juice in a gulp. "It was all documented by the Public Health Service and the Atomic Energy Commission. Dead fish in the Great Lakes, dead cattle and sheep in Utah—"

"Dead everything in Utah," Jimmy said, grimacing. " 'A is for atom. B is for bomb. C is for Cancer. D is for dead.' We used to say that on the way to school almost every day when I was a kid."

"The damage to livestock and humans was of course greatest in southern Nevada and Utah," Weber agreed. "Workers at the NTS were commonly overexposed and became very ill. Ranches in and around the main fallout belts reported horses and cows that were burned, lambs born with two heads. Men, women, and children contracted cancer well in excess of the national averages. Miscarriages and birth defects skyrocketed. Thousands of infantrymen were injured."

"Tell them about the pens," Jimmy urged.

"The AEC had no idea how the human body would react to a nuclear explosion," Weber said, "which was a big part of their problem. Negligence. Pure and simple. They were playing with fire and didn't take the appropriate precautions. Soldiers and technicians were routinely exposed to the blasts. More than forty thousand servicemen took part in the exercises. They watched them from close range and then were paraded right into ground zero—on 'atomic maneuvers'—before the dust had even settled. Some of the workers were forced to dig into hot holes to recover remnants of dirty equipment. It was all one big experiment and these people were just guinea pigs: the workers, the soldiers, the citizens in the fallout zone.

"Sometimes things really went awry. Instead of just long-term effects—cancers, thyroid problems, birth defects—people got horribly sick and died days, sometimes hours after a shot. After visiting a hot area, a worker might complain of nausea. He would begin vomiting, maybe develop a fever, often a rash or a burn. The guy loses short-term memory and blacks out. The supervisors send him off to Mercury, to the infirmary. Since they didn't understand the effects of radiation, they didn't know how to treat the resulting sickness and many people died. In some cases, pens were constructed to—"

Weber stopped in midsentence as two men entered the restaurant. The first was overweight with slicked-back hair. His companion was thin, gangly, a sharp nose punctuating his face. Both were dressed in neat, blue suits. The doctor eyed them suspiciously, then declared, "Fibbies."

Vaughn looked them over. Maybe. Either that or businessmen, or military contractors, or off-duty Air Force, or any of a dozen or so other identities.

"They shadow me wherever I go," Weber explained in a hushed tone. "Anyway, they had these pens out in the middle of the NTS where they kept animals and people suffering from severe radiation poisoning: skin falling off, facial lesions, losing all their hair . . . They quarantined them so that they could maintain the falsehood they had perpetuated to the public—'There is no danger.'"

Vaughn sighed at this. An unabridged history of the NTS was bad enough. But this . . . this conspiracy business . . . Next Weber would be telling them that aliens had landed at Dreamland. He glanced at his watch, then at Parish. Phil was gazing out the window, a bored look on his face.

"You don't believe me," Weber said to Vaughn.

"Well . . . it's a little far-fetched," Vaughn answered.

"I'm not making it up. I have documentation." He thumped his folders. "And I'm not alone in my criticisms of the DOE. One author called the nuclear era at the NTS the 'most prodigiously reckless program of scientific experimentation in U.S. history.' And I wholeheartedly agree. Think about what they did.

"They detonated weapons of unprecedented power on a regular basis just to see what would happen. People watched. They were stationed yards from the blast area and told to look the other way." Weber chuckled at this. "Have you ever witnessed an atomic bomb detonation firsthand?"

Vaughn shook his head. Parish was concentrating on the traffic outside on the street.

"I've seen four. And let me tell you . . ." Weber paused as Denise swept past, filling cups. He waited until she was two tables down the aisle before continuing. "And let me tell you," he repeated in a hoarse whisper, "it changes your view of life. Even with your eyes closed and your back turned, when that baby goes off, you can see right through your skin." He paused for emphasis. Leaning forward, he narrowly missed the cereal bowl with his elbow. "It burns the back of your neck. The heat is so intense that if you're within a certain range, you can't wear a watch or any jewelry because it will melt them right into your skin.

"Then comes the shock wave. Think of the worst earthquake imaginable, then multiply it by ten. You're down in this plywood-reinforced observation trench, and when the pressure wave hits, the thing starts dancing like a ribbon and you have to scramble out before it collapses on you. Then you see it."

Weber sat back in his seat, the blood draining from his face as he remembered. "It's like nothing on this earth: a ball of fire containing every color in the rainbow. The flames race up into the mushroom cloud, and the entire thing starts to boil. Black, green, purple . . . all churning upwards into the air at two hundred miles per hour." He shook his head at the vision. "It's spectacular . . . beautiful . . . breathtaking . . . utterly hellish . . . a preview of Armageddon. It's a humbling sight to behold." Weber swallowed hard and appeared to be fighting back a wave of tears.

"But that was over thirty years ago,"Vaughn pointed out.

Weber shook his head. "No. Above ground was over thirty years ago. Below ground has been going on ever since. The shots are merely set off in holes, tunnels, and vertical shafts. The thinking was that by detonating these beasts deep in the earth, the radiation would be contained. Unfortunately, that wasn't usually the case. Though it was seldom made public, the tests often vented, releasing lethal clouds of nuclear particles into the atmosphere, where they were driven along by high-altitude winds, toward St. George, Salt Lake City, as far as the East Coast.

"The reason you never read about any of this is because the AEC—now the DOE—maintained a strict media blackout. Operating under the guise of 'national security,' they basically had a free hand. And still do. They can conduct any sort of nuclear experiment they desire and keep it quiet by stamping the project classified."

"I have a hard time believing that our government could pull that off—a cover-up of that size and scope," Parish said, breaking his self-imposed silence. "Look at Watergate, for pete's sake. They couldn't even burglarize a hotel, much less contaminate the entire country for decades without anyone noticing."

"Oh, the people in Utah noticed," Jimmy assured him. "They just didn't make a fuss."

"And why's that?" Parish sighed.

"Because they're patriots," Jimmy declared, as if this explained everything.

"Patriots?"Vaughn wondered.

"Mormons, people who value family, who take pride in their country," Jimmy said.

Weber nodded and opened his mouth to reply, but Denise appeared with the check.

"If there's nothing else I can do for you boys," she purred mischievously, "I'll be your cashier." Her short, frilly skirt fluttered and danced as she strode toward the kitchen. Every head in the room followed her. Even Weber seemed to appreciate the bouncy waitress's energetic walk.

He cleared his throat as she went through the swinging doors. "They were told that the tests were for the good of the country, that the development of nuclear weapons was essential to the security and future of the United States. To speak up or complain would have been viewed as being disloyal to the government. These people wanted to support their country. And they did so, often blindly and to their own detriment."

Weber gazed at Vaughn, then Parish. "It's all right here in this material. Stories of men armed with Geiger counters slinking across the Southwest, sampling livestock and humans for radiation, telling small towns to stay indoors on test days, telling them to keep their children inside when the cloud passed over. And most of all, telling them there was nothing to worry about."

Vaughn considered this as he slid the check in Parish's direction. It was interesting in a morbid sort of way. But mostly, it was weird. Too weird. Weber was clearly a conspiracy theorist who thrived on researching the perceived sins of the almighty, ever-wicked government. And Vaughn had long ago grown weary of listening.

"What does this have to do with Quad 217?" he asked.

"Nothing," Parish whispered out of the corner of his mouth. He dug out a twenty and set it on the table for Denise.

"If something's buried out there," Weber continued unabated, "I'll bet you money it's accident related."

"It's what?" Parish wondered.

"Accident related: the clean-up of a nuclear incident," Weber said with a straight face. He glanced at the two men in suits. "You said the people who violated the zone were fossil hunters. Did they find anything?"

Vaughn shrugged, unsure how much to tell this nut. After all, their work was "classified." They weren't even supposed to be talking about contacts with non-military, uncleared individuals. "Maybe."

"Bones?"

Another shrug. "So what if they did?"

Weber grinned for the first time, revealing a top row of crooked, yellow teeth. He looked like a decrepit old tom cat that had finally trapped a bird. "They may well have stumbled onto the hiding place."

Parish laughed at this.

"The what?"

"They had to hide the accident victims somewhere," Weber insisted. "They quarantined them in pens—like animals. We know that. But what did they do with the bodies after they died? They most certainly buried them. We've just never discovered where."

Denise whisked by, snapping up the check. "Back in a sec with your change."

Weber watched her strut toward the cash register. "My guess is that they tossed all the bodies into a big hole somewhere and covered them up with a bulldozer. Maybe those fossil hunters found the hole—the mass graveyard."

Vaughn shook his head at the doctor. It was time to end this ridiculous conversation. "First of all, if the government had killed a bunch of people with radiation—which I seriously doubt—how could they have kept it so quiet? No way. Second, if people did die and the DOE wanted to get rid of the bodies secretly, why would they bury them in the zone? Why not in the T-tunnels or something." He paused to sigh at Weber's warped logic. "None of it makes sense, Doctor. The business about the pens—that's hooey. I grew up in Vegas and I've worked at the Site for seven years. Never once have I heard a thing about that. No, what you're suggesting is an atrocity that ranks right up there with the Holocaust. Do you really think our government is capable of that?"

It was plain from the expression of triumph on Weber's pasty face that he did.

"Here you go," Denise said, pouring the change onto the table. "Now you boys be sure to come back and see me, ya hear?"

Four heads nodded their agreement and watched as she applied her charm to a table of new arrivals. Parish doled out an extra-healthy tip for her.

Vaughn checked his watch in a polite attempt to end the discussion. "Wow, look at the time. We've got to be going." He rose from his seat. "Nice meeting you, Doctor."

"Yeah, nice to meet you," Parish grunted, scooting out of the booth. "You coming, Jimmy?"

The Truck shrugged apologetically at Weber, then stood. "Thanks for coming, Jack."

Weber muttered something and began gathering his material into piles. He was still refilling his box when they left the restaurant and climbed into Vaughn's Jeep.

"That guy is a wacko," Parish announced. "Imagine: accusing the U.S. government of mass murder! What a nutcase."

"I'll second that," Vaughn said.

"Okay, so Jack's different," Jimmy conceded.

"Different?" Parish exclaimed, chuckling. "Certifiably different, I'd say. The men in the white coats need to have a talk with him."

"But you have to admit," Jimmy tried, "he has some interesting things to say."

"Interesting," Vaughn grunted. "Humph."

"Who's to say he's not right?" Jimmy argued. "Maybe there was a cover-up back in the fifties or sixties. Maybe they did bury the bodies out there in the zone."

"Yeah. Maybe," Vaughn muttered, nodding. "And maybe your friend Dr. Weber was Napoleon Bonaparte—in a former life."

Twenty-One

IN THE HARSH NOONDAY SUN THE TENTLIKE PAVILIONS OF THE DENVER International Airport resembled a collection of enormous Indian teepees. Behind the sharp, brilliant spires a layer of purple-brown haze hung low and thick, transforming the city skyline and the foothills of the Front Range into a pale, impressionistic painting. On the horizon, the Rockies stretched northwest in an uneven line: rugged peaks dappled in white with thin veins of snow running away toward hidden streams.

Melissa took it all in as the plane circled and landed, unable to shake the feeling that she was coming home. There was little doubt that she missed it: Colorado, the mountains, the deep-blue, high-altitude sky, the ever-present sun. Life in the Rockies was unique, fitted with its own flavor and attitude. People here worshiped the outdoors, they dreamed of adventure, they tested themselves against the elements, against craggy rock faces, steep, off-road bike trails, raging white-water rapids, and icy double-diamond ski runs.

The plane reversed its engines, bending the passengers over their seat belts, then began the long taxi toward the gate.

More then anything else, more than the incredible scenery or the never-ending opportunities to enjoy nature, Melissa missed her two former loves. Nigel and paleontology. Coming here plunged her back into that mindset, into that pool of emotions . . . Returning sent her back in time, to the joys she had experienced here, and the sorrows that had accompanied them.

Closing her eyes, she shook off the memories, determined to focus on the true purpose of the trip. She wasn't here to reflect on "the good old days," to nurse past wounds, or to rehearse painful disappointments. She was here to do a job—to be about her Father's business. Specifically, she had come to offer a condemned prisoner a full pardon. Her mission was to tell him about the immediate freedom and future security available to him in Jesus.

When the plane finally rolled to a stop at the gate, passengers shot out of their seats and began fighting their way to the door as if the cabin had caught on fire.

"It was nice talking to you," Melissa told her seatmate as they waited for the line to move forward. The man gave her a suspicious look and nodded slightly. He acted as if he were afraid that she might be contagious, that if he got too close, something bad might rub off.

Melissa followed the trail of people into the terminal, along the moving sidewalks, onto a shuttle bound for the rental car area. When she arrived she chose the shortest line—Hertz—and ten minutes later was climbing into a maroon Tercel.

The drive to Boulder would take thirty to forty-five minutes, she calculated as she started the vehicle and began navigating through the maze of ramps and parking levels. She made two complete loops through the garage before the exit presented itself and she escaped into the light.

Five miles from DIA she met an imposing traffic snarl. Cars were lined up on both sides of the freeway, bumper to bumper, barely rolling. *A wreck,* she thought. Except there weren't any flashing lights. Road construction? No orange signs or flagmen. Maybe things had simply gotten more congested in her six-year absence. At this rate it would take her at least an hour to make it to Boulder and the CU campus.

She dug a map out of the glove compartment. There had to be a better way.

CAN YOU SEE HER?"

"Yeah."

"Is she still in the right lane?"

"Yeah."

Tito was fighting with the climate control panel, switching levers in an attempt to draw cool air from the vents. According to the device, the temperature outside was ninety-four. Inside it was a balmy eighty-four—and climbing. He punched a series of buttons, then swore as he put his hand to the vent: warm air. It felt like the heater was on.

"This car is a piece of junk," he declared, rolling down the window.

"Poor baby. What's the matter? Miss your Vette?" Vince teased.

They were driving a Camry, the best car the agency had to offer on such short notice. Still, it wasn't much in comparison with a tricked-out Corvette. No CD stereo system. No custom steering wheel. No padded leather seats. No 450 overdrive engine. Almost no power when you stomped on the pedal. And worst of all, the air conditioner was obviously shot.

Tito tried the panel again before noticing that the engine was getting warm. The needle on the gauge was in the upper reaches of the acceptable range and seemed to be inching toward the danger zone. He turned off the air conditioner fan and poured his energies into finding a decent radio station. "See if there's a map in the glove compartment."

"A map? What for?"

"In case we lose her. This traffic is horrible. It's impossible to tail someone when you can't even change lanes. We may have to pick her up again at the University."

Vince sighed heavily, as if searching for a map was a huge imposition. He dug through the glove compartment, withdrew a thick stack of paper, and ultimately found what he was looking for. "Where are we?"

"DIA."

"No kidding. But where's that? Which end of town?"

Tito shrugged at him, then began looking for a highway sign. "We're on I–70, going . . . west, I think. And we need to get to Boulder."

"Boulder? Man, that's way over there. Could take all day in this mess."

"Great." Tito found a classic rock station and cranked up the volume. What a day: forced to play gumshoe, following some teacher to Denver, getting stuck in traffic, boxed up in a rolling sauna. He glanced at the temperature gauge again. Perfect. The needle was in the red. They were about to overheat.

$\big($ELEBRATE DIVERSITY.

Melissa had been studying that bumper sticker for nearly ten minutes, wondering what it was supposed to mean. She had seen it decorating bumpers all over Vegas, but had never really stopped to contemplate the concept. Now, stuck behind the Acura, staring at the message over the Tercel's hood, she found herself confused. What exactly did the driver mean by "diversity"? Diversity of what? Nationalities? Ethnic heritage? Traditions? Beliefs? She was all for "celebrating" the "diversity" of God's creation, of appreciating mankind in all of his uniqueness and variety. Somehow, though, she didn't think that was what the sticker intended to communicate.

On the other end of the bumper was the silver outline of a fish. She had originally mistaken it for an ichthus: the symbol Christians had used since the catacombs to make other believers aware of their faith in Christ. Close examination revealed that the fish had small feet and was filled with the letters: D-A-R-W-I-N.

By the time the traffic snarl dislodged itself and the Acura disappeared into the fast lane, Melissa had decided that both the bumper sticker and the evolution fish were statements against Christianity—against God himself. The former was apparently an attempt to condone sin by changing the terminology and celebrating it. The latter was, in effect, a rebellious creature thumbing his nose at his Creator.

Yes, she thought with a smile, there's no mistaking Colorado. Home of the independent. Just wait until she got to Boulder. Like most college towns, it was a long-standing headquarters for anti-Christ philosophies—radical feminism, homosexuality, eastern mysticism, New Age thought . . . Off-beat gurus found receptive audiences for their quirky teachings among the young, idealistic, misguidedly zealous university crowd. As someone had once observed, colleges were where the squirrels came to gather nuts. And there seemed to be plenty of both in Boulder.

Though originally from Wales, Nigel fit in perfectly. He was the personification of the word *rebel*: stubborn, strong-willed to a fault, someone who was determined to do his own thing—his own way. Humanism was his god, and as a dedicated servant of that man-centered kingdom, he faithfully proselytized, imparting the theory of evolution to hungry-minded students as if it were the gospel truth.

Melissa considered this as she followed the interstate, dodging drivers who apparently thought they were competing at Indy. It was forty-five minutes before she saw the sign: University of Colorado—next right. Behind the sign the horseshoe of Buffalo stadium rose up like a Roman ruin.

She flipped on her blinker and took the exit. It spilled onto a parkway and a half-dozen blocks later she reached the edge of the campus. Slowing, she began the hunt for a parking spot.

It was only after she had captured a space in front of a beatnik coffee shop and fed the meter with quarters that she realized she didn't know what to do next. Finding Nigel seemed logical. But where? Would he be in his office? In a lecture hall? Maybe he had classes today. Or a lab. Or a field trip. It was Saturday. He might be at his apartment. A terrible thought struck her: What if he's not here? What if he's out on a dig? Or on vacation?

Standing there at the curb Melissa shook her head, amazed at her own stupidity. It was a summer weekend. What were the chances that Nigel was even in town? This was looking more and more like an exercise in futility.

Father, she prayed silently, *I'm floundering. I felt like I should come. I thought you wanted me to come. But now that I'm here . . . I just . . . I don't know what to do next. And if Nigel isn't around . . .*

Gazing up the block, she noticed the CU administrative offices—a series of mid-rise buildings that formed a neat square. Maybe someone in there would know Nigel's whereabouts. She locked her car and trotted across the street.

The buildings turned out to be a labyrinth of halls, cubicles, and counters, all of which were vacant. The place was quiet. As she went from one empty office to the next, Melissa began to feel slightly uncomfortable, like a guest touring a host's home—without the host.

After five minutes of wandering she heard voices and traced them to an office designated as "Scheduling." Inside, an obese Hispanic woman was standing behind a counter, listening as a girl with a backpack over her shoulder—presumably a student—told a tale of woe concerning her class schedule.

"There's nothing we can do," the woman announced when the girl paused for a breath. "Once you've registered, it's in the computer. You can't change unless you go through registration again."

"That's ridiculous," the girl protested.

The woman shrugged. "Maybe so, but that's the way it is."

The girl turned and left in a huff, muttering something unkind as she departed.

"Can I help you?" the woman groaned at Melissa, frowning.

"I hope so."

"Student number, please."

"No. I'm not a student. I'm looking for someone."

"This is scheduling," the woman explained through sleepy eyes. "I can give you a printout of our fall schedule, tell you if you got the summer classes you wanted—that's about it."

"I need to find a professor."

"Go talk to personnel," she said, moving away from the counter, toward her desk.

"Where's that?"

"Two doors down," the woman sniffed. "But they're closed today. Be open Monday."

"I need to find this professor today."

She didn't bother responding to this, her attention already turned to the computer terminal on her desk.

"Please. I just flew in from Las Vegas. Can you at least tell me if he's teaching this session?"

The woman rolled her eyes and sighed, then willed her bulk up from the chair in slow motion. "Name?" she asked, plodding to the terminal at the counter.

"Dr. Nigel Kendrick."

"Department?"

"Paleontology."

She entered the information into a keyboard and examined her fingernails as the machine searched its data base.

"He's teaching summer session," she said, plump face nodding. "In fact . . ." She squinted at the computer screen. "Looks like he's teaching today. Intro to Paleontology—Adams Hall. Auditorium three."

Melissa smiled at her—delighted, surprised, relieved. "Really?"

"Really," the woman said without enthusiasm. "Anything else?"

"What time is the class?"

"Uh—two to six."

"Great. Thank you so much."

"You're welcome so much," the woman deadpanned, returning to her seat.

As she left the building, Melissa tried to recall the location of Adams Hall. She had attended classes there in her freshman and sophomore years of undergraduate study. It was . . . on the west side of campus? The big stone building adjacent to the undergrad library? If so, getting there would require a fifteen- to twenty-minute hike. She glanced at her watch: 2:47.

Things are working out, she decided as she set out for the hall. Nigel was there. She was there. God seemed to be in control. It was all falling together.

Looking down at her hands, she realized that they had begun to tremble. The idea of seeing him, of speaking to him, of witnessing to him was finally sinking in. And it was utterly terrifying.

Here."

Vince studied the paper with a furrowed brow. "What is it?"

"That's where she sent the bones," Tito told him. They were seated on a stone bench in a treelined courtyard, pretending to appreciate a fountain. "When she comes out of there," Tito said, pointing toward the administration complex, "I'll follow her. You track that down. See if you can find the package."

Vince checked his holster, then asked, "Sonny mention anything about legitimate use of force?"

"No. Whoever's running the show still isn't ready to commit. They want those bones—for whatever reason—but won't go all out to get them back."

"Yet."

"Right. Anyway, try not to cause holy hell. Just slip in, get the package, slip out."

"And if I make a mess?"

Tito shook his head wearily. He was tired of waiting for the okay to do what needed to be done. "If you absolutely have to make a mess, just be sure and clean it up."

Vince smiled at this, satisfied, and set out in search of the paleontology lab.

Twenty-Two

"Tell me again why we're doing this."

"To prove a point."

"And that point is?"

"That Jimmy is a fool."

The Truck took offense at this, glaring at Parish. "A fool? *You're* the fool . . . sir."

"Yeah, well, we'll see about that, won't we?"

"We're driving into the desert in the worst heat wave of a decade, in a windstorm, on our day off, no less," Vaughn reviewed, hands draped over the steering wheel, "to settle a bet. *I'm* the fool for letting you two talk me into this."

"It's a matter of honor," Jimmy argued. "Nobody calls me a fool."

"It's a matter of money," Parish corrected. "I feel strongly that a man should put his money where his mouth is. Jimmy here thinks Dr. Weber is the Messiah, and—"

"I do not!"

"Okay then, the next Joseph Smith—"

"Sir! I'm warning you!"

"I say you're buying a line, that Weber is a con-man. Either that or a lunatic. The man shouldn't be loose on the streets. And this business about a mass grave . . ." Parish laughed heartily.

"I just think it's worth checking out," Jimmy said.

"Oh, so do I, now that there's a hundred bucks riding on it," Parish agreed.

"I warned you, Jimmy," Vaughn said. "Parish here will bet on just about anything. It's annoying, really. And if you're not careful it can be costly."

Parish grinned. "I'm a gambling man. So what?"

"Michael Jordan had a thing for gambling," Vaughn pointed out. "Look what it got him."

"A billion or so a year in endorsements?" Parish wondered.

"You know what I mean."

"Betting is one of the spices of life—it makes things interesting," Parish explained. "Jimmy thinks there are piles of dead bodies buried in Quad 217. I say that's hooey. We put a little wager on it—voila! Here we are, making an unscheduled excursion into the zone."

"Yeah, lucky us," Vaughn groaned. "Winner pays my gas."

"And buys the beer tonight," Parish added gleefully.

They rode in silence for the next twenty minutes—Jimmy stewing in the back, gazing off into the yucca spears, Parish napping in the passenger's seat. Vaughn kept the Jeep moving at seventy-five to eighty miles per hour. There were no other cars to speak of, no cops, and if they were stopped, base IDs and a creative story about running out to check on a military project in the zone would probably stave off a ticket. The police were usually sympathetic to other men in uniform.

Tomorrow's Sunday, Vaughn thought as he stared through the scrub oak and low, chalky hills. They weren't scheduled to report for duty at the bunker until noon. That meant he could sleep in, sip coffee, maybe drop in on Denise at the cafe. Either that or veg in front of the TV and OD on ESPN until it was time to head for the Site.

"I think it's the next dirt road," Jimmy advised.

Vaughn nodded, slowing the Jeep. He performed a hard right, and they bounced off the highway onto a furrowed double track that snaked through the sage, toward a distant mesa.

The jarring woke Parish up. He studied the road, then the speedometer. "We'll never get there at this rate. Let me drive."

"No thanks," Vaughn grunted. "I'd just as soon get there alive."

Jimmy registered his appreciation for Vaughn's humor with a deep chuckle.

"Jeeps are made to go fast. Especially off-road," Parish explained, ignoring them both.

"Maybe so. But you're still not driving." Vaughn pressed on the pedal, accelerating to forty-five. It was slow enough to keep the vehicle under control but hopefully fast enough to shut Parish up. The Jeep rocked and tilted with each new rut, the shocks groaning in protest.

A strong hot wind was pushing dust down the valley, blurring the horizon with a pale red fog. Miniature tornadoes lifted sand into the air, waves of rabbitbrush and wild grass shivering violently with each swirling gust. Overhead, thin, curling cirrus clouds hurried across the sky like frantic brushstrokes.

Vaughn followed the tracks as they veered left around the northwestern slope of the mesa.

"Someone else is here," Parish announced.

Vaughn followed the road with his eyes, then scanned the landscape. "Where?"

"I don't see it now. But there was a reflection. Right next to that mound." He pointed. "I think it was the windshield of a car."

They drove on, all three straining for a glimpse. The wind was increasing in velocity, transitioning into a full-fledged gale. The blasts beat on the Jeep, pulling at the canvas top.

"There it was again," Parish said. He aimed a finger directly out the windshield.

"I can't see much of anything," Vaughn admitted. He was bounding along at thirty-five, doing his best to stay on the road. The wind wanted to push them east and the dust made visibility poor, occasionally non-existent.

"Slow down," Parish told him.

Vaughn eased down on the brake, shifting into third. The needle on the speedometer fell: twenty-eight . . . twenty-four . . . twenty-two . . .

Particles of sand assaulted the Jeep with renewed vengeance. The car's top flapped as they rocked from side to side. The windshield was blank: a static, two-dimensional, monochrome rendering of airborne dirt.

"Maybe we better stop," Vaughn said. But before he could act on his own suggestion, the air cleared momentarily and he saw something: a flash of color, a burst of light, a shape . . . The other car appeared out of nowhere, like a ghost, magically materializing in their path.

Parish and Jimmy shouted in unison, urging Vaughn to react appropriately—and swiftly.

Stomping on the brake, he twisted the wheel and they went into a short but exciting spin. Sliding sideways, wheels locked, the Jeep threatened to flip before skidding to a halt just inches from the other vehicle.

Vaughn took a deep breath and silently cursed the idiot who had seen fit to park in the middle of the road. It was a bronze-colored compact that had to have been twenty years old. In between dents, the paint was peeling in strips. The chrome letters on the elongated trunk read: Valiant.

"What a beater," Jimmy observed.

"Good thing you didn't hit it, Steve," Parish said. "I have a feeling the owner isn't insured."

"Insured? The owner probably isn't living. What is that—a sixty-eight? Sixty-nine?"

"Right around in there," Jimmy agreed.

Vaughn popped his door open and climbed out for a closer inspection. The wind was blowing lustily, propelling sand pellets sideways, turning them into miniature bullets that stung the skin. He covered his eyes with a hand and circled the Valiant. Inside, the shabby seats were riddled with holes, the back window filled with papers and balled-up clothing. The Plymouth was either abandoned or served as someone's home. Possibly both.

Parish pulled the collar of his polo shirt up around his face and hopped out to join him. Jimmy followed, groaning as he squeezed his gargantuan frame through the tiny door of the Jeep.

"Talk about a slob," Parish shouted over the wind. He aimed a thumb at the interior of the car. Shoe boxes had been crammed into the backseat, leaning stacks that reached to the ceiling. The front bench was littered with crumpled papers, notepads, food wrappers, and pop cans. A pile of dull white underwear sat unfolded in the passenger-side floorboard, adjacent to a collection of unsorted socks.

"Not exactly a neatnik," Vaughn said.

"Sirs? This is it, isn't it?"

"What?" Parish asked.

"217."

Vaughn squinted into the wind, blinking away dust. "Hard to tell."

"Sure," Jimmy nodded, a thick hand over his brow. "Here's the mesa. There's the Cactus Mountains. I didn't come with you on the recon, but it sure fits the map."

"We're close," Vaughn agreed.

"But where's the ravine?" Parish wanted to know. "It should be right there." He pointed north, at a flat area void of plant life.

"It is," another voice replied.

Startled, the three men turned and saw a figure emerging from the curtains of dust. It was a man wearing faded dress slacks, a white dress shirt, and a tie. Held to his head by a hand was a gray felt fedora. It was Dr. Weber.

Parish scowled at him. "You scared me!"

Weber shrugged. "I didn't intend to."

"What do you think you're doing, slinking around out here?" Parish asked suspiciously.

"I'm not slinking," he said. "I'm gathering evidence. I came to examine the bone yard you described."

"It's not a bone yard," Vaughn protested. He was already growing irritated with Weber.

"Not anymore," Weber grunted. He started north. Vaughn, Parish, and Jimmy fell into step with him.

"You shouldn't be out here," Vaughn warned.

"Neither should you. Why are you?"

"It's . . . it's a long story," Vaughn replied. "But at least we have security clearances. You don't. There's probably a patrol out there right now, watching us."

"I doubt that," Weber said. "Not in this." He waved at the sandstorm.

"He's right," Jimmy nodded. "You know the way the sensors act in high winds. They go haywire."

Parish wasn't satisfied. "You go digging around out here and they'll haul you in."

"Maybe. But there's nothing to dig up anymore." He stopped and crouched, running a hand over the ground. It was unnaturally smooth. "This is your ravine—the place where those fossil hunters found the bones."

"It couldn't be," Parish said, shaking his head. He turned in one direction, then another, trying to orient himself.

"Trust me, it is." He stood and led them toward the first in a series of low mounds. "See this?" His arm traced a set of parallel marks in the earth. Each was made up of smaller rectangles.

Jimmy bent to inspect it. "Tank? Troop carrier?"

"Try bulldozer," Weber said. He led them up the mound. From the top they could see a tangle of blurred tracks on and around the flat, level section of dirt. "They buried it."

"Buried what?" Vaughn asked.

"The ravine. They buried it. With skip loaders and backhoes."

Vaughn studied the scene skeptically. "No. Even if this is the ravine, you couldn't bury the thing."

"Sure you could," Weber said. "With enough heavy equipment, you could build a housing project in the Grand Canyon."

"But we were here. Just yesterday."

Weber shrugged. "They're good. And they're fast."

"Who?" Vaughn wanted to know. "Who's they?" He immediately regretted the question.

"*They* is the federal government," Weber answered with fire in his eyes. He adopted an expression of righteous indignation. "*They* is the Department of Energy. *They* is the U.S. military. *They* is everyone who wants to cover up one of the greatest tragedies, one of the greatest catastrophes, one of the greatest atrocities in our nation's history. *They* is—"

"Not again," Parish moaned, hanging his head.

Vaughn waved the doctor off. "Okay. Okay. Simmer down. We get the picture. There's something horrible buried out there."

"Downwinders," Weber threw in. "Dead citizens. Casualties of the secret war. Victims of the nuclear holocaust. Human guinea pigs from radiation experiments."

"Yeah, right. The government obviously doesn't want anybody to find out that they've mowed down the masses with atomic fallout, so they stick the bodies in a hole in the desert. And when a group of dinosaur hunters accidentally digs up a bone or two, the government has the site dozed." Vaughn sighed. "Add in an extraterrestrial or two, and you'd have the makings of an episode of *X-Files.*"

Parish chuckled at this.

Weber glared at them. "Go ahead. Make fun of me. I'm used to it. But when the truth comes out, you won't be laughing anymore." He set off down the hill toward the cars.

"Where are you going, Jack?" Jimmy called after him.

"Back to town," Weber huffed, "to get a court order. I'll have a bulldozer out here undoing the damage by week's end. If there's evidence here, I'll find it. Thanks for all your help."

"Hey, don't go away mad," Parish called after him. His voice sank to a whisper and he added, "Just go away."

"No wonder you guys don't have many friends," Jimmy said as he started down.

Parish glanced at Vaughn. "What's that supposed to mean?"

"You don't really buy this stuff, do you, Jimmy?" Vaughn asked, trotting to catch up with the Truck.

"I don't know. Maybe." He was frowning, head pulled into his shoulders as he faced the wind.

"Think about it, Jimmy," Vaughn tried. "If there was anything there we'd know about it. We work here. This place is our turf."

Jimmy muttered something under his breath, shaking his head. Then he stopped and turned. "I'll agree it's a long shot. Jack is probably wrong. Our government wouldn't do something like that. But you two could at least . . . be nice. Jack is a veteran. Retired Air Force. You might try showing him a little respect."

Parish made a face, pretending to be stricken.

"Okay, smart guy," Jimmy said to him. "How do you explain this?" He gestured to the dozer tracks.

"Maybe you were right. Maybe they're from troop carriers. AF could have been running maneuvers out here last night."

"Right," Jimmy scoffed.

"Maybe the ravine was dangerous," Vaughn tried. "You know, a flash flood hazard. So they dozed it." Even he didn't buy that one.

The three of them watched as Weber's car spun in a semicircle and roared off, pushed by a cloud of dust.

"And that's why the brass at Nellis went nuts," Jimmy said, frowning. "That's why Henderson hopped out to the bunker. That's why they filled in a dry riverbed with bulldozers. Because it created a hazard. A danger to . . . to coyotes. Sure, that's it."

"Doesn't make sense, does it?" Vaughn admitted. "Something's not right."

"I guess the bet stands," Parish teased. "I can't collect . . . yet."

"If Jack turns out to be right . . ." Jimmy promised in a stern voice.

"I'll be out one hundred big ones," Parish said playfully.

"And I'll personally make you eat your words, sir."

"Oh, is that right? I'd like to see you try."

Vaughn heard it first: footsteps—boots running on loose rock. He started to turn around.

"Don't move!" a deep voice shouted. The command was followed by a series of metallic clicks: the unmistakable sound of M16s being locked and loaded.

The three of them froze.

"Hands on heads!" the voice demanded.

They complied.

"We're marines," Vaughn offered. "My ID's in my pocket."

"Reach for it and die!"

Vaughn decided not to reach for it.

"On your knees!" the voice ordered.

They knelt in the dirt, hands still poised atop their heads.

"I'm gonna get you for this, Phil," Vaughn whispered.

Twenty-Three

THE PALEONTOLOGY LAB TURNED OUT TO BE NOTHING MORE THAN AN oversized storage closet. Located in the basement of the natural sciences building, it contained a collection of musty boxes, most of which were sealed with clear mailing tape. A chair and a makeshift desk consisting of a knobless door laid across two short metal filing cabinets had also been crowded into the tight space. The door to the lab stood wide open. A hand-printed sign taped to it read: *Keep Out!*

Vince ignored this. Stepping between the stacks of cardboard, he found a wooden crate and examined its contents: yellow-brown rocks of every shape and size imaginable. After slipping on a pair of gloves, he raked a hand through the crate and picked out a long, thin rock—a petrified stick with slightly rounded ends. A bone, he suddenly realized. He pulled out another, this one shorter and thicker with a sharp end, as if it had been snapped off. They were all bones. There were a hundred or so of them in the crate. And if the other boxes held the same thing . . . He ripped at the tape of a nearby carton and peered inside. Bones. There had to be thousands of them in that one room.

He cursed softly at the nature of his task. Finding the bones he was after would be worse than hunting a needle in a haystack. At least needles and hay were different.

Vince looked about the room, wondering where to start his search and contemplating a fitting, hideously cruel punishment for Sonny. Next time he could get somebody else to do his grunt work.

He surveyed the door-desk. It held a magnifying lamp, a tray of file folders, several notebooks, and more bones. They had been loaded into three shallow plastic tubs, seemingly at random. To the side sat a miniature hammer, a tubular device with a pinpoint head and an electric cord, a dentist's pick, several sizes of paintbrushes, a toothbrush, and two unlabeled bottles of liquid.

What do the bones I'm after even look like? he thought. He was on the verge of giving up, already planning the complaint he would lodge with Tito, when he saw something protruding from the garbage pail beneath the desk: a red and blue poster tube. Pulling back the chair, he sank to his knees and checked the label: Fed Ex. Mailed from Las Vegas. Addressed to Nigel Kendrick. Sender: Melissa Lewis. Bingo!

He shook the tube. Nothing. Removing the round plug, he looked inside. Empty. He tossed it across the room. Of course it would be empty if it was in the garbage. Standing up, he scanned the desk, then began rifling the material in the paper tray. The paperwork from the Fed Ex package was one layer down, beneath a file. The bones had to be somewhere nearby. Didn't they?

Crumpling the Fed Ex receipt, he tossed it over his shoulder and dumped the first tub. Bones rattled across the desk and onto the floor. He stared at them for a moment, then threw the tub in disgust. It ricocheted off a box and bounced into the hallway.

"What am I looking for?" he shouted.

The second tub was overturned, then the third. Bones covered the desk and the tile below it.

Vince slumped into the chair and kicked one of the file cabinets. This was ridiculous. Insane. Why couldn't they just let him kill someone? That was what he was good at. Not this—this foolishness. They had sent him and Tito on a scavenger hunt, something you did at birthday parties when you were eight years old. Vince had never been big on children's games.

He retrieved the Fed Ex paperwork, smoothed it out, and reread the information. It said nothing about the size or shape of the bones. Not even how many he was supposed to obtain. Out of reflex, he took up the file labeled "PA Work-up" and flipped through it—back to front. Nothing but scientific jargon, graphs and charts, something about radioactivity. He was about to send the folder on an express trip across the room when he spotted the name: Melissa Lewis. The sheet was dated today. Near the bottom of the page a paragraph of tiny print explained that a "PA series" was being conducted on two fossils recovered by Lewis. The following pages contained drawings and Polaroids of the bones in question.

Vince nodded in satisfaction. Now he knew what they looked like. It was only a matter of—

"Hey! What do you think you're doing?!"

He turned toward the door. A stout Asian in a white clinician's smock was standing there, legs shoulder width apart, hands on hips—like the bouncer of the paleontology department.

"What are you doing in here? Can't you read?" He jabbed a thumb at the sign on the door. "Keeeeep Ouuuuut," he said, overenunciating the warning. "That means you, buddy."

Vince had to laugh. Who did this punk think he was?

"Are you hard of hearing, too?" the young man barked. "Blind, deaf, and dumb, huh?" He raised his voice to a shout, "Get out of my chair and get out of my lab before I—"

"Before you what?" Vince smirked, rising. He knew that, even though his stature was not especially impressive or intimidating, his face was. He'd been told he had the look of someone who could do just about anything: mean, incorrigible, without remorse. A lady friend back at Club Blue had once told him that the devil resided in his eyes. He took that as a compliment. And from the look on the face of this pimply, impertinent lab rat, the devil was about to come out and play. "What is it you're going to do?"

"I'll . . . uh . . . I . . . I'll . . ." the kid stuttered as Vince approached. "I'll call security."

"The question is," Vince said through a confident smile, "could you call them fast enough?"

Before the lab rat could respond or even blink, he found himself face-first against the wall, an arm twisted painfully behind him, a knife hovering at his neck.

"Now," Vince said nonchalantly, "I have a few questions I need answered. That okay with you?"

"Yeah," the kid whimpered.

"Good. First of all, what's your name?"

"My name? My name is Mark. Mark Chung."

"Okay, Mark. You keep cool and we'll get along just fine." Vince pulled the lab door shut and pushed Mark into the chair. "What are you? A teacher?"

Mark shook his head rapidly. "I'm—I'm a doctoral student."

"What do you do in here?" Vince motioned about the room with the knife. It had a broad, six-inch blade that shimmered under the fluorescent lighting.

"I help Dr. Kendrick. I'm a preparator."

"A what?"

"A preparator. Someone who prepares fossils. I sort them, catalog them, tag them, clean them, preserve them . . ." He lifted a trembling hand toward the table and started to say something. But his jaw dropped as he noticed the mess Vince had made.

"What about this,"Vince picked up the PA Work-up file and tossed it into Mark's lap. "You handling the Lewis bones?"

"Lewis bones?" He glanced down at the folder. "Oh, that.Yeah.The samples from Nevada. Dr. Kendrick asked me to run a stat PA on them."

"Stat PA?"

"Potassium Argon series." Mark took a deep breath. "It's a radio-metric dating method."

Vince made a face at this.

"As rock ages," Mark explained, relaxing slightly, "tiny isotopes inside them decay into other elements. Potassium breaks down into argon at a constant rate. We measure that to determine the age of a fossil."

Vince sneered. "Sounds about as interesting as watching grass grow."

"Well . . . it's . . . you know."

"So where are the bones—the ones from Nevada?"

Mark shrugged. "I guess Dr. Kendrick still has them."

"I thought you said you were testing them."

"We don't actually test the bones themselves. We test igneous rock recovered from the same strata as the fossil. There were a couple of small volcanic stones in the package we received. I sent it over to the chem lab to be tested for PA levels."

"So Kendrick has the bones?"Vince asked, confused.

"I assume so. He was pretty excited about the whole thing. Got me to come in on a Saturday just to get the PA series kicked off."

"Where can I find Kendrick?"

"He's lecturing over at Adams Hall."

"Who else knows you're doing this test thing on the Nevada bones?"

"You mean the PA series?" Mark shrugged again. "Just me and Dr. Kendrick. And Ruth, over in chemistry. She's almost as excited as Kendrick."

"Why's that?"

"Well, when she put the samples to a Geiger counter, it started to chatter."

"Chatter?"

"It reacted. That means the rocks are radioactive for some reason. A lot of fossils contain high levels of uranium. But these rocks—they were hot."

"So?" Vince still didn't get it. "What's that mean?"

"Who knows? It may just be a fluke. Or it could be important. It might even say something about the way dinosaurs died out. High levels of radioactivity in the rock this find was buried in might help confirm the asteroid-extinction theory."

Vince sighed at this, no longer even remotely interested. He retrieved the PA Work-up folder, the Fed Ex paperwork, and the mailing tube.

Mark eyed him warily. "Listen, if you're afraid I'll report you, don't be." He held his hands up to Vince in a gesture of good will. Sweat was trailing down his brow. "I won't say a word. Really, I won't."

"I know you won't." Vince put his knife away and started for the door. In one smooth motion he stuck his right hand into his pants pocket and withdrew the 9mm automatic. Spinning toward Mark, he gave the trigger two gentle tugs. Thanks to the thick silencer attached to the end of the barrel, the shots were accompanied by nothing more than a pair of muffled thumps. Mark slumped over obediently, blood already staining his white coat.

Vince smiled approvingly at his work before flipping off the light and locking the door. *Now that was fun.*

THE PROCESS OF FOSSILIZATION FOLLOWS A UNIFORM PROGRESSION: One, the animal dies. Two, the flesh rots off the bones. Three, sediment covers the skeleton and preservative minerals enter the porous spaces of the bones. Four, the sediment slowly compacts into rock. Five, the climate changes and erosion—wind, rain, freezes, thawing—exposes the fossil."

Melissa stood at the back of the darkened auditorium, waiting for her eyes to adjust. When the speaker paused, she could hear the scratch of lead against paper as students scrambled to take notes. At the front of the hall an oversized screen displayed a series of illustrations: a dinosaur lying on the ground, a dinosaur skeleton, the same skeleton covered with layers of earth . . . There was a click and the slide disappeared. Another click, and a new slide flashed onto the screen. This time it was a photograph of a paleontological dig site: an outline of shiny, coffee-colored bones rising up from a floor of brown sand.

"Here we see an exposed skeleton," the speaker continued. "What we don't see is the work that brought the fossil to this point—ready for extraction."

The slide projector gave a clunk, offering up a new scene: a rugged cliffside.

"Finding dinosaurs is perhaps the most difficult part of dinosaur paleontology," the voice continued.

Melissa felt her way down two wide steps and slid into an empty seat. Her eyes scanned the platform below for a glimpse of the speaker. Three slides later, she spotted a shadow at the edge of the stage. Even in the darkness there was no mistaking him. His voice was a dead give-away—the Welsh accent, the deep resonating tone. And his stance. It conveyed a sense of authority, of quiet assurance.

"Once the appropriate formation has been located," the speaker noted, "it becomes a matter of hunting. It isn't exciting. It isn't stimu-lating. It's tedious, sometimes exceedingly boring—especially when you don't find anything for weeks, even months on end. So if you've a mind to join up as a paleontologist one day, then go out and find some ridicu-lously important fossil the next, I'm afraid you will be sorely disap-pointed."

Polite laugher erupted from the unseen audience and the screen switched to a photograph of a man kneeling in the dirt.

"GDOAF," the speaker announced. "That is the key to fossil dis-covery: Get Down On All Fours. You have to get down in the dirt in order to find anything."

A fresh slide appeared: bone tips erupting from the ground.

"Before any digging or removal takes place, we examine the lay of the bones. This can tell us a great deal about how the animal lived and died, how it was buried. We call this taphonomy. It is important to remember that our aim is not to gather bones or compete to put together the best skeleton. Our aim is to learn about these extinct creatures."

New slide.

"Once we've gleaned all we can from the site itself, the digging begins. The first phase is to remove the matrix—the rock surrounding the find. This is done with picks, hammers, awls, trowels. The tool depends upon the type of sediment as well as the position of the fossil."

Melissa stared down at the shadow, listening to the lilt of his voice without hearing the words. It was a magical sound, a lyrical ring that caused something inside of her to rise up. A part of her felt like dancing to the cadence of his speech.

"At this point we spray the bone with a solution called Vinac. Vinac is a clear liquid which acts as a preservative, hardening the exterior of the bones. It also makes them unnaturally shiny. Unfortunately, even after a Vinac coat, the bones often remain soft and spongy, so great care is required."

Even from this distance—shrouded by darkness, cloaked in anonymity—she felt the tug. He was a galactic body, she a moon unable to break free of his gravitational pull. Without knowing that she was there, he was drawing her to himself. She could feel resolve crumbling, hope building.

"In order to 'jacket' the bone, we mix a plaster solution and spread it on bandages or paper towels and begin separating the bone from the matrix. Once the plaster has dried, it becomes quite hard."

Meeting would be awkward. Conversation difficult. At least at first. There were so many unresolved issues to deal with. She wondered how she would push past that, past the surface clutter, past the tangled remains of their dead relationship, to the subject of God. How would she breach the topic of salvation?

"We 'pedestal' the bone by cutting around and below it, removing any remaining matrix. Then we jacket the bottom."

Father, guide this encounter. Lead the conversation. Help me to say what needs to be said. Give me the right words. I want to be sensitive to what you're trying to do.

"As John Horner is fond of saying, it takes a 'soft touch and a good eye' to be a dinosaur paleontologist. Lights please!"

Suddenly the auditorium was ablaze in yellow, the harsh overhead lights transforming the "theater" into a bright, stark-walled lecture hall.

Melissa squinted against the glare. Blinking, she realized that she was four rows up from the class. The hall was only half full, and students were crowded into the seats near the platform.

Two long-haired kids hurriedly moved the podium back into the middle of the stage. Thirty seconds passed. The students conversed in hushed tones. Then Nigel made his entrance.

Melissa watched as he strode to the center of the platform: long legs, tall, slender frame, curly brown locks, square jaw covered in gray-black whiskers. The first time she had ever seen him she had thought that he personified the essence of the phrase "tall, dark, and handsome." And today, six years later, clothed in khaki shorts, Birkenstocks, and a CU T-shirt, he still did.

"Persistence is the key to paleontology," he announced, reorganizing his notes. Then he looked up at the class. "But you'll find that out in a couple of weeks, when we get out in the field."

He cleared his throat, checked his watch. "T. rex . . ."

The class repositioned themselves in their seats, backs straighter. This seemed to be what they had come to hear.

"Was he a predator?" Nigel asked, smiling mischievously. "Or a scavenger? Was he the chief exterminator of Triceratops? An agile, intelligent, birdlike hunter: forward leaning, s-shaped neck, tail in the air? Or was he a fat, slow, lumbering tail-dragger—the vulture of the Late Cretaceous?"

Pens flew as the pupils fought to keep up, pad pages flipping in their frantic effort to record copious notes.

Nigel paused, waiting. Finally all eyes were on him, pens ready. "We'll save that discussion for next time," he said.

A collective groan arose.

"Right now, I'd like to segue to the topic of evolutionary adaptation as it relates to various Mesozoic ornithischians. But first, are there any questions on the material we've covered thus far?"

Hands flew into the air.

Nigel picked through them with a finger. "Ah . . . Yes. You in the blue shirt. Yes. You."

An attractive blond stood up. "I'm not clear on the iridium layer and how it relates to the K-T boundary."

Heads nodded. Apparently many of the students were unclear about that.

"The iridium layer is a band of the element iridium that we find in sedimentary rock," Nigel began. "Iridium is not found in abundance on earth, but . . ."

He stopped, apparently losing his train of thought, and stared up into the seats for inspiration.

Melissa held her breath. His head swung left, then right, then it happened. Their eyes met; the connection was made. They acknowledged each other with a barely detectable nod, a miniature smile.

Students swiveled in their seats to find the source of the professor's amusement.

"But it is common on asteroids," he continued, still looking at her.

The note takers returned to their task, scratching out Nigel's answer, undoubtedly word-for-word.

"The K-T boundary is the point at which the dinosaurs died out— the end of the Cretaceous period and the beginning of the Tertiary period. What's significant about the iridium layer is that we find no evidence of dinosaurs living within one hundred thousand years of it. This suggests . . ."

Melissa steadied herself with a deep breath as he lectured on. Contact had been established. Now for the tough part: actually talking to him.

Twenty-Four

I T'S ALL A MISTAKE."

"A mistake?"

"We're part of the bunker team. Check our ID."

"We did. The problem we're having, Captain, is understanding what the three of you were doing in Quad 217—a restricted zone—in your off-duty hours."

Vaughn opened his mouth to reply, then closed it, unsure how to go about explaining. He was sure of one thing, though: he and his buddies were in serious trouble. Armed MPs didn't cuff you, load you into a personnel carrier, and cart you off to an interrogation room at the Nellis brig merely to congratulate you on doing a fine job. It would take some creative verbal gymnastics to extricate themselves from this mess.

"Where are Phil and Jimmy?"

"Lieutenant Parish and Sergeant Donohue are being taken care of," the major answered, studying her notepad. Major Wallace was a husky woman with stern features: pale, bony cheeks bordered by closely cropped brown hair. Her thick neck plugged into broad, muscular shoulders. From the back she might have been mistaken for a man.

"This is a big misunderstanding," Vaughn tried again. "We were just out goofing around—"

"In a restricted area," Wallace added, glaring.

"Okay. Yeah. But we have clearance. And 217 is yellow status anyway, so—"

"Was."

"Huh?"

"You weren't aware that it had been upgraded to red?"

"Red? No. When?"

"You're part of the bunker team—the crew in charge of NTS security—and you didn't know that quadrant was under a red flag?"

Vaughn sighed in frustration. The hole was getting deeper. "How were we supposed to know? The status must have changed after our shift was up. It's our day off, for crying out loud."

"Exactly. Which brings us back to the original question: What were you doing out there?"

"We were . . ." He shook his head. "It's stupid. You wouldn't believe me if I told you."

"Try me." Wallace stared at him with piercing green eyes.

"We were settling a bet."

"A bet?"

"There was a contact in 217 yesterday," he told her. "Stage three. We ran it down. Afterwards, General Henderson showed up to debrief us. We thought that was a little strange. So last night we're at this bar and we get to talking—"

"Who we?"

"Phil, Jimmy, and me. We were drinking beer . . . joking around . . . you know, having a good time."

From the expression on the major's face, it was apparent that she couldn't identify with the concept of "having a good time."

"Anyway, we got to wondering about what might be out in that quad. What was so important that it warranted Henderson's personal attention? To make a long story short, my partners wound up betting on this crazy notion, so we—"

"What crazy notion?"

"I'm embarrassed to tell you. It was outrageous. Just totally—"

The door swung open and Colonel Johnson entered, followed closely by General Henderson. Vaughn's heart sank. He was about to face the dragon.

"Commander in the room!" Colonel Johnson announced with a bellow.

The major leapt to her feet and offered a crisp salute. Henderson and Johnson returned it, then glanced at Vaughn. He shrugged at them helplessly. "I'd salute, sirs, but—"

"Lose the cuffs," Henderson grunted.

"But sir—" Wallace started to protest.

"Do it," Johnson insisted.

Wallace begrudgingly complied. Fishing a key out of her pocket, she yanked Vaughn out of his seat, spun him around, and removed the shackles.

"That'll be all, Major," Henderson told her.

"Sir, if I might speak . . . I've been questioning the Captain and I think—"

"That'll be all," Johnson repeated, nodding toward the door.

Wallace muttered a very unladylike phrase under her breath as she gathered her pad and pen and started for the door.

Henderson took her seat at the table and waited until the door had swung shut behind her. Then he looked at Vaughn and asked, "What were you doing out there, Captain?"

"Like I was telling Major Personality there, sir," he said, "we were settling a bet."

Henderson's face contorted at this.

"It was dumb, sir. We shouldn't have been there. We wouldn't have been there if we'd known the quad had been upgraded to red."

The general considered this for a moment. Vaughn held his breath, waiting to be consumed in a burst of fiery breath.

"Any idea what's out there, son?" Henderson asked in a calm tone.

The question caught Vaughn off guard. "What do you mean, sir?"

"You've been in the bunker . . . what? Five years now?"

"Seven," Vaughn said.

"Seven. Well, then, you know the zone. You know the quads. What about 217?"

"What about it, sir?"

Henderson leaned into the table. "A few fossil hunters wander into that quad. Next thing I know, I'm feeling the heat from Washington. Now according to my people, there ain't nothing in 217 but coyotes and rabbits. Never has been. It was never used as a testing area—not for above or below-ground devices. Which makes me wonder, what's out there that's got D.C. doing the dance of the Mexican jumping beans?"

"That's sort of how we ended up out there today, sir," Vaughn explained. "We didn't get it either. And that debrief yesterday—other than a drill, it didn't make much sense. Not on a stage three contact."

"Yeah, well—that wasn't my idea," the general muttered. "Neither was that business last night."

"The bulldozers?"

"What do you know about bulldozers?" Johnson asked suspiciously. There were three chairs in the room, but the colonel seemed reluctant to sit. He was content to pace and look down on the "prisoner."

"Just that somebody had been driving them around in 217."

Henderson studied the tabletop. "What in blazes needs dozing out in that quad?"

"I don't know, sir," Vaughn replied. "I assumed you did."

"Well, you assumed wrong. All I know is that people in high places are getting nervous. They're worried about a worthless piece of dirt in the middle of the Tonopah desert. And we can't figure out why, can we, Bill?"

Johnson shook his head. "No, sir."

"You have absolutely no idea what's out there, Captain?"

"No, sir."

"You wouldn't lie to me now, would you? Because as I see it, your rear is in a sling and I'm holding the rope. Granted, you fellas may not have known the zone was red, but technically, that's no excuse. I could still have you charged with criminal trespassing, even espionage. You'd be court-martialed by month's end, shipped off to a federal pen to serve, say, fifteen years to life."

Vaughn swallowed hard. "We were just goofing around, sir. That was all. Jimmy knows this guy who . . ." He paused, grimacing.

"Who what?" Johnson prodded.

"The man's a lunatic, okay? A real nutcase. Anyway, he thinks maybe there are . . ." His voice trailed off and he mumbled, "bodies buried out there."

"What's that?" Henderson asked, straining to hear.

"Bodies, sir. The guy thinks maybe there are bodies buried out there."

"Bodies?"

"Victims of radioactive fallout—from the fifties." Vaughn shrugged apologetically. "It's a ridiculous theory. Like I said, the guy's insane. But Jimmy's pretty naive, and he sort of believed the story, I guess. Phil and I thought the whole thing was loony tunes. But Jimmy and Phil got into it and wound up making a wager. So the next thing I know, we're headed out to 217."

"To look for bodies," Johnson confirmed.

"Well . . . yeah. Sort of. I guess."

"Bodies." The General chuckled. "That's a good one, Captain. I've been at Nellis nearly twenty years now and I've never heard that particular slant on the radioactive horror stories. Bodies. Buried in the zone. Incredible."

"Yes, sir," Vaughn agreed.

Henderson took a deep breath. "To be honest with you, Captain, I haven't the slightest idea what's going on with 217. Maybe it's home to an endangered kangaroo mouse. Maybe the BLM is trying to make it into a Native reservation. Maybe somebody started dumping high-level rad waste out there before getting the appropriate clearance. Who knows? I'm just an Air Force puke. They don't tell me squat.

"But I'll tell you something." He paused and looked Vaughn in the eye. "Whatever it is that has Washington all hot and bothered, it could get ugly before it's over. Federal scandals—if that's what it turns out to be—always do: investigations, committees, hearings, charges flying fast and furious . . .

"My advice to you, son? Watch yourself. Stay clear of that quad—especially when you're not on duty. Trust me, you don't want to get mixed up in this."

"No, sir."

Henderson rose with a sigh and the colonel hurried to open the door for him.

"Bodies," the general scoffed as he left. "Who thinks up that garbage?"

Vaughn sat there, alone in the cheerless room, confused, wondering what would happen next. The question was answered seconds later when the major reappeared.

She scowled at him, then grunted, "You're free to go."

Parish and Jimmy were waiting for him in the hallway. Parish was seething—a commissioned Spike Lee ready to lash out at a heinous injustice. Next to him, the Truck was stalled, head bowed, eyes dazed with fear. He looked like he was about to vomit. They left the brig in silence, avoiding the stares of the MPs and staff. When they were back outside, Vaughn was relieved to see his Jeep parked in a visitor's space.

Parish demanded, "What was that about?"

"We were in the zone," Vaughn explained matter-of-factly, climbing into the Jeep. "It was under a red. We violated."

"The Captain's right," Jimmy said, his deep voice driven deeper by melancholy. "We shouldn't have been in 217. It was our mistake."

"We're lucky they didn't lock us up and throw away the key," Vaughn said, pulling out of the lot.

That thought caused the Truck to sputter. His breath was coming in gulps now.

Parish shook his head. "Lucky? No. That's exactly what they want us to feel. This whole thing is screwed up."

"Phil—" Vaughn started to say.

"The fossil hunters weren't handcuffed," he pointed out. "They weren't arrested and interrogated."

"We weren't arrested," Vaughn argued, slowing for a red light. "We were detained. For questioning."

Parish said, "We could sue. We have clearances. Even if 217 was red, we've got the right to be out there."

"You guys want to stop for a beer?" Vaughn asked. "Man, I could sure use one."

Jimmy nodded enthusiastically.

"They're just trying to scare us off," Parish continued.

"Well, it worked," Jimmy replied. It was hot and the air conditioner was still fighting to catch up, but the sweat staining his shirt was the result of stress, not temperature. He presented a trembling hand to Parish. "See this. Talk about scared—man, if there's any place I don't want to go, it's to prison."

"They wouldn't dare," Parish said, still indignant. "It's all an act. They're trying to intimidate us. What I don't understand is why."

"Phil," Vaughn sighed. "Going out there was a stupid idea from the word go. The area is restricted—off-limits."

"But it's not enforced. We never—"

"If the powers that be suddenly see fit to enforce it—for whatever reason—we have to abide by that. That's life in the military. You don't ask questions. You just follow orders. And you try to stay out of trouble."

Parish muttered, "I think the whole thing smells."

"Sure it does," Vaughn agreed. He flipped on his blinker and braked for oncoming traffic. "But it got our attention, didn't it? And maybe Henderson is on the level. He told me he didn't know what the beef with 217 was."

"Oh, come on," Parish said, making a face. "Henderson is in on everything that happens in or around the NTS. If anybody knows what's out there, he does."

"Maybe so,"Vaughn said. A break in the stream of cars materialized and he turned into the parking area of the Buckaroo Tavern. It was only 4:30, but the lot was already over half full. "I'm not saying I understand what's going on. Just that we aren't paid to know. We do our job, we follow orders, we go home and toss back a few cold ones. Which is what I plan to do right now." He switched off the ignition and got out.

"Me too," Jimmy grunted, rolling out of the passenger's seat. "I seem to have developed a terrible thirst. I guess the brig has that effect on me."

Parish followed them, grumbling to himself.

The inside of the tavern was dark and loud, a cacophony of competing sounds: a jukebox belting out a Huey Lewis classic, a group of revelers celebrating at a corner booth, two women engaged in a game of darts, a dozen onlookers cheering them on, pool balls cracking, glasses clinking, the air conditioning system roaring as it struggled to keep the environs at an acceptable temperature. In the corner, a big-screen TV presented the early evening news to an array of empty tables. Over the bar, a small color set displayed the same anchorwoman seated behind the same desk. Her voice sounded tinny as she reported the top stories.

Vaughn and Jimmy slid onto stools. Vaughn waved three fingers at the bartender and a minute later a trio of ice-cold drafts arrived.

"Here Phil,"Vaughn said, pushing a glass his direction. "Have a seat and cool off."

Parish stood there, oblivious, watching the TV. He lifted his arm in slow motion, aiming a pointer finger toward the set.

Vaughn looked up. Most of the anchorwoman's report was lost in the noise of the tavern. But he caught the word "accident." Above her shoulder, a computer-generated box displayed a photograph of a man.

"Look!" Vaughn nudged Jimmy, then told the bartender, "Turn it up!"

When the bartender did, they watched in horror, listening as the anchor divulged the details.

" . . . approximately three this afternoon. The cause of the accident is still unconfirmed, but authorities now believe the man may have fallen asleep at the wheel. His vehicle was traveling south on the

Tonopah highway when it left the road and collided with a concrete embankment. The man was thrown from the car and found dead on the scene by a rescue crew. The police have identified the man as Dr. Jack Weber, a sixty-two-year-old resident of Las Vegas.

"In other news . . ."

The three of them shared a look of stunned astonishment.

Parish finally shook his head and sunk to a stool. He dug something out of his wallet and extended it to Jimmy: a hundred-dollar bill.

The Truck stared at it as if he had never seen Benjamin Franklin before.

"Go on, take it," Parish insisted.

"What for?"

"I always make good on my debts."

"What are you talking about?" Vaughn wondered.

"We had a bet, didn't we? I'm paying up." He grabbed Jimmy's slab of a hand and forced the bill into it. Then he took a long draw of his beer. "You win. Weber was right. There is something out there in 217. Something bad. Maybe even bodies. And whoever buried them doesn't want them dug up."

TWENTY-FIVE

He did what?" The question was rhetorical, of course. "Why did he do that?"

Tito waited, unsure whether Sonny really expected an answer. He was sitting on a warped wooden bench beneath an umbrellalike shade tree, phone to his ear, watching as students exited Adams Hall. Next to him, Vince was admiring passing coeds.

"You're sure he's dead?"

Tito relayed the question to Vince. "Yeah," he grunted, winking at a dark-haired beauty.

"He's sure."

Sonny responded with a flurry of profanity.

"What now?" Tito asked.

"Hang on," Sonny sighed.

Tito covered the phone with his hand. "Seen Lewis yet?" he asked his partner.

"Who?"

He followed Vince's gaze down the sidewalk to a slender blond. "Lewis," he tried again when the girl had disappeared around the corner.

"Oh . . . uh . . . no. Not yet. Man!" He pointed at the lecture hall where another coed in shorts was trotting down the steps. "I feel the sudden urge to go back to school. Get a degree. Any degree."

"Okay," Sonny sighed again. "First of all, Vince screwed up—royal. Killing grad students wasn't part of the plan. I cannot believe that idiot was ever in the military. He can't follow orders to save his life. The jerk. He's the one who needs to be shot."

"But?"

"But as it turns out, the order was already on the way down."

"The order?"

"To clean house."

Tito smiled at this. "It's about time. How extensive a cleanup are we talking about, Sonny?"

"Total. Anybody and everybody associated with the bones."

"Lewis too?"

"What did I just say? Do what you need to do. Just make it fast and neat. No witnesses. No trails of blood leading back here. Get the bones and come home. We've got a few other loose ends to tie up."

"No problem. Consider it a done deal. See you this evening."

Tito snapped the phone shut and watched as another wave of students poured through the doors.

"Sonny ticked off about my little job on the lab rat?" Vince asked.

"Of course. But you lucked out."

"How's that?"

"Whoever it is that's running the show—they want to clean house."

Vince's eyes lit up. "Everybody?"

Tito nodded. "Even Lewis."

"All right!" Vince stood and stretched, then started down the sidewalk.

"Where are you going?"

"To find the chemistry lab," he said, grinning. "I have an appointment with somebody named Ruth." He patted the pocket that held his 9mm. "It's show time!"

WHAT YOU'RE DESCRIBING IS A 'GIGANTOTHERM.'"

The young man scribbled this term down, then looked up, waiting for an explanation.

"That's a large creature that has evolved in such a way that it can maintain a stable temperature, retaining and conserving heat generated from the movement of its muscles. Now whether T. rex or any of his near relatives fell into that category is a topic of some debate. And I have certain opinions about the subject. But I'll get into that next week."

The fresh-faced kid nodded and stepped aside, still writing. The line lurched forward.

"Dr. Kendrick, about the Colorado Sea . . ."

The professor examined his watch, then waved a hand at the girl. "We're fifteen minutes over. The rest of you will have to see me in my office," he announced in a loud voice. "Stop by during my hours or make an appointment with my secretary."

There was a collective groan, then the shuffling of feet as the inquisitive youths made for the door. The girl stood her ground. "But Dr. Kendrick, if there was a shallow seaway covering the interior of North America, how—"

"Page 275 in the text," he told her grumpily. "Or make an appointment."

She frowned, then slunk into a seat in the first row of the auditorium and began paging through her text.

"Do I need an appointment, Nigel?"

Kendrick's head turned toward the voice. The scowl disappeared, replaced by a glowing smile—a mouth of icy, white teeth surrounded by a gray-black forest of whiskers.

"Bet you're wondering what I'm doing here."

He shook his head, then reached for his briefcase. Giving it an affectionate pat, he said, "I got your package."

"And what do you think?"

He chuckled at this. "I think it's wonderful to see you again, Melissa." He set the briefcase down and reached to embrace her.

Melissa hesitated, stiffening. She closed her eyes as he draped his arms around her, drinking in the familiar scent of his cologne, suddenly aware of how much she had missed him.

"Excuse me, Dr. Kendrick?"

The moment was cut short as he stepped back to face the persistent student.

"Page 275 talks about the nesting habits of duckbills."

Nigel sighed at her. "Try . . . 175." He shrugged at Melissa, rolling his eyes. "Come on." He led her up the stairs, into the entryway of the building. It was deserted.

"You look . . . fabulous. As beautiful as ever."

Melissa could feel her cheeks blushing.

"But you haven't come to have some old dinosaur-nut fawn over you—to flatter you and beg you to return to his side."

All she could manage was a thin smile. Actually . . . "No. Of course not. The purpose of my trip is twofold," she said, immediately regretting her choice of words. They came out sounding cold, businesslike.

"Both professional and personal in nature." She took a deep breath, trying to relax.

Nigel raised an eyebrow at this. The giddy, boyish expression on his face changed to one of serious concentration. "Tell me about the bones. Where did you find them? When? Is there a complete skeleton? How soon can I visit the site?"

"There's . . . there's no site. Well, not exactly. A student of mine found the bones on a field trip."

"Are there other bones?"

"Uh . . . yes. There were many other bones."

Nigel's eyes lit up.

"But they were like the small one I sent," she stipulated.

"The small one." He stooped and opened his briefcase. "This one?"

She nodded.

"There were more? How many?"

Melissa shrugged. "Hundreds . . . maybe thousands."

"Exposed?"

"Barely."

"On the same strata level as this one?" He lifted the longer, thicker bone for her inspection.

Another nod.

"You're certain?"

"Pretty sure."

"Extraordinary!"

"Why? What are they?"

Nigel started to say something, but stopped, his eyes growing wide. He glanced at his watch. "Are you hungry?"

"Huh?"

"Let me take you to dinner."

"Only if you promise to explain."

"Oh, I'll explain." The smile was back, along with an air of unbridled joy. He repacked his briefcase and slung it under his arm. Taking her hand, he led her out of the lecture hall. "You just might convert me yet."

Melissa stared at him. "What?"

"If these bones tell us what I think they do . . . Well, it's much too early to say, but I think—at least, I wonder—it could be that evolutionary theory, the philosophical framework so near and dear to my heart, is about to be toppled like so many dominoes."

Iᴛᴏ ᴡᴀᴛᴄʜᴇᴅ ᴛʜᴇᴍ ᴄᴏᴍᴇ ᴏᴜᴛ ᴏꜰ ᴛʜᴇ ʜᴀʟʟ ᴀɴᴅ ᴅᴏᴡɴ ᴛʜᴇ ꜱᴛᴇᴘꜱ, hand in hand like two lovers, their faces beaming. He waited until they were well on their way down the sidewalk before rising from the bench, then nonchalantly meandered after them.

Looking back in the general direction that Vince had gone, he tried to decide on a plan of action. How would he and his partner hook up if Lewis and Kendrick decided to leave campus? He would have no way of—

"Hey."

Surprised, he jerked his head around and saw Vince striding along beside him. His cheeks were pink, his hair matted with perspiration.

"Well?"

Vince offered a smile of success. "Poor Ruth never knew what hit her."

"Did you clean up the mess?"

"Of course. She's packed away in a broom closet. Probably won't be found for weeks."

"I don't suppose there were any reports or—"

Vince produced a crinkled file from his pocket. "Am I thorough, or what? Man, I'm good." Stretching his neck forward and back, then side to side, he asked, "So where we headed?"

"Good question. Lewis and Kendrick are on the move."

"Let's ice them and go home."

Tito nodded, slowing as Lewis and Kendrick paused at the corner of another lecture hall, absorbed in conversation.

"I could nail them right here," Vince offered, already reaching inside his slacks.

Tito shook his head. "Too public." They followed them down another long sidewalk to a parking lot. Kendrick produced a set of keys and started for a Ford Explorer.

"They're going mobile." Tito cursed, looking around. "Our rental is a mile from here. We'll never make it."

"Let's hot-wire something."

Tito shrugged. "Okay." He pointed at a Trans Am.

Vince laughed. "Low profile, huh?"

"Just get it started."

Vince pulled a rubber-coated device out of his pocket, jiggled the lock, and popped open the door. An alarm sounded once before he silenced the security system with a well-aimed kick to the dash. Hunching down in the floorboard, he fought with a nest of wires. Ten seconds later the car roared to life.

"Move over," Tito told him. "I'll drive."

"I started it. I should get to—"

"Move over!"

Vince swore at him, crawling across to the passenger seat. "Then I get to do the two targets."

"Whatever." He rolled out of the parking slot and made a right, keeping the Explorer in sight.

"Pull up beside them," Vince instructed, 9mm in hand.

"No. Not here. We can't do it on the street."

Vince sighed melodramatically, obviously disappointed.

"We need to be more creative," Tito told him. "We could shoot them both, sure. But we want to make the cops work to put this thing together. Four gunshot victims on the same campus on the same day? Piece of cake. Even a dope could figure out the link."

"What are you suggesting?"

Tito accelerated around a bus, pleased with the Trans Am's power, then shot through a red light, narrowly missing a pedestrian. The Explorer was rolling along a block ahead, its two passengers happily oblivious to their presence.

"I don't know," Tito said. "Any ideas?"

"No guns, huh?" Vince thought aloud. "How about something . . . explosive?"

Twenty-Six

"ARE YOU A RELATIVE?"

Jimmy nodded soberly.

"Brother?"

"Uh . . . cousin," Jimmy answered.

The uniformed woman at the counter scowled at him. "No."

"We just want to see the report," Vaughn tried. "Isn't it public record?"

"No."

Parish smiled boyishly at her. She was black, about thirty-five years old. "Listen, girlfriend—"

"I am not your girlfriend!" she snapped back.

"Okay, then . . . sister."

"Sister?"

"Fellow African American?"

"No."

"Oh, come on," Parish moaned.

"Is there a problem here, Sergeant?" A burly cop sidled up to the counter and glared at them. He was a blue square with no visible neck, not quite as large as Jimmy but twice as mean looking.

"These guys want to see the Weber report."

"Weber?"

"The accident victim."

"Alleged accident," Parish asserted. "We think it might have been foul play."

"Is that right?" The cop snickered at him. "You a detective?"

Parish shook his head.

"Did any of you witness the accident?"

Three heads swung left to right, right to left.

"Then why don't you go bother someone else?"

"We have reason to believe Dr. Weber's accident was intentional," Vaughn told him.

The cop sighed at this, then picked up the phone. "Sir, there are three men out here who think they know something about the Weber vehicular." He paused. "Yes, sir. No. No, they say it might not have been an accident." Another pause. "All right."

A thumb pointed toward the hallway. "Third door on your right."

"Now we're getting somewhere," Parish said as they followed the cop's directions. The door in question bore a plaque that read: Lt. Ronald Frazier.

Vaughn reached for the knob, but the door opened, seemingly of its own accord. A slight man with a tired face met them. "Ron Frazier. Have a seat."

There were only two chairs on the visitor side of the desk: rusted, gray metal, with bent stems. Jimmy wisely decided not to test their strength. Vaughn and Parish slid into them.

"What's this about the Weber accident? Do you boys have some information?"

"Not exactly," Vaughn answered. He hadn't wanted to come in the first place—it had been Parish's idea—and was now feeling uncomfortable. Hadn't General Henderson just finished telling him to stay clear of the whole affair?

"What do you mean, not exactly?" Frazier leaned back in his chair, fingers busying themselves with a pencil, eyes nearly closed.

"Just that—well, we didn't see the accident," Vaughn said. "But we did see him today."

"Is that right?" The detective seemed to be on the verge of sleep. "Where? When?"

"First at breakfast," Jimmy explained, taking up the narrative. "Then later out at the NTS."

Frazier woke up, sitting straighter. "The NTS?"

"We work there," Parish said. "Security. We're marines."

"And you met with Weber at the Site?" Frazier was taking notes now. "What was the purpose of the meeting?"

"Well, it wasn't exactly a meeting," Vaughn clarified. "Breakfast was. That was prearranged. But then he just showed up later when we drove out to look around at the Site."

The detective scribbled something, then asked, "What was he driving?"

"A Valiant," Jimmy said. "A bronze Valiant."

"Okay. So what's the deal? We got skid marks, tire tracks in the dirt, the Valiant plastered into an embankment, a hole in the windshield where Weber's body flew out, the corpse lying there—cause of death, severe head injury. It's not pretty, but accidents never are."

"Jack was a conspiracy theorist," Jimmy said. "He was working on this book—"

"Did you find his book?" Vaughn asked.

"What sort of book?"

"It was more research than anything else—a whole box of it. He must have had it with him."

"He said he took it everywhere," Parish added.

The detective flipped open a folder and paged through the Xeroxed material. "Let's see . . . Here we go. Boxes. He had twelve boxes in the car. Three contained newspapers. Five contained note cards. The other four held pop cans and soda bottles."

"Does it mention a small cardboard box—a file box?" Vaughn asked.

Frazier frowned, flipped pages, frowned some more. "I don't see anything about that."

"Jack told us this would happen," Jimmy announced.

"Told you what would happen?" Frazier asked.

"He said that they wanted his book, that they'd kill to get it."

"Hang on," the detective said. "Who wanted it?"

"The government," Jimmy answered. "It implicated the government in a massive cover-up."

"It did, huh?"

"Yeah. And they killed him to shut him up."

"They did?"

Jimmy nodded.

"You guys are military, right?"

They nodded.

"Off-duty?"

More nods.

"Been downing a few brewskies?"

"We're not drunk," Parish said, "if that's what you mean."

"Who's in charge of the case?" Vaughn asked. He was getting irritated.

"What case?" Frazier asked. "There is no case. It was an accident. We filed a report. The coroner took the body. That's it."

"There won't be an investigation?" Parish asked.

"Why should there be? Unless evidence warrants one, it's a waste of time and manpower."

"But we're here to tell you that it wasn't an accident," Jimmy insisted.

"Yeah. Right. You didn't see it. You don't know anyone who did. But you think Weber was murdered for some box of research."

"Exactly." Parish nodded. "Now you just need to do some detective work and find out who it was."

"You already told me who it was. The government." Frazier shook his head at them. "Listen, give me something solid, I'll go out and beat the bushes. Otherwise . . ."

"The least you could do is look into it," Vaughn submitted.

"Look into what?" Frazier sounded annoyed. "You haven't been listening. I need evidence in order to justify an investigation."

"That's backwards," Parish protested.

"Maybe so, but that's the American way," Frazier remarked, smirking. He rose and offered them each his hand. "Thanks for coming in, guys. I know you're just trying to help. Being good citizens and all that. I understand your concern. Now go home. Forget about this."

No one spoke as the three of them retraced their steps back past the precinct counter, through the entryway, and out to the parking lot. Vaughn unlocked the Jeep and they got in.

They had been driving for ten minutes when Jimmy said, "I hate to admit it, but maybe I was wrong."

"About what?" Vaughn asked.

"About everything. About Jack. Maybe he was just a paranoid nut. Maybe that book of his was nothing but baloney. Maybe his theory about a radioactive accident was pure fiction. Maybe he just dozed off and crashed on the way home from the Site."

"Maybe," Parish grunted. "And maybe this thing with 217 is just coincidence. Maybe our getting hauled in by the MPs had nothing to do with Weber. Seems like a lot of maybes to me, though."

"I've got another maybe for you," Vaughn announced, glancing at his side mirror. "Maybe that white Dodge a block behind us just happens to be going our way. Maybe it's a cop headed home and maybe he lives in the direction of the base."

Parish and Jimmy craned their necks, peering out the back window.

"Or maybe we're being followed."

THE FIRE WAS READY: A PYRAMID OF ORANGE, MESQUITE-STOKED FLAMES dancing up from beneath a blackened grill, the fickle breeze urging each glowing finger skyward. He jabbed the meat with a long, chrome fork, added a last dash of seasoning, a final squirt of marinade, then laid the slab carefully across the barbecue, as if it were still a living thing.

There was a hiss as flesh met fire. Blood fell to the briquettes in pale pink drops. Smoke billowed violently into the air. DiCaprio took a deep breath, savoring the smell. Satisfied that his creation was as it should be, he closed the top of the unit and checked his watch. The dinner party was slated to begin in fifteen minutes—at 8:30. Which meant that the first guests would arrive in approximately half an hour—fashionably late. The tri-tip was thick. It would take most of that time to grill through. And there were five other steaks and the fish still to cook.

The dark cumulous clouds that had built and boiled in the west for the better part of the afternoon had passed over without comment, without so much as a sprinkle. The sun was perched on the horizon, offering a parting blast of heat. As soon as it set, the temperature would drop. The evening would be cool, clear—perfect for a garden party.

Reaching for his drink, he took a sip and peered in the window. He could see his wife, Loretta, in the kitchen stepping to one counter, then the other, opening the oven, the refrigerator, doing something at the island. She hadn't changed yet. She was still wearing a grungy, oversized MIT T-shirt and a pair of khaki shorts. Over this she had tied an apron that was covered with stains. Despite her attire, she was still the best-looking woman he had ever seen: long dark hair, skin like silk, the trim, shapely body of a fashion model . . . Nearly fifteen years his junior, she was enough to make his colleagues and fellow politicians eat their hearts out. What they wouldn't give to have someone as young, supple, and—

Something flashed in the corner of his vision. The television. Loretta had left the big-screen set in the family room on. DiCaprio watched for a moment, sipped his drink, checked the steak . . . A face appeared on the screen. He squinted at it. The man was familiar some-how. He tried to place him.

The picture shrank into a box that fit into the empty space above the anchorman's shoulder. Beneath the photograph a name blinked onto the screen: Dr. Jack Weber.

Weber? Wasn't that the jerk who was always trying to scuttle the DOE, releasing hokey, contrived stories of misappropriation and foul-ups to the press?

DiCaprio set his drink down and started for the house to listen to the report. But by the time he arrived at the door, the television screen was already displaying a commercial for a local insurance company.

He went back to his barbecue, stared at it, then picked up the cel-lular phone that was lying next to his drink.

"It's me," he told the man who answered. "You ever hear of a guy named Weber?"

"As a matter of fact I have."

"Jack Weber? He was on TV tonight—on the news—for some-thing. I'm not sure what it was."

"Auto accident."

"Is he dead?"

"Very."

"You didn't . . ." His voice trailed off.

There was no response.

"You did." DiCaprio swore at him. "You idiots. You can't start a massacre just to cover your butts."

"We're protecting ourselves, Robert," the man explained in an even tone. "We're protecting the DOE. And most importantly, we're pro-tecting you. When you get to the Senate—who knows, maybe even the White House—you'll thank us."

DiCaprio looked up. His wife was waving at him through the win-dow, saying something. He ignored her.

"What else haven't you told me?"

"Can't think of a thing."

"No more bodies out there with your name on them?"

"Oh, bodies," the man said, joking. "You want a current tally or would you like to wait for a final count?"

DiCaprio cursed again. In the house his wife was waving frantically. He stifled her with a wave of his own. "Not now!" he shouted at her.

"How many?" he asked, sighing.

"As of today?"

"Quit playing around!"

"Listen, Robert. You don't need to know. It would be safer for you if you didn't know."

"I want to know, okay? Just tell me."

"Okay. Right now I see three casualties—two more in the offing. A maximum of another two or three after that. That's not counting our recent downsizing project in Vegas, of course."

DiCaprio shook his head in disgust. "You're talking about eight lives. Eight lives! For pete's sake! Why don't we just explain—"

"Why don't we just explain what, Robert? Huh? All of a sudden you sound like a man with nothing to lose. You even *think* about going public or trying to shirk responsibility, and I guarantee you'll regret it. Everything you hold near and dear—your houses, your little trophy wife, your job, your reputation, your bank accounts—it'll disappear." He snapped his fingers into the phone. "Just like that. Wham! Gone! You want to risk that, Robert? Huh? Do you?"

"No."

"Good. Then you will play along. And you will keep your mouth shut. And you will look the other way until this is over. Got that?"

"Yes."

"You do this for us, Robert, we'll take care of you."

Yeah, I'll just bet, he wanted to say. "I know."

"Honey!" his wife called out the door.

"Relax, Robert. We'll be in touch when this blows over."

"Honey!"

He hung up the phone and stared at Loretta. "What! What is it?"

She pointed at the grill and made a terrible face. DiCaprio turned and saw the cause of her concern. A column of thick, black smoke was rushing up from the barbecue. He lifted the lid, swearing as he burned his bare hand. When the smoke finally cleared, he surveyed the contents: a charred brick of something that had once been meat. It was less than half the size of the slab he had started out with. He cursed the grill, turned and told his wife to go back inside and get dressed, then proceeded to curse the crisis he was facing, his derailed career, his very existence. Everything seemed to be going up in flames.

Twenty-Seven

"RIGHT THIS WAY, DOCTOR."

They followed the young lady through a small, empty dining room, up three steps, through a larger room—this one containing a half-dozen patrons—and finally down a narrow set of stairs and out onto a flagstone verandah. Twenty round white tables sat like ships in dock, gleaming in the evening sun. They bordered a low, stone retaining wall that afforded unobscured views of Boulder on one edge, the Front Range on the other. Umbrellas shot up from the center of each table, colorful sails emblazoned with the names of foreign breweries. White, wire chairs had been crowded onto the patio to accommodate the hundred or so patrons. Books and notepads sat open—and largely ignored—on the tables, ringed by rows of depleted amber bottles. The customers, clad almost exclusively in shorts and T-shirts, were consuming burgers, nachos, and buffalo wings, conversing in loud voices, and guzzling from long-necks.

The girl led them to the far corner of the stone deck, to the only unoccupied table in sight. She handed them each a menu.

"John—your waiter—will be right with you," she promised before vanishing.

"I see your taste in restaurants hasn't changed," Melissa observed.

Nigel leaned toward her, straining to hear.

"I said, your taste in restaurants hasn't changed!" she tried again.

He grinned at her. "This used to be our place," he said in a raised voice.

Melissa nodded. It had provided the backdrop for their romance—as well as the setting for several heated arguments. In fact, it had been the site of their first and last dates. She had broken their engagement on this very patio. Sitting there now felt strange: pleasantly nostalgic and yet slightly disturbing.

"Nigel, before we talk about the bones, I have something else to—"

A burst of laughter from the next table and a dropped glass stole her words.

He looked at her, waiting for her to repeat it.

"I know you want to talk about the bones, but—"

"Oh, the bones!" His face took on an ecstatic quality, and he reached for his briefcase. Flipping it open, he used both hands to remove the larger of the two bones.

"Hi, I'm John. I'll be your waiter. Can I start you off with something to drink?"The tall, dark-haired young man tossed two cork coasters onto the table.

Nigel, still cradling the bone as if it were a precious gem, looked to Melissa. "Beer? Wine?"

"Iced tea," she said.

"Red Dog," Nigel told him. When the waiter was gone, his attention returned to the bone. "You shouldn't have left."

Melissa wondered if she had heard him wrong.

"You've got a good eye, Melissa. What has it been? Four, five years since you went to Nevada?"

"Six."

"And yet you still know a T. rex when you see one."

"Is that really what it is?"

He nodded proudly. "Piece of humerus from an adult, probably eighteen feet tall, around forty feet long. It's in good condition too." Nigel looked at it lovingly, stroking it with an index finger.

"What about the other bone?"

"That's the exciting part.T. rex remains aren't all that rare anymore. Full skeletons are, of course, and if one turns up at your site, it will be cause to celebrate. But this other one . . ." He replaced the first and took up the smaller bone. "You said it was in the same strata level."

"It appeared to be—discounting any disruptions in the layers."

The grin grew into a full-fledged smile. "Listen to you. You have paleontology in your blood."

Melissa shrugged at this.

"You found it on federal land, is that right?"

She nodded.

"Then we'll need an antiquities permit in order to excavate. Red tape." He made a face, as if he were suddenly in pain. "I hate red tape."

"You want to excavate?"

"Of course! I must excavate, if only to disprove the wild theory that's been running through my mind ever since I got your package this morning."

"What theory?"

The waiter arrived with their drinks. "Are you ready to order or do you need some time?"

Neither of them had even considered the menu. "We're waiting for someone," Nigel said.

We are? Melissa wondered. She opened her mouth to ask who they were waiting for.

"Hominid," Nigel announced, as if this explained everything.

"Huh?"

"It's from a transitional hominid. At least, it could be." He handed the bone to her gingerly, then downed the first third of his beer in a gulp. "Not ape. Probably not human. Early hominid. Don't have a date yet. But if you're right and they were on the same level—same age . . ." His voice trailed off and he gazed toward the mountains. A thin band of clouds was floating above the peaks, gilded pink and purple by the setting sun.

"What? What are you saying?"

"I'm saying that despite my beliefs to the contrary, it is at least within the realm of possibility that you have discovered proof of coexistence."

Melissa stared at him, mouth agape. "Coexistence?"

He nodded at her. "I'm trying to contain my excitement, mind you. The lab tests may put an end to the idea. But if the ages match . . . Imagine it: man's ancestors living during the same epoch as the late dinosaurs . . . That would wreak havoc with our timetables, wouldn't it?" He stroked his beard thoughtfully. "Either our take on dinosaurs is dreadfully off—they somehow survived well beyond the sixty-five million year barrier we have imposed—or our view of prehuman species is in error."

Melissa handed the bone back. This wasn't exactly the opening she had expected, but . . . "Or God created them both and instead of being millions of years old, both are merely thousands of years old."

Nigel laughed at this, then sipped his beer. He was clearly in a good mood. In the old days, a statement like that would have provoked a flurry of fiery evolutionary rhetoric. Instead, he merely raised his hands. "In light of this, almost anything seems possible."

He replaced the bones, carefully wrapping them in cheesecloth and closing the briefcase. "Here's what I'm thinking." He leaned toward her with a conspiratorial expression. "Say they did coexist—as incredible as that sounds. You mentioned that there were hundreds of these smaller hominid bones."

"Maybe even thousands."

"Okay, and we know a T. rex was in the vicinity. What if you stumbled onto a kill yard?"

"A what?"

"The jury is still out on whether T. rex was a scavenger or a predator. As you know, I am in favor of the latter. I believe he was a quick, aggressive hunter—the great white shark of the dinosaur world. If humans were around in T. rex's day, they would have been among his prey. Consider, for a moment, what would happen if a lone, male T. rex discovered a large herd of hominids. He circles, observing with those keen eyes of his, then attacks, paralyzing and killing with razor-sharp teeth. He spends weeks, maybe months thinning out the pack. And instead of eating his kills immediately, he behaves like a grizzly bear, storing away meat in a kill yard—stuffing bodies into the ground for later consumption."

Melissa made a face at the gory mental picture.

"I think those bones you described may well be the kill yard." He took a long draw of his beer, downing the last of it. "I must excavate this site of yours. It contained a T. rex arm bone. That alone makes it worth the price of an expedition. There's a good chance that I might find more of the animal close by. And if the dating comes back positive, connecting the T. rex with the hominid remains . . . Melissa, you could well have discovered the most significant paleontological find in decades."

Nigel signaled the waiter, holding up his bottle and motioning for another. Melissa had yet to touch her iced tea.

"Come back."

Melissa looked at him, confused. Had she heard him right? "What?"

"Come back to Boulder. We need you."

We? she thought. Was this a professional plea, or a thinly veiled come-on? Was he thinking about dinosaurs and science, or love? Had he actually missed her?

"We need good minds like yours in the classroom. And in the field. You obviously still have a fossil hunter's eye. You'd make a great instructor. Even work on your doctorate while you teach. I'm head of the department now. I could make it happen."

"I don't know, Nigel." She shook her head at the idea, her mind reeling. It was so tempting—her old life handed back to her on a platter. But she wasn't there to reclaim something she had lost. She was there to deliver a message.

It was time to get down to business, she decided somewhat reluctantly. They had discussed the bones. Now they had more pressing matters to talk about—matters of eternal consequence.

"Nigel . . ." She paused and took a deep breath, trying to decide how to start and what to say. *Father, give me the words.*

"Nigel, we need to talk about something."

He looked at her, waiting.

The waiter arrived with a fresh beer. "Can I get you an appetizer?" he asked above the din. "Buffalo wings?"

"No, thank you," Melissa said. When the young man had departed, she took another breath. "Nigel, there's something important I need to tell you . . ."

She lost concentration as a brunette made her way across the verandah, directly toward their table. The woman was in her mid-twenties with the slender figure of a movie actress. To Melissa's amazement, the woman stopped at the table and Nigel rose to greet her, offering a passionate kiss.

"I have something important to tell you, too," he said, his beard retreating to reveal gleaming white teeth. "Melissa, meet my fiancée, Cindy Grisham. Cindy, this is Melissa Lewis, an old friend from college."

Melissa rose, stunned, and shook the woman's hand. It was cold.

"It's a pleasure," Cindy said. But her eyes said something else altogether.

"Cindy is a palynologist. She does the pollen studies on our field work."

Melissa tried to think of something to say. But her brain was numb. All she could do was stare at Cindy.

"Honey, can I get you a white wine?" Nigel asked, fawning over her. He helped Cindy into her seat, then scooted his chair closer to hers. Cindy nodded and Nigel snapped his fingers in the air, alerting the waiter. "White wine!" he told the young man. The waiter nodded and set out for the bar.

"You . . . the two of you . . . you're . . ." Melissa stuttered.

"Engaged," Cindy announced. She wrapped her arm through Nigel's possessively. "Yes. The ceremony is set for late August. After the summer session."

"Congratulations," Melissa said. The sun had set and the light was quickly fading—deep purple dimming to black. The growing darkness was alive, swimming around her. She had the sense that she was floating . . . in limbo.

"I'm sorry," Nigel apologized. "You were about to tell me something important."

He and Cindy looked at her expectantly, and there seemed to be an audible lull in the boisterous party atmosphere. "Uh . . . I was going to tell you . . . Uh . . ."

Cindy was frowning now, her eyes inspecting Melissa and apparently finding her wanting.

"I was going to tell you . . ." She swallowed hard. "About Jesus."

Suddenly both of them were scowling—Cindy in disdain, Nigel in puzzlement.

Melissa closed her eyes and tried to compose herself. Embarrassment, shock, and most of all disappointment were making it difficult to think clearly. She had done her best not to get her hopes up, not to expect she and Nigel to experience anything even close to a revival of their relationship. But still, that glimmer had been there, that hidden, secret desire for him to fall on his knees in repentance when she presented him with the gospel, and then welcome her back with open arms. Marriage, children, a home in the foothills. It was all part of the fantasy—a fantasy that had yet to die. But this—this nightmare was reality.

When she opened her eyes, Nigel and Cindy were still there: four dark eyes peering at her with a mixture of curiosity, pity, and amusement.

Just tell him, she thought, resigning herself to the task she had agreed to perform. *Tell him and leave.*

"I had a dream about you, Nigel," she began. "You were in this burning room. And you couldn't get out. You were about to die. I tried to help you out. But you wouldn't let me. And there was someone else trying to help you out. It was Jesus. He was standing at the door of your home, banging on it, calling out to you. You had locked it and wouldn't unlock it—even though you were about to be burned alive."

The expressions on their faces had soured, as if they had both just been deeply offended.

"Whether the dream was 'prophetic'—sent to me by God—or not," she continued, "one thing is for certain, Nigel." She looked into his eyes, ignoring Cindy. "When you die, unless you know Jesus as your Savior, you go to a place called hell." The students, the noise, the patio itself had disappeared. "Hell is . . . darkness . . . fire . . . pain . . . a permanent state of heart-rending regret . . . a permanent state of separation from God.

"I'm here to tell you three things. First, this life is fleeting and tenuous. You will die one day. And that day could come at any time. Second, when you die, you will be judged. We are all sinners and will all be found lacking. God hates sin and deals with it severely with a sentence of eternal death. Third, God's wrath can be satisfied, here and now, his anger appeased, in the person of Jesus. God sent Jesus to bear the punishment for our sin. By accepting that sacrifice—his work on the cross—we accept life: both now and for eternity. Jesus provides the propitiation for your sins.

"It sounds complicated, but it isn't. If you will confess your sin and receive Jesus, you will have a relationship with God and be invited to heaven when you die. If you don't—then you've chosen hell."

Cindy looked as if she had just swallowed a worm. Nigel seemed less repulsed, more bored.

"That's why I came. The bones were just an excuse to see you." She paused, trying to read him. "Don't suppose you'd be interested in praying the sinner's prayer with me?"

He gave her a lopsided grin, then shook his head.

"Okay," she sighed. She was suddenly drained, relieved, exhausted, upset. She glared at Cindy. The girl had to be ten years younger than Nigel. She recognized the anger rising within, the resentment at having been replaced by this girl.

Rising, she took a first and only sip of iced tea. It was bitter with lemon—not unlike her encounter with Nigel.

"I've got to go."

Nigel stood and pled with her. "Stay! Have dinner with us. We can talk about your find." He turned to Cindy. "Melissa has discovered a rather startling find."

"Is that right?" she said coolly.

"It was nice to meet you," Melissa lied. "Good night."

"How will you get back to your car?" Nigel asked. "Remember? I drove you here."

"I'll walk."

"Actually, Nigel, she does look a bit pale. Perhaps the walk will do her good—stimulate her circulation."

Melissa turned to start across the patio. She was trembling, on the verge of tears.

"Why don't you and I go back to our place?" Cindy asked Nigel.

Turning back to the table, Melissa glared at them. "How long have you two been living together?" she asked, her voice cracking.

"Let's see . . ." Cindy smiled. "Next month it will be five and a half years, right, Nigel?"

Nigel nodded apologetically.

So he waited six whole months before shacking up, Melissa thought, frowning at Nigel. She could feel her cheeks blushing, but didn't care. Reaching under the table, she picked up his briefcase.

"What are you doing?" he protested.

She swung it away, out of his reach, then opened it. "These are mine," she declared in an even tone, removing the bones.

"Melissa," Nigel said. "Come on. Don't be like that. This isn't about us. It's about paleontology."

Melissa resisted the urge to curse, turned on her heels, and marched across the verandah. She made it through the restaurant and two blocks down the street before she broke down. Sinking to a bus stop bench, she buried her head in her hands and began to cry.

Twenty-Eight

Hurry up!" Tito whispered.

Vince's reply explained, in no uncertain terms, where Tito could put that order. "If I had a kilo of plastique, things would be different. I could hurry. But . . ." The voice trailed off and the two legs protruding from the underside of the Ford Explorer shifted as Vince repositioned himself.

Tito surveyed the area again. Aside from light traffic on the arterial a hundred yards away and an occasional cluster of college students entering or exiting the restaurant, all was quiet. Kendrick had parked on a tree-lined side street, affording them the opportunity to work in relative privacy. And it was dark. The closest streetlight had conveniently shorted out—thanks to a well-aimed bullet. It was the perfect environment. But it was taking too long.

"Have you got it yet?"

Vince swore at him again, his head and torso still hidden beneath the front end.

"Let me give it a try. I know more about cars than you do."

"Oh, yeah?" a voice replied from somewhere under the engine. "And exactly how many have you rigged?"

Tito didn't answer. He was well-versed in mechanics, a true car buff. He could fix just about anything relating to an automobile—no matter the make or year. But Vince was right. He had never actually rigged one.

"Where's the gas tank on these Explorers?" Vince asked.

"Back left."

"Fuel injection, right?"

"Yeah."

Tito watched as five figures stumbled out of the restaurant. All male. All drunk.

"We've got company," he announced in a whisper. "Group of kids. Blasted out of their minds. Coming right at us."

"Play it cool," Vince advised. "Car trouble."

Tito unlatched the hood, propped it up, and began tinkering with the engine, pretending to check the spark plugs.

He couldn't see the boys now, but he could hear them. They were laughing, getting closer, shouting something about Buffaloes reigning supreme. One of them howled like a coyote. The others followed suit. The first three went by without even noticing Tito. They were staggering down the sidewalk and probably hadn't even noticed the Explorer.

"I'm driving," one of them declared, dangling a key ring.

"Nope. You're drunk," another argued. He reached for the keys, missed, and performed a slow motion fall to the concrete. His companions hooted at this before helping him up. The three of them weaved toward a Toyota Four-Runner.

"Got a problem?"

Tito looked up into the bleary red eyes of a baby-faced frat boy. In his hand was a half-empty bottle of beer.

"Hey," the second kid said, blinking at the engine. "This . . . this is a car."

"Thanks, guys," Tito tried. "I got it covered."

"Listen, man," the first said, bracing himself against the grill. "I know a lot about cars. I had auto shop in high school. I can change the oil in my Miata."

"Is that right? I bet your parents are proud." Tito glanced at his watch, silently urging Vince on.

"Let's see," the kid slurred. "This is . . . it's the . . . uh . . . radiator . . . I think. And over here is the . . . uh . . . I can't remember what you call it, but it, uh . . ."

"I'm fine, guys. Why don't you go home and sleep it off."

They laughed at this. One of them dropped his bottle and it rolled under the truck.

Vince swore. "Get rid of those punks!"

The two of them looked at each other, their faces sobering. They backed off, hands held up. "Hey, be cool," they said.

"Sure, sure," Tito agreed. "Don't mind my friend. He's had a bad day."

They nodded, climbed quickly into their car, and disappeared around the corner, tires squealing.

Vince was swearing under the Explorer. "Spoiled brats. If their parents would just try teaching them some manners . . ."

"How close are you?"

"Pretty darn close. Give me two minutes."

"How about twenty seconds?" He quietly closed the hood.

"Huh?"

"Finish up and let's go. Kendrick and Lewis just came out and they're headed this way."

Tito heard something clank. Suddenly, Vince slid out from under the Explorer. "Let's go."

They walked casually up the sidewalk, away from the restaurant, into the deep shadow of a giant cottonwood.

I JUST THINK YOU COULD HAVE BEEN A LITTLE MORE—"

"More what? More friendly? To your old girlfriend?!"

"Okay, so it was a bad idea to bring her here."

"You bet it was, Nigel. Saturday night is *our* night."

"I know. I know. I just thought, under the circumstances—"

"She's a witch."

"No, she isn't. Actually she's quite nice."

"Nice? And what was all that about a dream? Why is she dreaming about you, Nigel?"

"I don't know."

"Because she still loves you. That's why."

"No. Cindy. That's crazy."

"You were engaged to be married, right?"

"Well, yes. But—"

"She's still got a thing for you. I can tell. And that weirdness about God and Jesus and—blah! Is she a Jehovah's Witness or something?"

"No. It's just . . . That was what came between us in the first place: irreconcilable religious differences."

"That gave me the creeps. It was like she was trying to get you to join a cult or something."

"Here I am. Where's your car?"

"I didn't drive. I told you that Janice was dropping me off."

"Oh, that's right. Get in."

"Get in? Aren't you going to get the door for me?"

"Okay . . ."

NIGEL DESERVED TO GO TO HELL. OR AT LEAST MELISSA THOUGHT SO. How could anyone be so thoughtless, so callous, so shallow, so uncaring, so . . . She had run out of tears five minutes earlier. Now she was beginning to run low on adjectives. Seeing him again had been intoxicating. Feeling his touch, looking into his eyes, being overcome by his smile . . . But had she really expected him to remain single, to stop dating? That was ridiculous, she realized now. But somehow, she had imagined him doing what she had done: becoming a spinster, seldom going out, never socializing, spending countless evenings alone in front of the TV . . .

The idea of Nigel cohabiting with Cindy enraged her. Unfortunately, the dismay and anger were already subsiding, leaving only a bleak, heavy sadness. No matter how she wanted to hate him, she couldn't. In fact, she still wanted to be with him because—though she hated to admit it—she still loved him.

Father, I don't understand. Did you ask me to come here just so you could humiliate me? You could have done that back in Vegas. It would have saved me airfare.

I'm sorry. I didn't mean that. But why did I come? I obviously missed whatever it was you were trying to accomplish. Or maybe the whole harebrained thing was my idea in the first place. Maybe you didn't ask me to come. I don't know. But I do know that this was a farce. Nigel . . . that Cindy . . . the bones. Oh, and that was a great exit back there at the restaurant—a sterling witness to follow up my little sermon: taking back my toys and stomping off like a pouting child. I'm sorry. That was stupid of me. I don't know what got into me. Anyway . . .

Father, what should I do now?

She looked down at the bones: two brittle, coffee-colored sticks lying in her hands. For one thing, she decided, she should take them back. Give them to Nigel. Apologize for her behavior. Act like a grown-up. In other words, eat crow—in front of Cindy. Now there was a thrill.

After wiping her eyes and taking several deep breaths, she rose from the bench and started back. As she walked along the sidewalk, she tried to decide what she would say.

I'm an idiot, came to mind. As did, *I lost my head, and I'm a jealous wreck who wishes we could get back together.* The latter was the most truthful, but also the most humiliating. Maybe she could try blaming the scene on PMS.

She hadn't decided which tactic to take by the time she reached the restaurant—just that the truth, spoken in love, was the best strategy. Mounting the steps, she reached for the door, then heard a car door slam. Turning, she looked up the street and saw Nigel's Explorer. The brake lights blinked on and a second later the ignition cranked.

The cool darkness retreated, eclipsed by the sudden rise of an artificial sun. A concussion wave sent tiny fragments of glass skyward. They sprayed the overhanging tree limbs, floating back to earth like ice crystals. Flames consumed the vehicle with demonic hunger, attacking the seats, the tires, the plastic interior. The bonfire crackled and roared, miniature explosions helping to further incinerate the Explorer. The ground surrounding the truck was soon littered with metallic debris as the sky rained car parts.

Melissa could feel the heat from where she stood almost a block away. And she could see the two forms inside the cab. In the first instant after the explosion, they shook and flailed violently. Then they grew still: silent captives resigned to their fiery prison. The furnace began belching smoke, obscuring the occupants in its effort to rise to the waiting stars.

There were frantic shouts and students poured out of the restaurant to watch. People appeared on the porches of houses along the street. In the distance a siren offered a mournful cry of hope.

But there was no hope, Melissa knew as she watched in horror. No hope for Nigel. He was gone—and Cindy with him. Burned alive. Just like in her dream. And tragically, he had never unlocked the door to his heart. He had never let Jesus in. Death had found him—tonight!—and he had freely chosen the road to hell.

The tears returned, streaming down both cheeks. It wasn't so much sadness as sorrow this time. An overwhelming sense of grief folded over her. The love of her life was no more. Another soul had slipped into the abyss. God himself must have been heartbroken. Melissa was.

She sat down on the step and wept for Nigel Kendrick.

WE SHOULD HAVE BROUGHT MARSHMALLOWS."

"You're sick," Tito replied, shading his eyes with an upraised hand.

"Maybe so. But I'm also pretty darned good at what I do." Vince smiled proudly at the fire, like a father watching his prodigy perform. "Admit it, I'm good."

Tito nodded slowly. "Okay. You're good." And he meant it. He had never seen such an impressive explosion that wasn't supplemented by plastic explosives or dynamite. "You just rigged the gas tank?"

"Yeah. Simple trick. We used to do it to Charlie supply trucks back in Nam. You pull the lead ignition wires out and string them to the tank. When the poor schnook turns the key, the spark sets off the gasoline. Looks like Dr. Kendrick had a full tank."

"I don't think we'll be getting the bones back," Tito said, gazing at the blaze in awe. "Sonny will be peeved."

"Sonny." Vince laughed, then cursed Sonny. "He said clean house. We're cleaning." There was another terrific bang and flames leapt into the air, licking up ash and cottonwood leaves. What was left of the rear window disintegrated in a cloud of fine glass.

"See," Vince joked, "we even do windows."

A fire truck arrived. As the firefighters hurried to unload their gear, an ambulance pulled up. Behind it three squad cars screeched to a halt. Rescue workers ran back and forth, illuminated by the uneven light of a half-dozen strobes. Police set up a boundary and pushed students and other onlookers behind it.

"I know how much you like to admire your work," Tito said as a high pressure hose was opened on the burning Ford. "But let's get out of here."

Vince took a long last look, savoring the scene as if it were his last bite of a sumptuous feast. "Sonny won't be peeved," he said, following Tito up the street. "He'll be overjoyed. Lewis is gone. Kendrick is gone. The bones are gone. All nice and tidy. Heck, they'll be lucky just to ID the victims."

"Dental records," Tito assured him. "They can identify them by their teeth. Teeth don't burn."

"I know that." Vince scowled. "But by the time they piece the fillings and crowns together, we'll be in Vegas, kickin' back at Club Blue, counting our money. What's Sonny paying us for this job anyway?"

"The usual." Vince opened his mouth to complain but Tito waved him off. "Plus a bonus."

"Better be a bonus. The usual would only cover tailing Lewis. You have us knocking people off right and left, you need to pay us appropriately. How much?"

"Twelve grand."

Vince considered this. "For four hits? Seems a little cheap."

"The lab attendants don't count."

"Why not?"

"Because they probably didn't need to die. Just think of it as six grand for Lewis, six grand for Kendrick."

"Apiece?"

"Apiece," Tito nodded. "Twelve Gs for you, twelve for me."

"I guess that's not so bad. Especially considering they were nobodies. Remember the congressman?"

"Yeah, I remember. But I don't think we should be discussing that out here on the street for everyone and their dog to hear."

"Twelve grand," Vince said dreamily. "Apiece. For one day's work. Now that's what I call an occupation."

"No kidding," Tito agreed. He stopped at a phone booth at the intersection of two moderately busy streets and dug some change out of his pocket.

"What are you doing?"

"Calling a cab."

"A cab? Why waste the money? We could lift something." His head swiveled around. "That Porsche over there for instance."

Tito paged through a battered copy of the yellow pages, wondering if his partner was serious. For such a skilled assassin, Vince could be downright stupid at times. Maybe he had been a victim of chemical warfare over in Nam. That would explain a few things.

"How about if we don't leave a trail of bloody footprints from here to Vegas," Tito grumbled as he dialed. "I'd rather not answer the door tomorrow morning and find a couple of suits shoving a badge in my face that says FBI."

Twenty-Nine

"FBI."

Vaughn squinted at the badge. In the glow of the porch light, it looked like the genuine article. And the two men behind it looked authentic as well: blue suits, burgundy ties, black shoes, even Polaroid sunglasses, despite the fact that the sun had gone down and the light was quickly fading. They were either G-men or Mormon missionaries. Vaughn didn't see any bicycles, so that ruled out the latter.

"Uh . . ." He opened the door a crack wider. "What do you need?"

"Captain Vaughn? Captain Steven Vaughn?" one of them asked.

"Yes." He was standing there in a terrycloth robe, a towel wrapped around his neck, hair still dripping wet. It was a wonder he had heard the doorbell from the shower.

The second man stepped forward. "I'm agent Morris. This is special agent Fuller. We'd like to speak with you, Captain. It's concerning a Dr. Jack Weber."

Vaughn stared at them. "Weber?"

"Yes. He died in an automobile accident this afternoon."

"Yeah, I know." He invited them inside. "Excuse the mess," he said, scooping up an armload of dirty laundry on his way back to the bedroom. "I'll be right with you guys. Game's on, if you want to watch." He nodded to the TV. On the screen a player was warming up, using three bats to take monster swings at an invisible ball.

Two minutes later he emerged in a pair of shorts and a Marine Corps T-shirt. The agents were standing in the center of the living room, backs to the TV set, still wearing their sunglasses.

"Have a seat." He pointed to the couch.

"How well did you know Dr. Weber?" Fuller asked as he sank into the cushions. He was a tall, thin man with a ring of silver hair and a sharp beak of a nose. On the low sofa he looked like a stork struggling to get comfortable: long neck craning, gangly legs boxed in by the coffee table, knees rising a little too high.

"Not well. Not well at all," Vaughn answered. He was trying to imagine why the FBI was concerned with Dr. Weber. Unless the guy hadn't been paranoid after all.

On TV the crowd was cheering. Vaughn turned around just in time to see Ken Griffey Jr. leap for a long ball—and miss. The tiny white sphere disappeared over the fence. The camera showed Jim Thome tossing his bat aside and trotting the bases, his arms waving in reaction to the shower of accolades. On the mound, Mark Huckins was beside himself, cursing the dirt.

Morris cleared his throat. "But you did meet with him this morning?" He was shorter and thicker at the waist than Fuller, with a receding line of jet black hair that had been combed back and anchored in position by a healthy dose of Vitalis. A miniature mustache decorated his upper lip. Taken as a whole, he came across as an oily used car salesman.

"Yes." Vaughn replied. *And just how did you know that?*

"What was the nature of that meeting?" Fuller wanted to know. Both agents had opened folders and were waiting for the answer with pens poised.

Suddenly it occurred to Vaughn—these guys were there, at the restaurant. They were the two men that had come into Jackie's while Weber was in the middle of his diatribe. They were the ones Weber claimed were FBI.

There was another flurry of shouts from the TV. Vaughn looked back and saw a ball bounce over the left field wall, ricocheting off a row of empty seats. A gang of children ran after it. The stadium erupted, the audio distorting. Fuller and Morris remained stone-faced. Apparently they weren't big baseball fans.

"Uh . . . We had breakfast with him."

"We who?" Fuller asked.

"Myself, Lieutenant Parish, and Sergeant Donohue." He paused as they took down this information. If they had been there to see the meeting, Vaughn thought, why were they bothering to ask? Were they trying to trap him? What were they after? Did it have something to do with Weber's book? Or 217? Or . . . "Listen, have you guys cleared this investigation with Nellis?"

"I wouldn't go so far as to call it an investigation," Morris said smoothly, offering a cool smile. His demeanor was as slick as his hair. "At this time, it's more of an informal inquiry."

"Well, have you cleared your inquiry with Nellis?"

"This is a federal case, Captain Vaughn, and it does not involve—" Fuller started to say.

"Case? I thought your buddy here just said it was an informal inquiry."

Fuller frowned, his eyes narrowing. The stork looked frustrated. "Captain Vaughn, Dr. Weber died in a vehicular accident on Highway 95. That isn't within the jurisdiction of Nellis Air Force Base or the Nevada Test Site."

"Or the FBI," Vaughn threw in. He watched as Fuller's face flushed slightly. This was starting to be fun. "I'm no lawyer, but I'd guess that an auto accident on an interstate would fall into the jurisdiction of the state trooper's office."

He snuck a look at the set. Albert Belle popped up and the inning was over.

The stork was glaring now. "You have a choice, Captain. You can either volunteer information, answer a few questions, and then go about your business. Or we can have a judge issue a subpoena, haul you in front of a grand jury, and force you to answer our questions. You'll be designated a hostile witness—and possibly be slapped with contempt of court for holding up a federal inquiry."

"Contempt of court means you go to jail," Morris pointed out helpfully.

Vaughn looked from one agent to the other, studying their faces. Both seemed quite serious. Fuller was scowling, hands on his knees. His greasy partner was wearing a thin-lipped grin that failed to reach his penetrating brown eyes. The threat—the business about a subpoena, a grand jury, jail—had to be a bluff. Still, Vaughn wasn't anxious to call it. These were, after all, Feds. It was probably in his best interest to cooperate. *Give them what they want, and maybe they'll leave,* he decided.

"We met Weber for breakfast. We talked over some of his bizarre theories. Actually, he did all the talking. We just sat there and listened."

"What sort of theories?" Fuller asked.

"Weird stuff about the NTS. About accidents and negligence during the atmospheric tests in the fifties."

They were both scribbling now, recording this vital disclosure.

"Anything about a book?" Morris asked casually, never looking up from his pad.

Vaughn hesitated. They know about the book? Maybe Weber hadn't been exaggerating after all. Maybe the FBI *had* been after him—and that book of his. At breakfast, the idea of the federal government caring, much less being worried about what Weber had in his shabby little file box seemed ludicrous. But now, with two representatives from the FBI sitting in Vaughn's living room . . .

"What sort of book?"

The stork stared into his eyes, searching for duplicity. Vaughn put on his poker face and stared back.

"As we understand it, Dr. Weber was putting together a book. Apparently it summed up these theories of his."

Oh, that book, Vaughn almost said. "Is that right? You suppose that's what got him killed?"

"Who said he was killed?" Morris shot back.

"Why investigate an accident," Vaughn responded, "if you don't suspect foul play?" Touché!

Fuller sighed at this. "We can have that subpoena by tomorrow morning," he promised.

"Fine," Vaughn replied. He'd had it with the intimidation tactics. Time for a bluff of his own. "I'll notify the legal eagles at Nellis." He reached for the phone.

Morris stopped him with an outstretched hand. He was smiling again, his lips upturned in an expression that reminded Vaughn of a televangelist. The man's mustache had disappeared into his fleshy lips. "Forget about the book for a minute. Let's go back to your contacts with Weber."

Contacts, Vaughn noted. Plural. These guys knew about Weber visiting the Site too? How? If they weren't working with Nellis, who were they working with? It had to be someone with authority, clout, and connections. Who was behind this "inquiry"? Before Morris could ask his next question, Vaughn's mind analyzed the puzzle and submitted a three-letter acronym that seemed to solve it: DOE.

"What happened after breakfast?" Morris wanted to know.

"We left."

"We who?" Fuller asked.

"Parish, Jimmy, and me."

"What about Weber?" Morris asked.

Vaughn shrugged at them. "He went home, I guess."

"Did you have any further contact with him today?" Morris asked.

As if you didn't already know, Vaughn thought. He was suddenly thankful that he hadn't had time to adequately dry off after his shower. Maybe the Fibbies wouldn't notice that he had begun to sweat.

"Yes."

"Where?" Fuller pressed.

"In the zone—out at the Site."

"Where exactly?" Morris specified.

"I can't say."

"Why not?" Morris wondered.

"Because the NTS is a high-security area. You have to have special clearance to work at the Site. You have to have special clearance to even discuss the Site."

"We're cleared," Fuller offered.

"Good. Then you can go over and have a nice long, top-secret discussion with General Henderson."

The stork readjusted himself on the sofa, swearing softly. Morris sighed and ran a hand over his oily head.

"Excuse us a moment, Captain," Morris said. He began to confer with Fuller in hushed whispers.

Vaughn took the hint, got up, and went into the kitchen. Jerks! No wonder people weren't fond of Fibbies. Talk about arrogant! This was his home, not theirs. And what was the deal with all the questions, as if he were the suspect in some crime. No answers. No explanations. Just an interrogation. Bozos!

He opened the refrigerator, suddenly aware that he was famished. Missing lunch and dinner probably had something to do with that. His only nutrition since breakfast had been the two beers he, Parish, and Jimmy had downed at the tavern.

Parish and Jimmy . . . As he searched for something that wasn't growing a culture of mold, he wondered if the Feds had been to see them. Doubtful. Parish would have called to let him know, and to gloat about how well he had handled the encounter, verbally outmaneuvering the poor chumps. Jimmy would have called too, most likely in a panic, having spilled his guts in order to avoid a prison sentence.

"Captain!"

He returned to the living room with a rectangular doggy box containing the remnants of a hamburger and fries he had neglected to finish at a fast food joint nearly a week earlier.

"French fry?"

The agents shook their heads glumly. "We have something to tell you, Captain," Morris said.

"Something concerning this investigation," Fuller added.

So it's a full-fledge investigation again, Vaughn noted. He tossed a fry into his mouth. It was cold, tough, and tasted like seasoned cardboard.

"We have reason to believe that Dr. Weber was murdered."

Vaughn glanced from one agent to the other. This was the big secret? He and his buddies had figured that much right off the bat. And if Weber could be believed, there was a good chance the FBI was guilty of the crime.

"Murdered?"

"His car was run off the road," Fuller said.

"How do you know?"

Morris glanced at Fuller in conspiratorial fashion before answering. "We had Weber under surveillance."

"What for?"

"That's not important," Fuller insisted.

"What did you do—sit there and watch him die?"

Morris shook his head. "The accident occurred in a gap between surveillance teams. All we know is that someone forced his car into an embankment." He paused, then answered Vaughn's unvoiced question. "We could tell that much from the skid marks and the dents in his car."

"Why would someone do that?"

Morris cleared his throat again. "We think it might have been to get the book."

"The book? Really?"

"Weber took it everywhere with him," Morris told him. "But it wasn't in the car when we found him."

Vaughn considered this. He remembered looking in Weber's car out in the quad. It had been full of junk: boxes, litter, clothing . . . "You sure? You went through all that stuff?"

Morris nodded. "It wasn't there."

"Any idea who could have . . . ?" Vaughn started to ask.

"That's the purpose of this inquiry," Fuller admitted.

"What we need from you is any information concerning your contacts with Weber," Morris explained.

Cheers were rising from the TV again, but Vaughn ignored them. "Like I told you, we had breakfast with him. Then later, he showed up in the zone. He had this . . . this crazy notion about . . ."

"About what?" both agents wanted to know. They were leaning forward in their seats.

"About why a certain dry riverbed had been bulldozed out there."

They glanced at each other. The stork was frowning again. Morris's eyebrows were raised, his forehead lined with furrows.

"He left. We didn't see him again until the news reports about his death."

"Did he show you the book?" Morris asked.

"This morning at the cafe," Vaughn said, nodding. "It was just a box full of papers and notes."

"Did he have it with him at the Site this afternoon?" Fuller wondered.

Vaughn shrugged. "I don't know."

"You don't know," Fuller sighed. He flipped his notebook shut.

"Thank you, Captain," Morris said, rising. He offered a smile, and his hand. "You've been a big help."

Vaughn almost laughed at this. "Well, maybe if you told me why you were so interested in Weber's book . . ."

"We'll be in touch," Fuller promised as they headed for the door.

Vaughn stood there, dazed, watching as they descended the steps and got into their car: a white Dodge sedan—the same Dodge that had been tailing them earlier? He was still standing at the front door, gazing out at the street, when the sedan rounded the corner and disappeared.

So Weber had been murdered. The Fibbies had confirmed that. And they thought the book was what had got him killed. If the FBI hadn't done the job—as Weber would have argued—then who had? For that matter, were the Feds really interested in finding the culprit so that justice could be served? Or were they just after that book? They seemed almost obsessed with it. Maybe it really did contain information that was scandalous to the government. Maybe the DOE was out to get it, to suppress it before it was leaked to the press.

Slamming the door, Vaughn went to the phone and dialed Parish's number. He and Jimmy needed to know about this. They needed to prepare themselves for a visit from Frick and Frack.

As he waited for the call to go through, another question presented itself. What if the book hadn't been the motive for Weber's murder? What if it had something to do with his trip to the zone? Dr. Weber had been killed just minutes after promising to get a court order and dig up whatever it was the dozers had buried out there.

What was hiding out in Quad 217?

THIRTY

LADIES AND GENTLEMEN, WE CANNOT, IN GOOD CONSCIENCE, PUMP radioactive waste into our oceans, as some have proposed. Neither can we launch it into outer space, for future generations to contend with. We do not possess the technology or the financial means to break down these materials with particle accelerators and specialized nuclear reactors. Though this strategy has merit and may become a reality sometime in the next century, it simply isn't an option at this time.

"Therefore, desert disposal is our only viable alternative. I believe that the proposal for an underground dumpsite at Yucca Mountain offers us the optimal solution: an environmentally friendly, cost-effective method of storing our nation's nuclear by-products."

Robert DiCaprio set the speech on his desk and leaned over it, pencil in hand. He was in his study, at home, practicing and punching up the presentation he would be making to the congressional subcommittee in the morning.

He glared at the final sentence. It wasn't quite right. Taking a sip of brandy, he considered calling his speechwriter. Maybe she could fix it. He reached for the phone, but a glance at the clock stopped him. It was late—after one in the morning. The young lady would be in bed. He didn't mind waking her up. But she would be groggy, her thinking clouded. No. He would work on it himself.

"I believe . . ." Too weak. Beliefs were for churchgoers. "Dumpsite." That had to go. "Nuclear by-products" was good. It sounded infinitely better than "radioactive waste." But "storing" . . . that word carried a negative connotation. The idea of "storing" rad-waste implied that it would be there for centuries to come, the dumpsite swelling, the potential for a nuclear accident mounting. All of that was true, of course. Which was precisely the problem DiCaprio would face on the Hill in approximately nine hours.

It was his job to convince Congress to allocate two hundred million dollars for the creation of an underground dump for mid- and high-level radioactive waste. The plan was nothing new. Two previous secretaries of the DOE had attempted to push nearly identical legislation through. But the Yucca Mountain bill had twice been killed. The members of the House weren't stupid. They understood the risks the project involved—both to the environment and to their political careers. No one wanted to go on record as having approved of the world's first permanent repository for nuclear waste. And a series of alarmist, largely erroneous scientific reports issued by opponents to the plan hadn't helped much. According to researchers at Los Alamos, burying rad-waste posed the chilling possibility of giving rise to a critical accident in which the material self-detonated, sparking a runaway nuclear reaction. The findings had been suspect from the start and were quickly discredited by DOE officials. But the damage was done. The reports had created a horrific mental picture of a time bomb: thousands of stainless steel canisters lying a thousand feet underground in some two hundred miles of tunnels, slowly eroding, leaking, contaminating the water table . . . plutonium decaying, neutrons being released, atoms splitting, a domino effect setting off a chain reaction that caused a spontaneous combustion—an entire mountain exploding.

The success of the project, the key to persuading the fickle congresspeople to give it a green light, was to focus on the numbers. Globally, intermediate and high-level nuclear waste products were building up at the rate of one million cubic feet per year. That equaled a hundred-by-hundred-foot block of radioactive pollution that had to be put somewhere. The thought of such a cube sitting—homeless—at Hanford or Rocky Flats or Los Alamos or Savannah River or a handful of other nuclear facilities was enough to make the representatives from those states vote for a dumpsite in Nevada. They wanted the rad-waste hauled as far away from their home states as possible. By accomplishing that, they would no doubt win the support of their constituents. The hard sells would be the folks from California, Utah, and, of course, Nevada.

DiCaprio finished his brandy in a gulp and refilled his glass. "Disposing of . . ." That was better than "storing." It sounded final, as if the waste was gone for good. He penciled it in. And "I am convinced" was stronger and more confident than "I believe." He crossed out "believe" and added the change in the margin. "Dumpsite . . ." How about "repository facility"? Not bad.

He took a sip of brandy, swallowed, and read the reworked sentence aloud. "I am convinced that the proposal for an underground repository facility at Yucca Mountain offers us the optimal solution: an environmentally friendly, cost-effective method of disposing of our nation's nuclear by-products." He smiled, pleased with the final product.

Rising, he cleared his throat and tried the speech again, from the top. The phone rang before he had completed the first page.

"DiCaprio," he grunted, irritated by the interruption.

"Robert. I hope I didn't wake you."

"No." He recognized the voice and sighed inwardly. Just what he didn't need at this hour on the eve of his congressional appearance. "What do you want?"

"I have good news."

DiCaprio doubted that. "Oh, yeah. What is it?"

"Our problem has been solved."

He blinked down at his desk. Problem? DiCaprio was exhausted and his brain seemed to be operating in slow motion. Three snifters of brandy hadn't helped. He was relaxed. Too relaxed.

"You do remember our problem?"

"Yeah." At this hour, it seemed more like an octopus. Which arm of the beast was the caller referring to?

"Remember, the schoolteacher? The bones?"

It finally came to him. "Right."

"It's been taken care of."

"How? What did you do?"

"That's not your concern, Robert. Just be assured that we cleaned house."

"Cleaned?"

"Thoroughly. Immaculately. The dirt has been eliminated."

In other words, DiCaprio thought, cringing, *more people have been murdered—in cold blood.* "Who did you 'eliminate'?" he asked with a sigh.

"The specifics aren't important."

"At least tell me how many casualties there were."

The caller laughed. "If you're that curious, Robert, try reading the newspaper in the morning. I'm sure our handiwork will receive some press."

"I can't believe you actually killed—"

"Now, now, Robert. You're not developing a conscience, are you? This is business. There's no room for ethics or morals in business. You should be thanking us."

"Thanking you? For massacring people?"

"For squelching a potentially career-ending scandal," the caller corrected in an even tone. "Listen, I'll let you go. I know you have a big day tomorrow. Now you have one less thing to worry about. You can focus your energies on Congress."

"How did you know—"

"We know everything, remember, Robert? And I might add that we're rooting for you. Yucca Mountain would come in very handy. All those tunnels. Plenty of room to hide things."

DiCaprio replaced the phone and slumped into his desk chair. A crisis had been averted. He should have been relieved. Instead, he wanted to cry. People . . . innocent people had been killed in order to cover up Quad 217. And he was an accomplice. No, he hadn't actually pulled the trigger—or physically participated in whatever means they had employed to do away with the witnesses. But he was in on it. He hadn't stopped it. He had allowed it to happen—even wanted it to happen so that the problem would disappear. Their blood was on his hands.

In effect, he had become a murderer the day he agreed to let the organization fund his college education. Had he realized then that he was selling his soul—exchanging his freedom for an upwardly mobile career? Had he know at that time that he would be owned? Perhaps. The implication was plain enough. But hadn't there always been the hope, however slim, that he would rise above it, breaking away from their control and using his position to do something worthwhile for society?

That foolish, naive idealism was no longer with him. He had long ago ceased to pursue "good"—whatever that was—becoming wholly obsessed with survival, with success, with obtaining and holding onto that elusive, slippery intangible: power. The organization had dangled it in front of him like a carrot, promising more and more in return for his cooperation—his loyalty. Like an idiot—or more accurately, a jackass— he had blundered on, taking what they offered, and doing what he was told. In essence, he had become a prostitute, trading favors for influence and clout. Maybe the old cliché was right. Maybe absolute power really did corrupt absolutely.

DiCaprio shook off this melancholy line of thought. None of that mattered. Not anymore. The reality was that he belonged to the organization. He was their boy and would continue to be for the rest of his life.

Finishing off his brandy, he picked up the speech. He was in no mood to practice it again. The pleasant buzz from the alcohol was subsiding rapidly, replaced by a growing sense of dread. Yucca Mountain, people dying, his political future, Quad 217, the organization . . . They swirled around him in an anxious haze.

He was in the process of emptying the liquor bottle into his glass when he heard something behind him.

"Honey?"

Swiveling in the chair, he saw his wife standing in the doorway. She was wearing a lace negligee.

"Honey, it's late. Why don't you come to bed?"

Ordinarily the idea of sharing a bed with Loretta set his heart pounding. He was wild about her. Not necessarily in love. But their physical relationship was out of this world. Tonight, however, not even Loretta could break through the depression that was imposing itself upon him.

He didn't want to go to bed. He didn't want to stay up. He didn't want to face Congress in the morning. He didn't want to continue his servitude to the organization. He didn't want to do anything—except fade away.

"I'll be in later. I have to finish this up," he told her. As he watched her leave, he made a decision. Some way, somehow he had to escape, to regain his life, or at least make an attempt to. He was a drowning man. It was time to either suck water and let the sea drag him down into the murky depths—or swim like mad toward freedom.

THE SCENE TOOK PLACE IN SLOW MOTION: A WOMAN FLOATING UP THE steps, reaching lethargically for the door handle, car doors slamming with thunderclaps, the woman turning, her head swinging inch by inch to the right—toward the sound, brake lights coming on like distant beacons, a mechanical click as the engine tried to turn over, and then

... fire. No sound, no color. White flames reaching into a black night, threatening to consume the universe.

Within the blazing tempest, shadows writhed in agony, their cries never escaping from the fiery tomb. The woman watched in horror, her eyes already wet, her heart already broken.

Suddenly she started toward the fire, impotent limbs churning against heavy air. Each step required her entire will. Each stride pushed her farther away. She reached out, but her arms seemed to sink into her shoulders.

Hysterical now, the woman opened her mouth, as if to shout. But nothing came out. Her lungs were empty. Her breath gone. So she formed the word silently, over and over again with her lips—in desperation, in denial, in prayer: Nigel!

"Miss? Excuse me, miss?"

Melissa opened her eyes and looked up into the face of a flight steward.

"Miss, we've landed," he told her.

She blinked at him, then glanced around at the cabin. The seats were empty. The last of the passengers were moving down the aisles toward the door a dozen rows ahead.

"Welcome to Las Vegas," he said.

Melissa nodded at him, too foggy-minded to reply. She stood up awkwardly and stretched. According to her watch, it was six A.M. She tried to remember when she had left Denver. Sometime around midnight. The only plane out had been a puddle jumper to Salt Lake City. She had spent several hours there before getting a red-eye to Vegas. The trip had taken three or four times that of a direct flight and left her stiff, her head pounding. But it didn't matter. What mattered was that she was home now—far away from Boulder.

As she retrieved her carry-on bag and exited the plane, the nightmarish events of the previous evening haunted her—hideous ghouls flittering in and out of her consciousness. She ordered herself not to think about it. She tried to concentrate on something else—anything else.

Father . . . I don't even know how to pray anymore. I don't understand . . . I just can't . . . Why did this happen? Why did you send me to Nigel—and then let him die like that?

Okay . . . I know you didn't kill him. But that doesn't change the fact that he's gone. I just . . . Help me to accept this. It's so hard.

She was inside the terminal, nearly halfway to the parking lot, when she spotted a newsstand. Would Nigel's death have made the morning paper? She picked up the latest edition of the *Rocky Mountain News*. The headline had something to do with the Middle East. But farther down the page, just above the fold, bold letters declared: "Famed Paleontologist Dies in Fire."

She picked it up and scanned the article, fighting back tears. It was short and contained only a general description of the tragedy. Dr. Nigel Kendrick had died in a car fire. A woman, Dr. Cynthia Grisham, had also died. No cause was given for the fire. Nothing about an investigation. The majority of the article concerned Nigel's background, his discovery of a T. rex, his books, his position at CU . . .

At the bottom of the piece there was a photo—the one from the jacket of Nigel's latest book. He was smiling. His handsome, bearded face seemed to glow. His eyes brimmed with contentment . . . success . . . life . . .

"You gonna buy that or just read it?"

Melissa flinched. Glancing behind her, she saw the newsstand attendant. "I'll buy it." She dug a pair of quarters out of her purse, paid him, and set off down the breezeway. When she reached the Land Rover she tossed her bag in the passenger seat, climbed in, and immediately began to cry.

Ten minutes and half a box of tissues later, she took a deep breath and dug out her keys. This was not going to be fun, she decided. Losing Nigel the first time had been bad enough. Losing him this time . . . She sniffed away a new wave of tears.

Instead of starting the car, she picked the newspaper back up and examined the article. It was like pouring salt in a wound: the description of the vehicle, the way in which it had burned, the great loss this would be to the paleontological world . . .

In the second paragraph she recognized her name. "The bodies were identified by Melissa Lewis, a former student at the University of Colorado who is currently residing in Las Vegas. Ms. Lewis was in Boulder to meet with Dr. Kendrick about a fossil discovery."

The press had arrived at the scene just minutes after the police— like vultures descending on road kill. She had been interviewed by a policeman, two detectives, then a reporter for the *Rocky Mountain News*, and finally by a TV news team. The endless questions had only served to make the experience that much worse. The people had no compassion. No sense of what she was going through.

"The cause of the fire is unknown at this time," she read again.

That seemed odd. Last night one of the detectives had explained that the car exploded as a result of being tampered with. She was surprised the press hadn't gotten hold of that little tidbit. And supposedly an investigation was underway to determine who was responsible.

That still made no sense whatsoever. Why would someone blow up a paleontologist's car? She could conceive of no logical answer—and wasn't particularly interested in pursuing it. Nigel was dead. No amount of investigation would change that.

She started the car and chuckled wearily as the driver's door creaked open on its own. The laughter quickly turned to tears.

Father, I'm a basket case. She inhaled deeply, held it, then prayed, *Only you can get me through this. Only you can enable me to cope with this. Lead me through . . .*

Rest. The word presented itself as if in answer to prayer. And she realized that it was precisely what she needed. She hadn't slept in approximately twenty-four hours. And the past forty-eight hours had been highly stressful ones: digging up fossils, having prophetic dreams about Nigel, hand-delivering a message of salvation to him, learning that the bones represented a significant find, meeting Cindy . . . That much would have been enough to tax her emotional and spiritual reserves. Add witnessing a horrible explosion that robbed you of the love of your life, and you had the makings of a nervous breakdown.

Bracing the door under her left arm, she navigated out of the garage, toward the toll booth.

Rest, she thought. What a wonderful idea. She would go home, crawl under the covers, and not come out until she was good and ready—and then only to get something to snack on in bed. For the next forty-eight hours, until the new track began at school, she would take it nice and easy—allowing herself to grieve and allowing God to facilitate the process of healing in the absence of distractions and stressful activities.

THIRTY-ONE

WHAM!

Tito flinched at the blow, suddenly aware that he was in intense pain.
Wham!

He groaned, cradling his head in his hands.
Wham!

Stars materialized and his skull pounded out a jungle rhythm.
Wham!

His lids trembled open and two bloodshot eyes looked up. The world was a blur, still moving, as if he were on the deck of a ship. The popcorn ceiling was alive, bending, floating . . .
Wham!

Eyes closed again, he reached a blind hand toward the night stand, toward the assailant.
Wham!

The receiver tumbled to the floor. Rolling to retrieve it, he nearly threw up. The throbbing behind his eyes seemed to shake the entire room.

A tiny voice called up at him, "Hello! Hello?"

Tito picked up the phone with one hand, using the other to massage his aching temples. His stomach continued to perform aerial maneuvers.

"Hello?" He retched again and started for the bathroom, staggering against the wall.

"Tito? You all right?"

"Yeah," he panted. "Hang on." He set the phone down and twisted the control on the faucet. After splashing his face and hair with cold water for a full minute, he pulled a towel around his neck and took up the receiver.

"Oh, man . . . You still there?"

"I'm here."

His brain finally placed the voice, and he instinctively glanced at the clock. Uh-oh. Why would Sonny be calling at this hour?

"Sounds like you did some celebrating last night."

"Yeah. We did," he sighed, wishing with all his heart that he hadn't tried to keep up with Vince in terms of alcohol consumption. "And I'm paying for it today. Vince is an animal." In the mirror he saw a vision of himself as an old man: lined face, pale complexion shiny with sweat, eyes ringed with purple . . . Most of his hair had escaped from the ponytail and taken on a life of its own. He looked like a street person or a drug addict or a mass murderer. A young, aspiring Charles Manson.

"I'm not feeling so hot this morning." He opened the medicine cabinet in search of the Advil bottle.

"Sorry to hear that."

Tito was sure something was wrong. Sonny didn't make small talk. And he never called just to chat. "What's up?"

"Well, I've got a little surprise for you. It's in this morning's *Rocky Mountain News*."

Tito took a deep breath, preparing for the worst. Here it came. "Really? What is it?"

"A nice article about your car bomb. The police have no suspects and aren't even sure it was a bomb. Good work."

Good work? Now Sonny was complimenting them on their work? Tito waited for the other shoe to drop.

"Too bad you didn't get Lewis."

"What? Sure we did. She and Kendrick both burned in the Explorer."

"Is that right? Funny. Lewis made a statement to the police after the incident. That would be kind of tricky if she were dead, wouldn't it?"

"She couldn't have, Sonny. Vince and I saw them come out and get into the . . ."

"And you visually IDed Lewis? You're certain it was her?"

"Well, it was dark," Tito explained, backtracking. "But she rode to the restaurant with Kendrick. Ate with him. Then they came out and—"

The profanity came in an avalanche. Sonny cursed him, cursed Vince, cursed their mothers . . . He described their stupidity in a squall of four-letter words.

Tito tried to think of what to say. He was tempted to ask: How could we have known the woman wasn't Lewis? Where did Lewis go? Who died with Kendrick? But these questions would have only fueled Sonny's wrath and further supported his supposition that they were wholly incompetent. Instead he asked, "What do you want us to do? Hit her?"

"No," Sonny answered sarcastically. "I want you to take her out for coffee."

"Where is she?"

"At home," Sonny told him. "Probably asleep. All you have to do is drive over and do her. You think you and bonehead can handle that?"

"No problem."

"No problem?" he muttered. "It had better not be a problem. You told me everything had been taken care of. I passed that up the line. Then I read in the paper that everything hasn't been taken care of. Now I have people breathing down my neck, asking me why this thing isn't over, why we didn't get Lewis.

"This is it, Tito. I'm not playing around. You and Vince do this lady—this morning. If it doesn't happen, I'm putting another team on it. And I may have them pay you a visit too."

Tito resisted the urge to lay into Sonny. He and Vince were the best people the organization had. To even suggest that they couldn't do the job, much less pressure them with another hit squad . . .

"We'll take care of it."

"You'd better," Sonny grumbled before hanging up.

Tito threw the phone. It sailed through the air, hit the far wall of the bedroom, and shattered. Bits of plastic fell to the carpet. Pulling on a pair of pants, he went into the kitchen and used the other phone to call Vince. A groggy female voice answered.

"This is Tito. I need to speak to Vince."

"He's asleep right now, honey. Maybe you could—"

"Wake him up!"

There was a rustling sound, then swearing. "Huh?"

"Vince? Tito. Get your rear end out of bed. We've got work to do."

"Work?"

"We missed Lewis."

"Lewis?"

"Yeah. I'll be by in twenty minutes. Pack whatever toys you think we might need. We have to make sure we don't miss her again."

_____

What are you doing here?"

Parish held out the Sunday paper, as if this explained his presence on the porch.

"You the new paperboy?"

"We have to talk. Are you going to invite me in?"

Vaughn glared at him, then swung the door back. "What are you doing here?"

Parish stepped inside and handed him the paper. "Read it."

Vaughn wiped the sleep from his eyes, then squinted at his watch. "We're not on duty for another five hours. You know that, don't you, Phil?"

"Read this." He pointed to the front page.

"Can I put some clothes on first?" He had answered the door in his robe.

"Look." Parish stuck the paper in his face.

"What?" Vaughn examined the front page. "More problems in the Middle East. So?"

Parish's finger pointed lower on the page. Vaughn followed it with his eyes.

"'Famed Paleontologist Dies in Fire,'" he read aloud. "So?"

"So," Parish said, unfolding the paper. "Down here it says one of the witnesses to the fire was Melissa Lewis. She ate dinner with this Kendrick guy before he died."

"So?"

"So she's our contact."

"Our what?"

"That's the lady who was in 217 the other day."

Vaughn stared at him, struggling to make sense of the revelation. "Phil, I honestly have no idea what you're talking about. It's too early for games. I was dead asleep when you started banging on the door."

"The woman who witnessed the fire in Denver," Parish said slowly, "is the same woman who was out in our zone on Friday."

Vaughn shook his head at this and a tired laugh escaped from his lips. "It's Sunday, Phil. I sleep in on Sundays. It's sort of a habit. And it also comes in handy when we pull the noon to midnight shift in the bunker—like today."

"Don't you get it? She was almost killed. It was the same woman."

"The same woman as what?"

"Try to follow me here, Steve. This Lewis was our contact in the zone. And now she's witness to a car explosion."

"So?" It came out as more of a whine than a question. "Phil—"

"She was on the news this morning. I saw her. It was the same woman from 217—the fossil hunter. I was getting ready to go to church, but I—"

"Church? You go to church? Since when?"

"Since I was a kid."

"You're kidding me."

"No."

"How come you never mentioned it?"

"You never asked. And it never came up, I guess. Anyway, I was supposed to usher at the 8:30 service—"

"What about beer?"

"Huh?" Parish made a face.

"You drink beer. I thought if you went to church, you couldn't do that."

Parish shrugged at him. "You want to discuss theology, or let me tell you why I'm here?"

"Okay. Go ahead."

"So I got up to get ready and I flipped on the TV, and there she was—Melissa Lewis. They were interviewing her about this paleontologist."

"So?" Vaughn asked, still confused.

"So I thought it was strange that a car she was supposed to be in blew up. She went to eat with Kendrick, but they left separately."

Vaughn rubbed his eyes again. "I need some coffee," he muttered, retreating to the kitchen. Parish followed him, paper in hand.

"Don't you think it's strange, Steve?"

"What's strange?" he asked, scooping grounds into the filter. "That you're in my kitchen at seven on a Sunday morning? Yeah, that's strange."

"No," Parish said. "All these coincidences. Think about it. Weber visits 217, decides to dig the place up. Then he gets run off the road and dies. Lewis visits 217, digs around, discovers a fossil. Then she nearly dies."

"I fail to see the point, Phil." He filled the carafe with water and poured it into the coffeemaker.

"The point is, something's wrong. Doesn't it make you just a little suspicious?"

"Not at this hour." He flicked the switch and the appliance surged to life, perking and sizzling. "Why don't you run along to church? We can talk about this on the way to the Site later this morning."

Parish was shaking his head at him. "We need to go see this Lewis."

"Why?"

"Because. Maybe she's in danger. Maybe she knows something. Maybe she could tell us what's out there in the zone. It's our duty to check into it."

"Listen, Phil, I'll admit that the thing with Weber is weird. And when the FBI showed up, that really started me thinking. But . . ."

"But what?"

"But . . . Well, for one thing we don't even know where Lewis—"

Parish handed him a slip of paper.

"What is this?"

"Lewis's address."

"How did you—"

"Remember my buddy down at the DMV? He ran the license plate from the Land Rover for me."

Vaughn stared at the address, frowning.

"Get your clothes on," Parish ordered. "Come on!"

"I don't know, Phil."

"Don't be a wimp, Steve. You're up, you've got nothing to do till we go on duty at noon. Besides, what have we got to lose?"

"The last time you said that," Vaughn noted, "I wound up in an interrogation room at Nellis."

"That was different," Parish argued. "Get dressed." He pushed Vaughn out of the kitchen. "Wear your uniform. It'll make a better impression."

"Better impression . . ." Vaughn started down the hallway, regretting ever having answered the door in the first place.

"Can I use your phone?"

"What for?" Vaughn slipped off his robe and selected a clean, pressed uniform from his closet.

"I want to call Jimmy."

"It's not enough that you're going to get the two of us sent to the brig. You want to ruin the career of a lowly sergeant as well?"

"You remember his number?"

Vaughn relayed it to him. Slipping on his pants and shirt, he began working on his tie. This was crazy, he realized. Following contacts off the Site, while off-duty . . . Accessing private information from the DMV . . .

"If Henderson finds out about this . . ." Vaughn called.

"He won't," Parish promised. "Besides, we're just going over there to have a talk with Ms. Lewis. An innocent visit. No harm—no foul."

As Vaughn fastened his cuffs, he found himself imagining plenty of harm and plenty of foul coming from this sort of craziness. Playing amateur sleuth, though appealing in the movies, could be dangerous business in real life. Especially if it involved going behind the backs of the Feds, the military police, fire-breathing superior officers . . .

Still, he couldn't stop himself from considering the implications. What if there was a link? What if Weber's death and Lewis's close call were somehow connected? Weber had been murdered. Perhaps Lewis's life had been threatened. Why? Had they both known something important, something classified, something scandalous . . . something that required that they be silenced—permanently?

Thirty-Two

I WILLINGLY BELIEVE THAT THE DAMNED ARE, IN ONE SENSE, SUCCESSFUL, rebels to the end; that the doors of hell are locked on the inside.

The words were a dagger plunged deep into her heart—sharp, cold, hideously true. She read them again, cringing at the mental image they produced: a man setting himself against God, choosing purposely to endure eternal suffering—separation and judgment—rather than bend the knee in submission to the Creator and his Christ.

Nigel.

Melissa looked at the clock for the tenth time in the past half hour, as if it might offer relief. She was exhausted; a heavy physical and emotional depression clouded her mind. Sleep seemed to be the answer, a welcome escape, a means of revival—if only it would come.

Setting aside the devotional, she took up her Bible again. She turned to Luke, the sixteenth chapter: the story of Lazarus and the rich man. As she read the account, she decided that Nigel Kendrick bore little resemblance to the uncaring, insensitive rich man. Nigel had actually been an active supporter of programs that assisted the poor, especially those that enabled students with little or no financial backing to attend college. Still, their ends had been the same. She winced at the description of Hades: torment, anguish, flames, a great chasm ensuring separation from Heaven . . .

A single tear ran down her cheek as she thought of Nigel, in hell, tortured by fire, crying out for a drop of water to cool his tongue. And she was impotent to do anything about it. She suddenly wished that she was Mormon and believed in the practice of being baptized for the dead. Almost anything would be preferable to this agonizing sense of helplessness.

"He locked the door," she told herself aloud. She knew that was true, that God was a just God, that Nigel had received a punishment befitting his sin. But it didn't change the way she felt.

Melissa dabbed at her eyes with a tissue, then checked the clock again. It was obvious that she wouldn't be sleeping any time soon. She wondered about going to church. There was plenty of time to get ready. But she wasn't sure she had the strength—to shower and dress, to be around people.

Father . . . I'm having a hard time accepting this. I know in my mind that Nigel had his chances. I know that I gave him the opportunity to call on the name of your Son just minutes before he died. And I know that he decided not to. He was stubborn. A rebel to the end. But—it just seems so harsh, the idea that now it's too late, that he's gone forever—to a place of horrible pain. If it was someone else, I would say that justice had been served. A sinner had been judged appropriately. But Nigel . . . I just . . . I don't know what to think, what to feel, how to react . . . I'm numb. I'm confused. I'm hurting. I need you.

$\int$TOP HERE."

Tito pulled the Corvette alongside the curb a full block from Lewis's apartment.

"Keep the engine running. I'll just be a minute." Vince pulled a 9mm pistol from the shoulder holster under his sports jacket and attached a long, thin silencer.

"Hey, I'm going too."

Vince shook his head, stuffing the gun into his coat pocket. "Just sit tight. I'll be right back."

Tito opened his mouth to object, then decided not to waste his breath. When Vince made up his mind, there wasn't much use arguing. Besides, two men would only double the chances of being spotted and identified later on. And it would only take a single bullet to end Lewis's life. Whether that bullet came from Vince's gun or Tito's didn't much matter.

"Okay. Make it quick."

Vince hopped out and started up the sidewalk.

$\int$LOW DOWN."

Vaughn complied, easing down on the brake. "I still say this is nuts."

Parish ignored him. "What's the number on that complex?" He pointed at a set of condos with tiled roofs.

"Seventeen hundred," Jimmy offered from the back seat.

"Then it's on the other side," Parish said. He looked past Vaughn. "There! That must be it."

Vaughn pulled into a parking spot. "We're just going to knock on her door? Cold call?"

Parish shrugged. He swung the door open and got out. "Why not?"

Jimmy struggled free of the Jeep, a giant emerging from a steel cocoon. "Excuse me, sirs, but I'd like to get one thing straight before we get up there."

"What's that?" Parish asked.

"What are we going to say?"

"We introduce ourselves," Parish answered, "flash some ID, then tell her we're conducting an investi—"

"No." Vaughn was shaking his head. He slammed the driver's door. "No, Phil. Having a little chat is one thing. But pretending to be conducting a military investigation, impersonating military police—we could really get into trouble for that. Henderson would court-martial us."

Parish sighed at this and rolled his eyes. "Stop worrying about Henderson. Besides, we won't claim to be official. We just say that we're looking into some things. As long as we sound sort of official, but aren't specific, there's no problem."

"No problem . . ." Vaughn muttered.

The three of them crossed the street and started into the courtyard.

THE KNOCK CAUGHT MELISSA OFF GUARD. WHO WOULD BE STOPPING BY at this hour on a Sunday morning? When it came again, this time with more authority, she hurriedly pulled on a pair of faded jean shorts and an old psychedelic T-shirt that declared Jesus to be Lord.

As she approached the door, she regretted that she didn't have a peephole. There was no way to determine who was out there before opening the door. That presented a safety issue for a single woman.

Reaching for the knob, her arm froze. The bronze sphere was turning of its own accord. Above it, the bolt clicked, then magically slid back. She took a step backwards, gasping as the door inched open. It stopped when the chain jerked taut. Throwing her weight against the door, she slammed it shut.

An instant later, Melissa was hurtling across the room, tumbling to the floor. Behind her, the door flew open with a loud crack, wood splintering as the gold chain was severed from the facing. Light streamed through the opening, rays from the newly risen sun igniting dust particles and giving the room a phosphorescent glow. A shadow stepped into the glare. She opened her mouth and inhaled, ready to scream.

"Don't," the shadow warned. The figure pushed the door shut with a foot. It kissed the frame, but didn't latch. The light retreated. Melissa could see him now. It was a man. He was short, wiry, with a harsh, angry face. His hair was black, shaped into an angular crew cut by a barber's clippers. In his hand, he held a gun.

"What do you want?"

He placed a finger to his lips, urging her to remain silent, then cocked the pistol. "On your knees," he whispered. "Hands on your head."

Melissa assumed the position, closed her eyes, and felt the metal barrel press against her temple.

"Where are the bones?"

"The what?"

The barrel dug into the side of her head. "The bones," he said in a low, hoarse voice. "Do you have them?"

"Yes."

"Where are they?"

"They're on the—"

There was another knock at the door. The man swore softly. Melissa held her breath, eyes clamped shut. Then she was airborne, yanked up by an elbow and dragged to the bedroom. The man was looking around, small eyes darting to the window, the bathroom. The gun was still pointed at her head.

There was a creaking sound. Melissa recognized it: the front door opening. Whomever had knocked was coming inside.

P<small>HIL</small>!"

"It's open," Parish argued, whispering.

"But that doesn't give us the right to just barge in," Vaughn countered, incredulous. "This is someone's home."

"It would constitute breaking and entering," Jimmy said calmly.

"Who asked you?" Parish sniped, glaring. "Besides, we didn't break anything. The door was open." He reached out and pushed it a little wider, causing the hinges to sing again.

Jimmy pointed at the carpet. The security chain was on the floor, screws still in their holes in the bracket. "Looks like someone broke something."

Parish glanced at Vaughn. "What if Lewis is in danger? What if whoever tried to get her with that car bomb thing came back to finish the job?"

"Then we find a phone somewhere and call the police," Vaughn answered. But it was too late. Parish was already inside, stalking across the darkened living room.

"Phil!"

THE MAN WAS SWEARING, WAVING THE GUN BACK AND FORTH, CLENCHING his jaw. Melissa looked up at him from the bed, too terrified to wonder who he was or why he cared about the bones. Her sole thought was survival.

Dear God, don't let me die!

"No back door in this place?"

Melissa shook her head.

"Who's out there?" the man asked, pointing with his pistol.

She shrugged. Her arms were shaking, her knees trembling as if they had just received a jolt of electricity. She felt sick to her stomach.

"The bones—they're out there, right?" He jabbed the barrel of the gun toward the bedroom door.

She nodded slowly.

The man cursed again, his face intense, the words barely whispers.

LET'S GET OUT OF HERE!" VAUGHN INSISTED. HE WAS STANDING JUST A few inches inside the front door, his head swiveling as he looked outside for signs of trouble, then inside to see what Phil "the Lunatic" Parish was up to. Jimmy was leaning against the kitchen bar, hands in pockets, frowning. He seemed bored. Vaughn wondered how that was possible.

"Come on, Phil! Before we get caught!"

"She's not home, Lieutenant," Jimmy agreed. "Let's come back later."

Parish was oblivious. He examined the dining table, then picked up something. "Check this out."

"What? What is it?" Vaughn asked, glancing over his shoulder at the pool area. Thankfully, there was no one out there yet.

"It's a bone," Parish announced.

Takin' care of business ..."

Tito tapped the stereo, engaging the CD player. BTO was silenced. Seconds later the Steve Miller Band cranked up a live version of "Jet Airliner" and the Bose, three-way speakers rocked the car. Nothing like golden oldies to pass the time.

He eyed his watch. What was taking so long? Vince had been gone for nearly ten minutes. Even allowing for a cautious approach, careful penetration of the front door locks, doing Lewis, hunting for the bones—he should have been back by now. What was the stupid ox doing?

Tito considered going in after him.

The opportunity presented itself suddenly, and lasted only an instant. The man glared at her, muttered something, then turned to the door. Peering out, he kept the gun aimed in her direction. But his back was toward her.

Without thinking her actions through, Melissa took hold of the heaviest object within reach—the brass lamp on the nightstand. Lifting it in one smooth, swift motion, she swung it down with all the force she could muster.

There was a dull clank as metal met bone. The man clutched at his skull, staggered, and cursed loudly when he saw the blood.

"Help!" she shouted.

Reeling, the man held the pistol at waist level, cocking it.

"Why you little—"

When Vaughn heard the cry, he reacted instinctively, dashing down the hall and thrusting open the door. The knob collided with something inside the room. There was a flash, a muffled thud, the smell of something burning. He reached for the light switch, but found himself flying backwards, driven by the impact of a blow to his head. Flat on his back on the floor, he reached up and touched his nose. It felt like it was on sideways. Blood was flowing freely, staining his uniform. He stared up at the ceiling, lightheaded, wondering if he had been hit by a bus or a Mac truck.

As stars filled his vision, he heard Parish shout, "Hold it!" Glass broke in the living room. Parish swore. "Get him, Jimmy!" Then there was a crash, as if an entire wall had been torn away by a wrecking ball.

THE BULLET MISSED HER—PRAISE GOD! BUT NOT BY MUCH. SHE HAD heard it whiz by, heard it burrow into the wall behind the bed. Blinded by the flash, she had rolled to the floor praying that she would not die.

God deliver me!

That was when Melissa felt it: warm, heavy, steel . . . the gun! The man had dropped it in the confusion. She had never in her life wielded a gun. She had never had a desire to. Until now.

Clutching the automatic with both hands, she pointed it at the door, expecting the man to come back. When he didn't, she used the barrel to nudge it open. The hallway was dark, empty. Then she heard voices—in the living room.

"You okay?" one asked.

"I'm not sure," another answered.

"What about you, Jimmy? Jimmy?" the first voice asked.

Melissa started down the hall, the gun jiggling in front of her. She was shaking uncontrollably, breath coming in gulps. Her T-shirt was soaked through.

A half-dozen steps later, she found them: three men in uniform. One was prostrate beneath the bar, covering his face with both hands. Across the living room another was kneeling below the picture window—or rather, where the picture window had once been. It was now missing, glass shards strewn about the carpet. Blood dripped from a ragged gash on the man's forehead. Two thick khaki legs protruded from the kitchen. The wall next to them was dented, the sheetrock creased inwardly.

"Jimmy? Jimmy? You okay?" the kneeling man asked. He tried to stand, but staggered and fell, cursing as he cut his palms on the glass.

In the kitchen, the sleeping giant flopped, turning over. "Oh, man. What happened?"

"Ahhh!" It was the man under the bar. He had raised up to a sitting position and was sniffing back blood, clutching at his face.

"Freeze!" she ordered.

VAUGHN TURNED TOWARD THE HALL, THE APARTMENT SWIMMING around him. "Who's there?"

"I said freeze!" A figure emerged from the darkness: short, hunched over, holding something. A woman. She was aiming a gun . . . at his head.

Even through watery eyes, he recognized her. It was their contact from Quad 217: Melissa Lewis.

Thirty-Three

TITO WAS FIDDLING WITH THE CD PLAYER, TRADING STEVE MILLER FOR the Doobie Brothers, when he saw Vince coming down the sidewalk. He was walking funny, his steps uneven, one hand on his head.

"What's the matter?" Tito asked, jumping out of the car.

Vince blinked at him, shook his head jerkily, then cursed. "I'm not sure."

"Did you get her? Did you get the bones?"

He was wincing in pain now, rubbing a spot on the back of his scalp.

"Did you get her, Vince?" he repeated.

"What? Uh . . . no." He removed his hand and examined his fingertips. They were wet with what looked like red paint. He swore again. "Everything was under control. But then somebody showed up."

"Who?"

"Bunch of marines."

"Marines?"

Vince went to work on the bump again, gingerly massaging it with his middle finger.

"They beaned you?"

He sighed melodramatically. "Lewis beaned me. The witch."

Tito waited for an explanation. When it became clear that Vince wasn't going to offer one, he asked, "So did you get her or not?"

"No! I didn't get her!" He squinted against the pain. "And I lost my 9mm." Reaching into the Vette, he pulled a .44 magnum from the floorboard. "Get your equalizer," he told Tito.

"What are you planning to do?" Tito asked. He opened the glove compartment and withdrew a .357. "If the cavalry's here, maybe we should—"

"Maybe we should blast them to kingdom come," Vince snarled, stuffing the gun into his jacket. "Come on. It's time to finish this."

"We won't have silencers," Tito pointed out. The large caliber revolvers were for emergencies only. "Target elimination" was carried out with smaller, quieter weapons—usually 9mm Berettas. "We're going to wake the dead if there's a shoot-out."

"Then let's wake 'em," Vince said, grimacing. "Nobody crowns Vince Scapelli and lives to tell about it."

It's okay," THE MAN UNDER THE BAR SAID, HANDS LIFTED. "DON'T shoot."

Melissa kept the pistol aimed in his direction as she surveyed the other casualties: the soldier on his knees beneath the window was wavering, probably about to lose consciousness; the khaki slacks and black military-issue shoes were still horizontal.

"Who are you?" she demanded, a trembling finger on the trigger.

"Captain Steven Vaughn. Lieutenant Phillip Parish. Sergeant Jimmy Donohue. We're marines. Assigned to Nellis. We work at the NTS— on security detail."

"What are you doing in my house?"

"Good question," Vaughn said, offering a meager smile. "We came to talk to you about the zone."

"About what?"

"The area where you and those kids were looking for fossils on Friday."

The gun drooped slightly. "How did you know about that?"

"You were on the Site. So we had you under surveillance."

She shook her head at him. "We weren't on the Site. We didn't cross any boundaries or go through any gates."

"The Site isn't completely fenced or guarded. There are large sections that you can just four-wheel into and never know you had crossed into secure territory."

Melissa considered this, still aiming at a point between Vaughn's eyes. "That doesn't explain why you're in my living room—uninvited."

"No, it doesn't," he consented, pinching his nose. "It's kind of difficult to explain."

"Try."

Vaughn wiped blood on his sleeve. "There have been some . . . incidents concerning the zone—the area you were in. The LT here," he motioned toward Parish, "read about what happened yesterday—the car explosion. He thought maybe it had something to do with your expedition. So we decided to come by and ask you a few questions—see if you could help us out. When we got here, the door was open, so—"

She waved him off and let the gun fall to her side. Sinking to the love seat, she said, "That guy broke in. He had a gun. This gun." She lifted it, offering Vaughn a side view. "I thought at first he was a burglar, but then he started talking about the fossils we found the other day."

"Those bones?" Vaughn asked, gesturing to the two elongated rocks on the dining table.

Melissa nodded.

Vaughn made it to his knees and picked one of them up.

"Gill found them," Melissa explained.

"Who's Gill?"

"One of the students that was on the field trip. Anyway, for some reason, that guy was interested in the bones." She shrugged.

"They came from the zone?"

Melissa nodded.

"What are they? What kind of bones?"

"One of them is a dinosaur bone. Nigel said . . ." She paused and swallowed hard. "Dr. Kendrick—the man who died in the explosion yesterday—he said that the large one is from a T. rex. The other one's humanoid."

Vaughn made a face. "So this Dr. Kendrick examined them?"

Another nod.

Across the living room, Parish tried to stand up again, groaned, and fell against the wall.

"I think he needs a doctor," Vaughn told Melissa. "Can I use your phone?"

"Sure."

"I'm all right," Parish protested, knees threatening to fail as he attempted to rise. He succeeded this time and braced himself against the window frame. A red-black crust was trailing from the cut on his forehead, snaking down his cheek.

In the kitchen, the Truck sat up. "Where am I?"

"We should report the break-in too," Melissa told Vaughn.

"Hold onto these," he said, handing her the bones. Then he picked up the phone and dialed 911.

Is THERE A BACK DOOR?" TITO ASKED, STUDYING THE APARTMENT.

"Nope."

They surveyed the courtyard, the pool area, the surrounding units. The place was deserted. Just another quiet Sunday morning. "What if they called the police?"

"We'll be long gone before a squad car shows up," Vince assured him. "Lock and load." He started down the path, toward Lewis's apartment.

"Doing servicemen doesn't thrill me," Tito admitted, a step behind. "It's only a few notches down from hitting cops or Feds."

"Don't get soft on me now."

"I'm not getting soft," Tito shot back. "It's just that—"

"No prisoners," Vince vowed. "This thing ends here. Now."

---

911. WHAT IS THE NATURE OF YOUR EMERGENCY?"

Before Vaughn could answer the woman, the front door burst open and a gun looked in. It was followed by a man—the same man who had broken into the apartment minutes earlier. Vaughn dove for cover, rolling behind the couch. As he did, the first shot erupted from the man's gun, a deafening explosion that seemed to rock the building.

Instead of retreating, Melissa rose like a zombie, lifted her gun, and began tugging on the trigger. Wood and bits of plaster flew into the air as bullets ate away at the door frame and surrounding walls. When she stopped, the man was gone.

Vaughn motioned Parish toward the hallway with his thumb. Forgetting his injury, Parish leapt over the couch and disappeared. Tugging on Jimmy's foot, Vaughn whispered, "Get to the bedroom!"

The Truck, eyes wide now, nodded nervously and began commando crawling in that direction.

After sneaking a glance around the couch, Vaughn jumped up and pulled Melissa into the hall, pushing her through the bedroom door.

"Now what?" Parish wanted to know.

Vaughn shrugged, breathing hard. He looked like he had just returned from combat duty, his shirt dark with a mixture of sweat and blood.

"We're sitting ducks in here," Jimmy noted, his face pale.

"Yeah, I know," Vaughn said. He looked at Melissa. "How much ammo you have left?"

She handed him the gun. "I don't know."

He checked the clip. "Three."

Melissa pointed up at the windows. They were about eighteen inches tall and ran the length of the bedroom. "They open to ground level. The bushes back there are full of thorns. But we could get out that way . . . if we have to."

"We have to," Vaughn said. He helped her crank the right window open, then assisted her up and through it. Parish went next.

"I don't think I'll fit," Jimmy sighed, studying the opening.

"You'd better." Vaughn gave him a boost and started pushing. "Suck it in, Jimmy."

The Truck did. Melissa and Parish each grabbed a beefy arm and pulled. Vaughn put his shoulder into Jimmy's rear end.

"I'm too big!"

Vaughn heard a noise in the living room. Voices. "Get up there, Jimmy!" he demanded.

"Sir, I—"

Vaughn took three steps back, then ran at the legs and buttocks hanging from the window, as if they were part of a tackling dummy. Jimmy groaned and popped through the window, taking the metal frame with him.

There was a clump in the hallway. Vaughn fired a shot through the closed door. Someone cursed. Ascending the nightstand, he crawled out the window. An instant later, the bedroom was blanketed with bullets.

"Run!"

Jimmy led the way, bounding awkwardly toward the street. Parish was on his heels, one hand attending to his wound. Vaughn pulled Melissa by the hand. When they reached the Jeep, they tumbled inside: Jimmy and Parish falling into the back in a tangle of arms and legs, Melissa rolling into the shotgun position, the bones in her lap, Vaughn climbing over her en route to the driver's seat.

In the distance, sirens wailed. But they were too far away to offer any assistance. Vaughn fumbled with the keys, trying to distinguish between the ignition and the door keys.

"Hurry!" Melissa shouted.

"I'm trying."

In the side mirror she saw two men dash out of the pool area, guns in hand. "They're coming. Two of them."

The men looked right, then left, then sprinted for the street.

"Hurry!" she repeated.

Vaughn forced the key into the ignition and twisted it. The engine cranked but wouldn't turn over.

In the backseat, Parish swore. "We're dead."

"They've seen us," Melissa reported, watching in the mirror. The men were racing towards the Jeep now. One of them stopped suddenly, dropped to one knee, and lifted his gun.

"Get down!" Melissa yelled, ducking.

There was a terrific boom, and the back window exploded.

Vaughn twisted the key again. The engine made a pretense of running, then died.

"Please God!" Melissa prayed aloud. "Get this thing started!"

"Amen!" Jimmy chimed as he brushed glass from his uniform. Next to him, Parish had his eyes clamped shut, as if he were wishing the nightmare away.

On the third attempt, the Jeep roared to life. There was another boom. The vehicle rocked from side to side. Vaughn shifted into gear, pushed the pedal to the floor, and they tilted off down the street.

"They must have gotten a tire," he observed, fighting for control.

Melissa stuck her head out the window. "Yep. Right rear. Flat as a pancake."

"Well, I'm not stopping to change it."

"Where are we going?" Jimmy wanted to know.

"Beats me," Vaughn admitted. "Away from here."

"To the police," Parish submitted.

"Where's the closest station?" Vaughn asked Melissa.

She shook her head. "I have no idea."

"There's one on Charleston," Jimmy said.

"Too far," Parish noted through closed eyes. "There must be something closer."

"What about the federal building downtown?" Melissa asked.

"No. We can't trust the FBI," Parish muttered.

"Why not?" Melissa twisted in her seat and glared at Parish. Then she looked to Vaughn for an answer.

"This guy named Weber was killed yesterday," he explained. "He'd been doing research into the subject of radioactivity at the Test Site. We had breakfast with him and he was telling us about how the FBI was after him, that they were trying to suppress the information. He claimed they would do just about anything to keep his research from becoming public knowledge."

"You're not saying the FBI—"

"Murdered him," Parish said. "Anybody got any Tylenol? I've got a splitting headache."

"Join the club," Jimmy grumbled.

"Somebody killed him," Vaughn continued. "That much is certain. We just don't know who did it. What we do know is that some weird things have been happening. Weird and dangerous things. Like that car fire your friend was in. Like what we just went through with those thugs. And it all seems to revolve around Quad 217."

"The place where we found the fossils?" Melissa asked.

"Right."

Melissa sighed down at the bones lying in her lap. "What do they have to do with anything? I don't understand."

"Neither do we," Vaughn admitted.

VINCE SHOUTED A CURSE. "GET THE CAR!"

Tito ran to the Vette and thirty seconds later they were screeching down the block in pursuit of the targets.

"Where are they?" he asked frantically. He accelerated to seventy on the empty residential street.

"Go right," Vince said.

Tito spun the wheel and the car fishtailed around the corner. "There." He pointed through the windshield as the Jeep slipped onto a busier boulevard. The needle rose to eighty-seven before he tapped the brakes and skidded his way into traffic. Horns blasted behind them.

The cellular buzzed and Vince swore at it. Tito repeated the profane sentiment. They both knew who it was—and it was bad timing.

Ahead of them, the Jeep was limping along, riding on three tires and one rim.

Tito picked up the phone on the second ring. "Yeah?"

"I'm calling to congratulate you."

"What are you talking about, Sonny?" Tito cut off a delivery truck and took up position two cars behind the Jeep.

"Well, by now, surely you've finished the job," he said in a patronizing tone.

"We're working on it."

Sonny swore at him. "Working at it? Just how hard is it to nail a schoolteacher, for pete's sake!"

"She got away," Tito confessed. "But we're going after them."

"*Them?*"

"She has some marines helping her."

Sonny ranted for a full minute. "You screw-ups!"

"We're taking care of it," Tito promised.

"Yeah, I'll just bet. What about the bones?"

"Lewis has them. We're sure of that."

"Get the bones. Do Lewis."

"What about the soldiers?" Tito slowed the Vette and put on his blinker, following the Jeep through a green left turn arrow.

"I don't care about them. Do whatever you have to do. Just do it quickly. And do it right this time." He offered a parting curse.

Tito replace the phone and muttered, "Same to you."

"What's the matter?" Vince asked. "Sonny got a problem?" He had already reloaded and was caressing the .44 as if it were a favorite pet.

"No. We've got a problem. And if we don't solve it in the next hour or so, we'll be in the doghouse—big time."

THIRTY-FOUR

"WE'VE GOT COMPANY."

"Where?"

Melissa gestured to the side mirror. "Three cars back. Red Corvette. It's following us."

Vaughn squinted into the rearview mirror. "You sure?"

"Pretty sure. It's been with us for the last mile."

"Make a left," Parish instructed.

"But that'll put us on the Strip," Vaughn argued. "We need police, not hotels."

"We need people, noise, crowds, cars. Those jerks—whoever they are—are less likely to blow our brains out in public."

"Good point," Melissa said.

"I can't believe we can't find a police station," Vaughn grumbled, taking a left. "We should have just gone to the base."

"It's a little late for that now," Jimmy observed.

They reached the Strip and waited at the light. "Is the Vette still there?"

"Yeah," Melissa answered, watching it in the mirror.

"Can you see the license plate?"

"No. And I can't see inside either. The windows are too dark."

Traffic began to move. The bare rim was grinding on the pavement, the Jeep jerking back and forth.

"We can't lose them," Vaughn thought aloud. "Not without four good tires."

"You couldn't lose a Vette no matter what," Jimmy threw in. "Especially not in a Jeep."

"Pull in over there," Melissa advised. She was pointing at the tall, Greek statues bordering the grounds of Titans Temple—one of the newer theme hotel casinos. "Let's see if they follow us."

Vaughn got into the right-hand lane and turned down the long, curving driveway. The fountains were shooting into the sky, water droplets dancing like crystal beads against the bright morning sun.

"Here they come," Jimmy observed.

Behind them, the Vette was rolling smoothly along, a cherry red shark moving in to attack.

"Time to abandon ship," Parish advised.

"What?"

"Even if we knew where a police station was, we couldn't get to it. They'd run us down. Let's ditch the Jeep."

"Good idea," Melissa agreed. "We can go into the hotel. Alert security."

"Have them call a SWAT team," Jimmy mumbled.

"Park right in front," Melissa directed. "They aren't going to shoot us out here, in broad daylight."

"At least we hope not," Vaughn sighed. He brought the Jeep to a halt next to the main pathway leading to the hotel. They popped open the doors and hurried away from the vehicle.

"You can't leave your car there," a young valet admonished. "If you'd like me to park it for you . . ."

They ignored him, walking briskly up the colonnade toward the gaudy entrance.

"THEY'RE GOING IN." TITO STOPPED A CAR LENGTH BEHIND THE JEEP AND slammed his fists down on the steering wheel. "Great!"

Vince grinned and opened the door.

"What are you doing?"

"Going after them."

"Right. Like we're going to hit them in the busiest joint on the Strip."

Vince shrugged, stuffing his gun into his pocket. "Why not?"

"Vince!"

"We don't do them in the middle of the slots or on top of a blackjack table," he said. "We push them into a corner, take them in the back room, and . . ." He imitated the sound of his pistol firing.

"And the hotel staff is just going to look the other way?"

"Titans is owned by Antonio Ghiradelli, right? Give Sonny a call. Tell him to contact Ghiradelli's people. In five minutes, the security team will roll out the red carpet for us. They'll close down the building."

Actually it wasn't a bad plan, Tito decided. The casino was the organization's territory—just about everything on the Strip was. Maybe Vince wasn't quite as stupid as he acted. "I guess it's worth a try." He picked up the phone and punched the speed dial button. "Stay with them. I'll be there in a minute."

Now what?"

The group was stalled in the entryway, momentarily directionless, stunned by the overwhelming array of audiovisual chaos: blinking lights, glowing neon, loud colors, faux Greek pageantry, live and canned music, the jingle of coins, the plastic click of chips, voices, and movement—everywhere, movement. Despite the day and the hour, the casino was writhing with activity. Accomplished gamblers and tourists with money to blow stood shoulder to shoulder, leaning against padded tables, yanking on one-armed bandits, doing everything within their power to guess which number a small marble would land on, or what card the dealer would toss at them next. It was a mixture of short-lived ecstasy, winners abounding in the joy of their windfalls, and utter dejection: sweaty faces, slumped shoulders, red, vacant eyes staring at rectangles of bright green felt.

"Over there!" Melissa said, answering her own question. She started toward an overweight security guard propped against the wall behind the baccarat tables. The others followed, snaking through the slots, the bingo lounge, winding around tight knots of gamblers hypnotized by ivory cubes, their bodies hunched toward the business end of crap tables.

The guard was seated on a stool, one level up from the main floor, looking sleepily across the casino. He wore a sidearm, an extra fifty pounds, and a scowl. There was a flicker of interest in his eyes as he noticed the group approaching.

Melissa reached him first. "Someone's trying to kill us," she blurted out.

The guard's eyebrows rose, the frown disappearing. "Come again?"

"Someone's trying to kill us," she repeated breathlessly. "Call the police."

He stared at her with a mixture of curiosity and skepticism and glanced at the sticks she was carrying. "Kill you?"

"Us," Vaughn said.

The guard's eyes darted to Vaughn's swollen nose, to his bloody uniform, to Parish's forehead, up and down Jimmy, then back to Melissa. He edged off of his stool and thumbed the mike attached to his chest. "Frank, this is Baker. I got a situation here." He tapped his earpiece with a finger, listening to the response.

Parish elbowed Vaughn and nodded behind them. A dozen large, muscular men in dark suits were striding in their direction, drawn from the four corners of the casino. Each bore an earpiece and a thin, lightweight headset mike. Ten seconds later, they were surrounded, dwarfed by the intimidating security team. Even Jimmy looked average against the forest of brutes.

The guard, who was by far the least impressive member of the team, was still speaking to his chest, listening, gazing past them at the sea of glittering lights and spinning games of chance. "Yes, sir. I'll take care of it."

He addressed them with a fresh smile. "If you will follow these gentlemen . . ." And the wreath of muscle-bound robots began herding them toward a mirrored door to the right of the main hallway.

"Do we have a choice?" Parish muttered.

"What about the police?" Melissa asked one of the suits.

"The men chasing us are armed and dangerous," Vaughn emphasized.

"You're safe with us," the man assured them. He used a security card to green-light the door and it opened automatically. "Right this way, please."

As they started through the doorway, Vaughn paused and rose to his tiptoes, peering over and between the security men. What had become of their assailants? It was difficult to make out individuals in the cavernous room. And there wasn't time to study the area. But he did spot the rotund guard perched on his stool, fifty paces behind them. And for the briefest of instances, he caught a glimpse of the short, wiry figure standing next to him.

Following Melissa into the corridor, he considered the image: the guard grinning, pointing in their direction, nodding. And the other man. Could it have been . . . ?

"I think we might be in trouble," he whispered to Melissa.

Iᴛᴏ ᴍᴇᴛ Vɪɴᴄᴇ ʙᴇʜɪɴᴅ ᴛʜᴇ ʙᴀᴄᴄᴀʀᴀᴛ ᴛᴀʙʟᴇs. "Sᴏɴɴʏ sᴀɪᴅ ʜᴇ ᴡᴀs sure Ghiradelli's people would cooperate."

"They already are."

"Really?"

"Yeah. They're putting our four friends in a holding room in the back."

"No police?"

Vince shook his head. "All in-house. The manager will be out in a minute. He'll take us to them."

Tito breathed a sigh of relief. "I'll be glad when this is over."

"Good. 'Cause it's fixing to be."

Tʜᴇ ᴄᴏʀʀɪᴅᴏʀ ʟᴇᴅ ɪɴᴛᴏ ᴛʜᴇ ʙᴏᴡᴇʟs ᴏꜰ ᴛʜᴇ ʙᴜɪʟᴅɪɴɢ, ᴛᴏ ᴀ ʟᴀʙʏʀɪɴᴛʜ of bleak, tiled hallways, unmarked doors, and dim stairwells. They explored the maze for five minutes without speaking, ascending two flights of stairs in the process. Finally, the suits ushered them into a plush lounge containing three large-screen TVs, a wall-to-wall wet bar, several leather couches, and an oversized hot tub. Through a window on the far wall they could see a control room where four more suits sat with their backs to the glass, studying a floor-to-ceiling bank of glowing video monitors.

They stopped at a door to the left of the security suite. When the lock had been satisfied, they were led into a room that held a long, oak conference table and a dozen armchairs. A tray bearing a glass pitcher and an array of crystal tumblers sat in the center. A small square of safety glass offered a side view of the control room.

"Please have a seat," one of the suits said, gesturing to the table. As they complied, the door behind them was shut, the bolt clanking into place.

"They locked us in," Jimmy observed. "I don't like being locked in places. I get claustrophobic."

"What about the bunker?" Parish asked, looking around the room. "Underground, plenty of locks . . ."

"That's different. That's work. And I try not to think about it."

"There's no phone in here," Melissa noted.

"Bet they have one in there,"Vaughn said, gazing through the window. In the darkened control room, the men were frowning at the monitors, watching as surveillance cameras offered fleeting views of the poker tables, the bingo arena, rows of slots . . .

Melissa reached over and rapped on the window. One of the men glanced over, then returned to his job. The others ignored her completely. She tried again, this time miming a phone conversation when the suit on the end looked at her. Nothing. No interest, no recognition.

"Maybe they don't speak the language," Parish said.

Vaughn stood and began to pace. "I don't like this."

"Don't tell me you're claustrophobic too," Parish sighed.

"No. But something's wrong."

"At least we're safe for the moment," Melissa offered. "Even those gun-toters would have a hard time getting past all this security."

"I'm not so sure. Right before we left the casino . . . I could have sworn I saw the guy that broke into your apartment."

"Persistent, aren't they?" Melissa said.

"I think I saw him talking to the guard."

"So?"

"So the two of them looked like they were having a friendly talk. Real chummy."

"Are you saying hotel security is in on this?" Melissa asked, her face contorting.

"I don't know. But I'd feel a whole lot better if we could call the police."

Melissa rose and began banging on the window with her fists. Two suits reacted, looking back, then chuckled as they returned their attention to their work.

"See?"Vaughn said. "They won't let us out."

Melissa turned, and their eyes met, exchanging a look of dread.

Don't worry. They can't get away," the manager snickered. He was an aging Italian with a halo of silver hair that encircled a poorly fitted black toupee. His face reminded Tito of his father's: a worn, insincere smile and thick, fleshy cheeks sagging beneath tired, violent eyes. Tito wondered if this man was as volatile as his father, if he had beaten his children unmercifully for the slightest disobedience.

"You're sure?" Vince asked, following him through the mirrored door.

"You boys aren't the only ones with problems," he said, puffing on his cigar. "Operating a casino, we run into all sorts of touchy situations that require creative solutions. If you take my meaning." He burst out laughing.

Tito nodded and chuckled politely. Even the man's hoarse, smoke-robbed voice brought back unpleasant memories.

"We've got them squared away in a conference room," he continued. "No way out. Security doors. Good place to let them sit and stew. Good place to ask questions too. Then, whenever you're ready, we can have them moved to the room. It's nothing but four walls of concrete with a drain in the middle. Opens to the physical plant. That way if there's a mess, you just spray the place down, load the remains into grinders—or whatever." He sucked on the cigar. "We're a full-service hotel." More laughter.

"Listen, I'm doing you boys a favor," he declared, his leather shoes scuffing along the corridor. "I need you to do me one."

"What's that?" Vince asked.

"Tell Sonny that I cooperated with you," he said, smiling. His teeth fanned out like an alligator's. "He'll tell the big boys. That'll be good for Mr. Ghiradelli. And anything that's good for him, is good for me. Know what I mean?" Smoke belched from his nose as he snorted at this. "Can you do that for me, fellas?"

"Yes, sir," Tito responded. In the few minutes since he had met this man, he had already grown to loathe him. It would have been satisfying to blow the jerk's head from his shoulders—if only to vicariously get back at his father. "We'll be sure and do that."

JIMMY TOOK THE SILVER KNOB IN TWO BRAWNY HANDS, SQUEEZED IT, and began to twist. His entire body tensed, muscles flexing, back and legs bending awkwardly as he struggled to force it open. "There's no way," he finally sighed, releasing it. "I can't get it open."

"Maybe you could knock it down," Melissa suggested.

The Truck bumped his weight against the surface, testing it. "Nope. That thing won't budge. I'd dislocate my shoulder."

"What about the window?" Parish tried.

Jimmy pounded on it with the flesh of his fist. "Reinforced glass. Even if we broke it with a chair, it wouldn't go anywhere. Besides, there are four security men in there."

"Guess we'll have to wait and see what happens," Parish said.

"Yeah. We're stuck in here," Melissa agreed.

"Well, we better get unstuck," Vaughn said ominously. He was looking past them, into the control room. "And fast." He pointed at the monitors. "Recognize anybody?"

They all stared at the bank of screens, watching as black and white images appeared and disappeared. One of the small squares displayed a poorly lit view of a hallway. Three men were walking down it, toward the camera: a stocky, older gentleman in a blazer that bore the hotel's logo; a handsome man with a long, black ponytail; and a short, stringy guy with thinning hair. The angle changed, shooting them from the rear.

"That's him!" Melissa gasped. "On the far right! That's the one that broke into my apartment. And that other guy . . . the one with the long hair . . . that's his buddy. He blew your tire out."

Parish swore.

"The dope in the Titans' jacket is leading them right to us!" Jimmy exclaimed.

Vaughn nodded. "They're in the corridors. They'll be here in a couple of minutes. Maybe sooner." He glanced around the room nervously. "We have to get out of here. Now!"

Thirty-Five

*D*EAR GOD . . ."

The men were striding away from the camera, down the corridor.

"Heavenly Father . . ."

The scene changed. Now they were approaching. In the black and white monitor, the stout man with the thick, fleshy face withdrew a card from his pocket.

"In Jesus' name . . ."

From yet another angle, the trio stopped in front of a door and the trollish leader slid the card through the scanner.

"We need a miracle," Melissa begged.

"Amen!" Parish and Jimmy agreed.

In a second monitor, a door swung toward the camera and the three men entered a short hallway—the hallway leading to the suite of rooms.

"Well, it may not qualify as a miracle," Vaughn said, "but . . ." He withdrew the automatic from his waistband.

"What are you gonna do?" Parish asked. "Shoot your way out—with two bullets?"

"Maybe." Vaughn stepped to the door that led to the lounge and examined the knob, then the keypad next to it. "To coin a phrase—'It's worth a shot.'"

"What are you planning to—" Melissa started to ask.

"Stand back," he ordered. When the others had moved to the other side of the room, he faced the door. "Eeny, meeny, miny, mo . . . Shoot the lock or shoot the keypad?" Without further deliberation, he aimed at the latter. The gun emitted a muffled thump and the electronic security device erupted in a shower of sparks, a thin trail of smoke curling into the air.

Parish moved in for a closer look. "I think you killed it."

Jimmy tried the door. "It didn't work. It's still locked."

"They're coming," Melissa warned, eyeing the monitors.

"Should have shot the lock,"Vaughn lamented. He gave the keypad a jarring straight right, then aimed the pistol at the knob.

Before he could fire, the device beeped and there was a metallic click. Jimmy tried the door again, then smiled. "After you," he said, opening it wide.

They hurried through, into the lounge. Parish approached the door to the outer hall, then backed away. He pointed at it, miming a warning. "They're out there!" he whispered.

"Where can we go?" Melissa responded, looking about the room in a panic.

Right down here," the manager directed. He led them to the door of the suite. "If you need any help . . ."

"No," Tito said. "We can handle it."

The manager shrugged and pushed the door back, ushering them inside. "They're in here," he said. They walked across the lounge to the next door, and the man performed the security sequence: card, code . . . He reached for the knob.

"Huh . . ." he grunted.

"Something wrong?"Vince asked.

"Must have put in the wrong code."The manager switched his cigar to the other hand and started over. He tried the knob again. It wouldn't budge. He cursed at it. "Newfangled technology," he muttered. He stepped over to a phone. "Frank, get this stupid door open."

Thirty seconds later, with the door still shut, the phone buzzed. The manager picked it back up.

"What do you mean they're gone?"

Vince took this as his cue. Withdrawing his .44, he blew the knob completely off of the door and forced it open with a vicious kick. Inside, one of the men from the adjoining control room stared at him with wide eyes—his hands straight up in the air.

The manager dropped the phone and went in. "How could they have gotten out, Frank? The blasted door was still locked." He turned and found Tito studying the inner keypad.

"Small caliber, probably 9mm," Tito announced. "Wonder where they got that?" He frowned at Vince.

Vince cursed and marched out of the room. "Close this place down!" he ordered. "Seal off the entire hotel."

"Listen," the manager said, "Titans is a big place. We shut down, we lose money. And in case you didn't know, making money is our business."

Vince spun around and aimed the gun at the manager's head.

"I wouldn't do that if I were you," the man said, unfazed. He puffed on his cigar. "Mr. Ghiradelli takes threats against his employees personally. He'll have a squad out on you so fast it'll make your head swim." Here he offered a vile, toothy grin. "Let me put my people on this. I'll post guards at all the entrances and exits. They won't get out."

"They'd better not," Vince grumbled.

Tito looked around the conference room, then stalked into the lounge. Couches, big-screen TVs, hot tub gurgling . . . He opened the closet and flipped through clothing with the barrel of his gun. Nothing. He gave the bathroom a cursory glance. Empty.

Satisfied that there were no other hiding places, he holstered his pistol and asked, "Any idea where they might have gone?"

The manager shook his head. "Once they got out of the control suite, they could have gone anywhere. Most of the other doors between here and the casino are unlocked. They're only secure on the way in."

Tito considered this. "Come on, Vince." He motioned toward the door.

"Don't worry," the manager said. "They're not going anywhere." He put his cigar out in an ashtray next to the couch and followed them into the hall. The door clicked shut behind him.

MELISSA BROKE THE SURFACE FIRST, HER EMPTY, BURNING LUNGS sucking down oxygen. Next to her, Jimmy surfaced, choking, spitting water—a whale breaching. Vaughn and Parish popped up, gasping, heads back in agony.

"I thought we were dead," Parish managed between breaths.

"I think I am," Jimmy panted and coughed.

Vaughn helped Melissa out of the hot tub. "Nothing like a little whirlpool to relax you." He grabbed towels from a neat stack on the bar and handed them out.

"What now?" Melissa asked, rubbing her hair.

"Good question," Vaughn replied. "We gotta get out of here. But first . . ." Opening the closet, he began rummaging through the clothes. He pulled out a hanger bearing a glittery, red gown, and handed it to Melissa. "Try this on."

She stared back at him, incredulous. "This is a party dress."

"You're right." He tossed a black tux at Parish and found a white one for himself.

"Nice," Parish said. "But it doesn't match my shoes."

"We don't really have time to play dress up," Melissa pointed out.

"We're sopping wet. If we don't change, we'll leave a trail down the hall," Vaughn explained. "Besides, a lady in shorts and three soldiers in bloody uniforms tend to stick out in a crowd—wouldn't you say?"

"I guess you're right."

"Hurry up and get changed," Vaughn urged.

"What about me?" Jimmy asked.

Vaughn pushed hangers along the rack, searching. "This is the best I can do." He handed Jimmy a bright purple suit.

"Trade you for your tux," he offered, looking at Parish.

Parish ignored this. Slipping off his dripping uniform, he tried on the tux. The arms of the shirt were almost an inch too long. The pants puddled at his ankles. He decided to forgo the cummerbund.

"Is this the biggest you have?" Jimmy asked.

Vaughn nodded impatiently. "Yes!"

"I wear a fifty-wide in a jacket. This is a forty-six."

"Just put it on," Vaughn grumbled. "The idea is to be dry—not stylish." His tux was right on the money, a nearly perfect fit. Transferring the bones to his new clothing, he glanced into the mirror and saw a bridegroom with matted, wet hair, branches protruding from his waistband.

Parish laughed as the Truck donned his costume. "Jimmy the pimp: a really big mobster in a really little suit."

"I wouldn't talk if I were you . . . Mr. Baggy Pants. You look like a gang member going to a formal."

"If you don't mind . . ." Melissa said, clearing her throat. The three men stared at her. "Turn around!"

They complied. A minute later she said, "Okay."

"Wow!" Vaughn and Jimmy chimed in unison. Parish offered a wolf whistle. Even with a limp do, tired eyes, and no makeup, Melissa looked good in the dress. It was a full size too small and emphasized all of her curves. Beneath it, her feet were bare.

"Now that we're all dressed for success," she said, frowning, "let's get out of here—before the goons come back."

———

ANY SIGN OF THEM?"

Tito shook his head at Vince, out of breath from running the length of the corridor. "Nothing on one." They were standing on floor three, next to stairwell A.

"Two was clear," Vince reported. "What now?"

"Ghiradelli's people are guarding the exits. You sweep this floor, then take tower two," Tito directed. "I'll take tower one. We'll move up floor by floor until we find them."

"Up?"

"We know they didn't go down."

At the end of the hall the elevator opened and the manager appeared. "Anything?"

Tito shook his head. "You're certain they couldn't have left the building?"

"Absolutely. They weren't out of that conference room long enough to have gotten out. I posted my boys at every door." He shrugged, biting the tip from a fresh cigar. "It's only a matter of time until they're cornered."

Vince swore wearily under his breath at this assurance. "If they get away . . ."

"They can't. Think about it," the manager submitted. "They don't know the place. We've got them outnumbered. And really, how hard can it be to run down a woman and a few servicemen?"

"Harder than you think," Tito answered.

———

YOU SUPPOSE THAT GOES OUTSIDE?" PARISH ASKED, POINTING TO A FIRE door. The foursome was standing at the crossroads of two corridors.

Vaughn shrugged. "Maybe. But if it sets off an alarm—"

"The fire department would come running," Parish submitted, hands on the chrome door bar. "And the police."

"And they would probably get here just in time to find our bodies."

Parish made a face at this and released the bar.

"Over here," Melissa called in a whisper. She was standing ten yards down the hallway to the right, in front of another door. The sign on it said simply: Stairs.

Vaughn pushed it open and paused, listening. Convinced that the coast was clear, he motioned the others through.

Melissa started left, down the flight.

"No," Vaughn told her. "Let's go up."

"Up?"

"Yeah."

"But we're already up a couple of stories," she argued. "We have to go down to get out."

"Exactly. They'll be expecting us to go down. So let's go up instead."

She looked at him, unconvinced.

"Trust me," Vaughn said. "We can't just walk out the front door. They'll be watching for us. We have to think of a more creative means of escape."

"Maybe we can call the cops from a courtesy phone," Melissa thought aloud, climbing the flight to the right.

"Maybe," Vaughn nodded.

When they arrived on the fifth floor, Parish reached for the door. Vaughn warned him off. "Keep going up," he directed. "The higher we go, the safer we'll be."

Tito slipped through the door onto the fourth floor. It was quiet, the plush hallway deserted. Gun in hand, he sprinted along the thick carpet, past the numbered doors. He paused to eye the elevator. No. They wouldn't be that stupid, would they?

Satisfied that the area was clear, he completed the square and bounded back into the stairwell, taking the steps two at a time en route to the fifth floor. It was silent too. On the second leg of the square, a couple emerged from a room: a man in his sixties, a woman in her late twenties or early thirties. Tito slowed to a brisk walk, scrutinizing them out of the corner of his eye, shielding his gun behind a thigh.

Moving along the neat line of brass doorknobs, he wondered how hard it would be to break into a room. If Lewis and her bodyguards had somehow managed that . . . He cursed at the possibility. They could hide out indefinitely and nothing short of a room-to-room search would find them.

A room-to-room search of a five or six hundred room hotel . . . He swore again. Sonny would have a conniption fit. So would the organization. This was turning into a fiasco, he realized as he raced along the last leg of the square. Instead of a simple, straightforward job—staking out an apartment, pilfering a couple of bones—it had become a quagmire of problems and mistakes. He wondered when the series of unlucky mishaps would end, when this nightmarish job would be over. If they didn't finish it soon, if Lewis and her newfound friends somehow managed another escape . . . This would probably be their last organization assignment. He and Vince would be out of work. Worse, they might be six feet under. These people didn't issue pink slips. They issued contracts. They seldom forgave and they never forgot.

With that distressing thought racing through his mind, he hit the door and leapt up the steps, to sweep the sixth floor.

"SEVEN," PARISH ANNOUNCED, PANTING. HE PAUSED AND LOOKED TO Vaughn.

"Keep going," Vaughn replied. "One more."

Scuffing footsteps and labored breath accompanied them up the next flight of stairs. When they arrived at the eighth floor, Vaughn nodded. "This is probably high enough."

Parish checked the door. Gently tugging on the handle, he opened it a crack and peered through. "Looks okay," he whispered. The door creaked wider and he stuck his head through. After a side-to-side scan, he swung the door back. "Come on."

They followed him through, Jimmy pulling up the rear in his skintight, plum suit. At the corner of the floor, where two of the four hallways met, they paused.

"I don't see a phone," Melissa whispered.

"You two go that way," Vaughn told Parish and Jimmy. "Melissa and I will go back and try the other hall. First one to find a phone, call the cops. Tell them where we are and what's going on. We'll meet at the catty-corner in two minutes," he said, pointing again. "I think there's another stairway over there. That'll give us a way out—just in case."

"And if there isn't a phone?" Jimmy asked.

"We could always try knocking on doors," Melissa said. "Maybe somebody would let us use theirs. Or at least call the police for us."

"Maybe. Get going," Vaughn urged.

Parish and Jimmy marched off down the hall. Melissa looked at Vaughn, sighing heavily. He nodded back, agreeing with her unspoken assessment. They reached the end of the first hall and started up the second.

"Could be a phone up in that lounge area," Vaughn observed.

"I certainly hope so," Melissa said. Her shoulders slumped and suddenly she looked old and spent—more like a street person than a debutante: flat hair, shoeless, face weighed down by a mixture of fear and fatigue. "I haven't thanked you."

Vaughn's brow furrowed. "For what?"

"For saving my life. I'd be dead right now if it weren't for you and your two buddies."

"Yeah, well . . ."

"I'm serious. You're an answer to prayer. And I want to thank you."

Vaughn snorted at this. "Thank me if and when we get out of this alive." He slowed her with a hand and held a finger to his lips. Flattening himself against the wall, he approached the lounge cautiously, gun in hand. He hunched as he reached the opening to the room, swinging the small automatic through the air, warding off invisible foes.

"It's okay," he told her, rising. "There's your answer to prayer."

She followed his gaze past a couch, to a handsome end table. On it sat a phone. Melissa hurried over to it and lifted the receiver. Then she hesitated, depressing the button. "There's no dial. It's a house phone."

"So? Tell the operator it's an emergency and you need the police."

"But if the hotel people are in on this . . ."

"Yeah. You're right." He swung a fist in frustration.

"We could tell the operator there's a fire on the seventh floor," Melissa tried.

"No." He blew air at this suggestion. "That would be the same as opening a fire door. We'd get help. But probably not in time. No. We need something else."

"This would be a good time to be famous."

"Huh?"

"You know—a celebrity. If one of us was a movie star or something, we could have the entire Vegas PD down here in a flash. They cater to the stars."

Vaughn nodded, a faraway look in his eyes.

"What?" Melissa asked.

"Who's playing here?"

"What?"

"Who was on the marquee when we drove in here?"

Melissa thought about this. "Um . . . Whoopi Goldberg . . . Garth Brooks . . . Uh . . ."

"And if they're playing here—they're probably staying here."

"Probably."

Vaughn took the phone from her and toggled the button. "Hello . . . Yes . . . This is Garth Brooks," he said with a southern drawl. He paused to groan melodramatically. "I'm in the . . ." He looked at Melissa for an answer.

"Penthouse suite," she whispered.

"I'm in the penthouse suite." Another moan. "I think I'm . . . I think I'm havin' a heart attack." He dropped the phone, then hit the button, cutting off the call. He gave Melissa a victorious smile. "That ought to initiate some action."

"Now we just have to get to the penthouse."

Vaughn shrugged. "Another twelve or fourteen flights of stairs—and we'll be safe."

TITO BURST ONTO THE EIGHTH FLOOR AND NEARLY FELL ON HIS FACE. His shirt was dark with perspiration, his legs burning. He leaned against the wall and tried to catch his breath. Doing stairs and running square floor circuits like a madman was taking its toll. And he still had fifteen floors to go. He wondered how Vince was faring. Smoking and drinking had greatly reduced the guy's endurance and physical capacity. Vince was either conducting the search at a stroll or riding the elevator up. Possibly both.

He trotted right, shot a glance down the hall. Nothing. He trotted left, looked again, and was already moving for the stairs—choosing to let the extra hallways go uninspected—when something caught his eye. He stopped, took a deep breath, and squinted: hallway, doors, pictures on the walls, elevators, lounge area . . . people. He could see a man and a woman. The woman was wearing a glowing red gown. The man had on a white tux. It seemed a little early for such attire, but this was Vegas—land of round-the-clock casinos and twenty-four-hour wedding chapels.

Tito had already turned on his heels and was pushing open the door to the stairwell when he heard the voice.

"Anything?"

The reply was muffled. ". . . phone . . ."

His head swiveled back, his ears straining.

". . . you call?"

Two men appeared from the far corner of the floor and approached the couple. One was wearing an ill-fitting tux. The other was a bear of a man encased in a hideous purple jacket and matching slacks. From a distance, the latter looked like a grape Frankenstein.

". . . told them . . ."

Muted laughter.

"Garth Brooks?"

More laughter.

"So we . . . to the penthouse . . ."

Tito stared, contemplating the foursome. Could it be? No. Wrong clothes. And they weren't panicked. They were just standing there talking—laughing. But a woman and three men . . . And the woman . . . The hair was the right color, the right length. Tito squinted at them, unable to distinguish the details of their faces. No. It probably wasn't. Still, he had to be sure. And there was only one way to do that. Stuffing his gun back into his waistband, he wiped the sweat from his forehead and set off down the hall—toward the lounge.

THIRTY-SIX

"OH, THEY'LL COME ALL RIGHT," VAUGHN ASSURED THEM. "WE JUST need to—"

Melissa silenced him with an elbow to the ribs. "Someone's coming," she told him without moving her lips.

Parish and Jimmy glanced down the hall.

"Well?" Vaughn asked without looking. "Trouble?"

"It's hard to tell from here," Jimmy said, a false smile on his face as he snuck another glance. "It's not the guy who broke into Ms. Lewis's apartment."

"But he's about the size of the other one," Parish added. "Can't see a ponytail though."

"I'm not hanging around to check his hair," Melissa said.

"We'll all go that way," Vaughn said, pointing with his eyes to the near hallway. "We'll take those stairs." His eyes darted to the stairwell entrance.

"Okay." Parish nodded.

"If we get separated, we'll meet at the penthouse," Vaughn said. "Now, let's pretend like we're good friends just back from a party or something." He grinned and chuckled loudly, herding them toward the stairs. "And could you believe what Lillian was wearing?"

"You'd think at her age she would be a little more discreet," Melissa said, giggling.

"I noticed that Harry didn't mind," Parish said. "The wolf."

"At least the food was good," Jimmy tried.

They moved toward the stairs, generating loud, innocuous conversation. Twenty yards . . . Fifteen yards . . .

THE WOMAN'S BACK WAS TO HIM NOW. TITO STUDIED HER WALK, wondering if it was Lewis. Tough call. Vince would know. He was the resident connoisseur of the female gait.

Tito studied her movements, the dress. His eyes traced the shimmering fabric down to . . . bare feet? She wasn't wearing any shoes.

His gaze shot to the hulk in purple. There was a tear in the back of his jacket, right down the middle seam. It was too small—by several sizes. The shorter man's tux was baggy to the point of being clownish—a bona fide zoot suit.

Tito withdrew the .357.

HE'S GOT A GUN," MELISSA WHISPERED IN TERROR.

"Yeah. I know," Vaughn whispered back. "Keep going."

Ten yards . . . Eight yards . . . Seven yards . . . The door seemed to be caught in a space-time warp—retreating from them with every step.

"Ms. Lewis?" the man called.

Melissa tried to breathe, but couldn't.

"Go," Vaughn ordered.

Five yards . . . Three yards . . . The door was floating in limbo now, just beyond their reach.

"Ms. Lewis!"

"Run," Vaughn told them. He reached into the tux pocket.

"What are you going to—" Melissa started to ask.

"Run!"

Two yards . . .

"Stop!" the man demanded.

One yard . . .

"Run!" Vaughn shouted.

Parish hit the door hard. The metal core echoed a thud, the hinges groaning in protest as he forced it wide. Jimmy pushed Melissa through, guarding her body with his own.

There was a thunderclap, then a gust of wind: breath leaving collapsing lungs. Jimmy rolled into the stairwell, tumbled over Melissa and skidded across the tile, his head bobbing. Behind him the landing was smudged with a thick crimson film.

Vaughn spun and dropped to the floor, extending the gun and its last bullet toward the attacker.

The grape Frankenstein was down! Three to go!

Tito fired again, this time hitting the door. Paint and metal shot into the air as the bullet ricocheted into the stairwell. The door started to creak shut. He dashed toward it, the adrenaline pumping. He had them. He finally had Lewis.

A stride later, as his legs fought for momentum, he realized that the last man had paused. For some unknown reason, he wasn't following the others into the stairwell. In the time it took Tito to brace himself and react, the man dove, twisting in the air, rolling across the carpet. He had something in his hand.

Tito adjusted his aim and was in the process of tugging on the trigger when he felt it. There was no sound. Not even any pain. Just the sensation that something had reached up and bitten him in the arm. His .357 blew a hole in the roof. His vision blurred. He looked at his shoulder, puzzled at the sticky red substance that was oozing through the hole in his jacket. The hallway began to tilt one way, then the other.

Shoot him! his brain ordered. He raised the gun obediently. But the man was all over the place—bouncing, leaning . . . Tito fired. A shower of plaster erupted from the wall and a framed picture fell to the carpet. The man weaved toward the door. Tito shot at him again, shattering a light fixture. The hall flickered. He shot again. The carpet retracted, exposing a tile floor with a grapefruit-sized scar.

The hall became a tunnel, golden sparkles encroaching upon the edges, pushing away the walls. The tunnel narrowed. The man disappeared. Tito examined his wound. Blood was trailing down his elbow, staining the carpet. He heard the door to the stairs clunk shut.

Go after them! his brain demanded. He took one faltering step before crumpling to the carpet. His arms were limp, his legs nonexistent. The gun sat useless at his side. Above him the hall wavered and vanished in a blanket of stars.

Is he dead?"

Melissa felt for a pulse on Jimmy's ample neck. "No. But he will be soon if we don't do something."

Vaughn threw off his jacket and ripped at his shirt, sending buttons tinkling down the steps. Wadding it up, he pushed it between Jimmy's shoulder blades, into the gap that had once been his back.

"When that goon comes through the door, we're all dead," Parish observed. The gash on his head had been reopened and a thin vermilion snake was crawling down his cheekbone.

"I slowed him down," Vaughn said. The white dress shirt had disappeared, consumed by a crevasse of blood. Vaughn's arm was shiny red to the elbow.

"We've got to get help," Melissa said. "He's going to bleed out right here on the stairs."

"If our trick worked," Vaughn said, struggling to keep pressure on the wound, "there'll be a team of paramedics up at the penthouse in the next few minutes."

"And how are we supposed to get the Truck up a dozen more flights of stairs?" Parish wondered. "You wouldn't happen to have a forklift handy, would you?" He was leaning against the wall, blinking, dabbing at his forehead with his jacket sleeve.

Melissa closed her eyes and sighed, turning both palms up. "Father, we ask in Jesus' name that you would release your power to heal Jimmy." Then she gently placed one hand on Jimmy's head. Her mouth continued to move, but no words came out.

Vaughn watched her, curious, and despite his lack of faith—hopeful. Just about anything was worth a try at the moment. He shot a glance at Parish. Phil had his eyes shut, his head bowed reverently.

"Father, show us what to do," Melissa continued. "Show us how to get Jimmy to the help he so desperately needs."

Vaughn stared at the wall, listening to the shallow, congested breathing. Warm liquid continued to pulse past the drenched dress shirt, escaping around his tense fists. Melissa was right. Jimmy was dying. If there was a God, this was an opportune time for him to intervene.

It was at that moment that Vaughn realized what he was looking at. There was a gray metal door mounted into the wall of the stairwell behind Parish. No handle. No buttons. But he knew what it was.

"There's your answer to prayer," he said, nodding toward the door.

Parish turned around. "It's just the circuit breakers or something."

"Or something is more like it," Vaughn told him. "See if you can pry it open."

He and Melissa gripped the edges with their fingernails and yanked. The door didn't budge. Then Melissa noticed a six-by-six-inch plate on the adjacent wall. It had a silver clip. She pulled on it and was rewarded with a panel bearing three buttons. One was marked "open." Below it, the other two were marked with arrows—one pointed up, the other down. She pushed open. The gray door slid back mechanically, revealing a service elevator.

Melissa's head fell back. "Thank you, God," she told the ceiling.

"I'll second that," Parish agreed.

Vaughn judged the distance to the elevator. It had to be a good ten feet. "We can't lift him," he thought aloud. "We'll have to drag him." He looked up at Melissa. "Trade me places. Straddle Jimmy's waist and stick your hands in here. Phil and I can pull him and you into the elevator. That way we can maintain pressure on the wound."

"Okay." Melissa knelt down. "Ready?"

Vaughn waited until her hands were right above his. "On three. One . . . two . . . three . . ."

Blood spurted in the transfer, splattering the floor and wall as Melissa fought to plug the hole. It looked dull and brackish in comparison to the nearly fluorescent glow of her dress.

Parish staggered forward and took hold of Jimmy's arm. His face was pale, an unnaturally light shade of brown.

"You up to this, Phil?" Vaughn asked him.

Parish nodded, his eyes glassy. "I am if it's the only way to save Jimmy." He was already panting and they hadn't started yet.

"Here we go," Vaughn said, taking the other arm. "On three. One . . . two . . . three . . ." Jimmy lurched a foot, his head rattling against the floor of the landing. Vaughn readjusted his grip, cradling Jimmy's face in one hand. "Again. One . . . two . . . three . . ." The three hundred pounds of dead weight slid another six inches.

"Hang on," Parish puffed. "I'm lightheaded. Give me a minute."

WAKE UP!"

Tito heard the admonition but it was far away, beyond a bank of thick clouds.

"Wake up!" This time it was accompanied by a slap in the face.

Tito felt the sting on his cheek. He noticed that his arm was numb—throbbing.

"Come on, Tito!" the voice insisted.

He was being shaken by the shoulders, his head rolling on his neck. His eyes finally blinked open and he stared into the unshaven face of his partner.

Vince swore at him. "What happened?" He seemed more perturbed than concerned.

Tito sat up, wriggling away from Vince's grip. "I had them."

"And you let them get away?" Vince asked through wide eyes. "Why didn't you just shoot them?"

"I did. I hit one of the soldiers." He paused to clutch his shoulder. It was hurting now, fire shooting down past his wrist, all the way through his fingers. "They changed clothes."

"What?"

"They were in formal wear."

Vince snorted at this. "Formal wear. And how exactly did they get past you?"

"You see this?" he asked, pushing his shoulder toward Vince. He immediately regretted this, wincing in pain. "They shot me. With your gun!"

Vince told him where he could go.

"They couldn't have gotten far," Tito said. "I nailed the biggest one." He looked toward the lounge, down the hallway, then at the door to the stairs. He pointed at the door. "They went through there."

"Get up," Vince said, yanking him to his feet. "We're going after them." He picked up Tito's gun and thrust it at him. "Here. You'll need this."

VAUGHN LOOKED AT THE ELEVATOR IN DISMAY. DESPITE THEIR EFFORTS, it was still a good four feet away. Parish was tipsy, his wound oozing. The poor guy was probably on the verge of shock. Melissa was astride Jimmy, the lower third of her dress dark with blood, her arms and face covered with it as she kept her hands pressed into his back.

"Here we go . . ." he said with a sigh. He counted. They pulled. The Truck scooted another eight inches. He counted. They pulled. The

Truck scooted five inches. Count . . . Pull . . . seven inches. They ate away at the distance in tiny bites.

Parish braced himself against the wall, fighting for air.

"We can't stop, Phil," Vaughn prodded. More counting. More pulling. They closed in on the prize a half foot at a time until finally Jimmy's head reached the opening to the elevator.

"Okay, now . . ." Vaughn started to say. But his words died away as he heard the knob squeak. The door to the stairwell was opening.

Leaping over Jimmy and Melissa, he drove his shoulder into the door.

VINCE SHOUTED PROFANITY AFTER PROFANITY. THE KNOB HAD impacted his wrist, wrenching his arm to the shoulder before the door crashed into his head. He then flew backwards, tumbling against Tito, both of them rolling to the floor.

VAUGHN RACED BACK OVER AND TUGGED ON JIMMY WITH RENEWED energy. "Hurry!" But behind him, the door to the elevator hummed and slid closed. He stared in amazement.

"Push the button!" he ordered.

Parish banged on the open button. Nothing happened.

VINCE FIRED A SHOT THROUGH THE DOOR BEFORE HE EVEN GOT TO HIS feet. It was a warning . . . a promise of things to come. "You are dead meat!"

Tito righted himself and grabbed Vince by the arm. "Hold up. They've still got that 9mm."

"Big deal. I've got this," he patted his .44 affectionately. "And they can't have very many rounds left—if any."

"It only takes one," Tito said. "Listen, I'll stay here and watch the door. You take the other stairway." He pointed down the hall. "Go up a floor. Down to this stairway. And—"

"And blow their heads off," Vince said through clenched teeth. He started down the hall, massaging his wrist and cursing as he went.

---

*S*O MUCH FOR GOD," VAUGHN OBSERVED. THE ELEVATOR REFUSED TO open, despite Parish's insistent efforts.

Melissa looked at him, through him, looked down at Jimmy, at the blood . . . "Father . . ." She swallowed hard. "Father . . ."

"Help," Parish finished for her.

"Yeah," she panted. Her arms were shaking, causing the muscles of Jimmy's back to ripple.

Parish jabbed the open button with his thumb. "Come on!"

Suddenly the mechanism hummed again and the door slowly jerked back. Inside, a maid stood next to her cart. Her jaw dropped open as she saw them. She crossed herself and began chattering nervously in Spanish.

"Pull!" Vaughn insisted, ignoring her. He and Parish put their backs into the job, sliding Jimmy and Melissa into the elevator. His legs were still dangling in the stairwell when they heard a door creak open. It clicked shut, echoing through the stairwell.

The maid was close to tears now, talking rapidly in a high-pitched voice as she flattened herself against the back of the elevator.

There were footsteps in the stairwell: quick, light, approaching . . .

The maid screamed and darted out of the elevator. Suddenly there was an explosion of sound—a sonic boom that rocked the elevator. The maid fell back inside—hysterical.

"Let's go!" Vaughn said as he gathered Jimmy's legs.

Parish pushed the button. Nothing happened. The maid sobbed something and reached across him to press the "close door" knob.

VINCE REACHED THE LANDING BELOW THE NINTH FLOOR AND JUMPED the last half flight to the landing of the eighth. To his right a metal door was slipping shut. He turned and fired from the hip. The bullet blasted a softball-sized hole in the door.

"Up, please!" Vaughn said from the floor. He looked at the hole just inches above his head, then back at the shambles the bullet had made of the maid's cart. It had disintegrated her bottle of Lysol, raining plastic and cleaning solution on the occupants of the elevator. The woman would also need to obtain a new supply of bathroom condiments before she serviced her next room. The bin holding the miniature soaps and shampoos was torn in half, bars and bottles still tumbling to the floor.

Parish tried the up button again. The elevator lurched, then began its ascent.

Vince swore at it, emptying his cylinder into the closed door. Tito appeared from the hallway.

"Service elevator," Vince told him. "Going up."

Tito started up the stairs. He was nauseous now, and chilled. Goose bumps covered his arms.

"We can't lose them," Vince vowed, reloading as he climbed.

"We won't," Tito promised. He really didn't care about Lewis anymore, or the stupid bones, or Sonny, or the organization. Right now he just wanted to assume a horizontal position—to get patched up, go home, and stay in bed for a week.

They reached the ninth floor and Vince paused to peer through the door, into the hall.

"Don't bother," Tito told him, already breathing hard. "They're headed for the penthouse."

"How do you know?"

"I overheard them talking about it."

"Then what are we waiting for?" Vince took off, leaping up the stairs, two, even three at a time—gleeful at the prospect of visiting revenge on the targets.

Tito followed, weak-kneed, struggling to keep up, wishing the escapade would end.

Thirty-Seven

When the elevator opened at the penthouse level, the stairwell looked exactly like the eighth floor: linoleum, paneled walls, stairs, door.

Vaughn released Jimmy's feet. "Wait here."

The maid chirped something in Spanish, made several gestures with her hands, and disappeared down the steps.

Vaughn moved to the door and pulled it back an inch. There were people in the hallway. Men in suits huddled near a lounge. A woman talked into a cellular phone. And a medical team stood cross-armed next to their equipment. One of them was talking into a radio. The others looked bored.

Vaughn stepped through the door and signaled to one of the paramedics.

"I've got a gunshot victim in the service elevator!"

Without asking questions, the team sprang into action, two of them dashing towards Vaughn, the others taking up their heavy equipment boxes and following at a slower pace. Within seconds they had descended upon Jimmy, encircling him.

Melissa relinquished her position, backing away into the stairwell as the team took vitals, hooked up an IV, shouted instructions to each other, and worked frantically to save the patient's life. The medic with the radio was conversing with a helicopter pilot, coordinating an airlift that would transport the victim to the nearest trauma center. A female medic looked Parish over and began attending to his forehead.

"Maybe there is a God," Vaughn said, watching the flurry of activity.

Melissa opened her mouth to reply, to assure him that there was and that he was responsible for their survival thus far, when she noticed something over Vaughn's shoulder. Three men appeared in the penthouse hallway. The first was short, overweight, wearing a bad toupee, sucking a cigar. The other two towered over him, wide shoulders, nonexistent necks.

"Isn't that the guy we saw on the monitor?"

Vaughn glanced back at the cigar smoker. "Yeah. The guy who led the goons right to us." His head swiveled, surveying the rest of the hall. "And no police in sight."

"What should we do?" Melissa asked.

With great effort, the paramedics loaded Jimmy onto a stretcher and wheeled him onto the penthouse level, to a door that led to the roof. As they did a helicopter swooped down and landed delicately on a pad outside.

"See you guys at the hospital," Parish promised, smiling weakly as the medic pulled him past.

"Can we go too?" Vaughn asked.

The medic with the radio shook her head. "Chopper's full," she grunted, hurrying to catch up with the team.

They watched as Parish and Jimmy were loaded onto the helicopter and it floated skyward.

Mr. Cigar was still there, still conversing with the brutes. As he talked, he scanned the floor, narrow eyes darting back and forth. Suddenly they locked on the stairwell—on Vaughn and Melissa. He raised an arm, and the two men started in their direction.

"Time to go," Vaughn said. He let the door swing shut and took Melissa by the hand, nearly dragging her down the steps.

"Wish we could have gotten on that chopper," Melissa lamented, barely able to keep up.

"Yeah. Me too."

They ran down five flights before they heard distant voices.

Walk it off!" Vince demanded.

Tito wiped his lips on his sleeve. His mouth was dry, his throat burning with bile. Thankfully he hadn't thrown up on himself—just on the landing and wall of the thirteenth floor.

"Man, that stinks," Vince added, jerking him along.

Tito was shaky now, his vision strangely blurred. He didn't want to climb more steps. He didn't even want to stand up. He wanted to crawl into a hole somewhere and assume a fetal position.

"We're almost there," Vince lied. "You can make it."

OMEBODY'S COMING," MELISSA WHISPERED, FIGHTING FOR BREATH.

"Somebody's always coming,"Vaughn sighed, wiping the sweat from his eyes. He peered down the gap at the center of the stairs. The voices were accompanied by heavy steps and glimpses of hands gripping the rails. "Two somebodies." His head tilted back and he gazed skyward. More hands, the clatter of dress shoes descending. "Those two other somebodies are coming down."

Melissa snuck a look out the door, into the hall of the seventeenth floor. Three muscle-pigs in suits were striding along, tapping earpieces, mumbling into headsets. She closed the door carefully. "We're trapped."

Vaughn jabbed the button for the service elevator. It didn't light up. He tried the other buttons. "They've deactivated it."

"Any suggestions?"

"We have a gun but no bullets,"Vaughn reviewed. "We can't seem to contact the police. Those thugs are after us. And every goon in the hotel is joining in the chase." He shook his head. "I'd say it's time to give up—except that I firmly believe they plan to shoot us down in cold blood."

"There must be something we can do," Melissa said, trying to think.

The footsteps echoed, growing louder. They could hear breathing now, men laboring, in a hurry to finish a bothersome chore.

"Maybe if we gave them the bones," she tried.

He fingered the ends of them, still snug in his waistband. "They'll kill us anyway."

"You think so?"

"Yeah. I don't understand what's going on—the 'why' of it—but they're on a mission to eliminate everyone associated with the bones. Especially you."

Eight shoes slapping steps. Four pairs of lungs demanding more air.

"Give me the bones," Melissa said, hand extended.

"What for?"

"They want me. They want the bones. I'll give them what they want. You make a run for it."

Vaughn frowned at this. "Not a chance."

"You don't think you'd make it?"

"It's not an option. I'm not going to abandon you."

"But you don't even know me. Why should you—"

"It's a matter of principle. I'm not going anywhere without you."

Melissa's eyes met Vaughn's. She took hold of his hand, stroking it. "If I'm about to die, at least I get to go out with a man of integrity."

"Hey," he said, blushing, "I'm a marine. Semper Fi—always faithful. Besides, I may not know you, but I like you." He shrugged, then gave her hand a squeeze.

Soles hitting tile. Men panting. Arms bracing against rails three flights above. Hands pulling at rails two flights below.

"Captain, have you ever—"

"Call me Steve."

"Okay. Steve, have you ever heard the saying, 'The doors of Hell are locked from the inside'?"

He shook his head.

"How about the phrase: foxhole conversion?"

"Yeah."

"I think this might be a good time for you to get right with God, if you know what I mean."

"There they are!" someone shouted.

Feet moving frantically, death approaching.

Legs appeared on the landing below. Bodies. Arms. Guns. The two men from the apartment, from the Vette. The one Vaughn had shot was pale, his shoulder dark with blood. The other—the shorter, wiry man—was grinning, a cat delighted that he had finally cornered two special mice.

The two bodybuilders arrived, dancing down the steps toward them, guns raised.

"They're ours," the smiling man warned. He lifted a long-barreled revolver. "They're mine."

THIRTY-EIGHT

WHEN THE DOOR TO THE SEVENTEENTH FLOOR BURST OPEN, IT CAUGHT everyone by surprise. Six heads jerked toward it in unison, all curious, all startled at the rude intrusion. Four guns reached instinctively for the door, fingers anxious to send the unannounced visitor to an early grave. Three guns glared back at them. That it turned out to be three members of the hotel security team did not matter. Neither did the fact that no one fired and an unnecessary shoot-out was narrowly avoided. What mattered was the momentary diversion their arrival created.

IN THE FRACTION OF A SECOND IT TOOK VINCE TO REACT, TO AIM, visually identify the intruders, assess that they posed no threat, and return his attention to Lewis and her soldier friend, the advantage was lost. Even before his eyes reacquired the soldier, he detected something coming toward him, a large object hurtling through the air. In the absence of time, his gun was rendered as useless as a toy.

VAUGHN DIDN'T CONSIDER HIS COURSE OF ACTION. HE DIDN'T PLAN IT. He wasn't motivated by a surge of courage or chivalry. He didn't even think. It came naturally, the result of years of training and practice. The door opened, a sense of short-lived panic fell over the assailants, their faces registering shock, their eyes glittering with fear. And he did it. He sprang with the agility of a tiger, across the landing, down the steps, flying through space, directly at the chief adversary.

MELISSA MIMICKED HIM, ASSUMING A PARALLEL FLIGHT WITHOUT REGARD for safety or consequences. Without conscious thought. Her mind was blank. She uttered no prayer. She did not pause to call on God, his all-encompassing power, his legions of angels. She simply jumped, performing the acrobatic maneuver with the skill of a ballerina, the strength of a gymnast—all fueled by an overwhelming, desperate desire to live.

VINCE SAW MOVEMENT AND AN INSTANT LATER FELT THE IMPACT. A shoulder: muscle, cartilage, bone . . . rock hard. His head snapped back and he was suddenly airborne—moving backwards . . . down . . . falling . . . His arms flailed, fighting to maintain balance, to keep him from losing equilibrium. They worked in vain, like the wings of a lame bird. His body inverted: feet above, head below. He hit the landing hard, groaning as his neck stretched, bent, and threatened to break. Pain . . . Breath abandoning him . . . The metallic sound of his gun scraping across the tile, careening off the wall . . .

ITO WATCHED, HELPLESS, IMPOTENT. HE CRINGED AS HIS PARTNER LIFTED into the air and tumbled to the tile a dozen stairs below. Then a second shadow found him. He had time only to brace before being struck by a female missile. She was smaller, but in his condition her momentum was sufficient to knock him backwards, one knee loosening his two front teeth, the other connecting with his injured shoulder, propelling him into the wall. Overhead a fresh display of fireworks decorated the stairwell.

VAUGHN GRABBED THE DISCARDED GUN, TWISTED, AND KICKED MELISSA'S legs out from under her. She went down the next half flight of stairs on her stomach, like a human sled. The stairwell erupted in gunfire: sparks, bullets ricocheting, chips of paint lifting into the air . . .

Thrusting the revolver at the gunmen, Vaughn issued three rounds. The .44 kicked in his hands, a trio of deafening blasts. He leapt to the next landing, dodging Melissa's limp body.

Bullets answered back in crisp retort. Then someone screamed a curse. "You idiots! Don't shoot us!" It was the man he had cold-cocked.

Vaughn fired two more shots up the stairwell and was pleased to see the hit men diving for cover.

"Come on!" He pulled Melissa up and dragged her down the steps, through the door to the sixteenth floor. She was rubbing her chin. It was scuffed, bleeding.

"My jaw," she complained, working it back and forth.

"Run!"Vaughn ordered. They sprinted down the hallway, made the corner, and raced for the other stairwell. Suddenly the door popped open and two thick-headed men in suits looked through.

Vaughn shot and hit the door. The two men vanished behind it.

"We're still trapped," Melissa said. They were standing at the intersection of the two hallways, men in each stairwell ready to kill them.

"Got any other miracles up your sleeve?" Vaughn asked, his head swiveling from one door to the other.

"Dear God . . ." she started in a whimper. Her knees buckled, sending her to the floor where she began to cry. Too much stress and too many near-death experiences in too short a time span had finally taken their toll.

A chime sounded. Vaughn looked up and saw the elevator open across from the lounge area. It was empty.

"Thanks, God," he muttered, collecting Melissa. "Come on, here's that miracle."

They made it halfway to the elevator, halfway to freedom, before the stairwell door opened.

VINCE STARTED SHOOTING BEFORE HE SAW ANYTHING OR ANYONE. He just led with the barrel of Tito's .347 and pulled the trigger: once, twice, three times . . . He continued shooting until he was out of ammo. That was when he saw them. Two people flattened against the side of the hall, eyes closed against the flurry of lead. Lewis and the soldier. Lewis was crying. And she had good reason to.

He reloaded and moved in for the kill.

NO!" VAUGHN PUSHED MELISSA TOWARD THE WAITING ELEVATOR AND fired twice, missing the gunman both times, but winning his respect. The man disappeared around the corner of the hallway.

Melissa limped for the elevator and fell inside. Vaughn fired again and raced after her. He was ten yards away when the gunmen reappeared. Bullets whizzed by his head. Vaughn hit the floor and fired back. The door to the elevator started to close.

Melissa screamed. Rising to her knees, she shot a hand out, pushing the rubber bumpers back. The door opened. Then, almost immediately, it started to shut again.

Vaughn aimed at the man. The gun clicked. Empty. He scrambled to his feet and dove for the elevator.

VINCE DROPPED TO ONE KNEE, SET THE SIGHT, COMPENSATED FOR THE man's movement by leading him slightly—and pulled the trigger. It was Tito's gun, unfamiliar to him, not his usual tool. But his aim was true.

VAUGHN ROLLED INTO THE ELEVATOR AND GRUNTED AS HE COLLIDED with the wall. Melissa pressed the "close door" button. The doors responded, moving to meet each other in slow motion. Muffled footsteps filled the hallway. As the doors jerked shut, she caught a glimpse of an arm, a leg, and heard a curse.

"We made it," she announced, sinking back against Vaughn. Then she gasped. His left pant leg was wet . . . bloody. "You're hit!"

"Yeah, I know," he said. Lying face down, he blew air at the pain. "Hurts, too. I think I've had enough fun for one day."

"Me too." She ripped his pants and used the fabric as a makeshift tourniquet. "If only we could get out of here."

"Let's try the lobby."

"The lobby? But they'll be waiting for us down there."

"We'll outrun them," Vaughn joked.

"Uh-huh."

"It's noisy, busy—maybe we can slip out a back door."

"Inconspicuously, right?" she said, pressing "L." "Nobody will notice a woman in a red dress with no shoes, and a man with no shirt, wearing white tux pants that are torn to the knee—both covered in blood from administering emergency first aid to a gunshot victim. I'm sure they won't give us a second thought."

"Don't forget my broken nose," he said, rubbing it.

Melissa laughed—on the verge of tears again—and took his head in her arms.

"All we need is another miracle,"Vaughn submitted from her lap. "God's big, right? Powerful. He's got plenty of them to spare."

Melissa closed her eyes and let her head fall forward.

"What are you doing?"

"Praying for one," she replied wearily.

I'M NOT DOING A FLOOR-BY-FLOOR SWEEP AGAIN,"TITO SAID. HE AND Vince were riding the east elevator down.

Vince shrugged. "Let Ghiradelli's people do it." He cursed softly. "I need a drink. I need it bad."

"We should probably check in with Sonny,"Tito observed.

"Not yet. I say we do these people first."

"That's saying we can find them. And even then . . . Talk about pain in the neck.We've never had this much trouble fulfilling a contract.This is crazy. Ridiculous."

Vince helpfully finished the statement with a choice expletive.

"Exactly," Tito agreed. He fingered his wound, flinching as it throbbed in response. "At some point I need to see a doctor. I don't think the bullet is still in there. But it hurts like a son of a gun."

"Let me take a look."Vince ripped away at Tito's sleeve, exposing the injury. "Ah—just a scratch. Don't be a wimp."

Tito resisted the urge to clobber his partner.

WHY ARE WE STOPPING?"

Melissa shrugged. "I didn't do anything."

The light above the door stopped at nine, and the elevator chimed. Vaughn lifted the revolver, expecting shots to ring out. "Get down."

The compartment bounced gently and the doors parted. A middle-aged man and woman stood there, eyes wide as they stared at the contents of the elevator—at two partially clothed adults splayed on the floor, at the crust of blood covering their skin, at the huge gun aimed at them.

The man's mouth opened, as if he was about to speak, then he grabbed the woman with an arm and turned to usher her away.

"Hold it!"Vaughn ordered, extending the .44 magnum.

The man swallowed hard, color draining from his face.

"Miracle number seventy-seven," Vaughn told Melissa. He gestured to the couple with the barrel. "Get in."

"But . . . we . . . we . . ." the man stuttered, eyes glued to the revolver. "Get in!"

The woman nodded at him and stepped inside. The man followed. "We don't have much money," he protested, hands raised. "Just a few credit cards." He fished a wallet out and fumbled through it, tossing plastic rectangles at Vaughn. "That's it. That's all we have."

Vaughn shook his head. "We don't want your money."

The man glanced at his wife, panicked. "Please don't kill us. Please ..."

"Take off your clothes."

IF WE LOSE THEM . . ." TITO SIGHED, THEN SWALLOWED A HANDFUL OF aspirin, washing it down with Diet Coke. "I can't believe this is happening. Sonny will—"

"Get a grip," Vince said, frowning. "Forget Sonny. And don't worry. We'll get 'em." He gulped down his second shot of Scotch. "Sure, it's a little messier than usual. But some jobs are like that. Just the way life is. I remember back in Nam, we went out on this night mission one time. We'd been in that part of the DMZ dozens of times. Done the same out and back till we knew it cold. But this time, things really went bad."

As Vince continued his account, a story that Tito had heard numerous times and that seemed to grow with each retelling, Tito scanned the lobby and casino area for a glimpse of the targets. He wasn't a religious man, but if he had been, he would have been praying for them to surface, for them to give themselves up. Sonny was not easy to work for. He represented a group of people that expected excellence and punished mistakes. And so far, this job was one big mistake. Even if they flanged it up now, somehow managing to hit Lewis and the soldier, there were still the other two to worry about, the ones who had been airlifted to the hospital.

And the kid . . . Tito wondered if Sonny had forgotten about the kid in the photo—the one who was with Lewis when she found the infamous bones. What about him? Was someone else taking care of that?

And what about the bones? Why on earth did it matter if a schoolteacher lifted a few old bones from the desert? Why would that concern the organization? And why did everyone associated with the bones need to die?

Sonny seldom offered any answers on contract work. He didn't say why people needed to be eliminated. He just called with the basics: name, address, schedule. Occasionally he specified where the hit should take place, what type of weapon should be used. But usually that was left up to Tito and Vince. They did their job, delivered the stiff, and Sonny employed others to concern themselves with corpse disposal.

Sitting there on a stool, next to his partner in crime, Tito suddenly had the urge to shuck it all, to leave Vegas and never look back. He wondered if the organization would allow that. Probably not. People never really left. They just went on inactive duty—with the understanding that they would be called upon if and when their services were again needed.

Maybe after this particular job was over, they could take a vacation. Go somewhere quiet, warm, tropical . . . Someplace far away from Las Vegas.

The manager appeared at the bar, smiling. It was an expression that bordered on vehemence—as if he were a lizard that had just bitten off an insect's head. "We're sweeping the entire building," he told them. "Top to bottom."

"'Bout time," Vince grunted. He used a finger to get the bartender's attention and ordered another shot of whiskey.

"We'll either do them for you," he promised, "or flush them into your . . ." The manager paused, looking in the direction of the elevator. "What the—"

Tito follow his gaze. Next to the main elevator a guard was talking to two half-clothed people: a woman in a shimmery red dress, a man wearing only white pants. They were waving their arms frantically, telling the guard something.

"Got 'em," the manager announced proudly, starting in that direction.

Tito shook his head as he slid from the stool. Even from that distance, he was sure it wasn't them. The clothes were right, but . . . "No," he said. "Something's wrong."

The three of them moved toward the guard.

"And they took our clothes!" the shoeless woman was saying when they arrived. "Our clothes!"

"Didn't want my wallet, her purse, the credit cards, traveler's checks," the shirtless man complained. "Just our clothes. Made us undress—right there in the elevator. What kind of hotel is this?"

The manager nodded, his face full of understanding. "How terrible." He extended a hand. "I'm Rich DeNiro, the manager."

"Bill Jacobs," the man responded, frowning. "This is my wife, Evelyn."

"Which way did they—"Tito tried to ask. The manager cut him off.

"Mr. and Mrs. Jacobs," the manager said, adopting a fatherly tone, "first let me assure you that we will do everything within our power to see that the perpetrators are apprehended and your clothes are returned. I apologize for this travesty. We here at Titans pride ourselves on running a safe, crime-free hotel and casino. A robbery . . ." He shook his head at the idea with an expression of distaste. "Never before has something like this happened on the hotel grounds."

"That doesn't help us much," Mr. Jacobs grumbled.

"No, no it doesn't," the manager agreed. "Perhaps making your stay here at Caesar's complementary—on the house—will help make up for the inconvenience."

Mr. Jacobs's lips rose, the frown inverting.

"Carl here," the manager said, patting the guard's shoulder, "will take you to our designer boutique and see that you are fitted with new clothing—at no charge, of course."

Mrs. Jacobs was grinning now.

"Where did they go—the people who robbed you?" Tito asked.

The Jacobs pointed across the casino. "They rode down with us," Mr. Jacobs explained, "and when the doors opened, they went that way."

Vince cursed loudly and sprinted off, pushing his way through knots of gamblers.

"The front door?" Tito wondered aloud, hurrying to keep up. "They waltzed right past us and walked out the front door? I can't believe it!"

Thirty-Nine

I CAN'T BELIEVE IT. I CAN'T BELIEVE WE WALKED RIGHT OUT THE FRONT door."

"Me either."

"And in these," Melissa added, waving a hand at her Hawaiian-style dress and sandals and Vaughn's new Panama hat, flowered sports shirt, khaki pants, and dress shoes.

"Just a couple of tourists out on the town," he said. He paused to squeeze his thigh, wishing away the pain that was shooting up from his wounded calf, then surveyed the long drive-through outside the hotel. "Now if we just had a car."

"Wonder what happened to yours," Melissa said. The space where they had parked was occupied by a white Lexus.

"Probably impounded," Vaughn said. They watched as a man accepted the keys to the Lexus, tipped the valet, and got in.

"They'll be coming after us. We have to get away from the hotel."

"Yeah, I know," he sighed.

"What about a cab?"

"No money. Should have kept that guy's wallet."

"We could hail a taxi and then stiff the driver, I guess," Melissa suggested.

Vaughn shook his head, then looked over his shoulder at the entrance to the hotel.

"Then what are we going to do?"

A handsome man with a full head of dark, curly hair emerged from the hotel and handed the valet a receipt stub. The valet, a kid in his late teens, ran toward the parking lot to fetch the vehicle.

"What are we going to do?" Melissa repeated.

"Steal a car."

"What? Steve, you can't—"

"Come on." Vaughn limped to the man in the suit. "Sir, do you happen to have change for a hundred?"

The man turned, inspected Vaughn and Melissa for a moment, then shrugged. Pulling his wallet out of a breast pocket, he checked the contents, and slipped out five bills. "Twenties okay?" When he looked up, he was staring down the barrel of a monstrous gun.

"What the . . ." The man glanced around, clearly amazed that he was being robbed in broad daylight, in a public place.

"We need to borrow your car."

The man's mouth fell open and he started to object. But just then the valet rolled up in a glossy black Lamborghini. The kid hopped out, smiling—until he saw the gun.

"Keys," Vaughn said.

The teen tossed them to him. They were still in the air when Vaughn pulled on the passenger's side door handle. The Lamborghini's alarm sounded, a deafening combination of horns and sirens accompanied by blinking headlights.

THEY WERE COMING THROUGH THE ENTRANCE WHEN THE ALARM went off.

"That's them!" Tito said. He directed Vince's attention to a couple in the driveway.

"The tourists?"

"Yeah."

"You sure?" Vince didn't sound convinced. But he raised his gun anyway.

WHEN THE SHOOTING STARTED, THE OWNER OF THE LAMBORGHINI AND the valet flattened themselves on the sidewalk, as did everyone within a hundred yards.

"Get in!" Vaughn shouted. He lifted the T-top and slid into the passenger's side. Melissa fell into the driver's seat, flinching as bullets ate away at the paint, upholstery, and windows. Vaughn inserted the key for her, and summoned the engine to life. The alarm stopped and after a brief struggle with the stick shift, Melissa pushed the pedal to the floor and the car screeched away in a cloud of burning rubber.

VINCE FIRED, SWORE, FIRED AGAIN, SWORE AGAIN.

"Get the car!" Vince shouted at the valet. The kid was shaking, face down on the concrete. "Don't kill me! Don't kill me!" he pled.

Tito grabbed the keys from the valet board and started for the lot, moving as fast as his injured body would allow. The pain was fading, but he was still lightheaded, weak from losing blood. His legs felt like overcooked spaghetti. Maintaining his balance as he ran was a trick. When he finally reached the car, Vince was waiting at the passenger's door.

"Hurry up!" he said. "They're getting away."

"No kidding," Tito muttered. They climbed in and he twisted the key. The 450 overdrive purred, then growled as Tito fondled the stick and pressed down on the accelerator. The Vette skidded out of the lot.

"Think you can catch a Lamborghini?" Vince asked, reloading his weapon.

"We'll catch them," Tito promised, gripping the wheel. "We'll catch them."

SEE ANYTHING?"

Vaughn looked back, out the rear window. A bullet had turned the small glass panel into a network of ragged splits. "It's hard to tell."

"Maybe we lost them."

"I don't know," Vaughn sighed, rubbing his leg. "Somehow, I doubt it."

Melissa ran a red light and waved her apologies to a truck driver that had to sheer down on his brakes to avoid sideswiping them. "Sorry."

The light at the next intersection was red too, but Melissa didn't bother to slow down. Horns blared and brakes locked as they shot through traffic.

"Who taught you how to drive?" Vaughn asked, hurriedly fastening his seat belt as they rocketed towards another intersection.

"You want those creeps to catch us?"

"No. But . . ." He gripped the armrest with both hands as Melissa pulled into oncoming traffic in order to pass a slow-moving compact.

"Where should we go?" she asked.

"I don't know."

"The police?"

"I . . . I don't . . ."Vaughn paused, then shook his finger at her. "Go right."

The Lamborghini went into a slide, the rear end nearly beating the front around the corner.

"We'll head for—"

"Uh-oh," Melissa interrupted. She was staring into the side mirror.

"What?"

"They're back."

Vaughn checked the mirror on his side. "Where? I don't see them."

"Right lane," Melissa reported. "About four cars back."

He checked again, then cursed as the red Vette tore around a slow-moving Toyota.

"What now?"

Vaughn shrugged. "Too bad Phil's not here."

"Why's that?" She watched as the Vette leapt in front of a pickup, leapfrogging its way toward them.

"He's a maniac behind the wheel. A regular Mr. Toad. He could lose them, I bet."

"A maniac, huh?" Melissa shifted, stomping on the pedal. The Lamborghini lurched forward, tossing them against the seats. They zipped around, past, between other cars. Melissa slammed on the brakes to keep from rear-ending a bus, shifted, and sped back to light speed. Behind them a Bronco sought solace in a ditch. "This thing's got power," she observed casually.

"And speed," Vaughn said between deep breaths. According to the speedometer, they were doing almost ninety.

———————

They want to play," Tito said, accelerating to keep the black sports car in sight.

"I'm tired of playing," Vince grumbled. "Get us close. I'll end the game."

Tito nodded. He twisted the wheel and the Vette shot to the right, moving by cars as if they were parked. They bounced along the rough, uneven shoulder, the needle on the accelerator climbing.

They're coming!"

Melissa glanced into the side mirror. There was a blur of red and suddenly the Vette was right beside them. She shifted into overdrive and accelerated to over a hundred. The Vette stayed with them, gliding along as if it had yet to tax its engine.

Melissa saw the gun and screamed, "Down!"

Vaughn hunkered in the seat as a shot rang out. The bullet glanced off the fender and made a spiderlike crack in the windshield.

Hold it still!" Vince ordered.

"I'm trying!" Tito eyed the speeding Lamborghini, then returned his gaze to the shoulder. "Oh, geez!" He swore as a delivery truck pulled into their path to make a right turn. Swerving wildly, the Vette did a 180, missed the truck, but went skidding through a four-way stop—backwards. It was only after careening off a minivan that they completed the 360 and Tito regained control.

"That was . . . interesting," he said, wiping at the beads of sweat that dotted his brow.

"Get me a shot!" Vince demanded, unfazed by the acrobatic maneuver.

I think we lost them," Vaughn announced. "Maybe you should slow down." He braced himself against the dash as the car jerked around a cement mixer.

"I'll slow down when we're safe. Which way?"

"Uh . . . take another right."

Melissa downshifted and they fishtailed wildly around the corner. The tires jumped the curb and squealed, fighting for traction. She twisted the wheel, nearly taking out a road sign. The metal post scraped the left side and back end, peeling up a channel of shiny, black paint.

"Oops."

"And I thought Phil was a maniac!" Vaughn said. "In case you haven't noticed, we're on the sidewalk."

The Lamborghini swooped by a bus stop, sending a half-dozen people into a panic. The waiting transit riders dove behind the benches, as if plywood could somehow save them from two thousand pounds of out-of-control steel.

At the end of the block, the car jumped off the curb. Back on the pavement, Melissa eased up on the pedal. She examined both mirrors. "Did we lose them?"

"I certainly hope so."

I DON'T SEE THEM!"

Tito shook his head. "Neither do I."

The Vette rumbled down the sunny boulevard, weaving recklessly through traffic. Tito slowed as they approached an intersection—not to prevent an accident, but to decide which way to go.

"We lost them," he sighed, making a normal left turn.

"Over there!" Vince pointed right.

Tito hit the gas and the Vette's tail swung wide. The car bounced over an island, the oil pan groaning as it bottomed out. "Where?"

"They turned at that next corner."

"Okay." Tito sped up in pursuit. Without warning he made a hard right, into an alley. Behind them a Honda slid helplessly into a fire hydrant. The Vette roared throatily down the narrow back street, skinning dumpsters and causing overstuffed plastic trash sacks to take flight.

"There."

Vince smiled. "Get me a shot and we can go home."

HELP!"

"What is it?" Vaughn twisted in the seat. "Oh, man . . ." Behind them, the red shark darted from an alley and took up chase.

Melissa pushed the Lamborghini, shifting into overdrive.

FASTER!" VINCE SHOUTED.

Tito shifted and the Vette leapt forward, closing on the Italian sports car. "You got a shot yet?"

"Almost. Get us a little closer."

The engine was howling now, rapidly approaching its limit.

"We can't outrun them," Melissa said, watching for traffic. Thankfully the street was nearly deserted. At the speed they were doing, any wreck would be fatal to all the parties involved.

"That's okay. We're almost there."

"Almost where?"

Vaughn pointed through the windshield and opened his mouth to explain. Suddenly the cherry red shark appeared at their side.

"Hit the brakes!" he yelled.

VINCE FIRED, STRIKING THE HOOD. THE BULLET PENETRATED THE STEEL and sent up a plume of steam. By the time his finger toggled the trigger again, the Lamborghini had performed an abrupt but convincing disappearing act. He swore as his shot hit a parked car, flattening the tire.

The black car was already a small dot in Tito's rearview mirror when he pressed on the brake pedal. They skidded for an eighth of a mile before coming to a halt. He shifted into reverse and the tires spun.

THERE IT IS!" VAUGHN SAID WHEN THE LAMBORGHINI HAD LURCHED TO a stop. He pointed at a gate two blocks away. "Go!"

Melissa shifted and the transmission hummed obediently. "Here they come."

The Vette was racing backwards, doing at least eighty—right towards them.

"Steve . . ." Melissa said uneasily.

"Keep going."

NOTHING LIKE A GAME OF CHICKEN," VINCE SMIRKED.

"It's not your car!" Tito objected. He accelerated, still backwards, aiming right for the Lamborghini.

STEVE . . . !" SHE URGED, WATCHING THE VETTE COME AT THEM.

"Keep going!"

The Vette was a hundred yards from them, fifty yards, twenty five . . .

FASTER!" VINCE INSISTED.

"You in a hurry to die?"

STEVE!" MELISSA CLOSED HER EYES, CONVINCED THEY WERE ABOUT TO die. Vaughn reached across and twisted the wheel. The Lamborghini swerved, nearly flipping over. It skidded sideways, around the Vette, then returned to its original course. A sign flew past: Nellis Air Force Base— reduce speed to ten miles per hour. Seconds later they crashed through the arm of a security gate.

A head popped out of the MP booth. Melissa saw a uniformed man waving at them in the rearview mirror. Two other uniforms took up chase in a jeep.

"You can slow down now," Vaughn told her. "We're safe."

TITO SHOOK HIS HEAD AT THEIR LUCK. IT WAS UNBELIEVABLE. SIMPLY UNBE-lievable. "What are these people? Superheroes? They're indestructible!"

Vince was muttering curses, squeezing his revolver until his hand turned white.

"We can't go in after them," Tito said. "Not on a base."

"Now it's time to worry about Sonny," Vince grumbled.

They stared at the gate in silence, watching as the Lamborghini dis-appeared around a bend in the road.

"He'll kill us," Vince finally whispered. "He'll hunt us down and—"

"Maybe not."

Vince looked at him. "Huh?"

"I have an idea."

"Let's hear it."

Tito sighed and put the Vette in park. "It's complicated. And it's a long shot. But it just might clear up this mess—and save our rear ends in the process."

FORTY

GRAND THEFT AUTO . . . POSSESSION OF AN UNLICENSED FIREARM . . . possession of an illegal firearm . . . AWOL . . . failure to yield at the base gate . . . reckless driving . . ." The major's voice trailed off and she shook her head at the clipboard.

"And out of uniform," Captain Renfro submitted helpfully.

Major Wallace swore at the list of infractions, then turned the page, scanning the form. Her eyes grew wide and she leaned in for a closer look. "Hit men?"

"Yes, ma'am," the captain nodded. "That's the story at least."

"Hit men . . ." Wallace muttered. She flipped through the report. "Unauthorized visits to the zone . . . car chases . . . shoot-outs with hit men . . . Been a busy week?"

Vaughn frowned up at her.

"Getting to know our MPs pretty well, too—eh, marine?"

He sighed at this.

Wallace set the clipboard down and glared at him. "You look like warmed over death, Captain."

"I feel like it," Vaughn replied. His nose was throbbing, swelling beneath the tape the nurse had applied. His leg was numb, a combination of bandages and painkillers. The latter were making him sleepy, his head heavy and thick. Having his arms bound behind him by handcuffs gave him the curious sensation of falling forward, toward the table. The interrogation room seemed to be retreating, the walls floating backwards.

"What time is it?" he asked. The episode with the MPs, being shackled and carted off to the infirmary, examined by a doctor, then transported to the brig . . . It all ran together. The drugs only added to the confusion.

The major glanced at her watch. Next to her Captain Renfro did the same. Agent Fuller from the Federal Bureau of Investigations didn't bother. From his seat at the end of the table, he enjoyed a view of all the participants, as well as the door and the clock directly above Vaughn's head.

On the table sat the infamous bones.

When his question went unanswered, Vaughn asked, "Where's Melissa?" He glanced at Wallace, then Fuller, back to Wallace.

Fuller shrugged. "Tell him." His long, thin legs were propped up on the table, arms crossed over his chest. Two gray-blue eyes looking dispassionately out from above his sharp nose. The stork seemed detached, indifferent.

"Ms. Lewis is being questioned," Wallace answered. She had been to the stylist since Vaughn's last encounter with her and the short, cropped cut made her seem even more masculine.

"I want to see her."

"Out of the question," Renfro said. He was a small man with dull, brown hair, tiny hands, and thin lips. His mannerisms made Vaughn wonder if Renfro had somehow sapped the major's femininity and injected it into himself.

"Maybe later," Fuller grunted.

"Am I under arrest?"

Wallace laughed, her eyes lighting up. "You better believe it." She seemed delighted with the prospect of holding a marine in her brig. "There's enough here"—she grinned, tapping the clipboard—"for a court-martial . . . and then some."

"Add a half dozen or so federal charges," Fuller threw in, "obstruction of justice, withholding evidence, interfering with a federal investigation . . . and you're looking at a few decades in prison."

The room was spinning now. Vaughn wished the meds would knock him out completely—and somehow wipe away this terrible nightmare.

"Unless . . ." Fuller baited.

"Unless what?"

"Unless you cooperate with us."

"But I am cooperating."

Fuller shook his gangly legs from the table and stood, his angular frame towering over Vaughn. "We need some answers, Captain."

"Why didn't you report for duty today?" Renfro wanted to know. "Where did you get the graphite gun? Why did you steal the car?"

"We've already been over that," Vaughn answered.

"We're going to go over it again," Fuller insisted. "And again, and again, until you tell us the truth."

Wallace fished a miniature tape recorder out of her pocket, activated it with the punch of a button, and placed it on the table. "Start at the beginning and tell us everything."

KIDNAPPING?"

"It's the only logical solution to the problem."

"But you said the problem was already taken care of."

"The situation has changed."

"Changed? You call losing the key target change? You call a shoot-out in a major hotel and a car chase through the streets of Las Vegas change? I'd say the whole sordid business has gone unequivocally down the toilet." DiCaprio paused to swear, then regretted his outburst. A narrow ring of fire stabbed at his gut, bile surging through an expanding perforation in the lining of his stomach. He pressed against the lower left quadrant of his abdomen with four rigid fingers, squinting at the pain.

"It's not a problem," the caller promised. "I just wanted to update you."

DiCaprio ignored this. He checked his watch. The meeting with the subcommittee on the Yucca Mountain project was only an hour away. He needed to leave now if he expected to get there on time. And he couldn't afford to show up late to a Sunday gathering, an "emergency" session that had been called specifically in order for him to present his case before tomorrow's vote. The outcome was already hanging in the balance, and tardiness would only serve to help the miserly congressmen nail the coffin shut on the project.

"Can't you just drop it?" he asked in exasperation. "Let the whole thing go."

"Let it go?"

"You've already killed how many people? Two?"

"Three."

DiCaprio cursed the number. "And now you've got your bone-breakers chasing marines? I've seen some idiotic things before, but this . . . It has to stop. You're digging the hole deeper and deeper."

"May I remind you, Robert, that you are up to your neck in this hole, shovel in hand. We fail, it goes public, you lose—big time. If anyone should be cheering our side on, it's you. You stand to lose the most."

"But I didn't do any—"

"Don't even start with that. Do you really think the ethics committee will care whether or not you knew the specifics of what we intended to do in 217? They find out you gave blind approval and you're out on your ear. And the FBI won't give a hoot that you didn't actually run Weber off the road, that you weren't in Boulder when Kendrick's car was sabotaged. You'll still be an accessory in the murders."

DiCaprio's ulcer was frantic, angry, shouting at him from its hiding place within his belly.

"Think about it, Robert. A grand jury indictment, forced to step down from your office, humiliated, disgraced, led away to prison in front of the gawking eyes of the press . . . And in the joint . . . Our people are there. They know what to do with back stabbers."

DiCaprio tried to swallow, but couldn't. There was a tap at the door and his secretary stuck her head in. "You asked me to remind you when it was time to leave for your meeting, sir," she said in a whisper.

He nodded, then watched her face disappear, the door closing again. "I . . . I don't know . . . I . . ." Rising, he took the jacket from the back of his chair and slipped it on.

"What's it going to be, Robert? Are you with us, or not?"

"I'm . . ." He closed his eyes. "I'm with you." Rubbing his belly he asked, "But kidnapping . . . is that really necessary?"

"Yes. It is. It's the solution to our problem. After that, 217 will be what it was intended to be: a secret. Eventually we'll want to move the bodies. Hopefully to Yucca Mountain. But as long as you keep that quad cordoned off, there shouldn't be any further trouble."

DiCaprio sighed into the receiver, then picked up the Yucca Mountain files. "Do it. Do whatever you need to. Just finish it." He hung up the phone and started out of the office. His secretary said something as he passed by, but he was oblivious, his mind engaged with a question. Which was worse, he asked himself: doing a song and dance to finagle money from parsimonious, selfishly ambitious congresspeople? Or bowing like an obsequious coward, attending to every whim of the organization? Both activities were humiliating, both chipped away at his pride and self-confidence. But at least the former was challenging, a frustrating, but often stimulating battle composed of small victories and small defeats. The latter ... It had nothing to do with war, everything to do with slavery. It was a wholly dysfunctional relationship that would never come to an end. The organization would be pulling the strings like a sadistic puppeteer until the marionette was in the grave.

Something had to be done. He had to break free. As he pressed the elevator button, he experienced an epiphany.

What if exposure isn't tantamount to death, he wondered. *What if it represents my only hope of liberation?*

THIS IS IT."

"Nice."

"Yeah. I could handle living in this neighborhood. Palm trees ... yards the size of football fields ... swimming pools ... a Beemer in every garage."

"And a Mercedes. And a Lexus."

Tito gazed enviously at the house they had come to visit. "This place has more square feet than a shopping mall."

"And better security," Vince said, nodding toward the tall, wrought-iron fence. Two closed-circuit cameras were perched above the gate. "Bet every home in this area has a system: motion sensors, cameras, maybe even heat detectors."

"Dogs too," Tito agreed. "Hungry dobies, or rottweilers, just waiting for some dope to hop the fence and make a run at the house."

Vince loaded his new 9mm and attached the silencer. "I've got something for them to snack on."

"With a little work, we can beat the cameras," Tito observed, loading his own Beretta. "But what about the sensors? They may even have lasers."

"Beams are overrated," Vince muttered.

"Maybe so, but we can't get past them. Not during the day. At night maybe, but—"

"There." Vince pointed up the street. "See that little box?"

"The phone cables? So?"

"So we overload the circuit."

"And that takes care of the phones. But what about the security systems?"

Vince sighed, frowning at him. "If we overload the phone cables with a big enough jolt, it'll surge to the electrical wiring—like a bolt of lightning. Zap! Take out the whole system. While it reboots and goes to backups, we rush the place."

"Good idea. But where are we gonna get that kind of juice?"

"We're sitting on it." Vince patted the dashboard. "You have jumper cables, don't you?"

Tito nodded, once again amazed at how adept Vince was at this. Despite his seemingly low IQ, the man had the uncanny ability to problem solve his way into and through any situation that involved guns and locked doors. If they were ever caught and thrown into prison—which Tito figured would happen sooner or later—Vince would find a way out and disappear like Houdini, probably robbing the guards in the process.

"Pull up and let's put the system down," Vince said.

Tito started the car and reached for the gear shift. As he did, an old brown Volvo appeared from around the corner and raced up the street toward them. It slowed in front of the house. The door popped open and a teenage boy jumped out. He waved as the Volvo rolled away, then turned to face the gate.

"That's him," Vince said. He waved the photo at Tito.

"You sure?" Tito examined the picture. Same hair color and style. Same build. And the kid was about to go inside the grounds—to his afternoon job as a groundskeeper.

"Must be running late today." Vince stuck the gun in his pocket and got out.

"What about the cameras?" Tito asked, climbing out.

"We'll have to get the kid to come to us."

They walked across the street and along the fence, stopping twenty feet from the gate. Suddenly Vince fell to the ground and began writhing with convulsions.

Tito stared at him for an instant, slow to play along. Then it clicked. "Oh, my gosh! He's having another seizure."

The kid was looking at them, curious, startled, his hand on the keypad lock.

Vince was groaning, limbs flailing wildly.

"Help! Help me! I've got to get him to the car! He needs his insulin!"

The kid hesitated, unsure what to do.

"Help! He'll die if he doesn't get his insulin."

The kid looked up and down the street, thought about it, looked back at the house, considered acting, then started toward them. The first few steps were halting, uncertain. The next were quicker. Finally the kid ran, a concerned Samaritan hurrying to their aid.

"Help me get him to the car!" Tito pled.

Vince shook violently, an epileptic on the brink of death—until the boy bent over him. Two arms shot out, taking hold of the kid's legs. Tito slipped one hand over the boy's mouth and used the other to immobilize his right arm. This left the boy's left arm free. The wide eyes grew wider, his face twisting into an expression of panic. He tried to scream, but the sound never made it past Tito's hand. Then he swung his free hand, striking Tito on the shoulder—his wounded shoulder. It was a glancing blow, but it brought tears to Tito's eyes, the boy's knuckles pulling at the makeshift stitches, unleashing waves of pain.

Tito responded with an elbow that emptied the boy's lungs of air. The kid bent over, gasping, coughing.

Vince held him under his arm, like a sack of cement, and sprinted for the car. Tito followed him, grabbing at his shoulder. The sleeve of his shirt was wet with blood, the gash reopened. He blinked at the stars that were threatening to crowd out the palatial homes, the palms, the street, the car.

Vince tossed the boy into the cramped back seat as Tito twisted the key in the ignition. The engine rumbled to life, and seconds later, the Vette lurched away from the curb, wheels spinning.

Tito looked into the rearview mirror. The street behind them was empty. No one in pursuit. A clean getaway. Then he pulled the mirror down and examined their bounty. The boy's face was beet red, his lungs still fighting for oxygen. He gagged but nothing came up.

"If you're going to throw up," Tito said, "don't do it on the upholstery."

"And don't hit me with it," Vince warned. "Aim out the window."

"What's your name?" Tito asked, watching him in the mirror.

The boy retched.

Vince held up the photo, studied it, then showed it to the kid. "That's you, ain't it?"

The prisoner squinted at the picture, panting. He fought off another retch before nodding.

Tito reached for the phone and tapped the speed dial button. "Sonny?"

"Yeah."

"Tito."

"Well?"

"We got him. And we're headed north."

Forty-One

Let's go over it from the top."

"I already told you everything."

"Tell us again."

Melissa's head drooped toward the table, her shoulders slumped. "I don't know what you want to hear."

"How about if we start with what you were doing in a restricted area," Captain Crispin suggested. He started the tape recorder that was sitting at the center of the table. "Why were you in a restricted zone, Ms. Lewis?" Crispin was in his early fifties, but looked younger. It was clear to even the casual observer that the man stayed in shape, and that weightlifting was a major part of his regimen. His chest pushed at his shirt, straining the buttons, and his neck looked pinched inside the starched collar. Only his silver crew cut betrayed his age.

"Ms. Lewis," Crispin prodded, jaw clenched. "This can go two ways: easy or hard. You can help us sort this out. Or you can spend time in our brig." He glared at her with steely blue eyes. "It's up to you."

Melissa looked toward the phone on the other end of the table. "I think I should call a lawyer."

Crispin cursed and shot out of his chair. He slapped the wall, swore again, then began pacing the interrogation room. His taut, leathery face was flushed, drawn into an expression of utter frustration.

"I'm serious about the brig, Ms. Lewis. Either talk to us or I'll make sure that you never—"

Agent Morris warned Crispin off with his eyes. Seated on Melissa's side of the table, he was playing the role of passive observer and had yet to ask a question or make a comment.

"Tell us what happened, Ms. Lewis," Crispin tried again, this time in a voice that bordered on civility.

"We've been over it three times now," Melissa sighed. "I don't see why—"

"Humor us," Crispin said. "We're slow learners."

"I need to call a lawyer." Melissa reached for the phone. She had no idea who to call, but had to do something.

Crispin shook his head, snapped off the recorder, and started pacing again: a big cat stalking back and forth in a small cage.

Morris shifted in his chair. "Ms. Lewis," he said in a fatherly tone. "You have the right to call an attorney. But in truth, I don't think that's necessary. We just need some information. Answer a few questions, and you can be on your way."

"Am I under arrest?" she asked, receiver in hand.

"No, ma'am. Not formally."

"Not yet," Crispin threw in.

"Am I charged with anything?"

"Not technically. But you witnessed and apparently participated in several events that may be connected with an ongoing federal investigation. As such, you are a valuable resource. We need your help, Ms. Lewis."

She looked at him suspiciously. The guy talked a good line, but his eyes, the pudgy face, and that oily hair . . . He looked more like a seedy insurance agent than a G-man. She begrudgingly replaced the receiver.

Crispin activated the tape recorder.

Morris paged through the report. "It says here that you were in the zone, Ms. Lewis." He followed a line with his finger. "On Friday. Is that right?"

"Yes."

"And why were you there?"

"It was a field trip. We were looking for fossils."

"Okay." He flipped pages. "What about Boulder?"

"What about it?"

"Why did you fly out there on . . . Saturday?"

She rubbed her eyes. "To visit an old friend."

"Nigel Kendrick?"

Melissa nodded. "I sent some bones to him. He's a paleontologist." She swallowed hard. *"Was* a paleontologist. And I . . ." Her voice trailed off as she fought off a wave of tears. She was exhausted, still shaky from a morning spent dodging bullets and running for her life—in no condition to face the recurring reality that she would never again see Nigel.

She desperately wanted to crawl into a cocoon and sleep away the events of the past seventy-two hours.

Closing her eyes, she recited a silent prayer to the Being that had walked her through the ordeal and would, she dared to believe, give her the courage and faith to endure to the end—whatever that turned out to be.

"Ms. Lewis!" Crispin said. He swore and turned the recorder off again. "You may not be under formal arrest yet, but if you don't start talking, I'll be forced to put you up on charges: conspiracy to commit grand theft auto, entering a military installation without proper authorization, trespassing on a government reserve, excavating without a permit—"

"That's enough," Morris growled.

Crispin told him where to go. "You're here as an observer. I'm in charge of this interrogation. This is my case."

"That's open to debate."

"Debate, my eye," Crispin retorted, glaring.

"I should call a lawyer," Melissa sighed.

"Trespassing on federal property is the Bureau's jurisdiction all the way," Morris explained calmly.

"Anything that happens on the NTS or this base falls under the military's jurisdiction," Crispin argued, the veins in his neck swelling.

"Relax, Captain," a voice warned. It was Major Wallace. She closed the door and sank into a chair.

Crispin bristled at this. "I have no intention of letting a Fibby—"

"I said relax," Wallace repeated. She opened a file folder.

"But—" Crispin tried to object.

"That's an order, Captain," Wallace said without looking up.

"And since you're taking orders," Morris said, "I'd like some coffee. How about you, Ms. Lewis?"

Melissa nodded, eyes closed.

"I take cream and sugar in mine," Morris told the Captain. "Bring plenty of both."

Crispin shot fire at Morris with his eyes.

"That's a good idea, Pete," Wallace said. "Take a breather. Go outside for a few minutes and cool off. Bring a pot back with you. We could all use some joe."

Crispin's face turned a bright shade of pink. He opened his mouth
to say something, but swallowed it. Turning, he left the room pouting
like a whipped dog.

Two minutes of silence passed. Melissa prayed. Wallace read the
report. Morris waited.

"Hmm," Wallace mumbled, looking up at Morris.

"How's it going next door?" he asked her.

"Hard to tell. He's cooperating, but . . ."

"But what?"

"Well, it's a bizarre story. Pretty far-fetched."

"Are you talking about Captain Vaughn?" Melissa asked.

Wallace nodded, then returned to the report.

"Are you ready to get started again, Ms. Lewis?" Morris finally asked.

Melissa took a deep breath. It came in gulps. "I guess."

Morris nodded at the recorder. After Wallace had started it, he
leaned forward and rested his elbows on the table. "Okay. Start back on
Friday. The field trip. Describe it for us."

"We left Vegas—" Melissa began.

"Who's we?" Wallace wanted to know.

"Me, the two girls, and Gill. I already—"

"What time?"

"Does it matter?"

"Maybe," Morris grunted.

Melissa shrugged. "I don't know . . . between six-thirty and seven."

"The kids missed school to do this?" Wallace asked. She was scribbling notes on a legal pad.

"No. They're on a year-round track. Last week was part of their
quarter break."

"What was the purpose of the trip?" Wallace asked.

"It was a field trip," Melissa said, weary of the questions. "Like I told
you several times, I'm a teacher. The kids were students from my tenth
grade science class. We were going into the desert to look for fossils."

"Anything eventful happen en route?" Wallace asked.

Melissa shook her head. "No. We just drove . . . ate a few snacks . . .
talked."

"Talked about what?"

She looked at Morris for relief. He raised his eyebrows. "We need
to hear the whole story."

"Again?"

He nodded, then smiled sympathetically.

"It was a science field trip," she told them with a frown. "We talked about . . . science."

"What time did you arrive at the fossil site?" Wallace asked.

"About—"

The phone rang, interrupting her answer. Morris and Wallace glanced at each other, confused. Morris answered it on the second ring.

"Hello? What? Yes, she is . . . Who is this? I'm afraid she can't . . ." He pulled the receiver away from his ear and stared at it for a moment. "It's for you." He offered it to Melissa, then made hand motions to Wallace, mouthing: *Where's another line?* She rose quickly and led him out of the room.

"Hello?"

"Melissa Lewis?"

"Yes."

"There's someone here who would like to talk to you."

"Who is . . . ?"

"Ms. Lewis?"

"Gill?"

"Yes, ma'am."

"How did you know where I . . ."

"These men . . . they . . . they picked me up . . . and . . ."

"What men? Where are you?"

"They say they're going to hurt me if you don't give back the bones."

"The bones?"

"Yes, ma'am."

There was a rustling sound, then, "Did you catch that, Melissa?"

"Who is this?"

Click! At first Melissa thought they had hung up.

"Hello? Hello?"

"I'm here. But tell your friends to get off now . . . or else."

"Friends?" Melissa didn't understand. "Is there someone else on this line?"

Click!

"Good. Now here's the deal," the caller continued. "We have you-know-who. Everything will turn out fine, if you'll simply give us the items in question."

"But I can't . . . I'm under arrest . . ."

"No. You're merely being held for questioning. Agree to return our property, and we'll see that you're released—within the hour. Go home. Wait for our call. We'll contact you to set up a meet."

Melissa didn't know what to say. Did she have any choice?

"Do we have a deal, Melissa?"

"I . . . I guess. Yes. I mean, I'll do whatever you need me to. Just don't hurt Gill." She waited for a response. "Hello?" The line was dead.

Moments later Morris and Wallace returned; behind them Crispin appeared, bearing a tray of coffee and a scowl. As the interrogators took up their places—the fed and the major seated, Crispin leaning against the wall—Melissa considered this strange twist. Someone had kidnapped Gill? Why? For the bones? Why were the bones so important? Were they the reason Nigel had died? Were they the cause of the morning's excitement? Why would someone commit murder, attempted murder, kidnapping . . . just to get their hands on the ancient remains of a T. rex? The fossils were valuable, but in a scientific sense only.

"Would you care to explain that call?" Wallace asked.

"It was my lawyer," she lied. How did they know where I was?

"Your lawyer?" Morris asked, smirking.

Melissa nodded. Better yet, how could they get me released?

Morris shrugged. "Let's take up where we left off. You were telling us about the field trip."

They have Gill. How did they even know that Gill had been with me when we discovered the bones?

"Ms. Lewis?"

The camera! It wasn't in the Rover. They must have stolen it, developed the film, and seen Gill in the picture. But they still would have had to identify him—to match his face with a name and an address.

"Ms. Lewis!" Crispin urged, gripping his mug of coffee.

Who are these people? Who has that kind of clout, those connections? The police? The FBI? The military? Vaughn mentioned something about the DOE. Could they—

"Ma'am?" Morris tapped her arm gently.

"I'm sorry. Uh . . . Where were we?"

"What time did you reach the Site?" Wallace asked, her pen poised.

Melissa shook her head and tried to think. "Um . . . Oh, about, uh . . . I guess ten or so . . . I don't remember exactly."

"And what did you do there?" Wallace continued.

"Looked around for fossils."

"Did you find any?"

"Not at first. Just a few shells. Nothing significant until . . . maybe two. One of my students went down in a dry riverbed and discovered a crevasse. In it was a T. rex humerus and . . ."

"Do we have the names of the students?" Wallace asked, flipping through the report.

"Yeah," Crispin grunted. "They're in there."

Wallace found the information. "Beth, Sydney, and Gill. Which one found the bones?"

"Gill did," Melissa said. Gill's face flashed through her mind, and with it came the hellish vision of thugs beating him. *Lord God, be with Gill . . . Keep him safe . . . Send your angels to guard him . . .*

"What time did you leave?" Wallace asked.

"Maybe three . . . I guess."

Wallace paused to jot down notes.

"Now . . ." Crispin said, seizing the moment. "About the explosion in Boulder . . ."

Morris waved him off. "We've been over that. So have the authorities in Boulder. It's under investigation."

Crispin's jaw twitched and he took a gulp of coffee, ostensibly to quench the fire building inside.

"Let's move past that and talk about today," Morris said. "I'm interested in the two men who were chasing you." He bent and retrieved his briefcase from beneath his chair. Placing it on the table, he opened it and withdrew an oversized, hardcover binder. He pushed it toward her. The title read: Federal Bureau of Investigation, Official Use Only, Criminal Record Album, Number 334.

"Go ahead," Morris said. "Open it and look through the mug shots. See if you can ID either of the assailants. We have a theory about who might have been trying to kill you. But we need confirmation."

Melissa opened the cover and stared at the first two criminals: unshaven faces, red eyes, stern, merciless expression. They looked mean, even depraved, fully capable of committing all manner of atrocities. But they weren't the men who had pursued them. She turned the page, glanced at the mug shots, turned another page. She was a third of the way through the book when someone knocked on the door to the interrogation room.

All four heads looked up as a female sergeant entered. "Excuse me," she said with an apologetic smile. She handed a note to Major Wallace and left. Wallace read the note. Her expression soured as she scanned it again, then handed it to Morris.

"What?" Crispin wanted to know. "What is it?"

"It seems that this concludes our session here, Ms. Lewis," Morris announced.

Crispin snatched the note from him. He cursed as he read it.

"Your attorney has requested to be present for all questioning," Morris explained. "Therefore we have to release you and reschedule a meeting in order for your attorney to be in attendance."

Attorney? Melissa wondered. *What attorney?*

"I should warn you that if you leave the state, a warrant will be issued for your arrest," Morris said matter-of-factly. "Hang around Vegas. We'll talk to your lawyer and arrange another little get-together."

Melissa stared at them. "I can leave now?"

Morris nodded. "They'll sign you out at the desk at the end of the hall," Wallace told her.

"Thanks for your help," Morris said. He ushered her to the door and closed it behind her.

THIS STINKS!" CRISPIN PROTESTED. HE WAS LIVID, THE VESSELS IN HIS neck threatening to burst. "Why don't we charge her? We've got enough to hold her overnight."

Wallace ignored this. She made a last note, closed her folder, and rose to leave. "Captain, would you mind taking that tray back to the kitchen?"

Morris smiled at this, patting Crispin on the shoulder as he made for the door. "Good coffee, Captain."

Crispin swore at them both under his breath and began collecting the cups.

"Do you guys have any idea what this is all about?" Wallace asked in the hall.

"A little," Morris answered.

"But you're not going to let us in on it?"

"It's an open case. We can't disclose everything."

They walked three doors down, pausing in front of another interrogation room. "We have grounds to arrest Vaughn," she said. "Any thoughts on that?"

"I don't think it would accomplish much," Morris confessed. "He and Lewis aren't the problem. They're just bystanders who were in the wrong place at the wrong time—or so we believe."

"Doesn't that mean they're in danger?"

"You bet it does. And if the people we're dealing with turn out to be who we think they are, Vaughn and Lewis need protection."

"So why are we releasing them?"

"Don't worry. We're putting a team on it. They'll both be tailed, their homes staked out. They won't so much as sneeze without our knowing about it. If something goes down, we'll be there—with bells on."

Forty-Two

MELISSA WAS STANDING IN THE PARKING LOT, SQUINTING INTO THE setting sun, when Vaughn appeared at her side.

"What an ordeal," he groaned. "I feel like I've been gutted and fried."

"I don't have any way to get home," she said rather mournfully, and immediately the tears she had been holding back came: a mighty river flooding its banks, breaking through a dam.

Vaughn held her. "Hey, it's okay. I'm stranded too. I'll just call a cab. We can share it. How's that?"

Melissa was sobbing now, her chest trembling with every gasping breath.

"Really, it's okay. I'll make sure you get home." He gave her shoulder a consoling squeeze and led her to a nearby pay phone. As she continued to weep, he called a taxi.

"They said it would be about ten minutes," he told her after he hung up. He directed her toward a wooden bench, but she refused to sit. Looking at him through bleary eyes, she tried to say something. The words were unintelligible, slurred hisses.

"It's going to be okay, really." He embraced her, her head resting on his shoulder.

She hissed again.

"Did they hurt you in there?"

Her head jerked back and forth, her mouth weighed down into an exaggerated frown.

"Were they mean? Did they badger you?"

Another shake of the head.

"Then what's the matter? We're safe now. Nobody's shooting at us. And we're not in jail—yet. I'm in serious trouble for being AWOL. And for stealing the car. And for the gun. But other than that . . ." He displayed the bones, as though they were some great prize. "They gave us these back. That's something."

She gulped in a breath. "They . . . they . . . they have . . . Gill," she managed between sobs.

"What?"

"Gill."

"Who's Gill?"

She slipped through his arms and sank to the bench, burying her head in her hands.

"Who's Gill?" Vaughn repeated, sitting down beside her.

"He's . . . my . . . student . . ." she whimpered.

"Okay. And?"

"They . . . have . . . him . . ."

"Who? Who has him?"

"The ones . . . the ones that . . . that tried . . . that tried to . . . to kill us . . ."

Vaughn's face twisted, his eyebrows falling. "Those thugs have your student?"

Melissa nodded, rubbing at the tears with her palms. The torrent was beginning to subside.

"Are you saying they kidnapped him?"

"Yes."

Vaughn thought this over. "How do you know?"

"They called me."

"Here?"

She nodded. "And . . . I think . . . that's how we . . . got out. They . . . they arranged it."

"They would have to be pretty darn powerful to do something like that. I mean, the FBI was there. Who could force the FBI to let us go?"

"It was . . . a legal thing," Melissa explained, still sniffing away tears. "A technicality. Something about . . . about having a lawyer . . . present."

"Really?" Vaughn looked out across the parking lot. The sun was perched on the horizon, about to hide behind Red Rocks and the La Madre Mountains—a fiery sphere waning. "Why would they kidnap your student?"

"The bones."

"The dinosaur bones?"

Melissa nodded. "They want them back." She breathed through her mouth as the tears wound down, pushing her hair back from her face.

Neither of them spoke until the cab arrived seven minutes later. "Come on," Vaughn said, helping her up. "We'll go to my place."

"No. They're going to call. I have to go home . . . alone."

"I'll go with you."

She kissed him on the cheek. "Thank you. I owe you my life." Turning, she started for the cab.

"Melissa! I'm going with you." He opened the door of the cab and she slipped past him, slamming it behind her.

"It's my problem, Steve. I'll take care of it myself."

"Right . . . Like a marine is going to let you meet with a bunch of armed criminals—by yourself." He jerked open the door. "Scoot over!"

Fuller slid into the Dodge and gently pulled the door shut. "Did I miss anything?"

"Nope. You're just in time," Morris told him. He started the engine. "Our lovebirds are in that cab."

"Lawyers . . ." Fuller cursed the entire profession as he strapped in. "I can't believe they got them out of there so fast."

"Glean anything useful from our friend Vaughn?"

"No. What about Lewis?"

Morris shrugged. "I don't know." He waited until the taxi had rolled out of the lot before shifting into gear and pulling the Dodge away from the curb. "We might have been getting somewhere. I'm not sure." They took up position a quarter mile behind the cab.

"No time to ID the perps?"

"Huh-uh. Had her in the mug book, but . . ."

"Still see this as family business?" Fuller asked. He readjusted himself in the seat, trying in vain to find a place to stow his long legs.

"Think about it." Morris slowed the car as they approached the gate, fishing his badge out of his jacket. "Perp One: muscular, medium build, ponytail . . ." He flashed his badge at the soldier in the guardhouse and nodded as they were waved through. "Perp Two: shorter, older, wiry, balding . . . Both Italian . . ."

"Okay. Even without a lineup, I'll give you that much. It fits Vispeti and Scapelli to a T. But my problem is, why? Why would the family care about Lewis? For that matter, why would they care about Weber?"

"I'm guessing that the good doctor was on to something."

Fuller's face wrinkled as he considered this. "You can't be serious."

"Why not?" Morris said, giving him a sideways nod.

"Because Weber was a paranoid nut," Fuller said, "that's why not. He was anti-government—a dissenter." He paused to swear. "The guy threatened to sabotage the NTS if the administration didn't go public with his imaginary 'cover-up' story. Sure, he warranted Bureau attention. But he wasn't on to anything."

Morris didn't reply. He just kept driving.

"Don't tell me you believe the little rat," Fuller prodded. "You don't buy his wild tale about the big bad government conducting nuclear experiments on humans, hiding atomic accident victims . . ." He shook his head at the idea. "Weber was out of his tree."

"Agreed. I didn't mean I bought his conspiracy theory. Just that maybe he was on to something."

"I don't follow."

"The guy visited Quad 217 of the NTS, right?"

"Right. So?"

"So you spoke to Vaughn, you heard what Weber was up to."

Fuller shrugged at this. "He was gonna dig up the place—to find all the bodies the DOE supposedly buried out there."

They rode on in silence, each analyzing the scenario.

"You think there really is something buried out there?" Fuller finally asked.

"Maybe."

"And he was going to dig it up . . ." Fuller thought aloud. "Okay. Maybe that got him killed. What about Lewis and Vaughn? Why chase a paleontologist and a marine around town?"

"The bones," Morris said. "Lewis said she unearthed some dinosaur bones in 217."

Fuller frowned at this, his sharp, gaunt features bending south with his lips. "And that made somebody nervous."

"Exactly."

After a pause, he said, "No. It's too outrageous. Even if there was something out there . . . what you're suggesting is a co-op between the mob and the government. The DOE hiring mob hit men to pop people. No way. The CIA maybe. But not the Department of Energy."

"Who said anything about the DOE?"

Fuller's brow filled with wrinkles. "You lost me again."

"I'm thinking this is 'all in the family.' "

"But that brings us full circle. Why would the mob care about a patch of desert in the NTS?"

"Beats me. I haven't figured that out yet." They watched as the cab performed a left and sped down a boulevard.

"Tell you one thing," Fuller said, still fidgeting, his knees rubbing the dash. "No matter who's sending out the terminators or what the reason is, Lewis and Vaughn are in over their heads."

"Way over their heads."

THE IDEA CAME TO HIM AT THE DINNER, FULL AND SWEET, LIKE A SUMMER rose. Somehow, his brain managed to water it, nurse it, and appreciate it from various angles while his mouth was fully engaged, his tongue offering the chairman of the subcommittee an eloquent, soft-sell description of Yucca Mountain and a low-key but earnest plea for the funds necessary to make it a reality. The idea unfolded, petals curling back one by one to expose a firm, unblemished stamen—aromatic, calling to him with the scent of freedom.

The debate began in earnest on the way home from dinner. As his wife chattered away, gossiping incessantly—mindlessly—about what her peers had worn, who was having an affair with whom, how she planned to join another diet plan, he sank deeper into himself. His emotions were warring with common sense, wrestling with the notion of shaking off the heavy shackles, with the horror of losing everything he held dear: job, career, political aspirations . . . home, reputation, bank accounts . . . His wife would leave him in a heartbeat. Without gold cards, dinner parties, and Beemers, there was no reason for her to stay. Love—if they shared such a thing—was not enough to hold them together. Certainly not enough to see their relationship through an arrest, a trial, a prison term. Prison. Incarceration: walls . . . bars . . . tiny cells . . . There was a good chance he would be indicted and put away for decades. If he made it that far. Betraying their trust would bring punishment—swift and severe. He might never reach court. They might come for him . . . silently . . . in the night . . .

Was it worth it? Was freedom worth the price? Was it worth risking imprisonment? Was it worth risking his life? He was still fighting the battle, jousting with these questions, leaning one way, then the other, when they pulled into the garage. He switched off the Lincoln and sat there as the automatic door groaned shut behind them.

On the ceiling above, the light blinked, then flashed, burning out. The door crunched shut and the darkness seemed complete.

His wife got out and felt her way toward the front of the garage. When she reached the steps, she unlocked the door and cracked it open. Amber light streamed toward him. She turned and peered into the car. "Robert? Are you going to sit there in the dark? Or come inside?"

The choice seemed plain enough. Even to his wife. She chuckled at him and went in before he could answer. The door slammed shut behind her and total night returned.

Make a decision! he told himself. Light—with a hefty price tag? Or darkness—with no hope of ever seeing the sun?

His wife was right. Only a fool would sit in the garage: blind, trapped. It was time to go inside: to confess his sins and seek forgiveness. Confession was frightening, humiliating. But with forgiveness came liberty.

He got out of the car and followed the line of the hood to the door. His trembling hands fumbled for the knob. When he found it, he paused and drank in a long, deep breath, sobered by the knowledge that he was standing in the breach. A simple twist of the cool, brass knob, and the obstacle in his path would swing back on silent hinges. There was nothing keeping him from crossing the threshold, save his own will.

Do it! an inner voice urged. At that very moment, the conflict ended, one side surrendering, raising a white flag to the overwhelming desire of a man intent upon regaining a part of himself: the title deed to his own soul. Ethics, morality, shame, and guilt . . . these virtues played no role in the conquest. This was a decision based on need. On self. He had to do it before he ceased to exist.

He felt the knob turn, felt legs moving. He sensed that he was walking, traveling the hallway like a zombie, eyes open yet unseeing. He found himself in the study. A hand paged through an address book. An arm reached for the phone. A finger dialed a number. A numb, disoriented frame fell into the chair. The line rang.

"General Henderson's office," a woman answered.

"Put me through to the general, please," a voice replied. It sounded a little like his own, but it was small and broken.

"I'm sorry. General Henderson is in a meeting at the moment. May I take a message and have him return your call?"

"I have to talk to him . . . now."

"May I inquire as to your name and the nature of the call, sir?"

"This is Robert DiCaprio."

The woman clearly didn't recognize the name. "And the nature of your call, sir?"

"I need a priest."

"Excuse me, sir? Did you say priest?"

"This is Robert DiCaprio, Secretary of the DOE," he said with as much courage as he could muster. "I need to speak with the general."

"Yes, sir. Can you hold for just a moment, please?" There was a click, then a tinny version of a John Philip Sousa composition filled the line.

As DiCaprio listened to the march, he glanced around the room—at the photo of his smiling wife, at the plaques, the picture of him shaking hands with the president . . . It was like a dream: foggy, happy, fleeting. And it was about to disappear.

———————

*S*O WHAT ARE YOU TELLING ME, MAJOR?" JOHNSON SNORTED. "ARE YOU telling me we just released a civilian and a marine who confessed to grand theft auto, illegal firearm possession, and entering the base illegally?"

"Yes, sir." Wallace nodded glumly, then turned to Crispin for support. The captain was staring at the floor, doing an in-depth study of the tiles.

Johnson glared at the report. "Oh, and the marine was AWOL." He shrugged and made a comical face. "Why should we bother detaining a soldier who decided not to report to his post?"

"Sir, if I may—" Wallace tried.

"You may not!" Johnson growled. "Vaughn was in here just yesterday because he was in the zone while off-duty—without permission.

Now the general is just as forgiving as the next guy when it comes to his people. Vaughn said they were settling a bet, that they didn't know beans about 217. Okay. It sounded innocent enough. But this . . ." He slapped the folder down on the table. "Coincidence? I don't think so. Neither will the general. Vaughn seems to be the man of the hour around here." The colonel shook his head and muttered something. "Released to consult with legal counsel . . ."

"Sir, the FBI—" Wallace started to interject.

"The FBI?" Johnson grumbled. "Who's running this show? This is an air force base, Major! This"—he beat the folder with a fist—"is our problem, not theirs."

"Yes, sir, but—"

"The general wants to know what's happening in 217. Why people are making pilgrimages to that quad . . . Why people are shooting at each other . . . Why soldiers under his command are running around Vegas . . . around . . ." He paused and flipped through the report. "Around Titans Temple, for pete's sake! Playing cowboys and Indians! What in blazes is going on?"

Wallace swallowed hard and joined Crispin in examining the linoleum. They were both visibly relieved when someone tapped on the door to Wallace's office and it creaked open.

"Excuse me, Colonel. There's a call for General Henderson on line one."

"The general is . . . indisposed. So am I for that matter. Unless it's the president, take a message," Johnson replied glibly, still smoldering.

"It's Robert DiCaprio, sir."

Johnson sighed at this.

"He's the Secre—"

"I know who he is." He glared at Wallace and Crispin—a father in the middle of chewing out two errant teens. "I'm not finished with you. Stay put." Then he followed his secretary down the hall to his own office.

He fell into his chair, cursing his luck—why now?—and picked up the phone.

"Hello, Secretary DiCaprio."

"General?"

"No, sir. This is Colonel Johnson."

"Well . . . I . . . uh . . . I really need to speak with Gerald . . ."

"He's attending a social event this evening, sir. Could I give him a message? Have him call you, perhaps?"

"I . . . There's something that I . . . I need to tell . . . uh . . ."

Johnson sighed inwardly. It had been a long day. He was tired, in no mood for games. "Yes, sir?"

"It's . . . Well . . . I suppose I . . . Uh . . . I'm not sure how to . . ." DiCaprio blew air into the phone. "This is . . . ah . . . It's a difficult subject . . . I apologize for . . . but . . . uh . . ."

Johnson was tempted to shout: *What is it?* Instead, he waited patiently. It was clear that the man had something important to say. He just didn't know how to say it. And he sounded . . . strange. The usual confidence—the arrogance—was missing. The secretary sounded depressed . . . maybe a bit drunk—or both.

"It's . . . it's about the zone."

The statement hung in the air. "The zone, sir?" Johnson prodded when nothing else was forthcoming. "What about it?"

"I haven't been . . . well . . . uh . . . It's . . . It's concerning . . . concerning what's out there . . . Uh . . . concerning what's . . . buried . . . in Quad 217."

Forty-Three

"WHERE ARE YOU?"

"About ten miles from town—and closing fast."

"When can you be at Lewis's?"

"Probably thirty minutes or so," Tito replied, "depending on the traffic."

"Okay." Sonny paused to think. "You're on Lewis. Who can we put on the soldiers?"

"I've already made the arrangements. Mario's handling the black guy. Julian's on the moose at the hospital."

"Julian?"

"Yeah, Julian. Got a problem with that?"

"For crying out loud, Tito. Julian's just a kid. He couldn't do a schoolgirl—much less a marine the size of Rhode Island."

"Julian can handle it," Tito promised.

Vince snatched the phone away. "You aren't running down my nephew are you, Sonny? 'Cause I wanna tell you something, he's a good kid. Just like his father was. And he's on the job."

From his side of the Vette, Tito could hear Sonny cussing a response. Vince swore back and returned the phone. "Jerk!"

"Sonny . . . Sonny . . . Cool off!" Tito waited for him to simmer down. When he finally did he added, "Don't worry. He'll do fine."

"Whatever," Sonny replied. "I don't care who does what. I just want this thing to work."

"Yeah, well . . . You're not the only one."

"I got chewed big time for the Titans fiasco," Sonny grumbled. "You idiots . . . I can't believe you couldn't . . ."

"Not now, Sonny," Tito grumbled. "We're on Lewis and her soldier friends. We're taking out the Fibbies. Is that it?"

"That's it. Keep me posted. And keep that barbaric partner of yours on a leash."

Tito hung up the phone.

"Sonny," Vince muttered with an expression of disdain. "I'd love to meet him in a dark alley sometime. Just him and me."

"I know. So would I. But forget about him for now. Try to focus," Tito advised. "Do we need to stop off for anything before we get to Lewis's place? How are we on weapons and ammo?"

Vince twisted in the seat and pulled a leather bag out of the back. Unzipping it, he withdrew a revolver, several boxes of hollow-points, another pistol, a silencer . . . "You still got your .357?"

Tito nodded.

"Shotguns are in the trunk. More ammo too." He shrugged. "I'd say we're ready to rock and roll."

"How we gonna lose the Feds?" Tito asked, slowing the Vette. They had reached the outskirts of Vegas and traffic was picking up, headlight beams and ruby taillights glowing as dusk faded to night.

Vince loaded one of the guns, snapping a clip into place. "Piece of cake."

This is it."

The driver pulled up to the curb and the cab squeaked to a stop.

"Sev-onteen-seexty-won."

"How much?"

"Sev-onteen-seexty-won." The accent was heavy, the words indistinct. The man was dark skinned, obviously Asian.

"I'll have to go in and get it."

"Lady," the driver sighed, "you no stiff me, uh?"

"No," Melissa said, climbing out. She leaned on the open window of the passenger's door. "I just don't have any money with me."

"What 'bout boyfriend here? He broke too?"

Vaughn got out. "Stay here," he told her. "Give me your keys. Tell me where some cash is."

"Sev-onteen-seexty-won," the driver said, growing impatient.

"I can get it," Melissa protested.

"Huh-uh. For all we know, this is a trap. They could be waiting in there . . ."

"Sev-onteen-seexty . . . They?" The driver's face contorted.

"With guns."

"Gons?" the driver repeated suspiciously.

"I doubt it," Melissa argued. "They want the bones."

"Boones?"

"They wouldn't have bothered to kidnap Gill—"

"Keednap?"

"—If they planned on killing us when we came back."

"*Keelling!*"

The cab jerked away from the curb and raced down the street.

"Takes care of that problem," Vaughn observed. He followed Melissa across the courtyard, through the pool area, to her apartment. The door was decorated with wide, yellow police tape.

"Do you have your keys?"

Melissa shook her head. Reaching for the door, she gave it a push. It creaked open. "Guess I don't need them."

They climbed through the crime scene tape and Melissa flipped on the light. The place was a mess, the floor covered with glass and wood shards, the carpet stained with blood.

"At least nobody looted the place," Vaughn offered. "That's something."

"Yeah," Melissa groaned. "Something."

"Now what?"

She brushed glass from the love seat and fell into it. "We wait."

"Got anything to eat?" Vaughn asked, already moving toward the kitchen.

"Not much. But help yourself."

"I'm starving. How about you?"

"Yeah. But I'm more tired than I am hungry."

Vaughn opened the pantry and surveyed the contents: Fruit Loops . . . Corn Nuts . . . a mostly empty bag of Fritos . . . M&Ms . . . "Don't suppose you have any real food." He tried the refrigerator: pickles, mustard, four eggs, a block of moldy cheese, mayonnaise, two shriveled apples, a carton of milk . . . The vegetable drawer contained a sack of rubbery carrots, a kernel of iceberg lettuce, and a cardboard crate of mushrooms. He checked the freezer. The walls were thick with ice crystals. Two ice-cube trays sat empty to one side. In the center, there was a pint of gourmet yogurt and a package of frozen, boneless chicken breasts.

"How about if I whip up something?"

He got out the eggs, the cheese, the mushrooms, a chicken breast . . . and set to work. After twenty minutes of clanking, cutting, and commotion, he slapped two handsome omelets on plates, grabbed a couple of forks, and returned to the living room.

"Voila!" He presented his creations with a flourish.

Melissa was slumped across the love seat, legs propped up, eyes shut, snoring.

"Oh, well . . ." Vaughn set one plate aside and inhaled his own entree. When he finished, he looked at the phone expectantly, then at his watch. It was almost eight.

He picked up the receiver, listened for a dial tone, replaced it.

"I need to check on Phil and Jimmy," he told Melissa's sleeping form. "But I don't want to tie up the phone . . ."

He peered through the broken window, toward the pool area. Luminescent blue washed back and forth, throwing wavy patterns of light up on the surrounding apartments. In the corner, next to the pool house, he saw a pay phone.

After borrowing a handful of quarters from a plastic bowl on the counter, he limped out to it. The directory attached to the booth was beaten, much of it missing. He tried to look up Memorial Hospital, but the *M*s were gone. Everything past *J* had been torn out. Thankfully, he found emergency medical facilities listed in the front.

He deposited a quarter and swore softly as the coin clinked back to him and dropped into the change bin. He retrieved it, fed it in again, and was rewarded with a dial tone. Punching in the number, he turned to watch Melissa's apartment. Though her theory about the thugs leaving them alone until they got the bones seemed to make sense, he wasn't about to let down his guard.

"Memorial Medical Center. How may I direct your call?"

"I'm trying to check on the status of a friend of mine."

"Was your friend admitted today?"

"Yes. To the ER or the trauma unit, I guess."

"Can you hold for one moment?"

Vaughn watched the surface of the pool perform a mesmerizing dance as he listened to a tinny, anemic version of Vivaldi's "The Four

Seasons." It almost sounded like it was on the wrong speed. He glanced at Melissa's apartment. No movement. He looked across the courtyard, at the street. It was quiet and dark. He could hear noise coming from the closest row of units: voices, water running, a TV blaring . . .

"Trauma Unit."

"I'm trying to find out about a friend of mine who was brought in to—"

"Name?"

"Jimmy Donohue."

A keyboard clacked on the other end of the line.

"James Donohue?"

"Yeah. That's it. How's he doing? Is he okay?"

"Let me transfer you to ICU."

Whiny strings fought like cats, transforming Vivaldi into obnoxious noise. Vaughn's eyes darted back and forth: street, Melissa's, street, Melissa's . . .

A car made the corner, blinding him with its high beams. It parallel parked and two women got out. They crossed the street and entered a set of townhouses.

"ICU. This is Linda."

"I'm checking on James Donohue"

"Was he admitted today?"

"Yes."

There was a long pause. "Here we go. Are you related or—"

"I work with him. He's a friend."

The nurse seemed to hesitate.

"I just wanted to find out how he's doing."

"According to his chart, he's in stable condition."

"Stable? What's that mean?"

"His vitals leveled out after surgery."

"Surgery?"

"Yes. To remove a bullet."

"But he's okay now?"

"He's stable. Making progress. He'll be with us for a while, however."

"Can I talk to him?"

He could hear her flipping pages. "Sorry."

"What?"

"There's a note here. He's not to be disturbed. And . . ."

"And?"

"A guard has been posted at his door. I shouldn't even be giving you this information. Looks like it must be a police matter. Probably gang related. If that's all . . ."

"Actually, it's not. I also wanted to check on Phillip Parish. He was admitted today also."

"Parish . . . Parish . . . No. He's not on this unit. Let me reconnect you with the main desk."

There was a click, then an out-of-tune rendition of Mozart's "Eine Kleine Nachtmusik." In the apartment, Vaughn saw a shadow rise from the love seat.

"I'm out here!" he called, waving.

Melissa stumbled to the door and looked out at him.

"There's an omelet for you on the counter."

She nodded and disappeared.

"Memorial Medical Center. How may I direct your call?"

"Do you have an admissions department?"

"One moment."

Mozart blasted from the receiver, violins shouting at one another. They were still battling it out when a voice interrupted."

"Admissions."

"I'm checking on the status of Phil Parish."

"One moment." Pages turned. Someone tapped a computer keyboard.

"Lieutenant Phillip Parish?"

"Yes, ma'am."

"Admitted this morning at . . . 11:49."

"Good. Could you connect me with—"

"Discharged at . . . 5:22."

"Discharged?"

"Yes, sir."

"Oh . . . Okay. Well, thank you." He hung up and dropped another quarter in the slot, punching in Parish's number.

On the street, a nondescript white car found a parking spot. No one got out.

Parish answered on the third ring. "This better be important," he grumbled. "If you're selling something . . ."

"Phil?"

"Steve?"

"Yeah. Are you okay? I called the hospital, but—"

"Insurance!" he said, as if it were an obscenity. "I get my head bashed in, but since I don't need to go under the knife, they run a few tests, patch me up, and send me home. They don't care if I'm in pain. They don't care if I need constant attention from a nurse. They just want to keep the hospital stays at a minimum. Save money. The greedy—"

"Are you in pain?"

"Well, not exactly. The docs wrote me some prescriptions. I down a handful of drugs every hour or so. They seem to keep me pretty . . . happy." He chuckled at this.

"Apparently so. Then you're okay?"

"I won't be skywalking to the hoop for a while, but the docs said they expected a full recovery. Hey, tell me what happened. I was worried about you. I tried to call but there was no answer."

"Long story. Melissa and I got away—sort of."

"Melissa?"

"Ms. Lewis. Anyway, we ended up at Nellis. The FBI and internal affairs grilled us for a while but . . ."Vaughn watched the white car. He couldn't make out anyone inside. Maybe they had gotten out when he wasn't looking.

"Listen, I need your car."

"What?"

"Mine's . . . who knows where. And Melissa's isn't in good shape. The door's busted."

"Where are you planning on going?"

In the white car, there was a brief burst of orange. Vaughn saw two figures in the front seat. Darkness quickly enveloped them again, leaving behind two tiny red dots: cigarettes.

"I can't explain right now. But . . . We need a car. I don't know why I'm asking you this. You can't drive. Not in your condition."

"Sure I can. The fine print on the meds said not to operate heavy machinery. My Z28 isn't heavy machinery."

"Phil . . ."

"I'll slip something on and be over there in a flash."

Vaughn considered this. It wasn't smart. But then, neither was agreeing to meet kidnappers . . . alone . . . at night. "Okay."

"See you in a few minutes."

"Okay. Be careful." Vaughn hung up the receiver and gave the white car a parting glance. The specks of fire glowed, faded, glowed, almost in unison.

In the apartment, he found Melissa on the phone.

"Yes . . . Yes . . ." She was scribbling on a scrap of paper. "I understand . . . Okay . . . Yes . . ."

Vaughn mouthed to her, "Is it them?"

She nodded. "Yes . . . Okay . . . Then what? All right . . . Yes . . ." There was an extended pause. "I understand." Melissa put the phone down and stared at it.

"Well?" Vaughn prodded.

"We're supposed to leave here at exactly 8:30. These are the directions." She waved the paper at him.

"We? You told them I was coming?"

"I asked them if you could come. They didn't have a problem with that. Anyway, we're supposed to bring the bones. And if we call the police or the FBI, they'll . . ." Her eyes flashed fear. "They'll kill Gill."

"They sound like a cheery bunch of folks."

"Yeah . . . real cheery."

"Where? Where's the meet?"

Melissa sighed. "Tonopah."

Forty-Four

Houseman? This is Fuller. What's your status?"

The radio crackled with static. Then, "Status green. Everything's clear over here. No movement. House is dark. I think the guy's down and out for the night."

"Give us a call if you see anything: vehicle circling the block, somebody milling around . . . anything suspicious."

"Roger that."

Fuller replaced the radio mike and flicked the butt of his cigarette out the window. "Where'd you put that other pack of Marlboros?" he asked, rifling through the glove compartment.

"They should be in there," Morris replied sleepily.

"Well, I don't see them. This will be one heck of a long stakeout if we run out of smokes."

"Tell me about it."

"It's bad enough that we don't have coffee . . ."

"I forgot the thermos," Morris said, frowning. "So shoot me."

"I may if I don't get some coffee soon."

"You and your caffeine addiction."

Fuller shifted in his seat, huddled his knees together, then fought with the adjustment knob, trying in vain to slide the seat back. "Piece of junk . . ."

"Why don't you check on Waters," Morris suggested, suppressing a laugh. "Before you break that thing."

Fuller cursed the seat, then took up the mike. "Like someone's going to walk into a public hospital and do a hit," he muttered. "Waters? . . . Fuller." He sighed melodramatically. "Status check."

Out of the static, Waters's faraway voice replied, "Status green. The place is quiet. Cafeteria closed two hours ago. I'm starving."

"You got a cup of coffee?"

"You betcha. There's a machine right down the hall here."

"Then don't complain," Fuller said. "That's more than we've got."

They could hear Waters laughing. "You know, I wish I could be there with you guys—sitting in that hot car, instead of here in the cool hospital, watching candy stripers go by as I sip my joe . . ."

Fuller told him where to go.

"Roger. I'm halfway there. Over." More laughter.

"Jerk," Fuller muttered as he put the mike back into its caddy.

"Get a little testy without our java, do we, Ed?"

"Don't start with me." He renewed his search for the Marlboros. "Here they are."

Headlights flashed behind them. "We got company," Morris observed. He nodded as a red Corvette rolled slowly past. It parked a half block up the street. "Looks like Tito Vispeti's car."

HERE THEY ARE." TITO WATCHED THE DODGE IN THE REARVIEW MIRROR.

"They see you?" Vince asked from his place on the floorboard.

"I think so."

"Good."

"I'll go first," Tito reviewed, as if he were explaining something to a schoolchild. "We run and play, you do your thing."

"Okay."

"And remember to call the other guys and tell them to go."

Vince shook his head, flipping open the phone. "Doesn't seem fair. They get to ice their targets. We have to 'disable' ours. Sure would be easier just to shoot them."

"Yeah, well, we can't," Tito said. "Not while Lewis is still in there."

"Her too."

"Huh?"

"We could put Lewis and any Feds in the area down. Bang, bang, bang . . . It's over."

"But like Sonny said, how would we know Lewis had the bones? What if she hid them somewhere? We have to wait. At least, until she brings them to the meet."

Vince grumbled something profane and started dialing. "You sure you can handle those two morons by yourself?"

Tito chuckled at this. "With one arm tied behind my back." He popped open the door. "See you in five." Slamming it shut, he activated the alarm. After it chirped, he started across the street, toward the apartment building, in full view of the Fibbies.

That's him. That's Vispeti," Fuller announced.

"And he's alone," Morris noted. "Want me to call in backup?"

"No time," Fuller answered. "Besides, we know where he's going. Let's go after him."

Morris discarded his cigarette and opened the door. As he got out, he unlatched his holster and withdrew his 45. Fuller did the same. They walked up the sidewalk, weapons in hand, on a collision course with the perp.

Agent Richard Houseman was sipping lukewarm coffee from a thermos cup, using a penlight to perform an exhaustive study of the June issue of *Hot Rod* magazine, when a man emerged from the condos. He fit the description: African American, about thirty, trim, medium height, glasses . . .

"Parish," he muttered, setting aside his magazine. Houseman watched as Parish weaved drunkenly toward a black Camaro with a personalized license that read: U-BETYA.

He lifted the radio mike to call it in.

Thump!

"What was that?" he wondered aloud, his head swinging from side to side. It sounded almost like a footstep. But just one. And then the Dodge had rocked ever so slightly. Or had it. Maybe it was his imagina—

A hand swung down from the roof of the vehicle and Houseman had just enough time to identify what it was bearing—a hunting knife with a long, shiny chrome blade—before the weapon slashed at him.

Tito twisted his head in an exaggerated fashion, looked directly at the Fibbies, pretended to panic, and bolted. Sprinting up the block, he heard them yell, "Stop! FBI!"

He waited until he was around the corner and had covered two more blocks before stealing a glance over his shoulder. And there they were: two federal agents in serious oxygen debt. The portly guy with the dark, greased-back hair seemed to be running in mud, his legs bouncing in time with his gut. Beside him the scarecrow was a picture of inefficiency: gangly arms and legs flailing wildly, as if he was swimming and would soon drown. Both of the men were drinking down air, their faces flushed, their eyes desperate.

Tito pulled up and limped along, acting as though he was winded, hoping to fool the two lead-legged Feds into thinking they might actually catch him. In another couple of blocks, he would hit the gas and leave them in the dust—like the road runner always did to the coyote in the Warner Brother shorts. Beep-beep—zoom!

VINCE DEACTIVATED THE ALARM, GOT OUT OF THE VETTE, AND WALKED casually to the Dodge. Without hesitation, he reached through the driver's side window and tugged the hood latch. The hood gave a metallic pop and jumped up an inch. Swinging it open, he peered inside. He nodded at the engine before yanking a wire loose. He used a wrench to work a spark plug free. Thirty seconds later half the Dodge's plugs were in his pocket. He pushed the disconnected wires out of view and closed the hood, then sauntered back to the Vette.

Starting the car, he eased away from the curb. After making the block, he parked in an alleyway between two apartment complexes. The position was out of the Dodge's field of vision, but offered a straight-on view of Lewis's building.

He had just cut off the engine when a black Z28 pulled up on the street.

HE'S HERE!" VAUGHN CALLED. HE WAS STANDING OUT ON THE WALKWAY, near the pool area. "Let's go!"

Melissa chewed at a fingernail. "You have the bones, right?"

"Yeah." Vaughn patted the lump under his shirt.

She stood there, reticent, surveying the floor, as if the broken glass and blood-stained carpet might offer up an answer to the crisis—if she paused long enough to listen.

"It's time, Melissa,"Vaughn prodded, stepping back inside. He presented his watch, but she was staring vacantly at the floor. "We have to leave now."

"I know," she replied drearily. "It's just . . . this is . . . I . . . I . . ." Her breath was suddenly coming in gulps, her shoulders quaking.

Vaughn draped his arm around her. "Hang on for another couple of hours and this whole mess will be over."

"That's what I'm afraid of," she said, sniffing back tears.

"Hey, where's that God you've been talking about? Huh?"

Her eyebrows rose and her lower lip crested forming an odd expression, something between a lost puppy dog and a frightened child.

"You've got the Almighty on your side—and the marines,"Vaughn joked. "Nobody can beat that combination."

She smiled at him, a single teardrop escaping down her cheek. "Will you pray with me?"

He looked out the door, toward the street where he knew that Parish was waiting, then glanced at his watch. Opening his mouth to object, he turned back toward Melissa and was melted by her gaze—two teary, brown spheres—her pretty face weighed down by concern, lined by exhaustion.

"Sure," he said, caving in. "But let's hurry, okay?"

She reached for his hands, took them in her own, and bowed her head. Distracted by her beauty, he watched as she prayed—the way her lips moved, her smooth round cheeks, the curve of her neck . . .

"Father, we're in trouble. Gill's in trouble. Please . . . please act. Show us what to do to bring about his release. Protect us as we go blindly to his rescue. Be our strength. Be his strength. Father, please deliver Gill from these evil people. Amen."

"Amen,"Vaughn chimed. He pulled her out the door.

"Shouldn't we lock it?"

He jabbed a thumb at the broken window. "What's the point?"

PARISH WAS WOBBLING OUT OF THE CAMARO WHEN THEY REACHED THE courtyard. They watched him try to close the door, then lose his balance and begin staggering backwards. He swung his arms in the air, as if fending off some unseen assailant, before tripping on the curb. He was about to hit the pavement when Vaughn caught him.

"Nice save," he said, looking up at them dreamily.

Vaughn righted him. "Thanks for bringing your car, Phil. Keys?"

Parish tightened his fist around them. "Not so fast."

"We don't have time for games," Melissa urged.

"No game. Just a stipulation. You can use my car . . ."

"If . . ." Vaughn groaned impatiently.

"If I get to go along."

"No!" they both responded in unison.

"Fine. Then find another car."

"A boy's life is at stake," Melissa explained.

"Exactly. That's why I'm going along. You need backup, Steve. And you need these." He staggered to the car and bent across the seat. When he stood back up, he displayed two side arms. He handed one to Vaughn. "I'm a decent shot."

"When you're not doped out of your mind." Vaughn shrugged at Melissa. "I don't know . . . What do you think?"

"We could use the help . . . I guess."

"Okay," Vaughn agreed. "But I drive."

"Fair enough."

FULLER WHEEZED A CURSE. HE TRIED TO SWEAR AGAIN, TO GIVE IT THE volume and intensity it deserved, but couldn't. Bent over, hands on knees, his lungs burned as he sucked in air.

Six feet away, Morris was sprawled on the curb, gun abandoned on the sidewalk, head back in defeat. His skin glistened with sweat as he panted.

"I . . . I think . . . I'm . . . going to . . . to throw up," he said between gasps. His shoulders flinched as he retched.

Fuller gestured, pointed with a finger. He tried to speak, but couldn't bring himself to waste the energy it required. Instead, he coughed raspingly.

A minute later, Morris rose awkwardly, retrieving his gun. "The car," he nodded, still laboring for every breath.

As they started back, Fuller withdrew the fresh pack of cigarettes and offered one to Morris. He took it and they both lit up.

"He's fast," Morris said. He wiped perspiration from his forehead and exhaled a curl of white smoke

"Very," Fuller agreed, filling his lungs with nicotine.

"Maybe if we kicked these," Morris suggested, "we could keep up."

Fuller shook his head. "Wouldn't make any difference. We could go to the gym five times a week, eat like rabbits, and shun all worldly pleasures." He paused to clear his throat, spitting away the product. "Guys like that would still leave us in the dust. We're just too old. And too darn slow."

When they finally rounded the corner, Morris announced, "He's gone." He pointed to the spot where the Vette had been parked.

"You surprised?"

"No. But—" He stopped and pointed. "There's Lewis and Vaughn! Get in!"

They jumped into the Dodge and watched as Lewis and Vaughn got into a jet black Camaro.

"Run the tags!" Morris ordered. He began fidgeting in his seat, thrusting hands into his pants pockets in search of the keys.

"Dispatch, this is Agent Fuller. We need to run a tag."

The radio crackled back, "This is dispatch, go ahead."

Morris found the keys, jabbed one into the ignition, and twisted. The engine cranked but didn't start. Up the block, the Camaro fired to life and rumbled away.

"Let's go!" Fuller demanded.

"This is dispatch," the radio repeated. "Go ahead with the tag."

"U as in Uniform. B as in Bravo . . ."

Morris tried again. He pumped the accelerator, turned the key. The ignition clicked. The engine barked rhythmically . . . but failed to catch.

"Come on!"

"There's Vispeti!" Fuller said.

The Vette emerged, wolflike, from the alley and prowled up the street, following the Camaro around the corner.

Fuller twisted the dial on the radio. "Houseman! Houseman! Come in! This is Fuller!" Static filled the pause. "Houseman!" More static. "Houseman! Do you read me?" He swore.

"Try Waters!" Morris suggested, jiggling the key frantically.

"It would take him twenty minutes to get here from Memorial— even with a strobe on the roof."

Morris turned the ignition a dozen more times, then slammed his hands down on the steering wheel. Shaking his head in disgust, he popped the hood and got out to take a look.

"Dispatch," Fuller said wearily, readjusting the radio dial. "This is Fuller. We've lost the subjects. Repeat—we are no longer visual. Agent Houseman is off the air. Are there any teams in the area that can take up pursuit?"

After a burst of static, the voice replied, "Negative. The closest team is over on the Strip—on a treasury department stakeout."

Fuller punched the dash. "Can you tell what the problem is?"

"Yeah," Morris sighed. "We're missing some plugs."

They both grumbled obscenities at Tito Vispeti.

"Dispatch," Fuller finally muttered into the mike, "put an all points out on a black, late model Z28 Camaro—license U-B-E-T-Y-A." He paused, then: "Request a tow truck be sent to our position immediately. We're dead in the water."

Forty-Five

"I'VE ALWAYS WANTED TO BE A NURSE."

"Is that right?" Junior Agent Waters nodded at the pretty young student. She had a dark complexion, silky black hair, and a figure that pushed the limits of her drab uniform.

"This is part of my internship."

Another nod. Her perfume was intoxicating.

"They always put students on night shifts." She rolled her eyes. "Totally destroys your social life. But . . ."

"Hey, I hear that," Waters sympathized. He gestured toward the chair behind him. "Here I sit. Probably all night. Alone . . ." Here he adopted a forlorn expression, intended to elicit pity. "Then I get to go home to an empty apartment . . ."

"You're not married?" The girl seemed surprised—pleasantly so.

Waters shook his head, frowning.

"Seeing anyone?" she asked flirtatiously.

"Nah," Waters responded. "Like you said, the night shift pretty much ruins your love life."

"Ginger!" a voice called from down the hall.

"Oops! Gotta go." She started down the hall, then turned back toward him. "I'm off at five. If you're still around . . . maybe we could grab some breakfast or something?"

Waters smiled at her. "Sure. I'd love to." He watched her continue down the hall, then retook his seat, happily preoccupied by thoughts of romance. Breakfast with an angel . . . Things were definitely looking up.

THOUGH IT WAS HIS FIRST JOB, JULIAN MOVED LIKE A SEASONED PRO: quietly, swiftly, his prey never even suspecting his presence until it was too late.

He lifted the billy club and brought it down with all the force he could muster. There was a thud as the hard, leather weapon met bony skull. The man groaned slightly as he slid out of the chair and onto the floor. There was no blood.

Julian stared, uncertain what to do next. Suddenly he was a novice again. Kill him, or leave him? The orders said to "eliminate" the guard at the hospital door. But why murder a federal agent when you could neutralize him and finish the real job: hitting the primary target.

Stepping over the fallen Fibby, he gently twisted the handle and pushed open the door. It was a private room. Only one bed. No chance of making a mistake. Of course, the target would have been easily recognizable in a warehouse full of hospital beds: male, Caucasian, mid-twenties, three hundred pounds . . . The leviathan under the sheet was obviously Sergeant James Donohue.

Julian checked the bathroom. Empty. He pulled out his 9mm, checked the silencer, then the clip. Satisfied, he flipped off the safety and pointed the gun at the target. His hands were trembling. He was breathing heavily, as if he had run all the way from the parking lot. Sweat trickled down his temple.

Julian had never killed a man before. He had never even shot at anyone. He'd seen others do it, heard plenty of stories . . . but never actually pulled the trigger. He licked his lips and flexed his trigger finger. There had to be a first time for everything. And if he expected to be part of the family . . .

He took a deep breath. Another. Swallowed.

The poor guy in bed just lay there, his face serene—sleeping.

Julian mentally rehearsed the lessons he'd gotten from Vince: Use a silencer. Got it. Shoot to kill. Aim for the head or the heart. Okay. He pointed the barrel at the man's eyes, then balked. Pulling back the sheet, he aimed for the left chest. Gripping the gun with both hands, he remembered the last tips: do it fast and get out. Oh, and whenever possible, do it in a contained area. Good. The hospital room was perfect.

He looked back at the door. It had a lock. He reached to push the button in.

$\int$TARS . . . PAIN . . . FOR AN INSTANT, WATERS DIDN'T KNOW WHERE HE was—or who he was. Throbbing . . . vertigo . . . Consciousness returned in pieces. Haze . . . nausea . . . His fingers examined a thick, tender lump on the back of his head. Seconds later, his training began to push past the pain and the accompanying disorientation, urging him to take action. Without fully understanding what had happened, he instinctively reached for his gun. He rose like a lush on skid row and staggered for the door.

As the hinges sang and the door swung open, there was a brief moment of indecision on the part of both combatants. Eyes locked, faces went blank, adrenaline flowed freely.

In the bed, Jimmy snored peacefully, oblivious to the confrontation.

The spell was quickly broken, weapons reacting, jumping to attention, eager to be used. It became a quick-draw contest: two modern-day cowboys drawing down on each other.

The more experienced, practiced gunslinger fired first. And despite being rushed, his aim was true. The opponent winced as the bullet bore into his belly, chewing through flesh and muscle before piercing digestive organs. Still, as he fell backwards, he managed to pull off a shot of his own. The small caliber hollow point hit a bony hip and spun the body counterclockwise, into a spiral that ended in an ungainly, slow-motion collapse to the floor.

As THE ROOM TUNNELED DOWN AROUND HIM, DARKNESS CLOSING IN like a clinched fist, Julian realized that he had just shot his first man. Unfortunately, from the feel of the steel in his midsection, it would probably be his last.

Agent WATERS'S LEFT SIDE WAS ON FIRE. HE HAD NEVER experienced such pure, undiluted pain. Using both hands, he pushed against the wound and watched as blood escaped between his fingers. He felt faint. Just before he passed out, he couldn't help thinking what a shame it was that he would miss breakfast . . . with an angel.

I MISSED PARISH."

"Yeah, we know," Tito replied.

"Huh? What?" The voice on the other end of the line sounded flustered. "How did you—"

"We're on him."

"You are?"

"Who is it?" Vince asked from the passenger seat.

"Mario," Tito told him. Into the phone he said, "Luckily for you, Parish picked up Lewis and Vaughn. We're playing convoy now, following them up to Tonopah."

Mario considered this. "You tell Sonny yet?"

Tito chuckled. "Not about Parish. You get to do that yourself, buddy."

"Yeah," Mario grunted. "I'd just love to."

"Better call him quick," Tito advised. "He may want you up north with us."

"Okay." The line went dead.

Tito handed the phone to Vince, then squinted up the highway, into the darkness. Red taillights formed a glowing trail across the featureless valley. They dipped and disappeared as they met the horizon. He spotted the distinctive lights of the Camaro four cars up—maybe a quarter mile ahead.

"Try Julian," Tito said. "He should have been in and out of the hospital by now."

Vince punched in the number and waited. "There's no . . ." He paused, looked at Tito, then hung up.

"What?"

"Fibbies," Vince said. He cursed and slammed the phone against his leg. "A Fibby answered Julian's phone."

Tito took the phone back and blew air at the windshield. Great . . . They drove on in silence for ten minutes. Then, guiding the steering wheel with his knees, Tito hit the speed dial sequence.

"Sonny?"

"And what's your problem?"

"I take it you talked to Mario. He tell you we're on Parish?"

"Yeah."

"So there's nothing to worry about," Tito said. "We'll herd the three of them right to you, then do them all at the same time."

Sonny grumbled something, then replied, "That's not the problem. The problem is the way this thing has been handled—or I should say, bungled—from day one."

"Hey, that's not our fault."

"Oh, yeah? Whose fault is it, huh? You can't get the bones. You can't hit Lewis. You miss a trio of marines."

"We put a couple of them down," Tito argued.

"Big deal. You and that barbaric partner of yours get paid plenty of money for these jobs. And so far, all you've done is screw up this one—over and over and over."

"What are you saying, Sonny? Are you saying we're fired?"

"I'm saying everyone has had it with your excuses. And now Parish is loose—"

"Hey, we're not the ones who missed Parish. And we didn't blow the hospital hit."

"What do you mean, blow the hospital hit?"

Tito swallowed hard. Great. Sonny obviously didn't know. "Vince just tried to reach Julian."

"And?"

"And he got a Fed instead."

Sonny burst into a fit of crude and abusive language.

Tito watched the road, passed an eighteen-wheeler, waited for the firestorm to pass. When it finally did, Sonny was almost speechless.

"I . . . I can't . . . I can't believe . . . This is . . . It's . . ."

"You want me to call you back?" Tito asked.

Air blew into the phone—a brief gust of manmade wind. "Do you have any idea what happened?" Sonny asked, suddenly unnaturally calm.

"No. Just that the Feds have his phone."

"If he does time," Vince vowed at the windshield, "or if he's dead . . ."

"I told you he was the wrong choice for the job," Sonny reminded in a guttural tone. "So let me review. Mario missed Parish—but did hit a Fibby. Julian apparently missed the Hulk at Memorial. Lewis and Vaughn are alive and well. We are still not in possession of the bones . . . Is that about the size of it?"

"I guess so."

"This is a nightmare," Sonny declared. He mumbled something. Then, "If things don't go exactly as planned in Tonopah, I promise you, some of us won't wake up from it."

"Don't threaten us."

"I'll threaten whoever I want to," Sonny steamed back.

Tito retreated and tried another tack. "Listen, don't worry. We're on top of Lewis and her friends. They're headed straight for you. It'll all be over in another couple of hours."

"You better believe it will." *Click!*

Tito returned the phone to its clip. "We're dead meat."

Vince looked at him. "What?"

"I said we're dead meat. Sonny is on the rampage. We screwed up. And even if everything turns out okay in Tonopah . . . We'll never hear the end of it. We're dead meat."

"Sonny's all air," Vince snorted. "He talks big. But . . . We deliver the goods tonight, and they'll probably give us a bonus on top of our usual fee."

"Yeah, a bonus. Like a head start out of town."

"We may not be blood to the DiCaprio clan, but we're part of the family. We always will be. And they take care of their own."

"Not when they screw up."

Vince shook his head at this. "We didn't screw up. This is a complicated job. A weird job. And remember, they were the ones who wanted Lewis 'watched' instead of hit. This whole thing would be over if they would have given us a green light and let us do her on Friday night. We wouldn't have missed."

Tito sighed at this.

"The problem is upstairs somewhere. Somebody panicked. Somebody had trouble making up their mind what to do about those bones. Whatever they are and whoever they're causing grief for, the bones are the reason for all of this. The bones created the situation. Not us."

"Yeah." Tito nodded glumly. "But the ax will fall on our necks. You just watch."

"Then maybe we should take steps to make sure it doesn't."

Tito glanced at him. "What do you mean? What steps?"

Vince shrugged. "The bones are the prize, right? So what if we capture the prize and offer to give it back—for a price?"

"Right. Like we're going to steal from these people?"

"Why not?"

"They'd kill us, that's why not," Tito pointed out.

"They'd have to catch us first."

Tito shook his head. "No way, Vince. That's the craziest thing I've ever heard. And the dumbest."

"Think of it as insurance," Vince said, picking up steam. "If they're peeved at us already, who knows what they plan to do. Maybe you're right. Maybe we're already dead."

"I didn't mean it literally. I meant out of a job."

"And if we're already dead," Vince continued, "what do we have to lose?"

"It's . . . It's stupid. It's a stupid idea."

"No. It's creative. If we had the bones, our safety would be insured. And from the effort they're putting into getting hold of them, I'll just bet we could parlay them into quite a little nest egg. We hand over the bones, they hand over a few mill. We head for parts unknown."

"And they find us and kill us in the slowest, most painful method imaginable."

"Tito and Vince—independently wealthy . . . millionaires . . ." Vince smiled at this.

"Tito and Vince—bodies found at the bottom of a lake wearing cement galoshes."

"Beach houses in the Bahamas . . . fine women in bikinis . . . all the rum we can drink . . ." Vince continued, relishing the fantasy.

"I want to live to see my thirtieth birthday," Tito complained.

Vince checked his watch. "How much farther to Tonopah?"

"About ninety miles."

"Good. Then you've got an hour and a half to make up your mind."

"It's already made up. We are not, I repeat, *not* making off with the bones."

Forty-Six

THE ROAD BLURRED . . . CRYSTALLIZED . . . FADED . . . VANISHED. THE Camaro picked up speed. The highway curved. The car continued boldly on its course, floating smoothly across the centerline.

"Watch out!" The warning was accompanied by the blast of a horn.

Vaughn jerked awake, blinking into the headlights of a tractor trailer. He swore and twisted the wheel. The truck driver hit the brakes, sending his rig into a skid. The Z28 rocked, jigged right, and barely missed the grill of the cab.

"That was close," Melissa sighed, rubbing her face. She had nodded off too. "Why don't you let me drive for a while. You need a break."

"I'm fine," Vaughn lied, still blinking. He shook himself and adjusted his rear in the seat—his heart still pounding.

"Fine my eye!" Parish chided from the backseat. He was spread out in the narrow space, head propped on a rolled-up coat. The horn had startled him out of a deep, foggy sleep. "You're gonna get us killed. Let her drive."

"I said I was fine. Just got sleepy there for a second. If it wasn't so quiet in here . . ."

"Turn on the radio or something," Parish suggested. He recrossed his arms and leaned back, eyes closed.

"We're all exhausted," Melissa noted. "This is crazy. We're in no condition to be traipsing all over Nevada."

Vaughn tried to suppress a yawn but failed. He toggled the window control and opened it a crack. Warm air streamed in, tickling his eyes.

"Even if we get there," Melissa said, "even if we give them the bones . . . I don't know. I just . . . I wonder if . . ."

"If what?"

"If they'll let Gill go. If they'll let us live."

"There's no telling," Vaughn replied. "It would help if we knew why they wanted the bones in the first place."

Wʜᴀᴛ ᴅᴏ ʏᴏᴜ sᴀʏ? Yᴏᴜ, ᴍᴇ, ᴀ ᴄᴏᴜᴘʟᴇ ᴍɪʟʟɪᴏɴ ᴅᴏʟʟᴀʀs . . . ?"

"I told you, it's nuts. Suicidal."

"But you can't help wondering if we could pull it off, can you?" Vince teased. "You can't help imagining the two of us in a tropical paradise surrounded by beautiful, bronze-skinned women."

Tito gazed out the windshield, over the hood, toward the parade of glowing ruby lights. It was tempting. But it would never work. They would never make it out of the country alive. And even if they did, the organization would hunt them down. Still, it would almost be worth it, just to stick it to Sonny—to leave him holding the bag.

"Come on, Tito. We're the best in the business. We pool our talents on this one job and . . . Man, oh, man . . . We'd have it made: riches, babes, everything."

But would we live to enjoy it? Tito wondered.

Gᴏᴛ ᴀɴʏ ɢᴜᴍ?"

"Glove compartment," a groggy voice from the backseat directed.

Melissa opened it and found a pack. She unwrapped a piece for Vaughn and handed it to him.

"Thanks." He began chewing it energetically, hoping it would help keep him awake. "Any theories? About the bones, I mean."

"Glove . . . compart . . . ment," Parish muttered. He sounded like he was still floating, held aloft by the potent array of painkillers.

Melissa shook her head. "I don't know."

"You found them in 217, right?"

"Yeah. On Friday when we went fossil hunting. Problem is, one of them is from a T. rex. The other is from a hominid."

"A what?"

"A hominid. They were precursors to humans. Transitional ancestors. Supposedly."

Vaughn glanced over at her. "You don't buy that?"

"I don't buy evolution in general. So when somebody tries to convince me that they've discovered a link between man and ape . . ."

"You mean, like . . . the missing link?"

Melissa nodded. "Basically. Whenever evolutionists discover something that doesn't fall squarely into the Homo sapiens or primate categories found today, they call it an intermediary. The problem is, the distinctions are pretty arbitrary—often based on fossil fragments, teeth, bits and pieces of skeletons.

"Look at Nigel. He was ready to call that little bone we turned up a hominid. But as a creationist, the only hominids I feel comfortable accepting would have been coexistors: primates that lived at the same time as human beings. Who knows, they might even have displayed humanlike traits, as some species do today."

Vaughn nodded, pretending to understand. "Is there a possibility that the one bone is human?"

"That's what I'm saying. It's either human or ape . . . in my opinion."

"But could it be . . ." Vaughn gazed into the darkness of the desert, trying to decide how to phrase his question. "Say it is human and not a monkey. Could it be modern?"

"Modern? You mean, Native American?"

"No . . . contemporary. You know . . . twenty or thirty years old."

"Doubtful." She stretched her neck, moving her head from side to side. "Nigel had the bones dated. Actually, he was in the process of having them dated when . . ." She paused, waiting for the tears to come. When they didn't, she realized that she was too tired to cry. "When he . . . was killed."

"So the hominid bit was never confirmed?"

"Not exactly. But he did know that they were radioactive."

"They were what?" Suddenly Vaughn was fully awake.

"Hot with radioactivity."

"Doesn't that strike you as a little odd?"

"No. Fossils are usually radioactive. The elements in them break down over time, giving off radioactive energy."

"Oh . . . I guess that blows that idea."

"What idea?" Melissa asked.

"We got involved in this because of Dr. Weber. Remember? I told you about him. He had these crazy theories about the federal government doing bizarre human experiments with radioactivity and then burying the victims out in the desert—in a mass grave on NTS soil."

"That's sick!"

"Yeah. And probably totally fictitious. Although the FBI seemed pretty interested in Weber's research."

They rode on without speaking for several minutes, the dull roar of the engine competing with Parish's snoring. Vaughn could feel himself sinking again. A sign flew past: "Tonopah—54 miles."

"Who would want the bones and why?" Melissa asked out of the blue.

"Huh?"

"Like you said, the bones are the key. All we have to do is figure out who wants them and why."

"Unfortunately, we can't answer either question."

"We haven't even tried," Melissa said. She twisted in the seat to face him. "Let's do who first. Who would want the bones?"

Vaughn shrugged. "A paleontologist."

"Right. Or an archaeologist. Maybe an anthropologist."

"What's the difference?"

"Doesn't matter. Besides, nobody in the prehistoric sciences would kill to obtain a few worthless bones."

"I thought you said one of them was from a T. rex. Wouldn't that be valuable?"

"To a handful of dinosaur nuts. Even more so if the fossil helped prove that hominids or apes or even humans were alive during the dinosaur epoch. That was what Nigel was so excited about."

"That's it, then. Some ruthless fossil hunter is after the bones."

Melissa shook her head. "Even if they wound up being the find of the century, I can't imagine a paleontologist committing murder to obtain them."

The tires hummed on the dark highway.

"I got it," Vaughn said.

"What?"

He gave her a knowing look. "Dogs."

"Huh?"

"The thugs we've been running from are working for a pack of dogs."

She glared at him.

"You know, dogs . . . bones. Maybe you dug up some pooch's stash."

"I'm serious." She took a deep breath. "Okay. Let's try the 'why.' Why would anyone care about a few old bones?"

Vaughn toggled the window shut. "Because . . . Because they revealed something criminal?"

"Maybe."

"Which brings us back to Weber's line of thinking. The big bad government is behind it all. They've got a miniature holocaust hidden out there and they want to keep it a secret."

"The government . . . That's too vague. Be more specific. Who would that involve?"

Vaughn sighed. "The administration . . ."

"Motivation?"

"Avoid a scandal."

"Good. The administration." Melissa put up her index finger. "How about the DOE?"

"The DOE for sure. If there really was a nuclear accident or radiation experiments, they'd be in on it."

Another finger went up. "Who else?"

"General Henderson . . . maybe. He oversees Nellis and the Site, so he'd know about it . . . probably."

A third finger sprung to attention. "Who else?"

"I don't know . . ." The highway curved again. This time, Vaughn followed it closely. "The Pentagon . . . the State Department . . . They'd be involved if there were casualties from atomic weapons tests."

"All right." Melissa displayed all five fingers, then put her hand back into her lap. "Now. Forget the nuclear cover-up angle. Forget about unsavory paleontologists. Where does that leave us?"

Vaughn blinked at her. "Nowhere."

How?"

"How what?"

"How would we pull it off?"

Vince laughed out loud. "I knew you couldn't resist. It's too sweet. This is going to be—"

"Slow down! I'm just asking a question. I want to know how you plan to make the thing work. Let's say I did agree to it—which I haven't yet—just how do you propose that we get the bones? What do we do with Lewis and her marines? How do we trade with Sonny—without getting ourselves killed in the process? And how do we get out of the country? We have to think it through, Vince."

"What do you think I've been sitting here doing—meditating? Shut up for a minute and listen."

Wᴴʏ ᴇʟsᴇ ᴡᴏᴜʟᴅ ᴀɴʏᴏɴᴇ ʙᴇ ᴄᴏɴᴄᴇʀɴᴇᴅ ᴀʙᴏᴜᴛ ᴛʜᴇ ʙᴏɴᴇs?"

Vaughn dismissed the question with a shake of his head. In the backseat, Parish sounded like an old man with a sinus disorder.

"What about the gunmen?" Melissa prodded.

"What about them?"

"They seemed to know what they were doing."

"Professional," Vaughn agreed.

"Who contracts hit men?"

"The CIA . . . Terrorist groups . . . The Mafia . . ."

Melissa's mouth fell open. "What if . . . what if . . ." She paused and stared out the blackened window.

"What if what?"

"The two guys that were after us . . ."

"Yeah."

"They were olive-skinned, dark-haired."

"So?"

"Could have been Italian."

"So?"

"Do you know very much about Las Vegas?" she asked.

Vaughn squinted at her. "I guess so. I grew up there."

"Who runs it?"

"What?" He was getting tired of this game. "I don't know."

"Think. Who runs Las Vegas?"

"The mayor."

"No."

"The city council."

"No. Think revenues."

"Gambling? Casinos?"

"Right." She leaned toward him. "And who owns the casinos?"

Aʀᴇ ʏᴏᴜ ɪɴ, ᴏʀ ɴᴏᴛ?"

Tito hesitated, common sense making one last appeal. Agreeing to the scheme was tantamount to signing his own death warrant. Cross the

organization? It was utterly foolish . . . reckless . . . exceedingly dangerous. Why go against the grain, against sound judgment, to act out a plan
concocted by a depraved—possibly brain-damaged—individual whose
primary pleasures in life revolved around sex and murder? The odds of
success were nil. They stood a better chance of winning the lottery.

On the other hand, what did he have to lose. His life? Yes. But what
kind of life was it? Living alone. Hanging out at Club Blue—with
Vince. Biding time between jobs. Performing contract work: blowing
away anyone and everyone the organization asked him to. Doing everything within his power to please his employers. The money was good,
sure. But it was still immoral. A form of prostitution. Worse, really. It was
brutal . . . criminal . . . horrific . . .

And what if they made it? What if luck smiled on them and they
somehow escaped the long arm of the organization? He could ditch
Vince and live out his days in a warm climate. No more killing. No
more guns. Maybe he would meet someone. Maybe he could invest his
share in a business—something respectable. Suddenly his mind was alive
with dreams of a life unblemished by murder and mayhem.

"Well? Are you in?" Vince repeated.

"Yeah," Tito nodded. "I'm in."

"Catch up to them."

"Now?"

"We're only forty miles from Tonopah. It has to be now. Let's go!"

Tito pressed down on the accelerator. The 450 purred and the
speedometer inched up. He pulled into the passing lane. Taillights
streamed by: dots of red suspended in space. To him, they seemed to
represent time—years—his future flowing by as they rushed toward
almost certain destruction.

THE MOB?"

"It fits," Melissa said. "Italian gunmen in Corvettes shooting at
us. Remember how the people at Titans Temple helped them try to
catch us?"

"Yeah." He considered this. "But what would the Vegas mob want
with old bones?"

"Maybe you were right. Maybe they're human bones. And maybe
they aren't so old."

"Huh?"

"What if . . ."

The interior of the car was suddenly ablaze with artificial light.

"Where'd he come from?" Vaughn wondered, squinting into the rearview mirror. "The idiot has his brights on."

Night returned as the car zipped out and passed them, leaving them behind as if they were parked.

"The nut must be doing twenty or thirty miles over the limit," Vaughn said. He turned his attention back to Melissa. "Anyway . . . What were you saying?"

"I was just wondering if maybe . . ." Her head swiveled from Vaughn to the windshield. "Look out!"

Brake lights materialized out of the darkness: a car stopping in the middle of the road—directly in their path! Vaughn reacted by stomping on the brakes. The wheels locked and the Camaro skidded sideways, then backwards—a two-ton missile scraping its way down the shoulder at seventy miles per hour. It had completed a 360 and was sideways again when the tires lost the pavement and went airborne over a steep ravine.

Forty-Seven

THEY WERE WEIGHTLESS, ASTRONAUTS FLOATING IN ORBIT. ONE FLIP . . . Another . . . The fuselage returning to earth . . . Shocks groaning at the impact. A second, shorter flight as the tires leapt from the ground, then kissed it again. Dust . . . A rocking motion . . .

Ominous silence.

Slowly, the sound of air entering and leaving three lungs filled the void. Breath . . . It notified them each that they were still alive, that they had survived the journey through space.

"Is everyone all right?" Vaughn asked, his face pale, his heart pounding.

Melissa held her face in trembling hands. "I . . . think . . . so."

"I was up close and personal with the roof a few times there," Parish reported. "But considering I wasn't belted in . . . What happened? Did you nod off again?"

"No," Vaughn groaned.

"A car stopped right in front of us," Melissa said, still shaken. "In the middle of the road!"

Vaughn popped open the door and examined the body by the dim light of the interior lamp. "Believe it or not, Phil, I think your car's okay. Might need a front-end alignment or fresh shocks, but otherwise . . ."

Behind him another car turned off the highway and rolled toward them. Vaughn put a hand to his eyes and squinted through the glare. It was low and sleek. A sports car. He couldn't make out the color.

The car stopped, its headlights still straight on, and both doors swung open. They were long, like those of the Camaro. The engine idled throatily.

"You folks okay?" a male voice asked.

"I think so."

"Who is it?" Parish wanted to know. "Is it the police?"

"No."

"We saw what happened," another voice said from behind the glare. "Nasty spill. You folks are lucky to be alive." Shoes moved in the dirt and two figures stepped past the hood, into the high beams: dark outlines against horizontal shafts of white. Dust particles danced and swirled playfully.

Melissa was the first to notice that one of the men was holding something. It was metallic, gleaming in the headlights, and gave his right arm an unnatural, protracted appearance—as if his pointer finger was six or seven inches too long.

"Uh-oh . . ."

"What?" Vaughn asked.

"I think he's got a gun."

With that pronouncement, the shadowed car took on form: long doors, low chassis, scooped hood, contoured roof . . . A Corvette. *The* Corvette.

"It's them," Parish whispered from the backseat. "Get back in, Steve!"

Vaughn took a step backwards and reached for the door. The man on the right lifted his arm. There was a clicking sound.

"Don't even think about it!"

"Phil . . ." Vaughn urged without moving his lips. "Where are those pistols?"

"Hands in the air!" the man ordered. The figure beside him now had his gun raised.

"What should we do?" Melissa asked, frozen in her seat.

"Pray!"

"Move away from the car!"

Vaughn hesitated. The scene at Titans Temple flashed through his head: leaping out of harm's way, narrowly avoiding the bullets, escaping, protecting Melissa in herolike fashion . . . Could it possibly happen again? If only he had a gun. If only there was a distraction, something to avert their eyes, even for a split second. Then he could—

"I said move!" The revolver approached, a long, thick barrel silhouetted in the headlights.

"It's now or never," Vaughn muttered. His mind was racing, the adrenaline flowing: fight or flight! He looked to the backseat out of the corner of his eye. "Phil?"

"They're right here, Steve. But I'm not sure what you want me to do with them. Those guys aren't gonna just stand there while you reach back here."

"Do what they tell you to, Steve," Melissa warned. Her lips continued to move as she pleaded for God to intervene. "Lord! Protect us! Be a hedge around us. Send your angels to defend us against these men."

"This would be a good time for another one of those miracles," Vaughn said. His shirt was sticking to him, his skin damp and clammy.

"Move!"

He took three halting steps forward.

"Down! On your knees!"

"Dear God! Don't let him die!"

He knelt on the rocky ground.

"Hands on your head!"

Vaughn obeyed. He tried to say something, but couldn't. His lungs refused to hold air for longer than a second at a time. He was dizzy: headlights, shadows, dust, a canopy of stars overhead . . . they all seemed to be in motion.

"Lord Jesus! Please!"

One of the men aimed a revolver at the Camaro and its occupants. The other stood over Vaughn. He placed the barrel against Vaughn's temple.

"Oh, dear Lord—*No!*"

Melissa's shriek was the last thing Captain Steven R. Vaughn heard. Her panicked voice seemed to echo through the desert, careening from hill to horizon to sky, rocketing up into the Milky Way as the night exploded in a shower of sparks . . . The world flickered, disintegrated, disappeared.

---

*S*O WHAT'S THE BIG CRISIS, BILL?"

"A call from the Secretary, sir."

"I don't suppose it could have waited until morning."

"Uh . . . no, sir. I don't think so."

"Okay. Then cut to the chase. What did he say?"

"He said he knows what's in 217."

"And what might that be?"

"Bodies."

"Bodies?" General Henderson sank into his chair and began working the knot in his tie. He was still in his dress uniform, a broad square of colorful ribbons and badges decorating his chest. The urgent message from Colonel Johnson had reached him midway through the awards banquet. To his wife's chagrin, he had agreed to meet Johnson at command headquarters. He had abandoned his better half at the officer's club, left her standing there stewing, demanding with her eyes that he return within the hour—as promised—or else.

"Bodies?" he repeated. The knot finally gave and he tore the tie away from his neck. After unbuttoning his collar he asked, "He say how he knew this?"

"Yes, sir," Johnson replied, still standing. "It's all in the report."

"Bodies?" Henderson frowned at the folder on his desk, then leaned forward and flipped it open. Inside was a twenty-page manuscript. "I'm a dead man."

"Excuse me, sir?"

"Call my wife," he groaned. "She's at the club. Tell her . . . tell her I've been detained. I'll be back as soon as I can." He ran a hand over his face. "And get us some coffee."

"Yes, sir." Johnson left to attend to it.

While he was gone, Henderson scanned the material. The report read like a page out of the *National Enquirer:* Payoffs, bribes, favors, covert meetings, intelligence leaks, secret agreements and contracts . . . It was sensational. Unbelievable. Henderson would have dismissed it offhand had it not come from the Secretary himself. The final page was a faxed memo that amounted to a confession. The last paragraph promised a full testimony under oath in return for immunity and federal protection. The signature at the bottom read: Robert DiCaprio.

Johnson was back in five minutes bearing a chrome pot and two mugs. He poured Henderson a cup and set it next to the report.

"He admitted all of this?" the general asked, incredulously. "Just . . . out of the blue?"

Johnson shrugged. "Yes, sir."

"Why us?"

"Sir?"

"Why did he decide to spill his guts to us? Why not the FBI?"

"No idea, sir. I guess he trusts you."

Henderson snorted at this. He turned the report over, sipped at the coffee, and started at the beginning again, reading the material more carefully this time.

"When did he call?"

The colonel took one of the empty seats in front of Henderson's desk, cradling his mug. "About two hours ago."

"Two *hours*? Why wasn't I notified?"

"I notified you as soon as I could, sir," Johnson answered defensively. "In your absence, the call was routed to me. When I determined the nature of the Secretary's message, I asked if I could record the call. He agreed to that. After he finished the statement and sent the fax transmission, I took the tape over to the pool and had them transcribe and type it up. Then I tracked you down at the club, sir."

"Good gosh," the General mumbled, reading. He paused to flip the page. "I knew DiCaprio was related to the Teamsters and the Vegas mob, but . . ."

"His uncle's a casino don," Johnson threw in helpfully.

"But this . . ." Henderson shook his head at the report. "This is hard to believe. A man of his stature and intelligence . . . Why would he do something so stupid?"

The colonel shook his head. "No idea, sir."

"And this business out in 217 . . ." He paged through the report, searching. "Here it is." His eyes raced down the sheet. "This steams me. It really does. If the guy wants to play fast and loose with his career—scratching the mob's back in return for a quick trip to the top of the heap—that's his business. But he has no right to screw around with my zone. That's my territory out there. My responsibility."

"Yes, sir."

"I don't care who he is or who he works for. The Test Site is my show—a military installation, under my direct supervision."

"Yes, sir."

The general's cheeks were red, his eyes flashing with anger as he built toward critical mass. "You know what this does, Bill?"

"Sir?"

"It makes me look bad—like I don't know what the heck I'm doing. Like I'm incompetent. Like I don't pay attention to what's going on right under my nose."

"General," Johnson consoled, "you weren't even supervising the Site when DiCaprio 'annexed' 217."

"Doesn't matter," he mumbled. "Heads will roll over this. The whole thing will snowball, it'll crash through the DOE and land right in my office. Heads will roll. And mine might just be one of them."

"I hope not, sir," Johnson submitted.

The general glared at the report. "If the press gets wind of this before we can handle it internally . . ." He thought aloud. "There'll be heck to pay—from the administration right on down the line."

"Would you like me to try to reach Secretary DiCaprio?" Johnson asked.

"No. Not yet. I'm in no mood to talk to that little creep." He sighed and bent to remove his dress shoes. From beneath the desk he grunted, "Get the Bureau on the horn. And get Major Wallace in here." He sighed again as he slipped off his jacket. "We'll need more coffee, Bill. Barrels of it." After a pause he muttered, "I'm a dead man."

"Sir?"

"Arrange a driver for my wife. Tell her . . . Tell her something important's come up. Tell her to go home without me—and not to wait up. Looks like it'll be a long night."

Houseman had his throat cut. Waters was shot. He's in the hospital—occupying a bed instead of guarding a patient's door. And you lost Lewis, Vaughn, and Parish!"

Morris nodded sheepishly. "Bad night, sir."

Dick Foreman, the supervisor of the Las Vegas office of the Federal Bureau of Investigations, responded to this quip with a curt curse. "I'd say that's an understatement. Wouldn't you? More like something out of *Nightmare on Elm Street.*" He aimed a stern, admonishing glare at Morris, then at Fuller.

"And you still don't know what we're chasing. Is that right?"

"Well, sir," Morris said. "We know more than we did."

"Which isn't difficult." Foreman sank into his chair. "Anything is more than nothing."

"We made Tito Vispeti tonight," Fuller explained. He paused to light a fresh cigarette from a waning butt. "He's the reason we lost Lewis and the marines."

"He led us away from Lewis's apartment," Morris said.

"And you both followed him—leaving Lewis unprotected—without calling backup, because . . . ?"

Morris swallowed the lump in his throat and turned to his partner for an answer. "There wasn't time for backup, sir," Fuller said, puffing smoke with each word. "It all happened so fast."

"And we thought he was alone."

"We almost caught him too," Fuller lied.

"Yeah. I'll just bet." He shut the folder in disgust. "Vispeti is what . . . twenty-seven? Works out like a madman. And you two . . . Why, you're a couple of Olympic track stars when it comes to running down perps: Roly-Poly and Mr. Smokestack."

Morris ignored this. "We know that Lewis agreed to meet with someone who kidnapped her student."

"Tapping her phone was your one smart move," Foreman admitted. "But according to the transcript, the caller didn't mention where the meet would be."

"They're supposed to go to a phone booth in Tonopah," Morris said. "And wait for further instructions."

Fuller sucked on his Marlboro. "That's why we need the helicopter."

"It's already in the works," Foreman said, scowling. "The pilot's fueling it now. Problem is, I don't know who to send up there. You two . . ." He shook his head at them and seemed poised to launch into another verbal diatribe, when the phone on his desk rang. He looked at Morris and Fuller, as if they were responsible for the interruption.

"What is it?" he asked gruffly. "Who? What's he want?" Foreman's eyes grew into saucers. "You gotta be kidding . . ." His mouth dropped open as he listened. "Of course. Put him on."

Morris and Fuller watched, puzzled.

"General Henderson," Foreman said respectfully. "Yes, sir. I understand you have some important information for us?" There was a long pause, then: "Robert DiCaprio? *The* Robert DiCaprio?"

Forty-Eight

"Father . . . I . . . I need you. I . . . Oh, God . . . help."

"What was that?"

"Please, Lord . . . somehow . . . someway. . . ."

"What are you mumbling about?"

Melissa glanced over at the driver. He didn't look like a murderer: young, muscular, quite handsome, with a kind face and eyes that sparkled with charm. His long black hair was pulled back into a gleaming ponytail that dangled halfway down his back. When she imagined a thug, she thought of a big, sour-faced oaf who went around breaking kneecaps. But this guy . . . He was more like a leading man—Antonio Banderas's sibling.

She sighed and returned to her petition. "Oh, God . . . please hear my cry . . ."

"What are you doing?" he asked, clearly irritated.

"Praying."

"Praying?"

"To God. Maybe you've heard of him. And then again, considering your line of work, maybe you haven't."

He sat up straighter in the seat, gripping the steering wheel with both hands. "Hey. I know about God." His hand moved up, down, sideways, tapping his shirt as he outlined a cross reverently. "My mother raised me Catholic. I was a choir boy."

"I'm sure your mother is quite proud of you now," Melissa deadpanned.

"I still go to confession . . . now and then."

"Bet you wear out a couple of priests."

"Very funny."

A car horn sounded behind them. The driver glanced into the rearview mirror, then noticed the small, black box perched on the dash. It had sprung to life, blinking red.

"That Z must have a hot radar detector," he observed. "It beat mine by a good five seconds." He tapped the brake and waited for the speedometer to drop below eighty.

Melissa twisted and saw the lights from the Camaro. The other hoodlum was driving it, chauffeuring Parish, who was still in the back-seat—arms and legs bound with rope.

Melissa pulled at her own shackles. She was handcuffed to the arm-rest and the metal was digging into her wrist.

"What are you going to do with us?"

"You'll see."

A sign flashed by: "Tonopah—12 miles."

"We were supposed to go to a phone booth and wait for—"

"Yeah. I know."

"What about Gill? Is he . . ."

"The kid? He's fine."

"But you're going to kill all of us. Isn't that right?"

The man sighed wearily. "My partner and I aren't going to hurt you—as long as you cooperate. As for Sonny . . . I honestly don't know what he has in mind. We'll be handing you over to him. Then you're his problem."

"Who's Sonny?"

"Sonny? He's . . . well . . . head of family security."

"Family? As in the mob?"

The driver sniffed at this. "Sonny has a nasty temper. Swears like a sailor. He can be a monster—especially when things don't go his way. My advice? Be real nice to him. He'll be peeved enough after we fin-ish with him. Probably won't take much to set him off."

"Finished with him? What are you going to do?"

He ignored this. "Just tell him what he wants to know, and every-thing will be fine."

"What does he want to know?"

He shrugged. "About the bones, I guess."

"What is it with the bones?" Melissa asked. "Why does the mob care about dinosaur bones?"

Another shrug. "We're just delivery boys. Sonny gives the orders, we hop. Or . . . at least, we used to."

The Camaro tooted again—three short blasts of the horn. The dri-ver of the Corvette responded by picking up the telephone. He punched a button and then put the phone to his ear.

"Sonny? There's been a change of plans." Melissa could hear a tinny voice curse in response to this. "No, you listen. We've got the bones. We've got Lewis. If you want them . . ." Distant shouting, swearing . . . The driver waited for it to die down. "If you want them, this is how it's gonna go down. First, you're going to call the boys back in Vegas and have them put together a little package for us: four million dollars." There was a yelping sound, as if someone was beating a dog on the other end of the line. The man listened casually, guiding the Vette around a plodding fuel truck. On the dash, the radar detector was still going crazy—red lights flashing a silent warning.

"I really don't care how hard it is or what you have to do, Sonny. Just get the money. And make it big bills—G-notes. All in one bag." The man watched the speedometer as they drove beneath an underpass. A state trooper's car was parked just behind the concrete embankment. For a split second the headlights revealed the trooper inside: an outline of shoulders and a wide-brimmed hat, an arm out the window pointing a radar gun at the highway.

"Pigs," the man muttered.

Melissa couldn't quite make out what the voice on the phone was saying, but the tone was clearly one of anger.

"Are you finished, Sonny?" the man asked, smiling. He seemed to be in a good mood. "Because I have more for you." As he waited, he rolled his eyes, shaking his head. "Okay. One: get the money. Two: have it in Tonopah in one hour." The abused dog began howling in pain again. "I don't care. Ship it up by carrier pigeon if you want. Whatever. Just make the arrangements. We'll call you to specify the meeting place sixty minutes from now. If you aren't ready by then, we're gone."

He flipped the phone shut and shoved it back into the caddy. "Sonny's a real horse's rear." He used the soft flesh of his fist to hit the horn: three short blasts. The Z28 tooted back.

Guiding the Corvette with his knees, he slid a revolver out of his jacket, spun the cylinder, and laid the weapon across his lap.

"I thought you said you weren't going to hurt us." Melissa said, eyeing the gun.

"This isn't for you. It's for Sonny."

How much longer?"

Morris depressed the indiglo button on his Timex and the face glowed blue. "Eleven minutes."

"Where are they?"

"How should I know?"

Fuller shifted in his seat, knees brushing the dash. They had been airlifted to Tonopah via helicopter and were sitting in a rented Ford Colt—a car that made the Dodge seem spacious.

"Maybe the time was transcribed wrong."

"Doubt it," Morris grunted, struggling to retrieve a briefcase from the backseat. His wide form didn't fit in the compact any better than Fuller's.

"Communications made us a copy of the tape," he said, popping open the case. "I think it's in here somewhere." He pushed legal pads and folders around inside the four-inch-deep square. "Here." Two fingers offered a cassette to Fuller.

Fuller pushed the tape into the player inset next to the air conditioner controls. When nothing happened he said, "Turn the key." Morris did and the radio blared. After twisting the knobs and flicking the tape in and out of the device several times, Fuller surmised, "Doesn't work."

"I'll call Vegas." Morris typed the number into a cellular and waited. "Yeah, this is Morris. Could you play back the Lewis tape for me?"

"I'm surprised anyone answered," Fuller muttered. He cracked the door open and let his feet stretch to the pavement. Above them, the dome light illuminated.

"Close the door," Morris urged.

Fuller cursed and folded his legs back into the cramped floorboard.

"Yeah. I'm ready. Go ahead." Morris squinted as he listened. Then, "Thanks." He hung up.

"Well?"

He jabbed at his watch. "Ten minutes."

"Great." Fuller lit a cigarette, handed the pack across to his partner, then surveyed the area. They were parked a block from the phone booth, next to a hamburger joint that had been boarded up and abandoned. The booth was on the corner, in front of a pub, beneath a stop light. They had been watching it for almost forty-five minutes and had yet to see a patron come or go from the bar. Only two cars had been through the light.

"This place is a ghost town."

"Pretty much," Morris agreed, lighting up. He stared at the neon signs adorning the window of the pub: Budweiser, Coors, Bud Light, Red Dog . . . "I could go for a cold one right about now."

"Who couldn't?" Fuller sucked, held it, blew white rings through fish lips. "Didn't Foreman say something about support from Nellis?"

"Yeah."

"You see any support around here?"

Morris swung his head from side to side. "I just see us, stuck in this crummy little car." He shot a stream of smoke out the window.

Fuller took the phone and dialed. "You guys see anything?" he asked the other team. His frown became more pronounced. "Yeah. Okay." He replaced the phone. "Madson and Bishop got zip."

Halfway to the stars, an airliner rumbled past, tiny beacon lights winking.

"I'm hungry."

"Me too. Wonder if that bar has a grill?"

"Nah. It would say bar and grill if it did."

"Yeah. Probably."

"Bet they have coffee though," Morris suggested.

Fuller flinched, deeply offended. "Don't talk about coffee if you don't plan on doing anything about it."

Morris nodded, exhaling toward the moon. It was a third full. "What do they call that?"

"What?"

"The moon. It's not a quarter moon. Not a full moon."

"Half moon," Fuller said, shrugging.

"No. It's more like a third. But . . . third moon? I don't think that's right."

"Who cares?"

A Toyota rolled to a stop beneath the light at the corner. Thirty seconds later, under a green, it continued on, past their position.

"What time is it?"

"You got a watch. Ever try using it?"

"Doesn't glow like yours. Look." Fuller presented his wrist. "Can't see a thing. Just glare from the stupid crystal."

Two men emerged from the bar, weaving. They climbed into a pickup and rumbled down the street, past the phone booth, around the corner, into the night.

"How much longer?"

Morris sighed. "Seven minutes."

THIS IS . . . FANTASTIC . . . UNREAL."

"Yep," the general grunted, sipping coffee. The shock had worn off and he was anxious to take action. "The question is, what do we do about it?"

"With all due respect, General," Foreman said, "We don't do anything. I appreciate your help and your willingness to cooperate. But this is a Bureau matter. I don't foresee any military involvement—"

"Quad 217 is mine," Henderson replied, tapping his chest. "So is Vaughn. So is Parish."

"I understand that, sir, but—"

"No buts." Henderson rose from his chair and leaned over his desk, meeting Foreman's eyes. "When somebody buries corpses in my zone, then starts chasing my people all over the countryside with guns . . . That makes it *my* business."

"General," Foreman tried to reason, "the FBI has the resources and the expertise to handle this situation. We'll take care of Mr. DiCaprio and—"

"That's not saying much," Henderson scoffed. "The little rat confessed—in triplicate. He's sitting at home right now, sweating bullets, waiting for your people to knock on the door and enroll him in the witness protection program. My grandmother could handle it."

Foreman sighed at this. "DiCaprio is just the tip of the iceberg. If his accusations are true, then we've finally got something on the Vegas Mafia." When Henderson started to interrupt again, Foreman held him off with a hand. "We've been watching them for months. There's been an extremely high turnover of casino owners and operators in the past two years. People disappearing, dropping out of sight. A restructuring of the power pyramid. We think they're attempting to reclaim the territory they lost when the big corporations moved in during the eighties."

Henderson threw up his hands. "Fine. Go after them. Keep investigating. Issue grand jury subpoenas. See if you can put a few of the crooks away. What I'm talking about is doing something—now! Tonight! I'm talking about protecting my people, about keeping them from getting killed!"

Foreman hung his head and examined his shoes. "General, really, we can take care of it. I have men on top of—"

"I gave this to you," Henderson said, jabbing at the folder on his desk. "The least you can do is let me help."

Foreman opened his mouth to object, but the general waved him off. "First, I want a full rundown on the situation. On the phone you alluded to a kidnapping, a midnight meet with the mob. Spell it out for me. What's going on?"

"General . . ." Forman sighed, "this is an active FBI investigation. It's a matter of—"

"Don't bother giving me the old 'matter of national security' routine." Henderson retook his seat and shot Foreman a stony glare. "My security clearance is about five or six levels higher than yours, son. Furthermore, the situation involves the Nevada Test Site and two members of my security squad."

Foreman frowned at him. "All right. I'll outline things for you. But we really do have it under control. I have a team of my best agents assigned to the case. So although I appreciate the offer, General, I doubt that you could be of any help."

"Oh, you'd be surprised, Mr. Foreman."

Wнат тиме is it?"

"They're late."

"By how much?"

"Six minutes."

"A no-show. And no telephone call."

Morris studied the phone booth, as if it were about to perform a circus feat. "We could hear it ring from here, right?"

"We could hear it ring from ten blocks away. Listen." Fuller cupped his ear with a hand. "Nothing. Silence. The town's dead."

"Maybe the meet was changed."

"Maybe."

"But where does that leave us?"

"Holding a bag of air."

Forty-Nine

THE CIRCLE-B ON THE SOUTH SIDE OF TONOPAH HAD ONCE BEEN A working ranch—six thousand acres of sparse grazing land where cowpokes on horses herded a thousand beef cattle. After the death of the owner in the late seventies, it had been hacked up into a dozen or so swatches, rezoned and developed: low-rent apartment complexes, trailer parks, gas stations, bars, strip joints, convenience stores ... In the past twenty years, it had been adopted by various criminal elements—of late, transplant Chicago gangs—and was now a decaying maze of drugs, prostitution, illegal gambling, and racial violence. The average resident of Tonopah didn't venture into Circle-B territory at night without a very good reason.

At the center of this micro-ghetto was the Circle-B itself. The old ranch house stood on its original foundation, a broad wooden porch running the full length of the building. It was surrounded by concrete, next door to a tavern, across the street from dilapidated row housing that looked like something out of East L.A. A pink neon sign had been added to the roof. It flashed and buzzed in the cool night air, promising that the establishment was open "24 hours a day," and that it supplied the finest in "female companionship." The B in Circle-B, a handwritten board in the parking lot noted, stood for "Babes"!

"What is this place?" Melissa asked.

The driver acted as if he hadn't heard her. Beside them the Camaro parked and the other driver got out. He was short with a hard face and lifeless eyes. "Pop the trunk." The Corvette's tiny trunk snapped open and the two men walked back and began rummaging through it. Melissa watched in the side mirror as they loaded a black leather bag with small cardboard boxes, then pulled out two massive shotguns. There was a clunk as they closed the trunk, another as they rested their load on the roof.

The Vette's driver appeared at her door. "Get out." He unlocked the cuffs and yanked her from the seat. She rose stiffly, legs threatening to cramp. Before she could stretch, the man pulled her arms behind her and shut the cuffs on her wrists again.

"What about him?" the Camaro driver said, nodding toward the back seat of the Vette.

The man shrugged, his ponytail bobbing. "Take him inside, I guess. He's not going anywhere, but . . ." He bent and began working a pair of legs out. A shoe came off. Mr. Ponytail cursed. The other man—Mr. Ugly—laughed at this and started helping. They grunted, swore . . . Suddenly the torso slid free. Ugly caught the head just before it hit the ground.

"Wouldn't want him to have a headache," he joked, smiling. His teeth had a yellow sheen that pulsed green in the neon light.

"Come on," Ponytail said.

Melissa followed them as they carried Vaughn's limp body toward the building. Glancing back, she eyed the guns sitting on the roof. For an instant she wondered if . . .

"Don't even think about it," Ugly warned.

Ponytail fought with the door and it finally creaked open. Inside, the light was dim, smoky—tinted red. The place reeked of cigarettes and sour perfume.

Ugly led the way. "Ladies!"

Three "ladies" were seated on a shabby brown couch in the reception area—in various stages of undress. They looked cold and bored, on the verge of sleep.

Shaking themselves awake, the "hostesses" rose slowly to greet Ugly—thin smiles, lids batting over tired, prematurely aged eyes. They balked when they saw the body.

"We have need of your services," Ugly snapped. "A room, please."

The temptresses stood there, dumbfounded, staring.

"We need a room!" Ugly repeated testily.

Another woman glided through a door of hanging beads. She was comically obese, fat rippling over tight elastic bands, yet seemed confident in her tiny lace outfit. "Vince!" She strutted over to offer a kiss, but froze when she saw the lifeless figure.

"Oh, Vince," she lamented, shaking her head. "Have you been a bad boy again?"

Vince grinned back at her. "I'm always a bad boy." He chuckled hoarsely. "We need to borrow a room, Clara."

"And I thought you came to see me," she whined playfully.

"We got a little business to attend to," Vince informed her. "Important business."

"Mi casa, su casa." She turned and led them through the beads, down a dark hallway.

Ponytail urged Melissa forward with a stern nod. "Go."

She obeyed, moving with the parade, watching as Vaughn's suspended form floated forward. The smell of smoke quickly dissipated, replaced by a sick-sweet fragrance. Either incense or cheap cologne—she couldn't decide which. The hall contained at least eight, maybe ten doors. Melissa wondered what sorts of debauched acts were being carried out behind them. This disturbing thought, combined with the nauseating aroma, made her stomach churn.

As they neared the end of the hall, a door swung open behind them. A black woman with long braids appeared. Her shoulders were slumped, her face despondent. Clutching a roll of bills in one hand, she trudged toward the reception area.

"How's this?" Clara ushered them into a small, dank bedroom. A king-sized water bed had been wedged inside. She flipped on the light and they were bathed in a red glow. Above them the ceiling was one giant reflection: covered with mirrored tiles.

"Perfect," Vince said.

The two men dumped their load onto the bed. It rocked wildly, miniature tidal waves pitching the plastic mattress one way, then the other.

"Let me know if you need anything," Clara purred. She winked at Vince before leaving.

"Here." Ponytail slipped a key into one side of Melissa's cuffs, pulled her to the head of the brass bed frame, and hooked her to it.

"Let's go get the guns . . ." Vince said.

"And the other marine," Ponytail reminded.

"Yeah. Right. Then we'll give old Sonny a jingle."

"Don't go anywhere," Ponytail told her.

When they were gone, Melissa glanced frantically around the room, searching in vain for a means of escape. There was no window. Nothing that presented itself as a weapon. Aside from the bed, the only other object in the room was a dented TV set that was bolted to a steel platform. Next to it was another door, presumably leading to the bathroom.

Melissa tugged at the cuff, jiggling it back and forth on the bedstead. The brass frame felt solid. There was no way out. Nothing to do but wait—sit and wait for her captors to return.

A Bible verse materialized inside her head, the words more ominous than comforting: *It is appointed for men to die once, but after this the judgment.* Was this her appointed time? Would this night be her last on the earth?

Dear Lord . . . God . . . Father . . . Do something!

"Uhhh . . ."

It was a soft, mournful groan, the sound of a man attempting to climb out of the abyss of unconsciousness.

"Steve? Steve!"

He moaned again, a leg flopping, then sliding to hang from the side of the bed.

Melissa stretched to touch him, to console him, the cuff cutting into the skin of her wrist. Her free hand met Vaughn's head and she stroked it lovingly. The blood from the cut on his scalp was hard, his hair matted in an uneven circle.

"I'm here, Steve. I'm here."

He mumbled something and his arms struggled against the ropes, anxious to attend to his wound. When the bonds failed to budge, he rolled to his side. "Geez . . ."

"You're okay, Steve."

"No . . ." he managed. "I'm not."

Jesus . . . Send your Spirit to heal Steve . . .

"Oh, man. . . . And I thought hangovers were bad." He fought the ropes again.

"Be still. Just relax."

"What happened? Where are we?" His eyes blinked open, the pupils pinpricks. He looked up at Melissa and tried to focus. "Was I hit by a truck?"

"The butt of a gun," she explained. "We're in a . . . a . . . bordello . . . in Tonopah."

"A bordello?"

Coarse, throaty laughter wafted in from the hallway. "They're coming back. What should we do?"

Heavy footsteps approached.

"Close your eyes. Act like you're unconscious."

"Not much of a stretch," Vaughn sighed, heavy lids falling shut.

"We'll think of something," Melissa promised. "God will give us a way out of here."

"I hope so," he whispered.

The door clunked open and the two men came in bearing their weapons. Vince set the bag on the floor and began loading one of the shotguns. Ponytail popped shells into the other. Neither acknowledged Melissa.

"Where's Parish?" she asked.

"Did you bring in the phone?" Vince asked his partner.

Ponytail tapped his pocket and continued filling the gun with three-inch, red cylinders.

"Where's Lieutenant Parish?" Melissa repeated. "What did you do with him?"

Ponytail looked at her curiously, as if he hadn't noticed she was there before.

"Is he still alive? Did you kill him?"

"Ready?" Vince asked.

"Almost." Ponytail finished his work on the shotgun and inspected his watch. "Sonny's got . . . twelve minutes to get the cash."

"Twelve minutes . . ." Vince snapped the shotgun shut and leaned it against the wall. "Twelve minutes and we're rich men."

WHAT DO DR. WEBER AND HIS ACCUSATIONS OF A RADIATION VICTIM conspiracy have to do with it?"

Foreman shrugged at the general. "Nothing. We just happened to have Weber under surveillance when this other business started to unravel."

Henderson's face screwed into an expression of suspicion. "Right. Just coincidence, huh?"

"Weber was a nut," Foreman explained. "A real pain in our backside. The guy had it in for the DOE and the NTS. Who knows? Maybe a few of his less sensational claims were on target. The DOE is a beast. Any big arm of the government is bound to have problems."

"Conducting radiation experiments on humans, covering up cata-strophic nuclear accidents?" Henderson pushed. "Those aren't run-of-the-mill problems."

"No. But Weber . . ." Foreman shook his head. "He was insane. Para-noid. And quite possibly dangerous."

"Not anymore," Henderson observed. "So he was killed because . . . ?"

"Because he found out about 217 and was planning to sound the alarm. Or so we think. He had breakfast with Vaughn. Then went out to inspect the Site later that day. He was killed on the way back in. You be the judge."

Henderson leaned into his desk, staring into Foreman's eyes. "Who killed him?"

"That's what I've been trying to tell you. The mob."

"The mob . . ." The general frowned at this. "Let me get this straight. They put a contract out on that paleontologist and his girlfriend in Denver . . ."

"Boulder," Foreman corrected. "We think so. Along with two techs at the University of Colorado."

"And they murdered one of your agents, wounded another?"

"Right."

"And they're after Vaughn, Parish, and this Lewis woman as we speak?"

Foreman nodded. "That's the way we see it."

"Why?"

Foreman gestured toward the DiCaprio file. "Because of that."

Henderson rubbed his forehead, as if he had a splitting headache. He poured a fresh cup of coffee, then asked, "What do dinosaur bones have to do with anything?"

"The dinosaur bone is incidental. Lewis was out there digging around. And apparently she found something human along with the fossil. That's obviously what concerns them." He shrugged. "So they've been hitting everyone who touches the bones or who goes out to that site."

"They being the mob, right?"

Foreman nodded. "DiCaprio is mob backed. Has been since his col-lege days. We knew that, but couldn't prove anything. Besides, all they did was give him money. Nothing illegal in that. But over the course of the past decade, it's been payback time. They want information. He supplies it. They want an ear, eyes, a voice on the Hill, he's it."

"They want a place to bury their dead . . ." Henderson added thoughtfully.

"DiCaprio gives them one—in a secure area in the middle of the Tonopah desert. Far away from prying eyes."

"So those are former casino owners buried out there?" the general asked.

"Maybe. And anybody else the mob wanted to disappear. The Vegas Mafia has been 'eliminating' folks for years—since Bugsy Siegel founded the place. But they've been extremely careful and secretive about where they hide the evidence. Without bodies, we have no case against them—aside from an occasional conviction on income tax evasion or a violation of gaming laws.

"DiCaprio provided them with a new, highly secure location to stash the remains of their handiwork. Everything was working out smoothly—until the secretary decided to blow the whistle." Foreman smiled for the first time that evening. "Bet they didn't expect that."

Henderson's mouth was open, a question poised on his lips, when the phone buzzed. He answered it.

"For you." He handed it to Foreman.

"Yeah?" The FBI supervisor squinted at the floor, listening. Then he swore. "Nothing? Not even a drive-by?" Another pause. "Maybe they made you."

Henderson watched him, curious.

Foreman cursed again. "Stay there. Patrol the streets. It's not that big a town. I'll call the local cops and the state troopers." He listened again, his frown intensifying. "Just find them!" He slammed the phone down.

"What?"

"Lewis and the marines never showed at the phone booth."

"What does that mean?"

"It means we lost them. It means the plans have changed. It means . . ." His voice trailed off and he shot an obscenity toward the floor.

"Let me help. Let me do something."

"There's nothing to do—short of a door-to-door search of Tonopah . . . if that's even where they are . . ."

Henderson tapped his phone console.

"Yes, sir?" Colonel Johnson's voice chimed.

"Bill, get the state patrol and the Tonopah police on the line. Patch them through to my cellular." He paused to think. "Get the AWACS up. Scramble the special forces alert teams A and B. Copter-hop them to . . ." He paused and fished a map out of his desk drawer. "Set up a convergence point on the . . . southeast edge of town. I want them on the ground in thirty minutes."

"Is this a drill, General?"

"No, Bill. This is the real thing. Weapons ready—live ammo. Loaded for bear."

"But, sir—"

"Just do it!"

"Yes, sir. What about ground transport?"

"Yeah. We'll need troop carriers."

"There won't be time to line that up, sir. Not in half an hour. It would take two hours travel time—another twenty minutes to scramble the crews."

Henderson stared out the window, examining the sky. It was a black drape bearing pinpoints of flickering light. "Rent something up in Tonopah. Rent U-Haul trucks if you have to. Just make it fast!"

"Yes, sir."

"And have my flight crew placed on standby. I want my bird air-ready in ten minutes." He lifted his finger from the intercom and pulled a thin cellular from his breast pocket.

"Bird?" Foreman wondered.

"Harrier III."

"Where are you going?"

"*We*. We're going to Tonopah." He rose and started for the door. The FBI supervisor grabbed his briefcase and followed, confused.

"General, I don't think this is a very good—"

"Ever ride in a jump jet, Agent Foreman?" Henderson asked with a sly grin.

Foreman shook his head, eyes wide.

Henderson shot him an evil grin. "You're in for a thrill."

FIFTY

PONYTAIL EYED HIS WATCH, THEN FLIPPED OPEN HIS PHONE AND BEGAN to dial. Five seconds later he asked, "You got the money?"

"He'd better have it," Vince muttered. He slumped onto the bed and tapped Vaughn's cheek with his fingers. "Sleeping Beauty's still out. Must have hit him harder than I thought. Or maybe marines just aren't that tough nowadays. Back when I was in the Green Berets . . ."

"Shhhh!" Ponytail chided. "Good. Now listen closely. Here's how it's gonna go down. You're going to put the money in a case and deliver it to us personally." He cringed, pulling the phone back from his ear. "Tell you what then, we'll just give the FBI a call. I'm sure they'd be interested in examining certain bones and in having a little chat with Ms. Lewis here."

"What a jerk!" Vince said. "Let me talk to him!" He reached for the phone, but Ponytail leaned away.

"Yeah, she's right here. Just a second." Ponytail held the slim device to Melissa's ear. "Say something."

"What am I supposed to say?"

"Your name."

"Melissa Lewis."

"And tell Sonny we've got the goods."

"The goods?"

"The bones!"

"They've got the bones," she repeated with a sigh.

"How's that, Sonny? Satisfied?" he asked. "We're at the Circle-B. You know where that is, right? Bring the cash. Come alone. If we so much as sniff an ambush, we'll take defensive measures." Pause. "Let's just say that we haven't left ourselves without recourse. You mess with us, the FBI gets a nice little package in the mail." The line was alive with profanity. "Be

The noise of the trucks rose, then fell away as they passed behind the school facility. In their absence, other sounds disrupted the silence. First a high-pitched whine arose from the south—a giant mosquito moving in to attack. It was followed by a chaotic thumping—something akin to a sheet being beaten with an oar. In a matter of seconds, Morris and Fuller were surrounded, hemmed in by the roar of engines, enveloped by blinking lights.

As the trucks plodded up to the field, gears grinding, a military helicopter dove out of the sky like a bird of prey, touching down just twenty yards in front of the Dodge. Shadows leapt from the bay door, disappearing into the darkness, while the propeller continued to whip the air. Another Chinook fell gently to earth fifty yards to their right. More ghosts escaped onto the field. A third kissed the ground. A fourth. A fifth. A sixth. Dozens of two-legged figures raced across the grass, gliding in and out of the tiny white pools created by the aircraft beacon lights.

"Good gosh!" Morris said, awed by the landing. "It's World War III."

"And we've got front row seats."

There was a tremendous roar behind them, a floodlight momentarily transforming the night to day. Blinded, the two federal agents squinted through the back window. Dust whirled into the Dodge. Turbines hummed, then began to unwind.

Before they had blinked the dirt from their eyes, someone said, "Glad you could make it." The rear door popped open and a pair of men climbed into the back seat—one of them Dick Foreman.

"Have you two met General Henderson?" Foreman asked, panting. He looked pale . . . ill.

Morris and Fuller shook their heads, reaching back to shake his hand.

"General, this is Agent Fuller . . . And Agent . . ." Foreman stopped suddenly, then fought to open the door. He fell out, retching.

"I think the ride up here may have bothered his stomach a little," Henderson told them.

Morris nodded. "Agent Morris. It's a pleasure."

"Mind telling us what's going on, sir?" Fuller asked.

"Yeah, what's the story here?" Morris asked. He gestured to the line of men marching through the truck headlights. They were clothed in camouflage fatigues, carrying assault rifles, their faces smeared with black and green paint. "These guys look serious."

"Special Forces," the general told them with pride. "When Mr. Foreman explained the situation, I decided to send our best."

Outside the FBI supervisor was on all fours, bent over on the pavement.

"General," Morris said, "with all due respect, sir. Uh . . . We're dealing with the . . ."

"The Vegas mob," General grunted. "Know all about it. They've got a boy. They're trying to kill two marines and a civilian. It's a hostage situation. Mr. Foreman briefed me. That's why we're here."

"But, sir," Morris objected, "this . . . uh . . . this battalion . . ."

"Unit," Henderson corrected.

"It's overkill, wouldn't you say, sir?" Fuller said.

"Nonsense. You boys need support. Just think of this as a well supplied, impeccably trained SWAT team."

"But General," Morris tried, "we don't even know where these people are. It's a little premature to send in the . . . the cavalry—so to speak."

"What are you doing to find them?"

"Scouring the area around the meet location," Fuller answered. "But it's a lost cause. We'll never . . ."

"Never say never, son. It won't be so hopeless with my people assisting," Henderson said.

"But, sir . . ."

"What harm can an extra eighty men be?"

Morris sighed at this. There was obviously no point in arguing.

"Foreman!" the general called. "Come on, man! You can lose your cookies later!"

The supervisor made it to his feet, still breathing heavily, and clumsily climbed back into the car.

Henderson laughed at him. "You're still as white as a sheet. But you'll live."

"Maybe . . . I wouldn't be . . . so sick . . . if you hadn't done those . . . barrel rolls," Foreman whispered.

"It was a split-S. And to tell you the truth, even the best pilot gets a little green now and then. I've decorated my visor a time or two myself. The G-forces and the vertigo just mess with your equilibrium. You get queasy and . . ."

At this Foreman gagged. Henderson patted him on the back, like a proud father. "Let's get going."

"Where?" Morris asked, starting the engine.

"Tonopah is laid out on a grid," Henderson said, withdrawing a phone from his jacket. "We'll just fan out and sweep it."

"The whole town?" Fuller wondered.

"If that's what it takes."

"Mr. Foreman?" Morris asked, looking to his superior for approval.

Foreman nodded, a hand over his mouth. His cheeks were pallid, his skin clammy. "Do it."

Morris steered the Dodge out of the parking lot. Four bright yellow Ryder trucks fell into line behind them, forming a convoy.

". . . Send a team in each direction," Henderson was saying. "Calculate the center of town and work outwards."

"This is crazy," Morris told Fuller in a whisper.

"Stupid," Fuller agreed. "Like sending the Hell's Angels on a fox hunt."

"At least we're not getting chewed out."

"Yet. As soon as he quits barfing his guts out," Fuller whispered, nodding toward Foreman, "he'll start chewing."

"If we're lucky, maybe we'll find Lewis and he'll forget about bawling us out."

"Lucky? It would take more than luck. It would take a miracle. An honest-to-God miracle."

FIFTY-ONE

A MIRACLE, LORD. WE NEED YOU TO REACH DOWN AND SUPERNATU-rally rescue us from these . . . these maniacs. We need you to send your angels to show us a way out. To protect us. We need you to . . . to release your power . . . to somehow . . . save us. We need a miracle."

"Amen," Vaughn grunted. They were alone again, the thugs having left to attend to their business with the infamous "Sonny." But Vaughn's eyes were still closed. He was still flat on his back on the waterbed.

"How do you feel?" Melissa asked him.

"Like I went on a drinking binge and this is the morning after."

"Can you get up?"

"I don't want to."

"I know," Melissa conceded. "But can you?"

His eyes blinked open, then shut again, his face scrunching up against the pain. "Ohhh . . ."

"We have to try to get out of here. Otherwise they'll kill us."

"Right now, that doesn't sound so bad."

"Steve!"

"Okay. Okay." He propped open his eyes and attempted to sit up. Bending at the waist, he jerked forward. The bed jiggled, waves slosh-ing beneath the plastic, and he slipped to the floor with a loud clunk.

"Are you all right?" Melissa couldn't see him from her side of the bed.

Footsteps approached in the hallway. The door swung open and Clara peered in. "Is there a problem in here?"

"You've got to help us!" Melissa blurted out.

"Honey," Clara said, "if Vince and his buddy want to keep you two tied up in here, more power to them. If there's anything I've learned over the years, it's to mind my own business. Never question a customer. That's my policy. And never . . . *never* cross Vince Scapelli." She shut the door and they could hear her moving her girth back toward the reception area.

"We're not going to get out of this alive, are we?" Melissa lamented, her faith eroding. She pulled at the cuffs, clanking them against the tubular brass frame.

From the floor, Vaughn said, "There's got to be some way out."

"You wouldn't happen to have a set of handcuff keys on you, would you?"

"No. But . . ." He scooted across the floor and put his head against the wall next to the head of the bed.

"What are you doing?"

"Looking for a miracle." He grunted, pushing his face into the narrow gap between the waterbed frame and the wall.

She could see his legs and torso writhing. "What are you doing?"

"My grandmother used to tell me that you have to put legs on your prayers."

"Huh?"

"Well, I don't remember the exact saying. I didn't pay that much attention to old Grammy. But I think what she meant was that sometimes God opens doors—and we have to walk through them."

Melissa sighed heavily. "I have no idea what you're trying to say."

"Just that there don't seem to be any angels hovering around, offering to unlock your cuffs." He twisted around and began using his feet to kick at the frame. It wobbled in response. "No lightning bolts. No booming voices from heaven. But . . ." He continued kicking, legs tied together into a single foot. The brass headpiece shook violently.

"But what?"

Two more kicks and the headpiece tilted sideways, plowing a furrow in the wallboard. A final kick sent it toward the ceiling. It bounced against the wall, then fell onto the mattress.

Melissa stared at it, mouth agape.

"Voila! There's our miracle."

"You broke it!"

"It wasn't even attached. Just wedged in there—between the waterbed frame and the wall."

"Now what are we gonna do?"

"Escape," he told her, struggling to rise. He sat on the bed and held his feet up to her. "Untie me."

She began working on the knots. "But I'm still stuck."

"No you're not."

"I'm not?" She gestured to the headpiece. "I'm just going to drag that thing along behind me?"

"I'll help you carry it."

The knots finally gave and she unwound his feet. "Stand up and turn around." She began pulling at the knots binding his hands. "We're going to make our getaway trailing a brass bed frame?"

"Don't look a miracle in the mouth."

"That's 'don't look a gift horse in the mouth,'" she corrected. "I can't get these. They're too tight. We need a knife."

"Well, we don't have one. Come on," he urged.

"Where?"

"Let's make a break for it before they come back for us."

"We'll never make it," Melissa observed, stumbling as he led her toward the door. Vaughn walked backwards, helping her support the headpiece. "Not all three of us."

"Oh, man . . . I almost forgot!"

"Huh?"

Vaughn propped the bed frame against the wall. "Be right back."

"Steve? Where are you going?"

"To find Phil." He worked the door blindly, opened it, and slid through. "I'll be right back."

The door creaked shut and Melissa stood there dumbfounded—shackled to her brass companion.

P OP HIM."

"Huh?"

"As soon as he shows us the money, we pop him."

"Vince . . ." Tito paused to survey the street as a bus groaned past. They were squatting next to a dumpster in the parking lot of a boarded-up gas station, directly across the street from the Circle-B. "We can't just shoot him . . . in cold blood."

"Why not? He'd shoot us if we gave him half a chance."

"But we made a deal."

Vince cursed at this. "And you think Sonny's gonna keep his end? You think he's just gonna pull up and hand over four million in cash? Without a fight? That lying, no-good . . ."

Tito waved him off with a hand. "How's this sound? Sonny treats us nice—comes alone with the dough—we treat him nice. Let him go his way. Sonny tries to double-cross us—"

"Which he most definitely will."

"And we respond accordingly," Tito said, cocking his .357, then his shotgun.

"You bet we do. We put that dirty scumbag down." Vince aimed his shotgun at an imaginary target and pretended to shoot. "Blam! No more problems with good old Sonny."

A new Lexus rolled around the corner and slipped into the Circle-B lot. With the lights off, but the engine still running, the driver's window slid down two inches. Beady eyes stared out. Ten seconds later the motor died and the door opened. A short, overweight man in a suit got out. He surveyed the street nervously, then jogged for the door of the bordello, his hairless head glaring beneath the bleak light of the street lamps.

Vince leaned against the dumpster. "The key is surprise. We have to do this thing fast—put Sonny and any friends he brings along on the defensive, grab the money bag, get out of town. We can't let him dictate the pace. If we do, we're dead."

"What if he brings an Italian army and hits the Circle-B guns blazing?" Tito wondered. "What if he makes it inside?"

"He won't."

"But what if he does? If he gets Lewis and the bones . . ."

"He won't," Vince promised. "We won't let him get in. But if he somehow does, trust me, he won't be coming back out—except in a body bag."

A low-rider cruised by, the bass from its trunk-stereo thumping at their chests. Tito examined his watch.

"How long?"

"Fourteen minutes," Tito answered. He pointed at the mini-mart next to the Circle-B. "What about over there?"

"Yeah. That looks good—the right corner of the building. You can watch the back of the B from there. And it'll give us a cross-fire to take out any uninvited bad boys."

Tito looked over his shoulder, down the alley. "If the bottom falls out . . ."

"It won't."

They watched as another car parked at the B: a late model Monte Carlo with California tags. A man in a ball cap got out. He looked up and down the street suspiciously before going inside.

"If it does, you can disappear down this alley. I'll head around the back of the 7–11 and meet you a few blocks west of here."

"If the bottom falls out, we're not running away." He gave Tito a long, cold stare.

"Right."

"You better hustle. My guess is that he'll show a little early—to scope things out."

"Probably."

"And I'm telling you, he won't come alone."

"Probably not."

Vince extended his arm. "This is it, man," he said, gripping Tito's hand. "This is our big chance. Let's do it right."

Tito nodded, picked up his shotgun, and trotted up the sidewalk. Crossing the street, he darted into the fluorescent glow of the all-night convenience store.

P$_{HIL}$?"

Vaughn stood in the hallway, his ear up against a door.

"Phil?"

Nothing.

"Phil?" he whispered at the next room. Nothing. "Phil?"

As he glanced up the hallway, he considered giving up and going back to get Melissa. There were a half-dozen more doors to check. Phil could be behind any one of them—or none of them. Maybe they had killed him. Or maybe he was unconscious.

"Phil?" he asked another door. Silence.

Phil Parish was his best friend, his buddy, someone he would do anything for . . .

He stepped to the next door. "Phil?" A female voice responded, calling him a derogatory name. He moved on.

"Phil?" But this was ludicrous. He was endangering Melissa and himself on the off-chance that he could find Phil before the two thugs returned.

Voices reached him from the reception area. Another customer. Vaughn opened the door closest to him and hurried inside. He watched through the crack as Clara ushered a man in a baseball cap into the room directly across the hall.

"Steve?"

He swiveled in the darkness. "Phil? You in here?"

"Right here. On the bed."

Vaughn toggled the light switch and Parish materialized, washed in red. He was sitting up against the headboard, as if he was relaxing— about to read in bed. Except that his arms were behind him, his legs glued together at the ankles.

"What's going on?"

Vaughn shrugged. "The hit men went to meet someone. But they're coming back." He sat on the bed and began using his fingernails on the rope binding Parish's legs. "This is impossible. Maybe if my hands weren't tied . . ."

"That would solve a few problems, wouldn't it?" Parish leaned, twisted, and presented the rope restricting his arms. "How about this?"

Vaughn fumbled with the knots. "I can't see what I'm doing." Thirty seconds later he gave up. "It's no use. They're too tight." He stood and looked helplessly about the room. "Can you walk?"

"Right. I can't even get up."

"Try." Vaughn took Parish by the arm and shifted his weight, pushing up with his legs. The first attempt merely caused a squall, the waterbed sloshing on its frame. The second attempt was successful— sort of. They rose like two vaulter's poles . . . and continued forward. Vaughn tried to catch himself, tripped, hit the wall with his shoulder, and went down. Next to him, Parish did a convincing impression of a mummy: arms and legs impotent to stop his progress as he wavered, hopped, tipped, and fell—face first—toward the floor. His head bounced as a bony cheek smacked the hardwood.

"You okay?" Vaughn asked, horizontal at the foot of the door

Parish's reply took the form of a curse.

"Here. Let me help you up." Vaughn flailed, his legs pumping. He grazed the door with his nose and finally made it to his feet.

Three feet away, Parish was scrambling to his feet. "I'll do it myself, thanks." The right side of his face was already purple, swelling as the blood from a dozen broken vessels pooled just beneath the skin. Using the wall as a crutch, he leaned and grunted his way to a standing position. "Now what?" he asked, panting from the effort.

"Now we find Melissa and get out of here." He backed to the knob and opened the door. "Come on."

Parish sighed melodramatically, then started forward: hop, hop, miniature duck step, scoot, scoot, hop, waddle . . . He lost his balance as he reached the doorway, careened off the wooden frame, spun into the hall, and thudded against the wall—still upright.

"Shhh!"

"We'll never make it, Steve," Parish complained in a whisper. "I can hardly move."

Vaughn performed a 180 and offered two flipperlike hands to assist him. "You think you've got it tough. Wait until you see Melissa."

FIFTY-TWO

TITO SPOTTED THE EBONY TOWN CAR TWO BLOCKS AWAY. ACCORDING to his watch, Sonny was six minutes early. Across the street, Vince whistled and waved his shotgun. Tito gave a thumbs-up in response.

The long, sleek Lincoln rolled lazily up the street, as if the driver were sightseeing—out for a leisurely Sunday drive in the country. The car didn't even hesitate as it passed the Circle-B. It continued three more blocks, made a right at the light, and vanished.

When it reappeared two minutes later, the Town Car was moving slowly, cautiously—a vehicle on a mission. Pulling up to the curb a half block from the B, it sat idling, like a panther crouching, considering its prey, preparing to attack.

Tito watched, waiting, wondering what Sonny had up his sleeve. Vince was probably right. Sonny was too smart and much too vindictive to let them take the money and run.

Having assessed the situation, the Town Car crawled into the Circle-B lot. The headlights blinked out. The deep engine switched off. The occupant—or occupants—remained inside.

Tito was so distracted by the Lincoln that he almost missed the Seville. The short, burgundy coupe had emerged from an alley—lights extinguished—and taken up position in the lot across the street—just ten yards from Vince. With the Town Car still silent, the driver hidden, the Cadillac's doors opened like wings and men began filing out. Two, three, four . . . It was like the clown car at the circus. After six strapping strong-arms had dislodged themselves, the trunk jumped open and the gang began arming themselves for battle—strapping on extra ammo, loading clips into semi-automatic rifles, pumping shotguns . . .

This was going to be interesting, Tito decided. Vince was in the perfect place—the only place—to hamstring the unannounced infantry. But six! Even Vince wasn't that good. He might hit three, maybe four before they blasted him to kingdom come. Tito wouldn't be much help from a hundred yards away. He might nail Sonny—if that was who turned out to be inside the Town Car. But even so, even if the money was really in there, even if he somehow got his hands on it . . . The chances of escaping clean—and alive—seemed slim.

Steal the car? Take the Lincoln and head for the hills? Might work. Or hightail it right now. Turn and bolt. Forget the money. Save his skin. Either alternative meant abandoning Vince. Leaving him for dead. Unless the dope had the good sense to sneak into that dumpster and keep his head down in the garbage until Sonny and his clan pulled out. Vince wouldn't do that though. That wasn't his way. He was a fighter, not a runner. No matter the odds.

What to do? He had never liked Vince. The man had the personality of a wolverine. And they weren't friends, per se. But they were partners. Comrades. Professionals. No. He couldn't just leave. That wasn't an option. They had to figure out a way to get the money—if there was any—and get out alive.

I FOUND HIM."

"Good. What now?"

Vaughn took hold of the bed frame. "Let's go."

They clunked their way into the hall, Vaughn plodding, hands behind his back, grasping a brass crossbar, Melissa straining, using both arms—free and cuffed—to carry the headpiece.

"This thing's heavy," she grunted.

"What the—" Parish stared at them. "You've got to be kidding, Steve."

Vaughn glared over his shoulder. "Do I look like I'm kidding? I'd ask you to help us lug this thing, Phil, but . . . you seem to be all tied up at the moment."

"Hardy-har."

"This is much better," Melissa observed with a sigh. "Now instead of being trapped in the room, we're trapped in the hall."

"What now, Maestro?"

Vaughn glanced up and down the dimly lit corridor. "There." He nodded toward the far end—twenty paces away. A rectangle bore the darkened letters: E-X-I-T. Beneath the burned-out sign was a steel door with a roll bar. "I bet that leads outside."

"And if it doesn't?" Parish wondered.

Melissa shrugged. "Doesn't really matter. It will take us a year to get down there anyway."

"Then we better get started," Vaughn prompted. "Come on."

After the obligatory groans, the trio limped to action: Parish hopping, losing, regaining his balance, Melissa struggling to bear the weight of her brass encumbrance, Vaughn taking careful, blind steps, righting Parish, sliding the bed frame . . .

They bumped and clumped along, creeping past one door, past a second . . . The exit loomed in the distance, an unreachable goal. The headpiece scraped the wall, chipping the Sheetrock. Parish did a nose-dive. Vaughn helped him to his feet. Melissa dropped the bed frame—picked it back up. A minute ticked by, another . . .

Three doorways from the prize, a woman emerged from the room closest to them. She had flaming red hair that reached down her back, almost to her waist, and freckled, ivory skin. She looked at them with a quizzical expression as she tightened her robe. Her eyes darted from the bed frame to the handcuffs to the ropes on Vaughn to the ropes on Parish.

"Whatever," she mumbled, turning sideways to slide by them.

As she breached the bead doorway behind them, Vaughn urged, "Keep going!"

The brute squad fanned out: two men taking up position on the street side of the Circle-B, two more moving around to the back. The last pair stayed with the Seville, each dropping to one knee behind an open door. Metal crackled and popped in the quiet night air: clips checked and rechecked, safeties switched off, hammers cocked, cartridges shoved into place—the sounds of war approaching.

When the preparations were complete, the armed hit team now still—silent shadows with guns for upper extremities—the driver's door of the Lincoln glided open. Someone started to get out. Shoulders tilting and emerging, shoes tapping the pavement, legs flexing, a head rising above the Town Car's roof.

Tito smiled. Even in the dark, at that distance, there was no mistaking the man's identity: small stature, square frame, hard features, cold eyes ... Sonny Tarantino had graced them with a personal appearance—as promised. Of course, he had also brought a battalion of shooters with him. That wasn't supposed to be part of the deal.

After a slow, careful perusal of the area, Sonny stepped to the back of the vehicle and unlocked the trunk. His head swiveled again, his eyes surveying the street, the convenience store, the Circle-B. Finally he withdrew a fat, oversized, leather satchel.

Tito almost laughed out loud. Sonny had actually made the meet—instead of just sending in a team of hit men. And he had the money! Maybe this was going to work out after all. Maybe the wise guys were just an insurance clause—to watch his back. Maybe Sonny really wanted Lewis and those bones bad enough to deal. Maybe, Tito thought, just maybe he and Vince were about to be very rich ... instead of very dead.

The trouble now was how to handle the switch. According to Vince, there was really only one way to do it. Surprise attack. Tito was the strike force—Vince the support team. Eyeing Sonny and his gang, Tito decided that it would have to go something like this: he would sneak in on Sonny and hold him at gunpoint. Vince would pin down the two doofs kneeling at the Caddy. The other four ... Hopefully they would back off when they realized that there was a shotgun poised to scatter their boss's brains across the parking lot.

Taking possession of the money bag would be simple. Getting more than a few steps down the block without being filled with lead would be a little more difficult.

He was considering this, wondering if Vince was in synch, when something across the street caught his attention: an arm waving at him from behind the dumpster. He waved back. It was time. Time to rock and roll.

Tito took a deep breath, gripped the shotgun, and started forward. Bent at the waist, he moved around the corner of the mini-mart, leapt over the short dividing wall, into the Circle-B lot—and sprinted toward Sonny.

We'll never get there," Melissa gasped with labored breath. They were still five yards from the door, several concerted efforts away from freedom.

"Hey ..." Vaughn puffed. "You're the one who keeps praying for things ... for miracles."

"Getting to the exit is just the first step," Parish pointed out. He was leaning against the wall like a human walking stick, his shirt stained with sweat. "Making it to the door, having it be unlocked, then opening it to find a cab waiting outside ... An on-duty cab ... Now that would qualify as a bona fide miracle."

"That would qualify as a delusional pipe dream," Vaughn responded.

They heard something behind them, down the hall: Clara laughing.

"Hurry up!" Vaughn urged. "Go!"

The approach was flawless. No one saw him. No one heard him. All eyes were on the Circle-B. He made it into the parking lot, used the Lincoln for cover, and arrived at his target undetected. It was only as he pressed the dual barrel against Sonny's temple that his presence was realized.

Sonny cursed softly, the skin on his leathery face bunching into wrinkled rows. His eyes flashed with shock, recognition, then rage. Thick lips curled into a cruel smile—a king cobra blindsided by a mongoose.

"You guys are good," he acknowledged.

"Tell your gumballs to drop the cannons."

"Or?"

"Or I send your gray matter down the block."

"When you put it that way ..." He sighed, swore again, then: "Drop the guns!"

Heads turned, weapons coming with them. Tito kept his eyes on Sonny, his trigger finger ready to send two lead cartridges rocketing down the parallel steel tubes. But he could feel the eyes, sense six guns aimed at his skull.

"Do it!" Tito said. "Or I waste the man you're supposed to be guarding. Wouldn't that impress the big boys back in Vegas?"

He watched for movement out of the corner of his eyes. Nothing. "Vince? Maybe they need convincing!"

"Move and you'll be Swiss cheese," Vince's voice promised. "Drop the guns, like my partner asked you to."

Metal bounced on concrete, echoing off the abandoned gas station.

"That's two," Tito said, nudging Sonny's head with the barrel. "Let's hear four more."

Sonny cursed at them. "Do it!"

More guns clanked to earth. "Now, let's all come right over here." Tito gestured toward the Lincoln with his head. Hulking figures filed in from both sides of the building. Vince followed two giants across the street, each a head taller than their captor.

"On the ground," Vince ordered when the group was assembled next to the Town Car. "Hands away from your body, face to the pavement."

The goons complied—a herd of moose settling in for the night on an asphalt mattress.

"Good," Vince said, grinning. "Now everybody just mellow out. Get nice and cozy. Stay put and you'll all live to get your backsides kicked by old Sonny here." He stepped over to Sonny. "Long time no see, Mr. T." Vince put his face into Sonny's. "Did you bring the money?"

Sonny's response was vulgar.

Vince's eyes gleamed, the grin blossoming into a smile. "Oh . . . You wanna dance? Huh, Sonny? Huh?"

"Vince . . ." Tito warned. "Not now."

"I've wanted a piece of you since the day we met." Vince licked his lips as if he were starving and Sonny were a T-bone steak.

"Did you bring a leash for this mutt, Tito?" Sonny asked.

"Back away, Tito," Vince said, raising his gun. "Back away and let me waste this piece of . . ."

Sonny swore back at him. "Lose the squirrel gun and we'll see who's the man and who's the animal."

Vince offered his gun to Tito. "Here. Hold this while I teach this jerk a lesson. I'm gonna show you how they taught us to fight in the Green Berets."

"No, you're not," Tito said, refusing the gun. "Give us the bag, Sonny. Slow and easy."

The heavy satchel rose, hovered . . . Sonny muttered something profane, then dropped it—a yard from his feet.

Tito kept the barrel of his shotgun against Sonny's temple, his eyes darting to the bag. Vince reached a foot over, his shotgun at the ready, and kicked the case, scooting it away from the Lincoln, away from the prostrate men, away from Sonny . . . into the bleached light of the street lamp.

 P HASE ONE OF THE MIRACLE COMPLETE," VAUGHN NOTED.

"Yeah," Melissa said, her chest rising and falling. "Now if this door is unlocked . . ."

"And there aren't any stairs on the other side," Parish added. "I think I'd rather get shot by thugs than do stairs like this."

"Try it," Vaughn said, his back to them. He saw someone emerge from a room halfway down the hall. Someone large. Clara.

"Hey! What are you doing?"

"Try it now!" Vaughn insisted as he watched Clara's wide form approach.

"Vince!" she called as she bounded toward them.

Melissa extended her free hand and depressed the steel bar. It creaked and the latch mechanism slid away. The door swung open.

 V INCE WAS KNEELING NEXT TO THE BAG. HE HAD JUST SNAPPED IT OPEN and was in the process of lifting the lid to inspect the contents when they heard a thud—a metal security door clapping against a wooden frame.

Vince glanced up—to his left—toward the Circle-B. Sonny's head turned. Tito looked, his eyes leaving his charge, the rifle drooping slightly.

They saw the open doorway. Sonny shifted his weight. They saw an odd collection of ropes and brass. Sonny reached. They saw the trio. Sonny gripped a polished pearl handle inside his jacket. They saw Clara arrive. Sonny drew his weapon. They saw Clara open her mouth to speak . . .

But they never heard what she had to say.

FIFTY-THREE

THUNDER . . . LIGHTNING . . . LIMBS IN MOTION . . . BLOOD PEPPERING the ground . . . voices shouting . . . bodies reeling, rolling away from ground zero . . . bullets chasing feet . . . cannons sounding the alarm . . . noise, movement, confusion . . . Chaos.

Tito felt the bullet pierce his side and snap through his rib cage. The tiny slug seemed to linger in there, wreaking havoc with various internal organs before ripping free and exiting through his back.

Before the pain or blood arrived, before his mind had time to comprehend that he had just been seriously wounded, Tito pulled the trigger and the shotgun blew smoke and steel into the air—at the stars. Sonny was gone.

As his legs gave way, the night sky swiveled and twisted. It seemed to dip toward him, following him down to the pavement. Life gushed from his side, trickled from the hole in his back. He could feel himself fading away.

He saw Vince duck behind the Lincoln. He watched as the brute squad fled, only to reassemble across the street. Vince fired at them. They shot back. The case of money sat unattended—lonely. It was just a yard from Tito. He could have reached out and touched it—if his arms had worked. They were dead, unfeeling tree limbs.

Next to him, the shotgun was still smoking. Where was Sonny?

"GET BACK!"

A bullet pinged off of the brass bed frame, then skittered down the hallway.

Vaughn dove for the floor, pulling the headpiece and Melissa with him. Next to him, Parish toppled over Clara.

Another shot made it through the opening, creasing the frame before shattering the only light fixture in the hall. The door began to swing shut. Outside, a figure started for it—an outline growing at the end of a dark tunnel.

The door hissed on its hinges, jiggled, continued its slow-motion trip. The opening became a crack.

The man ran for it, dress shoes clattering on concrete.

The crack became a sliver.

He shouted, hand reaching.

The sliver disappeared and with it, all light. They heard the lock engage. The man fought with the door, kicked it, fired a round into it, another, then . . . silence.

B*UZZ!*

Morris and Fuller instinctively reached for their cellulars. When neither was blinking, they looked into the backseat. Foreman shrugged. His was quiet too. Next to him, General Henderson was already talking on one.

"And I want another team to—"

Buzz!

"Hold on." Henderson fished another phone out of his jacket and flipped it open. "Henderson here."

Morris eyed him in the rearview mirror as they drove west, toward Henderson's next intersect point.

"Is that right?" the general grunted. "Good work . . . You bet I do. Keep me posted. I'll be up in ten." He snapped the phone shut and stuffed it back into a pocket. "Turn us around!" he barked.

Morris glanced to Fuller, then Foreman for confirmation.

"What for, General?" Foreman asked.

"My AWACS just picked something up."

"AWACS?" Morris wondered.

"That's a radar plane, son."

"I know what it is. I just didn't realize you had one out for this . . ."

"They detected small arms fire about thirty clicks south of here."

"Really?" Foreman asked. "They're that sensitive?"

"You betcha. An AWACS can spot a beaver building a dam from thirty thousand feet up."

"Then they're definitely worth the multimillion dollar price tag," Fuller observed in a whisper.

"Turn us around!" Henderson repeated.

Foreman nodded. "Do it."

"What if it turns out to be gang war or something?" Fuller wondered aloud. "Can your radar plane tell who's doing the shooting?"

The general ignored this. Into his other phone, he said, "Redeploy south. I want everybody down there. Get the coordinates from AWACS."

Morris made a left turn, pointing the Ford south.

"I said turn around!" Henderson chided.

"But sir, we're headed south now."

"I don't want to go south. I want to go back to the school."

"Huh?"

"My bird, blast it!" he said. "Get me to my bird!"

Is EVERYONE OKAY?"

"I don't know . . ."

"I think so . . ."

"Get off of me!"

"Who's this?"

"Watch where you put those hands, buster!"

"Clara?"

"I said get off of me!" There was a clump as someone's head hit the wall.

"Ow!"

"Phil?"

"I don't suppose anyone has a flashlight?"

"Get up!"

"Who?"

"Everybody."

Clomp . . . grumble . . . bump . . .

"Clara?"

A heavy sigh. "What?"

"How do we get out of here? Is there a back door?"

"You were just there."

"Any suggestions?"

"Run like heck before those boys come in here and kill us all."
"Good plan."

"TITO?"

Vince fired the shotgun, missed a brute. Dropping the empty rifle, he let loose with his .44. The enemy wisely stayed down, waiting out the flurry.

"Tito!"

He reloaded, glancing at his partner from behind the Lincoln. Tito's eyes were open, glassy like a doll's. Beneath him a crimson lake was soaking into the asphalt.

Two strong-arms dashed out of an alleyway, hurrying to the cover of a pickup parked on the street. Vince aimed, pulled the trigger. The slower man dropped, clutching at his leg.

One bad guy down. A pair pinned behind the dumpster. One behind the truck. That left two on the loose. Not counting Sonny. Where was Sonny?

"IN HERE."

Clara opened the door and hit the light switch. A heart-shaped waterbed appeared in the pink glow. The trio scraped their way inside, the bed frame dragging behind.

"You wouldn't have a knife, would you?" Parish asked.

Clara gave him a cold stare. "Do I look like I have pockets in this outfit?"

"They'll come in here after us," Melissa said. "Is there another way out?"

Clara's stare was redirected to Melissa. "What do you think I'm doing, honey? Giving ya'll a tour?" She gestured to a window. It was blacked-out with paint, covered with steel bars.

"How are we supposed to . . . ?" Parish started to ask.

Clara was already pulling at the bars, flabby arms jiggling. She grunted, yanked, and they gave way in a cloud of plaster.

"Does it even open?" Vaughn wondered.

Lifting a leg, Clara removed a six-inch, spike heel shoe. The first swing shattered the glass. The second and third removed the remaining shards. Warm night air streamed in. "Does now." She turned to them with a bored expression. "Who's first?"

Ladies." Sonny smiled at the four scantily clad women huddled in the reception area. They flinched as he entered. He waved his Beretta at them. "Don't worry. I'm not here for you. Anybody call the police yet?"

Heads shook, assuring him that they hadn't. One of the women began to cry.

"You'll need to in a few minutes," he told them, starting for the hall. "To report a multiple murder."

Vince shot another round, then assessed the situation as he reloaded his guns: bag of loot, wounded partner, armed resistance, car, the absent chief devil . . . He'd been in worse spots in Nam. Far worse. And he'd lived to tell about them.

This one just required a little creativity, a few judgment calls. First, the money. No question there. He would do whatever it took to get it. Second, Tito. He glanced at his partner. Tito's face was ashen, the pool of blood spreading. Take him . . . Leave him . . . Tough choice. The car was the key. If Sonny had left the Lincoln open, the keys in the ignition, there was a chance.

The wild cards were Sonny and the missing bad guys. When the shooting started, Sonny had . . . what? Dived? Run? Flattened himself on the ground? Vince couldn't remember. It had happened too fast.

A head poked up from across the street. Vince sent it ducking with a near miss that made sparks jump from the dumpster.

And the other shooters? They could be anywhere. Or nowhere. Maybe they had wet their pants and run away. Maybe.

He hit the dumpster again, then sent one in the general direction of the pickup—to keep that guy honest.

Time to pull out, he decided. Money. Tito. Car. Tropical island. In that order. Raising the shotgun, he sent a slug into the broadside of the dumpster. The metal screamed, compressing inward, and the entire container rocked. Another shot reduced the windshield of the truck to a shower of glittering dust particles.

He dove out of the shadow of the Town Car, toward the satchel. His fingers found it, gripped the handle. He hurried back toward the Lincoln. Then . . . *Bam!*

THE FIRST AND SECOND ROOMS WERE EMPTY. THE THIRD AND FOURTH were occupied, but only by the "hostesses" and their customers. He cursed at them and continued his search. They had to be in there somewhere.

VINCE BLINKED UP AT THE MAN ABOVE HIM: TEETH, FAT, OILY FACE, DARK hair, no-neck—all wavering, like a buoy on a stormy sea. The image was still floating when the next punch came.

Lightheaded, his mouth throbbing from the first impact, Vince reacted from training rather than feeling. He rolled, his body moving quickly, nimbly, seemingly of its own accord. The fist narrowly missed his head and continued forward, hitting the asphalt with a sickening crunch. Above him, the face contorted, twisting in pain. His foot took advantage of this pause, striking the man between the legs. There was a grunt. Goliath dropped to his knees.

Shots rang out. Vince used the fallen redwood for cover, commando crawling back to the Lincoln. Safe in his hiding place, he reflected on his progress: the money bag was still three yards away, Tito was still lying there, unmoved, in his own blood . . . The only change was that he had determined the location of one of the missing bad guys. And, he noted, spitting a piece of pearly candy corn into his hand, he had one less tooth in his head.

I'M OUT," MELISSA SAID. "BUT I DON'T SEE THE POINT." SHE WAS standing on the back porch of the Circle-B, one arm draped over the window frame—still hooked to the brass headpiece. "It won't fit."

"We'll make it fit," Vaughn insisted. He and Clara helped Parish toward the opening.

"Get up there, Phil." Parish wriggled up and through the window like a worm, then dropped, hitting the wooden planks hard.

"Now . . ." Vaughn said, taking a deep breath. "The frame."

"No. Now you get out," Clara said. "I'll work on this thing."

Vaughn hesitated, then nodded. "Okay." He threw a leg over the window and hopped out.

"These frames unscrew," Clara was saying as she fiddled with the headpiece. "I put them together myself. But that was . . . ten years ago. I can't remember which part turns . . ."

THE DOOR CRUNCHED OPEN, WOOD SPLINTERS FLYING. A WOMAN screamed. The dim red lights came on. The man cursed and turned to another door. Crash! Empty.

He was about to use his shoulder to force the next one when he noticed that it wasn't latched. He could hear voices inside. Something clanking.

Finally!

FIFTY-FOUR

$\int$IRENS WAILED MOURNFULLY IN THE DISTANCE. VINCE SWORE. TIME WAS running out. He looked at the goon. The idiot was still nursing his injury, two size-fourteen clodhoppers heels up, close enough to touch. And the plan suddenly formulated itself.

Fueled by thoughts of imminent capture and incarceration, he did it. In one smooth motion, Vince fired twice into the air, lifted the man—all 250-plus pounds—to his feet, and gave him a push. The man staggered forward, toward the street. Three guns returned fire, anxious to subdue their foe now that he was in the open. The brute groaned, twisted, twitched, and fell. Realizing what they had just done, the other men hesitated—gawking at their handiwork.

It was all Vince needed. He fired, winged one of them. Fired again. Saw another fall. Fired a third time at the numskull behind the pickup. Missed. Lunged for the case. He grabbed it with one hand, clinched Tito's ankle with the other, pulled with all his might, and made it back behind the Lincoln before a hail of bullets dug holes in the fender and trunk.

Above him, the dark window of the Town Car hid the locking device. He rose to his knees and squinted at it. The lever was up. The car was unlocked! He reached for the door handle, but as he did, there was a thumping sound—the mechanism slid down.

Vince stared at it as if it were an apparition. Someone had just locked the doors. Someone was in the car!

Sonny?

THERE!"

The brass tubes slid apart like a puzzle, pieces clanking to the floor. "Go!" Clara shouted.

"No!" a voice from the door corrected. "Simon says stop!" The man was pointing a gun at Clara's head.

Outside, Melissa, Vaughn, and Parish froze.

The man shoved Clara aside and climbed through the window, joining them on the porch.

"Where are they?"

"Who?"

He swatted Vaughn with the butt of the pistol, cursing at him. "The bones. Give them to me . . . now!"

"We don't have them."

The small automatic found Parish's face this time. "Don't lie to me."

"We're not lying. Those other men . . . they took them," Melissa pleaded.

The man swore, then looked in the direction of the parking area. The night was alive with the sound of gunfire, of law enforcement officers approaching.

"Go!" he ordered, gesturing toward the lot with the gun.

"What are you gonna do to us? Where's Gill?"

"Hurry up or I'll shoot you right here."

VINCE TRIED THE HANDLE AGAIN, BEAT ON THE DOOR WITH HIS FIST, kicked it, cursed it. A face materialized in the tinted window, vanishing before he could get a good look at it.

"Sonny!" he demanded, pounding on the door. Then it struck him. If that was Sonny inside, why hadn't he started the car and driven away? For that matter, why hadn't he hopped out with a gun and blown Vince to bits?

Lifting the shotgun, Vince pulled the trigger. The window bent, flexed, then popped out of the square in one piece. Not even bulletproof glass could withstand a .20 gauge from point-blank range. After cocking the shotgun, he pulled up the door's locking rod, took a deep breath, and swung it open. A shadow huddled against the far door, head covered by arms.

"Get out!" Vince insisted.

The shadow began to shake, sobbing.

"Get out!"

He reached in and grabbed a handful of T-shirt. "I said, Get out!" He yanked and the occupant of the Lincoln tumbled out. The barrel of the shotgun followed the progress, coming to rest on the mystery person's chest.

"Geez . . ." Vince sighed.

"Don't shoot me," a small, frightened voice begged.

Vince swore at him. "Help me load my buddy here into the car." When the order went unheeded, Vince jabbed with the shotgun. "Help me load him!"

"Okay."

Together they folded Tito's bloody, limp form into the backseat. Vince leaned in, sticky, wet hands smudging the leather seat as he checked for a heartbeat. It was faint, but it was there. Tito was still alive. Barely.

"Keys."

"Huh?"

"Where are the keys?" He raised up and peered over the seat.

"I don't . . ."

"Ha! In the ignition. Thank you, Sonny!"

A terrified face stared at him, waiting to learn its fate.

"Get out of here."

"What?"

"Run. I won't shoot you." Vince lifted the money bag. "Go!" He fired another round from the shotgun, nailing the dumpster again. Dropping the shotgun, he used his revolver to further damage the body of the pickup truck. When he turned back around, he was alone.

Sliding through the passenger-side door, he scooted into the driver's seat and turned the key. The sound of the engine turning over brought the goons out of their hiding places. They rushed toward the Lincoln like roaches converging on a crumb in a dark kitchen.

Vince shifted into drive and hit the gas.

GUNSHOTS AND SIRENS FORMED AN URBAN SYMPHONY, EACH FIGHTING to carry the melody as Melissa and Vaughn and the rest of their group rounded the building.

The man swore at the Town Car, lifting his pistol to slow its departure.

"Don't shoot!"

Suddenly there was someone standing directly in front of him—just three feet away—hands in the air.

"Don't shoot me!"

The Lincoln spun out of the lot, tires smoking on the asphalt. Three men chased it on foot, firing wildly down the street at the shrinking taillights.

Sonny looked at the kid, shouted an obscenity, and assaulted the wall of the Circle-B with his foot.

"Gill!"

Gill squinted into the darkness, hands still reaching for the stars. "Ms. Lewis?"

Melissa started forward.

"Don't," Sonny cautioned. "Everyone back here." He gestured to the backside of the building, away from the light of the parking lot.

When they had complied—Melissa, Vaughn, Parish, and Gill lined up on the porch—Sonny began pacing frantically in front of them.

A police siren jumped in volume as a patrol car screeched around the corner three blocks away. Dress shoes tapped the pavement in the parking lot—roaches fleeing the light.

Sonny began mumbling, repeating the same profanity over and over and over. He looked up at them, a dazed expression on his face.

Another siren signaled the arrival of a backup squad. Engines rumbled from the other direction: trucks approaching.

Sonny stopped suddenly. "On your knees."

The four captives knelt.

"Hands on heads."

They obeyed: fingers intertwined, palms against scalps.

Sonny crossed himself, then put the barrel of his gun against Melissa's skull. "Ladies first."

"Father . . . have . . . have mercy on . . . on this man . . ." Melissa managed to pray.

She closed her eyes . . . prepared to die.

Hold your horses," General Henderson told Foreman via the headset intercom. With that vague warning, he took the Harrier down. It dropped like a stone—free-falling through space. The patchwork of black squares and streetlight-dotted avenues jumped up at them. A parking lot emerged, widening magically, like a welcome mat ready to receive them.

THE SOUND CAME FIRST: A ROAR, AS IF A RIVER WAS DROPPING FROM the sky. Then movement: something big, descending to earth—wings, tail, fuselage . . . The wind rose to greet the UFO, throwing dust into the air, into their eyes.

"What the . . ."

Vaughn pounced, legs springing, hands grasping for the gun. He hit Sonny full on, shoulder down—a linebacker attacking a quarterback, hoping to create a fumble. Blindsided, Sonny reeled, stumbled, and fell, his head bouncing against the wooden railing. Next to him the pistol rattled, spinning under the rail before disappearing off the raised porch.

Righting himself, Vaughn hurtled the rail. Sonny performed the same maneuver. They landed in unison on the thin grass—facing each other. Sonny threw a straight right that caught Vaughn flatfooted, tipping him back, into a bush.

Melissa kicked at Sonny through the pegs of wood. He bobbed away, then bent to retrieve the gun. Another foot flew at him, this time from Vaughn. It clipped his chin, pushing him onto his seat. Sonny reached for the gun. Vaughn dove forward. One gripped the handle. The other pulled on the barrel. They rolled on the ground, grunting, struggling for possession.

THE TWIN ROLLS ROYCE TURBINES WERE STILL WHINING WHEN Henderson popped the canopy and started his climb to the asphalt. In the cockpit, Foreman's head was buried in a barf bag, his face olive green.

Two squad cars raced in, sirens blaring. A Colt screeched into the parking lot. Morris and Fuller jumped out. Trucks rumbled around the corner a block away, troops hanging from the tailgate, anxious to disembark.

Three thugs were facedown against the asphalt in the middle of the street, subdued by representatives from the Tonopah Police Department who had reached the scene first—in response to an anonymous 911 call. Three unmarked white Fords pulled in at odd angles, doors flying open to form an uneven circle around the perps. Everyone in sight was bearing a handgun or a shotgun.

Henderson drew his sidearm and pointed to the back of the building. "There's movement around there," he told Morris.

Morris nodded and trotted forward, flab jiggling, gun aimed at the moon. "Let us handle it, General." Beside him Fuller ran stiff-legged, neck craned forward like a chicken.

Henderson followed them.

THERE WAS A CRISP, EXPLOSIVE POP. A SHOUT. ANOTHER LOUD POP.
"Steve!"

MORRIS, FULLER, AND HENDERSON FLATTENED THEMSELVES AGAINST the retaining wall at the back of the lot. Ten seconds later, troops dashed across the parking area. The general waved them past—into the black hole behind the Circle-B.

The men sprinted fearlessly into the void, M16s pushing at any demons lurking there.

"Go!" someone shouted.

"In position!" another voice responded.

Heavy breath, boots on wood . . . then, "Two down back here!"

"Medic!"

"Clear!"

"Clear!"

"Secure the building!" a deep voice boomed. Boots hurried away, into the Circle-B.

Henderson nodded. "Come on." They ran into the shadows and mounted the porch. Two soldiers stood—legs wide—guarding three people: a woman, a man, a teen. The woman was crying, her breath coming in gulps.

"Can someone untie me?" the man demanded. "Steve? Steve!" He was looking off the porch toward the bushes where three other uniformed men were busy attending to someone.

The teen slipped an arm around the woman. "We're okay now, Ms. Lewis."

"But . . . Steve's . . . not," she sobbed. "Oh . . . God . . ."

"Whattya got?" Morris asked one of the soldiers that was crouching on the grass.

"Gunshot victim," he replied without looking up. The soldier's hands were pressed against a man who was lying faceup on the ground. Blood was trickling from the man's lips, spurting from a wound to his belly. The soldier was red to the elbows. "I don't think he's going to make it."

"What about the other one?" Fuller asked.

A pair of special forces men were diligently attending to a body that was propped into a sitting position against a tree, as if the man was relaxing in a park. The eyes were open, but looked empty. He was bleeding from an unseen hole in his upper chest.

"Needs a medic, bad!" one of the soldiers responded.

General Henderson flipped open a phone. "Then let's get him one!" He began conferring with someone in hushed but urgent tones.

"What happened?" Morris asked the trio on the porch.

"That man ..." the woman sobbed, pointing. "He ... he was going to kill us. And ... And Steve," she pointed again. "He ... He ... saved us."

"I lost the pulse!"

"He's not breathing!"

"Start CPR!"

"He bled out ... He's gone."

"Oh, God ... Dear God ... don't let him ...!"

"Time of death ... 01:23."

WE HOP A PLANE IN TAHOE. FLY TO MEXICO. THEN ... THEN THE SKY'S the limit: Rio, the Caymans, Tahiti ..."

The Lincoln was doing nearly a hundred, flying up the highway towards Reno.

"What do you think? Where should we go first? Bahamas?"

There was no response.

"Tito?"

Vince craned his neck. The cushion and floorboard of the backseat were covered in blood. Tito's eyes were closed now. Vince watched, trying to decide whether his partner was breathing.

"Guess the first thing is to find a doctor," he sighed. "Tito?" Vince twisted in the seat and jiggled him. Nothing. An arm slipped onto the floorboard.

He slowed the Town Car and pulled onto the shoulder. Putting it in park, he left the engine running.

"Tito?" He shook him gently. Still nothing. "Don't croak on me, man. Not now. Now when we got this."Vince fingered the brass knobs on the money case, lifted the top, and withdrew a thick wad of bills. There was a clicking sound. Probably just the motor. He waved the currency over Tito, as if it might bring about some supernatural cure. "Hey, man . . . Don't let this go to waste."

Click!

He froze. "What *is* that?"

Vince switched off the engine, his ears straining at the noise. No more clicks. Instead, a muffled electronic sound. A beep. A beep repeating itself at regular intervals. Almost like a watch alarm. Except . . .

He jerked the satchel open and began fishing through the money. And there it was. Near the bottom. A small, steel box with an LED readout—red digits changing, keeping time with the beeps: 4 . . . 3 . . . 2 . . .

In the instant before it exploded, Vince smiled at the bomb. So much for worrying about doctors and destinations. He was in the process of cursing Sonny when the car evaporated. An angry fireball boiled up into the heavens, shuttling the inhabitants of the Lincoln to judgment.

FIFTY-FIVE

SIX WEEKS LATER

"More coffee, boys?"

"Yes, ma'am."

Jimmy's jaw fell as Denise began refilling the porcelain cups. She smiled at him, long, dark lashes batting.

"How you feeling?" she asked, eyes twinkling.

He looked stricken: cheeks flushing, a panicked expression on his face. "Fine . . . ma'am. Just . . . fine."

"How's your back?" She used her free hand to give his shoulder a squeeze.

Jimmy swallowed hard, flinching at her touch. "Uh . . . It's okay. Yeah . . . Rehab went great and uh . . . I put in a lot of time on the weight machines so . . ."

"I can tell," she said, nodding.

His cheeks were rosy now. Sweat was staining the sleeves of his shirt.

"When do you go back on duty?"

"Uh . . . The doctor says another week or so."

"Great." She turned her attention to Parish. "And how are you doing?"

"Not bad." Parish's hand unconsciously reached to his forehead, to the two-inch scar just above his brow.

"Where's your friend this morning?"

"Friend?"

"You know, the guy you two usually pal around with? Uh . . . What's his name?"

Jimmy's face fell at this. "You mean Steve . . ."

"Right. Steve. Where's he been? Haven't seen him in here in ages."

Parish sighed heavily. "I'm afraid Steve . . . he's . . . he's no longer with us."

Her face expressed genuine concern. "Really? What happened?"

"It's a long story," Parish said, mournfully. "He tried to help some-one—a schoolteacher. Got himself shot in the process."

"Shot!" She slid into the booth next to Jimmy, clutching the cof-fee pot. "How terrible!"

"Yeah," Jimmy lamented. "Poor old Steve."

"Another good marine bites the dust," Parish sighed.

Denise's mouth quivered. "That's . . . that's so . . . so sad." Suddenly she was bawling. Every patron in Jackie's turned their direction. Jimmy blushed again—embarrassed. The waitress leaned toward him, then buried her face in his chest. The Truck stalled: eyes wide in terror, arms paralyzed at his sides.

Parish gestured to him, mouthing instructions: pat her on the back, say something, you idiot!

A beefy paw tapped at her shoulder helplessly. "It's . . . It's . . . It's okay," he stuttered, grimacing.

"I'm sorry," she apologized through the tears. "I didn't even know Steve, not really . . . But . . . But I just . . . I just . . . I remember how it felt when my brother died . . ."

"Died?" someone asked. "Who died?"

Three heads bobbed up at the man standing next to the booth.

"You!" Denise shouted.

"What? What did I do?"

Parish slid over. "Have a seat, Steve."

Denise turned on Jimmy with eyes of fire. "You said he was dead!"

"No. I . . . I never said that."

"Yes, you did!"

"Their first quarrel," Parish announced in a patronizing tone.

"They told me you were dead," she argued.

Vaughn shrugged at her. "Well . . . I'm not."

"All we said was that he got shot," Jimmy tried. "And that he wasn't with our squad anymore. Tell her, Phil."

Parish nodded. "That's right. He's on sick leave because of the bum leg."

Vaughn stuck it into the aisle for inspection—a nondescript pant leg—then held out his cane. "Took a couple of slugs." He offered her a lopsided smile. "From different guns, on different days. But they hit the same leg. Put a kink in my hoop game for a while. Lost a few moves."

"You didn't have many," Parish jabbed.

Vaughn ignored this. "But my therapist says I'll be back on the court in another two or three months. Unfortunately, my days of guarding the zone are over."

Denise examined the evidence, glanced at the leg, the cane, at Vaughn's face. With tears still glistening on her cheeks, she shot out her lower lip. "You tricked me," she accused, slipping smoothly back into her flirt routine.

"No. Really. I didn't mean to," Jimmy pled.

"What about biting the dust?" Denise wanted to know. "What was that crack supposed to mean?"

"He said it," Jimmy accused, pointing at Parish.

Parish chuckled. "I just meant that Steve is effectively out of circulation. He's been reassigned to fly a desk. And, who knows, he may be out of circulation, romantically speaking too."

Vaughn rolled his eyes.

"Come on, Steve. You like her. Admit it."

"Mmm . . . Maybe . . ."

"Who?" Denise wanted to know.

"Don't ask."

Rising, she brushed at her uniform. "Coffee?" she asked Vaughn in a cool tone. Her eyes darted to Jimmy, then back again, admonishing him playfully.

Vaughn examined his watch. "No. We have to be going."

"I'll get the check." With that she strutted off toward the cash register.

"What did I do?" Jimmy wondered. "I didn't do anything . . . did I?"

"You're not due at the bunker until noon, right?" Vaughn asked Parish.

"Right."

Denise returned with the check. She placed it on the table and glared hard at Jimmy. Turning to leave, she winked at Vaughn and Parish.

"She hates me," the Truck moaned sadly.

"No, she doesn't." Parish threw a ten on the table. "She's just trying to get you riled up."

"Well, it's working."

The pretty brunette met them as they reached the exit. "Bye now. Come see me again real soon. You hear?"

Jimmy looked at her with sorrowful hound dog eyes, shoulders slumped.

"You come back too, big guy," she finally added, the pout becoming a smile. "I'll be looking for you."

The Truck grinned crookedly and floated out the door, flying all the way to Vaughn's car.

"Take my advice," Parish offered, climbing into the shotgun seat, "marry the girl."

The conversation degenerated from there, turning to women in general, then to basketball, and finally to a series of macho exaggerations concerning both subjects.

One hundred and fifty minutes—and a great deal of bragging and taunting—later they reached the turnoff.

Parish sighed at his watch. "My grandma could have gotten us here quicker."

"Huh?"

"At least she drives the speed limit. You . . . I swear, Steve, you're the slowest driver on the planet."

"What's the rush?" Vaughn gunned the engine and the jeep leapt off the highway, tires spinning, gravel spraying. "How's that? Better?"

Parish buzzed his lips. "Why don't you let me drive?"

"No."

"Come on. Give your leg a rest."

"It isn't my pedal leg that's the problem."

"You're right there. It's your attitude, Steve. You're too cautious."

"Yeah. Right. And that's why I'm being bumped to major. Because I was too cautious—especially when I was taking on that hit man in hand-to-hand combat, getting myself shot . . . all in an attempt to—"

"Don't say it!"

"Save your ugly mug."

"Oh, sure. Go ahead. Rub it in. Remind me that I owe you my life."

"Okay. Now that you mention it . . ."

They both burst out laughing. Parish reached a fist over and pounded Vaughn's shoulder affectionately. "Thanks, buddy."

"Shut up."

"I'm serious, Steve. Jimmy and I both owe you big time. Right, Jimmy?"

The question was met by a snore. The Truck had nodded off in the cramped backseat.

"Anyway, we'll miss you out in the zone. I can tell you that."

"Liar. You won't miss me. Now that you're in charge of security, Captain Parish, you'll be too busy to miss me."

"Maybe so. But I won't be too busy to give you B-ball lessons on Saturday mornings."

"We'll see about that."

The jeep bounced through a rut and Vaughn slowed to shift into four-wheel drive. They followed the two-lane dirt track around the first mesa. After climbing a knoll, the Site came into view.

"Thar she blows!" Parish called.

Three yellow-orange bulldozers were pushing earth on the horizon, puffs of smoke rising from their stacks. A mammoth dirt mover sat idle to the left of the site. Nearby, dump trucks were lined up in a neat row, waiting to be loaded. A pair of backhoes and a skiploader were working a shallow pit, rubber tracks sending trails of dust skyward as they moved jerkily forward, back, forward . . . From a distance, the scene resembled a nature documentary: busy insects fashioning a nest.

As the jeep bounded across the valley, a half-dozen cars appeared. Parked at odd angles a quarter mile from the heavy equipment, their windshields and hoods glared in the brilliant morning sun: five white Dodges and a clunky metal box—an old Land Rover.

"Feds . . ." Parish said, making it sound like a curse. "They aren't gonna grill us again, are they?"

"I doubt it," Vaughn answered. "They'll be preoccupied with their excavation. Probably won't even notice we're there."

"But somebody knows we're coming, right?"

Vaughn nodded. "We were invited."

They rumbled through a network of ruts, down into a dry riverbed. When they emerged the jeep struggled to ascend the final rise.

"Here we are," Vaughn observed, pulling up next to the Rover.

"Hey . . . Lover Boy," Parish called. "Wake up!"

"Denise . . ." he mumbled.

"Jimmy!"

"Huh?" The Truck blinked at them. "Huh? What?" He licked his lips and looked around, dazed.

"Sorry to disappoint you, Jimmy, but we're here."

"Oh."

They got out and started up the hill. A wide figure appeared on the ledge of a drop-off some fifty yards ahead. It gazed at them from under a hand, then started in their direction. Another figure—this one rail thin—materialized and trotted to the first man's side.

"Fibbies," Parish grumbled. "I knew we shouldn't have come."

"Let me handle it." To the men, Vaughn said, "Agent Morris . . . Agent Fuller . . . Good to see you again."

"This is a restricted zone," Fuller told them.

"Yeah. Sorry boys," Morris said, "but we can't let you . . ."

Parish and Jimmy offered up NTS ID tags. "We're cleared," they chimed in unison.

The agents frowned at this. "What about you?" Morris asked Vaughn.

"I was invited."

"Oh, yeah . . . by who?"

"That's *whom*," a voice corrected.

The huddle of men turned to see someone approaching: a wide-brimmed hat, a T-shirt bearing a Buffalo and the letters CU, shorts that showed off trim, tan legs.

"By her," Vaughn grinned.

Melissa greeted him with a hug and a kiss on the cheek. "Glad you could come, Steve."

"Hey! What about us?" Jimmy complained.

She threw one arm around the Truck, the other around Parish. "I'm happy to see you guys too."

Fuller glared at them. "I don't care if you all have personal notes from the president, this Site is part of a federal investigation. So—"

Morris waved him off. "Let 'em look," he told his partner. To the visitors he said, "Just stay away from the dozers."

"Yeah," Fuller added grumpily. "Try not to get run over. We've got enough bodies to clean up out here already."

As the agents returned to the north end of the ravine, Vaughn, Parish, and Jimmy followed Melissa to the south end.

"What's the story out here, anyway?" Vaughn wondered.

"Yeah. They wouldn't tell us diddly during the interrogation sessions," Parish complained. "The feds had plenty of questions, but no answers."

"I'm not really sure what it's all about," Melissa replied as they began scrambling down the side of the ravine. "Apparently the Vegas mob used this place for a burial grounds."

"For the people they murdered?" Parish submitted.

Melissa shrugged. "Guess so. According to the FBI, the mob's been revamping their Vegas operations—personnel wise—and depositing the people they found lacking out here."

"What about Weber's theories?" Vaughn asked. "The radiation victims . . . all that?"

"I don't know anything about that," she said. They continued the descent, backing down the steep grade on hands and knees.

"I don't understand how . . ." Jimmy started to say. His feet slipped out from under him and a miniature avalanche of gravel and dirt peppered the others.

"Hey!"

"Watch it!"

"Sorry." After regaining his balance, he asked, "How could they do it?"

"What? Kill people in cold blood?" Vaughn wondered. He reached the floor of the ravine and began flexing his bad leg. "I think you just get used to it. Your conscience goes numb and it quits bothering you after a while."

"And money is a pretty good salve," Melissa added, beating the dust from her shorts.

"No. I mean . . . practically speaking. How could they bury people out here—in our zone. We would have seen something. The sensors would have picked up the activity."

"Maybe they hid the bodies before the system was implemented," Parish suggested.

"No," Melissa said. "I haven't paid that much attention to what they're doing up the way there," she said, pointing at the dirt movers, "but I've overheard a thing or two. The bodies . . . some of them aren't that old. We're talking months. Weeks in some cases."

"Doesn't make sense," the Truck muttered, still perched on the side of the slope.

"Come on, Jimmy!" Parish urged impatiently.

Jimmy jumped the last three feet and landed with a grunt. "We would have picked something up. That's all I'm saying."

Melissa led them along the wall of the ravine. "Any of you guys ever hear of Robert DiCaprio? The FBI people have been tossing that name around a lot."

"Sure," Vaughn said, nodding. "Secretary of the Department of Energy."

"Former secretary," Parish corrected. "He stepped down about . . . six weeks ago."

"Yeah," Melissa prodded. "Six weeks ago. Ring any bells?"

"Should it?"

"That's when we were all running for our lives, being chased by hit men."

"So?"

"So doesn't it seem a little odd that DiCaprio 'resigned' right when this Pandora's box was being opened?"

"The papers said he retired for personal reasons," Parish reported.

"Yeah. Right. And since when are the papers ever accurate?" Melissa prodded.

"Last week on CNN they said his wife left him," Jimmy reported. "Just up and left. Filed for divorce. And I guess he didn't take it too well. Went into seclusion or something. They don't know where he is."

"Sounds like one of Weber's harebrained stories to me," Parish said with a sneer. "Big conspiracy . . . Government involvement . . . High officials losing their jobs . . ."

"And disappearing," the Truck added.

"That would explain it though," Vaughn thought aloud. "As head of the DOE, DiCaprio had the clout to down or at least punch holes in our security fence."

"And why in the world would he do that?" Parish asked, his face contorted. "The man was on an express trip to the White House. Everybody knew that."

"Why would he suddenly announce his retirement then?" Melissa pushed.

"Yeah . . ." Parish frowned at this, unsatisfied.

They rounded a bend in the bank and Melissa paused to gesture up the riverbed. "Right up there is where we found the first fossil. That's also where the FBI is digging up bodies. Looks like the mob stuffed them into a hole in the wall and covered them with a bulldozer. Problem is, this soil erodes so quickly out here. Flash floods, wind, the sun beating down, earthquakes . . . A combination of forces pulled the hole open again and voila! Bones began erupting out of the sediment."

They all gazed north, watching as a backhoe picked at layers of earth, waves of rock cascading to the floor of the dry riverbed.

"How can you work when they're ripping the place up?" Vaughn asked.

"We can't. At least, not up there. Not yet." She turned and ushered them into a narrow gap in the bank of the ravine. "It's tight back here."

The men turned sideways and began pushing in.

"I'm stuck!" Jimmy shouted. When Parish yanked him forward, pebbles rained on their feet, a fog of dust rising to choke them.

The fissure went back fifteen feet before opening into a wide pit encircled by vertical walls of stone. Straight above, the sun shone out of a cloudless, blue sky.

Three students were bent on the ground, dental instruments in hand, chipping away bits of soil from a pedestalled oval that contained what appeared to be a three-dimensional carving.

"What is that?" As the question hung in the air, the answer began to materialize: a long, snaking trail of vertebrae, a tangle of leg bones, one stubby forearm, neck curving upwards and back, a skull lying a yard to one side—a jaw, two pillar-like teeth, a baseball-sized eye socket staring up at them.

"It's a dinosaur!" Jimmy exclaimed.

One of the students glanced over his shoulder at them. "Not just any dinosaur. A T. rex."

"Meet Gill."

Gill had his face an inch from the ground, examining an incongruity in the earth.

"We've met," Vaughn said. "In Tonopah. Remember?"

"No," Melissa said. "Our T. rex. His name is Gill. When we came out about a month ago, the FBI wouldn't let us survey the original site. So Gill here"—she motioned to the student—"he wanders off and finds this little . . . cave. Except it's not exactly a cave. Anyway . . . Next thing I know, he's digging up his second T. rex." She shook her head at him. "The kid's fifteen and he's already found two T.'s."

"So far," Gill muttered without looking up.

"How'd you persuade the feds to let you excavate?" Vaughn asked.

"I didn't. CU did." In answer to their puzzled expressions she added, "University of Colorado Department of Paleontology. We took a few pictures. Sent them out to Boulder. They offered me a grant. I assume they pressured the FBI into an antiquities permit." Melissa shrugged, eyebrows lifting. "They want to pay me and give me credit toward my doctorate—I don't ask questions. It's just weekends. So I can still teach. It's perfect for me."

"Sounds perfect," Vaughn said.

"Oh . . . and look at this." She led them to the side of the well and knelt down, placing her hand into a depression.

"What is it?"

"A footprint."

"Kind of little for a Tyrannosaurus, isn't it?" Jimmy wondered.

"Yeah. But not for a man." She shifted, slipping her Nike into the mold. "There's a chance that the impression was made during the same time period that this beast"—she aimed a thumb over her shoulder—"roamed the earth."

"Men and dinosaurs . . . living at the same time?" Parish exclaimed.

"Why not?" Jimmy asserted. "Just like *The Land That Time Forgot.*"

"Yeah," Parish scoffed. "Just like it."

"Looks like you have quite a dig going," Vaughn observed.

Melissa nodded. "Problem is, I don't have enough help. After we expose the find, we'll have to cast it and try to remove it. It'll be a lot of work. And I can't expect these guys to come out every Saturday."

"We don't mind," Gill said.

"Still . . . Know anybody with some free time on their hands?" Melissa offered Vaughn a coy smile.

Jimmy nudged the major with an elbow. Parish cleared his throat in an exaggerated fashion.

"Well . . . yeah . . . I guess I do have some free time . . . I'll be on vacation for a couple more months . . . but . . ."

"What do you know about dinosaurs?"

"Absolutely nothing."

"Want to learn?"

"That depends."

"On . . . ?"

"On who my teacher is."

"Maybe we should leave you two alone," Parish said, rolling his eyes at Jimmy.

Melissa ignored this, her attention on Vaughn. "About tomorrow . . ."

"Tomorrow . . . ?"

"Church . . . You promised you'd go."

Parish and the Truck snickered at this.

"I did?"

"Yeah. Remember? When I visited you in the hospital?"

"Oh, yeah . . . I guess I did. Don't suppose I could take a rain check?"

"No. You're going. After what God brought us through, the least you can do is show up for church: say thanks, get that leg prayed for . . . get to know him . . ."

"Mmm . . ."

"Service starts at nine."

"Nine," he repeated with a sigh.

"Sharp. And I expect to see you there."

"Yes, ma'am."

"Nailed," Parish whispered.

"I'd keep quiet if I were you," Vaughn warned.

"Hey, I go to church," Parish replied.

Melissa gave him the evil eye. "Oh, yeah?"

"Really, I do!"

The eye turned on Jimmy. "I went when I was a kid," the Truck pled. "Does that count?"

"We're not talking about brownie points here, guys," Melissa said. "We're talking about a Person . . . about a vital bond . . ."

The three men stared at the ground, clearly uncomfortable, anxious for a diversion—anything to avoid discussing the threatening, unmanly duo: spirituality and relationships.

"Can we help?" Parish offered, suddenly interested in the dig. "We've got an hour before we need to head for the bunker."

Melissa admonished them with a glare. "Okay," she sighed. She handed them each a trowel and a small, stiff brush. "Welcome to Dinosaurs 101. First rule: take things slowly. Be patient," she explained, taking Vaughn's arm on one side and Parish's on the other and guiding them—with Jimmy following meekly—beyond the pedestal where the sweating teenagers worked.

"Everything under control here, Gill?" she asked as they passed.

"Yes, Ms. Lewis," the boy muttered, clearly preoccupied.

Melissa steered the three men toward the far side of the pit and a narrow continuation of the ravine. "Paleontology's a lot like detective work," she said as she pushed them ahead of her into the opening. "We're searching for clues to the past—no matter how subtle—that might help us unravel the mysteries of God's creation. What I need you to look for ..."

Her voice faded as the four of them disappeared into the ravine. Gill looked up after them from the patch of ground he was scratching at, smiled, shook his head—and returned to the search.

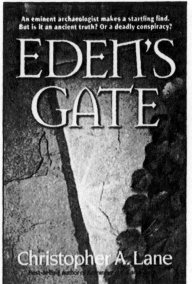

An eminent archaeologist makes a startling find.
But is it an ancient truth? Or a deadly conspiracy?

EDEN'S GATE

Christopher A. Lane
Best-selling author of *Appearance of Evil*

When Dr. Richard Grimm, the noted archaeologist, disappears in the Middle East under mysterious circumstances, Dr. Ben Lawrence is called in to take his place. A Christian and creationist, Ben is used to being pushed aside and ridiculed. This dig is his big break—the chance to discover the birthplace of humankind. But the trail of Dr. Grimm leads straight into enemy territory: northern Iraq.

Meanwhile, Jennifer Rogers is none too thrilled about her new boss on the dig. As the rebel daughter of Chinese missionaries, she considers Ben Lawrence as not only her opposite, but also her enemy. So why does she find herself so attracted to him?

Unknown to Ben and Jennifer, more than one person has a stake in this obscure Babylonian dig. A high-powered businessman, a TV news celebrity, FBI and CIA agents—all of them have an interest in the operation. Power, money—even lives—are at stake. And Jennifer and Ben are caught in the middle, battling forces beyond their control.

Pick up your copy of this explosive page-turner today at your local Christian bookstore.

Softcover 0-310-41161-0

We want to hear from you. Please send your
comments in care of the address below. Thank you.

ZondervanPublishingHouse
Grand Rapids, Michigan 49530
http://www.zondervan.com